chulito

chulito

Charles Rice-González

MAGNUS
BOOKS

Magnus Books
Cathedral Station
PO Box 1849
New York, NY 10025

Library of Congress cataloging-In-Publication Data available.
Printed in the United States of America on acid-free paper.

First Magnus Books Edition 2011

Edited by: Donald Weise
Cover by: Scott Idleman/Blink
Cover photo by: Ricardo Muniz/Coquichulo Images

ISBN: 978-1-936833-03-0

www.magnusbooks.com

Dedicated to

The one and only Freda Rosen, who said,
"Charles, if anyone can write this particular story and get it
published, it's you."

And to my Troika of Support

Cassandra
Arthur Aviles
My mom, Maria Narvaez

chapter one

Chulito awoke with a hard-on as usual. He looked down his smooth, brown chest past the black strands sprouting around his navel to see the head of his dick poking up at him through his bed sheet. He greeted it with a firm gentle squeeze. "Hola, papito."

The old window shade in his tiny room cast a Creamsicle glow from the sun rays that shot off a big metallic sign from one of the many auto glass shops that lined the street across from his building.

The sounds of trucks revving and barreling along Garrison Avenue mixed with the cries of "auto glass! auto glass! auto glass!" from the guys who competed with each other to lure cars with broken windshields, cracked mirrors or busted headlights into their respective shops.

Chulito stood naked in front of the full length mirror on the back of his door. That spring, with just some push-ups and sit-ups, smooth hard muscles came out of nowhere and he looked like a

Latino, hip hop version of Michaelangelo's David. He crossed his arms over his chest, fingers underneath each armpit and thumbs pointing up to the ceiling. He shifted his weight onto his right hip, tilted his head, tucked his chin into his neck, and contorted his pretty boy face into a mean gangsta snarl.

He then popped a CD into his system and mouthed out the words along with Big Pun. When the percussion popped into the song, he bopped his head and challenged his own image in the mirror.

As Chulito slipped into the bathroom across the hall from his room, his nostrils filled with the comforting smell of freshly brewed Café Bustelo. He heard his mother, Carmen, talking in the kitchen with Maria from upstairs about her son Carlos, who was coming home from his first year at college. All week he'd heard Maria's slippers make sounds like sandpaper scratching on the bare wood floor as she prepared Carlos' room, which was right above his.

Chulito was excited, too. Carlos used to be his boy. They were real tight from the day Carlos and Maria moved into the building. Carlos was five, almost a year older than Chulito, and would come home from kindergarten and teach Chulito the songs he'd learned. Growing up, they played together all the time—snowball fights, trick-or-treating on Halloween, going to Joe's for ices, or sneaking into El Coche Strip Club and laughing real hard when they got chased out by the old Irish owner.

But that was before all the shit came down.

It started when they went to different schools. Chulito went to Stevenson High School, the local school that everyone in Hunts Point attended, but Carlos got accepted into the Bronx High School of Science in the North Bronx, a school for the gifted and intelligent. Maria threw him a party when he got accepted and took a second job to buy him a new laptop. Then Carlos started dressing differently, like one of those white boys in the J. Crew catalogs. Chulito didn't care, at first; he thought Carlos looked cool and sophisticated. They still spent time together. Carlos helped him with homework and they rode the number six train to Parkchester to see movies on the weekends. They were always together. Then people in the neighborhood started calling Carlos a pato.

"We should kick his faggot ass to show him a lesson," said Looney Tunes, one of the fellas who hung out on the corner and lived in Chulito's building. Looney Tunes earned his name because as a kid he ran home from school to watch cartoons. He even watched them on videotape, sang the songs and imitated the noises and sound effects. He grew out of it, but the name stuck.

Chulito stared Looney Tunes down. "Yo, Carlos is my boy and he from the 'hood, so cut that shit."

"Protecting your boyfriend?" Looney Tunes teased. Chulito responded with a punch that knocked Looney Tunes on his ass and required three stitches on the inside of his mouth. So everybody left Carlos alone—including Chulito. It was just what he had to do to be correct with the fellas. Carlos tried to stay connected, but he was placed in pato exile—no one looked at him or talked to him.

Chulito hated treating Carlos as if he were invisible whenever he ran into him in the Bella Vista Pizza Shop or saw him walking up the block. Chulito got heated when the fellas made "faggot this" and "faggot that" comments when Carlos passed the corner, but he kept it in check. He'd successfully avoided Carlos until one day, while coming out of the bodega, he collided with him. The fellas were on the corner right outside the door watching. Carlos looked surprised at first, then the corners of his mouth curled into a smile. Chulito wanted to say "sorry" or "excuse me" but instead said, "Watch where you're fucking walking." The fellas laughed. The hurt in Carlos' eyes haunted him for the next week.

He finally went to meet Carlos at his school, which was safely a world away from Hunts Point. He was worried that things with the fellas could get out of hand. He wanted to protect Carlos, so he told him to get correct and stop fagging out.

Carlos looked down at his fitted yellow Polo shirt, straight-legged jeans and red Adidas sneakers with the white stripes and held out his slim arms. "There's nothing wrong with me, Chulito. There's nothing wrong with not wearing drooping pants and Timberlands all the time. Look around, people dress all different kinds of ways. And I'm still the same Carlos. It's the neighborhood that's fucked up."

Chulito checked out Carlos' friends waiting nearby with their mohawks, dread locks and fuschia dyed hair. He looked back at Carlos. He wanted to confess that he missed him, he missed the movies and the walks near the empty industrial streets of the Hunts Point Food Market, the laughs, and the long telephone conversations where Carlos told him the storylines of the books he was reading, but instead said, "I'm just trying to look out, 'cause the fellas be getting worked up." Chulito shoved his hands deeper into his pockets and looked at the ground.

"Thanks for looking out for me, Chulito. I know you're not like the rest of those assholes."   Carlos touched his shoulder. Chulito's heart quickened.

On Carlos' graduation night, Chulito was hanging out on the corner with the fellas when Looney Tunes said, "Oh shit! Look,

Carlos is holding hands with a dude." One of the auto glass guys sarcastically called out, "Oh, qué cute," which opened a flood gate of catcalls. When Chulito saw Carlos holding hands with his date a rush of anger swept over him. Is he messing with that dude? It was the same guy with the long blond dreads from his visit to Carlos' school. As the pair crossed the street, the auto glass guys and some of the fellas on the corner blew kisses at them. Looney Tunes walked around with a limp wrist and called out Carlos' name in falsetto.

"That's right." Papo, one of the other fellas on the corner shouted, "You better walk fast before we fuck ya ass up, Carlos."

Carlos looked over his shoulder at Chulito, then kissed his date on the cheek. Chulito had trouble breathing and the neighborhood became a blur.

"Who the fuck does he think he is doing that shit over here?" Papo asked. "This ain't the Village." He picked up a bottle and hurled it. Carlos and the blond guy jumped as it shattered a few feet behind them. The auto glass guys and the fellas laughed. "You see that, Chulito? You stick your neck out for him and this is what he does. He's a fucking faggot. A dirty pato." Then Papo handed Chulito a bottle and gestured with his head to throw it. "Throw it!" one of the auto glass guys yelled. Then someone else said, "Throw it, Chulito." From all around Chulito the "throw its" shot like arrows. Carlos turned to see what was happening and noticed Chulito holding the bottle. They made eye contact. "Throw it, Chulito!" Papo urged. Chulito wished Carlos had done this when he wasn't around, then ran three steps forward and hurled the bottle into the lavender sky. As the bottle left his hands he wanted to fly with it and stop it mid-air. The bottle hit the blond guy on the shoulder, bounced off and crashed on the ground. The hecklers erupted into laughter, hissed and doubled over. "Bull's eye." Papo winked at Chulito.

The guy turned to confront the crowd. "What? Looks like that faggot wants a showdown. Let's get 'im fellas." Papo charged into the street. Chulito followed. He wanted to hurt that guy. He wanted to show him who's top dawg. Carlos tugged his date's arm and the two ran down Hunts Point Avenue. Papo laughed and stopped, along with the other fellas, in the middle of the street. "You betta run, faggots."

Chulito continued to sprint after Carlos and his date as they crossed under the Bruckner Expressway and dashed down the steps to the train station. The honking from the oncoming traffic under the highway made him stop. He stood on the median gasping and coughing. His lungs burned and his body tingled, then he pressed his eyes to keep back the tears. He thought, How could Carlos disrespect the neighborhood like that? But he felt personally betrayed.

Chulito didn't talk to him again, and later that summer Carlos left for school on Long Island.

A year later and about a month before Carlos came home from his first year at Adelphi, his mother got sick. She thought she was having a heart attack, but it turned out to be some bad pork in the mofongo she ate from the 97 Café. That night they learned how popular that mofongo was when three people in their building also got sick and ended up in the emergency room. Chulito's mother took Maria to the hospital and asked Chulito to call Carlos because they hadn't reached him.

Chulito sat in his room and stared at his phone. Carlos' number was still his first number on his speed dial. He pressed it, but before the phone finished dialing, he closed it. Would he just keep it business and say "Your mom got sick but she O.K.?" What else would he say? He felt like Carlos had dissed him and owed him an apology. He pressed number one again. When Carlos came on, Chulito's thoughts became a tangle of apologies and questions.

"Hello?" Carlos repeated. "Chulito?"

Chulito must have still been in Carlos' phone. Chulito closed his eyes and took a deep breath. "My moms asked me to call you, 'cause your moms got sick from some food, but she O.K." Chulito slipped off his loosely tied Timberland boots, laid back on his bed and looked up at the ceiling that had the original light fixture which looked like a lotus flower covered in quarter inch of thick white paint. He pretended that Carlos was right beyond that light fixture, in his room, resting on his bed.

"I saw there was a missed call from my mom and called her back but there was no answer. Are you sure she's O.K.?"

"Yeah, she didn't want to worry you 'cause it ain't serious. They should be on their way back from the hospital."

Chulito liked hearing Carlos' voice. He wanted to say so, but held back. He could still see Carlos holding that blond guy's hand, kissing his cheek.

"Well, thanks for calling." Carlos sounded distant and cold.

Neither spoke.

Then, as if someone had hijacked Chulito's brain, he started speaking. "Yo, sorry I haven't called you." His throat dried up.

"You've got something to say?"

"Nah."

"Well, why were you going to call me?"

Chulito sat up. His ears got hot and his nostrils flared. He wanted to tell Carlos that he should be apologizing, too, for bringing that dude to Hunts Point, holding hands in the fucking street and kissing the nigga. "To say sorry and shit. Ain't that a good enough reason?"

"No, Chulito, it's not. I appreciate you calling me about my mom, but you're acting like you didn't throw a fucking bottle at me. So, if you just want to say sorry for being a stupid asshole, then say your pitiful 'sorry' and go back to the corner with the fellas."

Chulito jumped up from his bed. "Carlos, why you always gotta be steppin' off and shit?"

"What are you sorry for? Are you sorry for what went down? And how you went along with all those assholes? That shit hurt. David wanted to have your ass arrested for assault."

Chulito paced in his room. "Fuck that dude! I threw the bottle at him not at you."

"Same difference. You threw a bottle at the fags, right? I don't care about those fellas, but you? I thought you were different. You were my friend. Why did you turn on me?"

"Me? You fucking turned. I did what I had to do!" Chulito slammed his phone shut. The room clouded with his tears. He let his anger take over, because it was easier than confessing that he wanted to be the one holding Carlos' hand. Not in public or anything, but he wanted to be in that dude's place. But he couldn't admit that.

Their brief conversation swirled in Chulito's mind for days before he called Carlos and left a message.

"Yo! I'm sorry I hung up. I just..." Chulito paused. He was still conflicted between wanting to be near Carlos and needing to stay away. "I just feel mad mixed up, bro. We were bloods, but you changed. And I don't understand what happened with you. I'm sorry about the bottle. I never meant to hurt you. So, if you want, let's talk. Just you and me like it used to be. Peace."

Moments later Big Pun chimed on Chulito's phone and Carlos' name in blue letters streamed across the screen.

"Hey, Chulito, I got your message," Carlos said matter-of-factly.

Chulito was expecting Carlos to sound happy, not distant. "I felt real bad about hanging up on you, but you get me so heated sometimes."

"What gets you so heated?" Carlos asked flatly.

Chulito thought about Carlos' question. He was straight up jealous. He had never felt like that before. Instead he intertwined his feelings with those of the neighborhood. "I keep thinking about that night when you walked out holding that dude's hand. You never told me about any shit like that. And I keep seeing you kissing him and I get pissed. How you gonna go and do something like that all out in public and shit?"

"Chulito, I want to be who I am."

"C'mon, Carlos, you know how you supposed to act around here and you go off and do some shit like that—kissing a dude?"

"It was on the cheek. What's the big deal? I see you guys hugging each other, and when I came home for Christmas, I saw that Kamikaze guy kiss you."

"What?" Chulito heard a hint of playfulness in Carlos' voice but held back from playing back. "Carlos, you know that's different. It's bro shit. Kamikaze kisses me on my forehead. He's just playin'. What you did was straight up and down gay. Niggas are crazy. They don't go for that shit. And I knew when the fellas started to make fun of you it was gonna get serious. I should have just said cut the shit. I mean you from our 'hood."

"They see me as just a pato." The playfulness was gone from Carlos voice and he sounded like he was simply stating a fact.

"Don't say that."

"It's true. Do you see me like that, Chulito?"

Chulito sighed. Carlos being gay was an understanding they both shared but they'd never talked about up front. As long as it was in the realm of rumor, Chulito could still hang with Carlos. But Carlos fucked everything up by bringing that dude. Now that it had been confirmed it would be impossible to keep his friendship with Carlos public.

"I don't want to see that part. I just wanna remember the fun we used to have."

"But that's part of me, too, Chulito. On the one hand I'm different and on the other I am still the same. You want to relate to the me who's still the same and the fellas want to relate to the me who's different. I'm relating to all of me."

"Is that what you're learning in college?"

"Somewhat."

Chulito sat at the kitchen table as he sketched Carlos' name graffiti style on a napkin. "I get what you saying."

"How?"

"Well, that you are the old Carlos and a new Carlos at the same time." The name on the napkin had thick letters and the bottom of the "s" wrapped around the word. Chulito chuckled. "You the real gangsta."

"Oh, yeah?"

"It's like you don't give a fuck. You gonna do ya thang at any risk."

Carlos laughed. "You think I'm gangsta? I love it."

Chulito liked hearing Carlos' deep, bubbly laugh. It reminded him of the first time he heard it full out and hearty when they went to see *Ace Ventura: Pet Detective* when they were kids. Their mothers had dropped them at the theater in Parkchester, given them money for popcorn and a soda, then went window shopping until the movie was over. At every stunt and joke, Carlos' laughter gushed out of him. He rocked in his seat and his stringy hair danced around his head. Chulito laughed, too, but it was more guarded. Then, he started to imitate Carlos and laugh loudly along with him. It felt good. The laugh was not just in his head, but in his chest and body. There were moments where they just looked at each other and laughed. Carlos' mouth was wide open and Chulito tossed a piece of popcorn. It landed on Carlos' tongue. They played the popcorn game a bit, then bumped heads when they leaned over at the same time to sip from the soda they shared which made them laugh even louder.

Chulito smiled at the memory. "I changed, too, ya know." He ran his hands over the ripple of muscles on his chest and abdomen. "My moms treats me like I'm a kid, but I ain't a kid anymore. Ya know, I'm turning sixteen soon."

Their conversations continued every day and Chulito's heart skipped three beats every time he answered the phone and heard Carlos' "Hey." He knew where this was going and couldn't wait to see Carlos when the semester was over.

Chulito walked into the kitchen with a bath towel wrapped around his waist. "Yo, mamis, I hope you left some cake for me." His mom and Maria were finishing their coffee and some leftover birthday cake from the night before. Carmen had cooked a special dinner of pernil with arroz con gandules and gotten him his favorite cake from Valencia Bakery. Chulito loved that sweet frosting, all cold with a thin, crispy coating from being in the fridge overnight.

"I'm gonna have me some of that." Chulito pulled the cake out of the refrigerator.

Carmen smacked his bottom. "Put some clothes on."

Chulito smiled and flexed. "Chill, Moms, Maria's family right?"

"They grow so fast." Maria sighed and sipped her coffee.

Chulito offered cake to the women. They shook their heads. "We better save a piece for Carlos 'cause ya know he digs this shit, too."

"I'm glad you two are friends again," Maria said.

"Well, it's gonna be birthday celebration Part Two tonight. I don't know what we gonna do 'cause Carlos says it's a surprise."

Chulito took the cake and a cup of fragrant coffee into his room and looked in his closet. He had shirts and jerseys by Mecca, Tommy Hilfiger, PNB, FuBu, Rocawear, and all the hottest designers organized by color. He got dressed, strapped on his Fossil watch and clipped on the gold neck chain with his name on it, then slipped on his religious beads, red and white for Chango, the Orisha god that his grandmother said was his protector. He tied a red bandanna around his head and topped it off with a fitted Yankee cap. He pulled the cap down low on his brow. Too hard. He flipped it with the rim to the back. Too casual. He brought it back to the front, cocked it slightly to the right and brought it down toward his right eyebrow. Bingo. His look had to be perfect, because for as much as Carlos liked wearing Polo shirts, khaki pants and boat mocs, he had a feeling Carlos would like seeing him tough and thugged out.

When he stepped out onto Garrison Avenue everything was the same. The auto glass guys with their tight glistening bodies were chasing cars with cracked windshields, a group of old men sat in front of his building playing dominoes on a card table, and further down Garrison he could see the spray of a fire hydrant and hear the squeals of the kids darting in and out of its refreshing, cold stream.

He slipped on his favorite Yves Saint Laurent shades with the bright gold tint that were more style than function against the high summer sun. He nodded to Martha, Brenda and Debbie who sat on a car on one end of the block, and bopped over to Papo, Looney Tunes, Chin-Chin and Davey who were hanging out in front of Rivera's bodega on the other end of the block.

"Yo, Chuli-to! Happy birthday, nigga." Davey clap-shaked hands and bumped shoulders with Chulito. "You sixteen now, te estás poniendo viejo." Two years older than Chulito, Davey had a baby-face with large eyes with long lashes and full, rich dark lips that he licked constantly. He lived in the Virgin Mary building around the corner from Chulito on Manida Street. The building had earned its name because its residents maintained a lit water fountain with the Virgin Mary in the front. The statue itself was encased in Plexiglass and surrounded by multi-colored plastic flowers—yellow roses, white mums, pink carnations, orange bird of paradises, lavender lilies, and orange royal orchids—that were kept spotless, dust free and replaced at the first hint of their color fading. Outside the case, the Virgin was surrounded by tropical plants and flowers illegally transported from El Yunque rainforest, including the golden yellow and white lily ginger and the fiery orange and red lobster claw heliconias in large pots that were moved indoors during the winter. From the security bars of all the first floor windows there hung massive ferns in pots turning the front of the building into a lush fragrant mini rain forest for their beloved Virgin Mary.

Chulito slid his arm around Davey's neck and pulled him close. "You heard right, sucka. My moms had a little cake for me last night and shit, but tonight who knows what could happen?"

High fives were served all around. Chin-Chin, the shortest and the oldest of the group at four feet and ten inches and twenty-four years old, said, "Well, if you want to play with tetas, you lucky you got friends to hook you up."

"What? Nigga, I ain't wasting my time with those tired, saggy tetas over at El Coche or The Wedge. Tonight I have special plans." Chulito pretended to wipe dust off his bare arms.

Papo, considered one of the more serious guys around, chimed in, "Oh, we know about the special plans." He made a sexy slurping sound with his mouth. Papo was the tall perfectly put together kind of guy whose body was slim and solid from playing football in front of the house he lived in on Manida Street. On some level he turned everybody on. His skin was a little on the blanquito side with a sprinkle of freckles on his long nose. His brown eyes lit up and looked freaky when the sun hit them and had a way of looking at you dead on, that made you want to ask, "What?"

The guys, except for Looney Tunes, erupted in laughter.

"What's so funny, yo?" Looney Tunes smoothed back his unkempt hair.

"Let's just say there is no way we gonna serve up saggy tetas to our boy here." Davey licked his lips, leaving a smooth shine on them. "We goin' out! Way out!"

"Hol' up, fellas. I told you I got some special plans tonight, but tomorrow I'm down for whatever you guys want."

Papo crossed his arms, making his chest swell through his tank top, and scanned the neighborhood while the rest of the guys high-fived each other. "Special plans? Bro, forget that 'cause what we got planned is gonna rock your fuckin' world."

"I'm down." Looney Tunes did a little dance.

"With what money?" Davey asked. "Yo, you never have money. Not even to hang out on this corner."

They all laughed again.

Papo waved Looney Tunes away. "You a lazy mo'fo' because I tried to get you a job working maintenance with me over at Hostos, but you too lazy to get ya ass up for work."

Looney Tunes shrugged. "I don't want to be at work at five o'clock in the damn morning, and I definitely don't wanna be cleaning up after dumb college kids."

Papo shook his head. "Always got an excuse. We do what we gotta do. Right, fellas?" He held up his hand and Chin-Chin slapped it.

Davey nodded in agreement. "Fuck, next month after I graduate from Stevenson High, I'ma go full-time at Dunkin', but just for the summer 'cause you hookin' me up at Hostos, right Papo?"

Papo held up a fist and Davey bumped it. "Done deal."

Looney Tunes slipped beside Chulito. "Why don't you put in a word with Kamikaze and I could work with you two?"

They all laughed.

Martha, Brenda and Debbie approached the corner, waved and stood right by them as they waited for the light to change so they could cross the street.

Chulito interrupted the fellas's laughter. "Forget that. Yo, listen up, fellas. I am down and Ready Freddy to hook up with you guys tomorrow but not tonight."

"What you doing?" Papo looked him in the eye the same way as when he had handed Chulito the bottle.

"It's a secret man. Besides, tomorrow's Saturday. A way better night to go bug out, right?"

The fellas all looked at each other and considered the possibility.

"So what you doing tonight, Chulito?" Davey asked.

The traffic light changed, but Martha and her posse paused to hear the answer.

The question reverberated through Chulito's head. "Chillin' with Carlos who's coming back from school" is what he wanted to say. "A special date."

The "ooooh's" rose and fell from their throats in perfect harmony.

"With Catalina?" Davey gave his lips another lick. Catalina was the girl who worked at the Salome Ureña Nail Salon. Everyone thought she was Chulito's girl, including Catalina.

"Yep." Chulito did a hump dance where he pumped his hips and pretended to spank whoever he was pumping. The women exchanged glances and crossed the street.

"What?" Chin-Chin asked incredulously. "You could fuck that chick any time. You goin' out with the fellas, hear me?"

"O.K., hear me out, fellas." Chulito called them over in a huddle. "It's someone else."

Another chorus of "ooooh's" from the fellas as they separated.

Papo knitted his brows. "Pussy you could get any time. We organized this shit and tonight we going out. Way out." High fives were served up again.

The clapping sounds of palms meeting palms were like gun

pops shooting down his plans with Carlos. Chulito couldn't cancel on him. Maybe I could invite Carlos to come along? Would that be so bad? It would be a disaster. Besides he wanted to be alone with Carlos to share his thoughts. Carlos always had a way of knowing what he wanted. He knew Carlos would help him understand.

"O.K., here's the deal, fellas. You get the party started and I'll meet you at the spot later."

They exchanged glances and nods.

"I guess so, just as long as it's not too late." Papo moved in close to Chulito and put his arm around his shoulder. "Damn, she must be something special if you don't want to break that date."

"It's just that, you know how chicks get when they make plans, especially for birthdays and holidays." They all nodded.

"Shit. This is gonna cause a problem," Davey said. "It's not just us right here." Some of the auto glass guys had arranged to take off work early so they could get cleaned up to go and many of the guys in the neighborhood were prepping as they spoke.

"You're right, Davey. Nah, Chulito, it ain't gonna work," Papo said. "Everybody is ready to go tonight and you can't be showin' up all late. We all gotta go together."

Chulito wished he'd just stayed in his room and waited for Carlos.

Just then, Notorious B.I.G.'s booming rap vibrated the air around them and drowned out their conversation. They all turned to see Kamikaze roll up to the corner in his special order Royal Blue Lexus LS from next year's line. The sun reflected off all the chrome accents and the tinted mirrored windows making the car sparkle like a giant jewel crawling along Garrison Avenue. Kamikaze rolled down the window and yelled, "Wassup, bums?"

Chulito thought Kamikaze would be just what he needed to

escape their plans. He was Kamikaze's boy and even though Kaz was cool with everybody, he rarely did the group thing with the fellas.

"Yo, Kaz," Davey called out as he approached the car. "Lookin' good, bro. Sweet running suit. Adidas?"

Kamikaze smiled and looked down. "Nah, man, it's Armani. But what up, D?"

"Chulito has plans, man," Davey said.

Kamikaze turned off the music. "I know. He's going out with us." He leaned toward the passenger window, pulled down his blue tinted shades and stared Chulito down.

"Kaz, I didn't know," Chulito said.

Kamikaze stepped out of the car. "That's because it was supposed to be a surprise, nigga. Show a little gratitude. I don't normally do this shit, but I'm making an exception and even organized this motherfucker 'cause you my pana."

Being taken out by the fellas was a coming of age rite, a boricua bar mitzvah thrown by your buddies. Chulito knew that to have a party posse organized for his birthday meant that he had gained an important position in his neighborhood, even though he was just sixteen. Davey hadn't had one yet and he was eighteen. Chin-Chin never had one and he was twenty-four. Papo had one only a year ago for his twenty-first birthday. And Looney Tunes would never have one.

Throughout Hunts Point word had spread that Kamikaze had organized a party posse and arranged for Chulito to get into a strip club in Yonkers. There was always an electric excitement in the air when all the guys in the neighborhood gathered to go out together. His party posse was growing by the minute. Tats Cru, a team of graffiti muralists who had their "headquarters" around the corner, were joining the posse. His buddies on the corner would leave their posts to attend. Those who had wives or girlfriends would leave them home or give them money to do their own thing.

Then the guys would all meet at a designated spot, the cars would line up, Hennessey would be passed around, the fellas would be dressed up, cologned down and blinged big time. The stories would live on for days.

Chulito began to think that the conversations he'd had with Carlos and their plans were a mistake.

"C'mere, Chulito." He walked slowly to Kamikaze.

"So you going tonight, punto." Kamikaze offered him his fist and Chulito bumped it with his own. "Good, I don't wanna hear nothing about other plans, O.K.? I'll be by around eight."

As Chulito tried to think of another excuse to delay his arrival, he saw Catalina—all big hair and hips—stomping across the street with Martha, Brenda and Debbie.

"Chulito, you motherfucker!" Catalina's presence parted the guys. "Who you fucking tonight? 'Cause if it's supposed to be me, this is the first time I'm hearing about it."

Her eyes were wide and her nostrils stretched to their max. Her manicured hands were crossed in front of her ample Dominican tetas. "Well?"

Everything stopped. The only sound came from Chulito's cell phone when Big Pun's "Still Not a Player" began to chime. Chulito looked at Carlos' name flashing across the phone's screen.

Catalina lunged for the phone, which fell out of Chulito's hand and spun across the pavement. Looney Tunes picked up the phone.

"Give it to me!" Catalina and Chulito yelled at the same

time. Looney Tunes passed it to Davey, who passed to Papo, who tried to pass it to Kamikaze, who didn't accept it but pointed to Chulito. Just as Papo moved toward Chulito with the phone, Martha plucked it out of his hand just as it stopped ringing.

"Answer her," Martha demanded. She commanded attention as she held the phone high in the air with one hand and pressed her fist to her waist with her other. She glared with a low tolerance for bullshit. She once played Rizzo, leader of the Pink Ladies, in Junior High School 125's production of *Grease* and the role stuck. Now she attended Bronx Community College, was the president of its Latina Movers and Shakers Club and wanted to single-handedly deliver her neighborhood sisters from macho oppression. "Enough of your stupid games, Chulito. You are supposed to be a man now, according to these knuckle heads. Own up, Mr. Man."

Then, out of the corner of his eye, Chulito saw Carlos stumble out of the passenger's seat of a new white Range Rover in front of their building. He was laughing and dialing his cell phone. He looked a little different, maybe a little skinnier. Chulito felt excitement and dread. He hoped no one from the corner would notice Carlos.

Kamikaze walked over to Martha and held out his hand. She held the phone out, and he took it and gave it to Chulito. "Handle your shit, pana."

"What are you doing tonight, Chulito?" The anger in Catalina's voice had gone from a volcanic boil to a low simmer.

Big Pun's beat chimed out of his cell, again. Looney Tunes danced to the beat.

Carlos held his phone to his ear while he unloaded a big suitcase, a bunch of shopping bags and two stacks of books tied with a thick heavy twine. Maria popped out of the building and gave her son a hug. She went over to the Rover and waved hello to the driver.

"You gonna answer that, bro?" Davey asked.

Chulito noticed Papo staring at the front of his building.

"Oh shit," Papo said. "There's Carlos. He must be back from college. Go get a bottle so we can welcome his ass back home."

The fellas laughed.

Chulito hit the silence button.

"Chulito, look Carlos is home. Come say hello." Maria yelled over to the corner.

The guys erupted into laughter.

"But hol' up yo, check out his ride. That shit is sweet," Davey said.

When Carlos saw Chulito on the corner, he flipped his phone shut.

"Chulito, come here," Maria said.

Chulito took a few steps.

"Don't even think about it, Chulito," Catalina growled through her teeth. "We're not finished."

"I don't want to disrespect Carlos' mother." Chulito walked away.

Catalina turned and crossed the street back toward the salon, swearing in Spanish. Martha, Brenda and Debbie followed her.

"Yo, pana," Kamikaze called out as he got into his car. "I'll see you at eight, right?"

Chulito turned to face Kamikaze and slowly nodded yes. The fellas hooted and hollered. "The party is on!"

As Chulito approached the building he saw that Carlos and his mom had gone inside and the driver, a tall, slim guy with curly blond hair, was carrying the two stacks of books inside. He was wearing cut-off jean shorts, sandals and a loose black concert T-shirt that had "Nina Simone, Carnegie Hall, June 28, 2001" written on the back with a big picture of Nina Simone on the front. He reminded Chulito of the guy with whom Carlos held hands and his heart tightened into a fist. Carlos appeared in the doorway, took one of the stacks from the driver and smiled at him. Then he paused and looked at Chulito, who stopped in his tracks.

Back on the corner, Looney Tunes asked the crowd. "Who's that? His boyfriend?" The guys burst into convulsive laughter and gave Looney Tunes high-fives.

Carlos glared at Chulito a moment, then went into the building with the driver. Chulito felt the cake and coffee he'd eaten earlier rising and he swallowed to keep it down.

He quickly flipped open his cell and called Carlos, but he didn't answer.

chapter two

As he prepared for the party posse, selecting his finest threads, Chulito kept dialing Carlos. He knew no one was upstairs because he didn't hear any footsteps. Where did Carlos go? And who was that dude in the Range Rover?

It was a half hour before Kamikaze would pick him up. The cars had already begun to congregate across the street in front of Master #1 Auto Glass. From his window, Chulito saw that they'd begun passing warm, amber bottles of cognac around. Chulito checked his phone for the hundredth time to see if he'd received a response from the texts he'd sent to Carlos.

Carmen appeared in his doorway. "I can't stop you, right?"

"Don't worry, Ma. Kamikaze has got my back."

"What happened to your plans with Carlos?"

"I didn't know about this," he said gesturing out his window.

Carmen entered the room and touched Chulito's face, but he flinched. She patted his shoulder and smiled. "You look nice." Part of him wanted his mother to hold him like when he was a little kid, when she would take him into her lap in the rocking chair and hold him close. Swinging back and forth and singing boleros by La Lupe and Hector Lavoe. Another part of him wanted her to ground him and say that he couldn't go out. He wished that she was high strung and more emotional like other Latina moms who yelled at their kids and might say something like, "Just try to leave this house and I will slap you so hard you will see the Virgin Mary." But after growing up in a household with lots of yelling and fighting, and then later dealing with his father's drunken binges, she preferred peace. Carmen retreated and disappeared into the dark hallway. There was no one to save him.

Chulito sat on his bed and looked at the doorway as if he could still see her image there smiling at him.

As the daylight faded, Chulito's room became an ethereal blue. It was the time of day where a lamp light could dispel shifting shapes in its the dark corners. Outside, Chulito heard Fat Joe thumping though speakers before he saw the blue Lexus roll up to the corner. The moment Kamikaze stepped out of his Lexus, he leaned against it and a group of the guys gravitated toward him as if he had a hook in each one and was reeling them all in. Kamikaze was dressed in his signature blue—sky blue Kangol hat, baby blue button down shirt with matching shorts and pale blue Timberland boots. Under his hat he wore a bright yellow bandanna.

The bandanna reminded him of the first time he actually met Kamikaze. Everyone knew him. They knew Kamikaze had run corners in the Lower East Side, El Barrio and the South Bronx, but that was back in the day when he was twelve years old. He quickly moved up and now he rolls with the big boys and has crews selling his packages out on the corners and in several exclusive night clubs and gentlemen spots. He personally handles the top level clients including rappers, politicians and some hip hop fashion designers.

Chulito had always seen him in the neighborhood, but they connected one unusually cool day the previous summer. It had been a few days after the bottle throwing incident, and Carlos had gone to Puerto Rico for the rest of the summer. Chulito was sitting on the steps in front of his building and the earphones from his iPod drowned out the sounds of the street with Trick Daddy's ode to being a thug.

Kamikaze walked quickly around the corner of Hunts Point and Garrison Avenues and made eye contact with Chulito. As he passed him, he dropped a small bundle and a gun into Chulito's lap. Instinctively, Chulito slipped the package and the gun inside of his hoodie. The gun felt warm against his bare belly. There had been no sound of gunshots, so it must be warm from Kamikaze's body. That thought caused his dick to swell.

When Kamikaze reached the next corner two plainclothes cops stopped him. Then two more cops appeared. Chulito's heart thumped twice as fast as the beats from the song. He wanted to get up and run inside; instead he tried to relax and bopped his head to the music. The cops pushed Kamikaze against the wall and frisked him. Finding nothing on him, they let him go. The four men walked down the block toward Chulito. With every beat his heart climbed up his throat. There were two Latinos, a Black and a white cop. The white guy was red-faced and as he passed Chulito he said, "Stay away from scum like that, little brother."

Chulito wanted to deck him. He definitely was not little and he was not his brother. Chulito watched the cops disappear around one corner and Kamikaze around the other. The gun and bundle shifted inside of his hoodie, and as Trick Daddy sang about baggy jeans, gold teeth and saying "fuck!" to the police amidst a chorus of children agreeing with his every word, Chulito knew he'd crossed a line.

Kamikaze reappeared, walking slowly this time. He wore a bright yellow running suit with sky blue tank top underneath it, matching sky blue Timberlands and a bright yellow bandanna— definitely not a cop-dodging outfit. Without needing to be told, Chulito stood up and went inside his building as Kamikaze followed. He reached under his hoodie but Kamikaze touched his arm.

"You live here, right?" Kamikaze asked.

Chulito nodded. "My mom is out."

When they got into the apartment, they went to Chulito's room.

Kamikaze howled and hooted as he looked out the first floor apartment's window. "Your name is Chulito, right? You just saved my ass, little bro. Big time. Those stupid fucks almost had me." As if the room were his, he plopped down on the bed.

Chulito lifted his hoodie, and the bundle and the gun dropped next to Kamikaze.

"Thanks, bro." Kamikaze sat up and put his feet on the floor. "I owe you."

Chulito uttered, "Nah" and the word got caught in his throat. His underarms began to sweat, and, as one cold drop slid down the side of his body, he collected himself. "It's cool. You don't owe me nothing."

"Bullshit! My ass was grass, bro. I was thinking, 'what am I gonna do,' and then I turned the corner and boom! There you were. I was hoping you were smart. I was right." Kamikaze looked up at the ceiling and whispered. "Thank you, my nigga." He turned to Chulito. "Yo, I know my boy Willie was looking out for me 'cause I'm wearing his color today. You musta known him? He lived in this building."

"I knew Willie," he said simply.

Everybody knew Willie. He and Kamikaze were always together and Willie always wore yellow. Not gang gold, but yellow, nice and bright. He did wild shit like wear snake eye contact lenses and gold teeth that looked like fangs. Willie also had a sweet face and by the time he was seventeen he could stop traffic just by stepping out of the building wearing a tank top. The girls swirled around him, and he played with them all. It was a miracle that he didn't leave any Willie juniors behind before he died in a car accident racing revved up low riders over on Edgewater Road.

Chulito remembered when the makeshift shrine went up in front of his building—a couple of cardboard boxes and plastic milk crates filled with candles, pictures of Willie, flowers (both plastic and real), Hennessey bottles, 40s, and cigars. The centerpiece was a picture of Willie dressed in yellow and Kamikaze dressed in his signature blue toasting with piña coladas out at City Island for Willie's nineteenth birthday. A snapshot version of that photo hung from Kamikaze's rear view mirror.

Willie died the previous summer on August 22nd. For one whole month Kamikaze wore Willie's yellow and had Tats Cru make T-shirts that read "Willie R.I.P. I miss you." Now the 22nd of every month, Kamikaze wore Willie's color in his memory.

Kamikaze tightened the yellow bandanna around his braids. He looked out the window and since they were only about six feet up from the ground it took little effort to scope out what was happening. "It's been almost a year and I miss the shit out of him." Kamikaze let the shade drop as he turned to face Chulito. "Check me out, getting all open and shit about Willie." He got up from the bed and shook himself like a dog shaking off water. "Whew!" Then he put an arm around Chulito. "Besides, if they caught you with the stuff they couldn't do much. You are like what, fifteen, right?"

Chulito nodded. "My birthday was last month."

"They would have just taken the shit and the gun and called your mommy to come pick you up."

Chulito crossed his arms, narrowed his eyes and clenched his jaw.

Kamikaze stepped back. "Oh, sorry, bro. Didn't mean no disrespect. You can handle yourself. You proved that shit straight up and down." He pulled out his wallet and removed two one hundred dollar bills. "Here, go buy yourself some sneakers."

"Nah, that's cool."

"Bro, don't disrespect me."

Chulito accepted the two crisp bills as Kamikaze smiled. He looked at the posters on Chulito's walls of Fat Joe, Big Pun, Ja Rule and Jennifer Lopez. They connected over their favorite rappers and songs. Chulito couldn't believe that he was chilling in his room with Kamikaze like they were old friends. His mom would definitely lose her cool if she caught him in the house.

"Yo, Chuly-chu, can I call you that?"

Chulito nodded.

Kamikaze said that he liked Chulito's instincts and his clean, tough rep in the hood. Then he said that he needed help running deliveries.

"Are we in business or what?"

Chulito shrugged. He was afraid because, like every kid in his neighborhood, he knew drug life was rough. He had taken a puff from a joint every now and then with the fellas, but he'd never bought drugs or been this close with a dealer before. But he was also excited because he would get mad props from the fellas when they saw him rollin' with Kamikaze and he would have his own loot so he could help out his mom who worked in the lunch room at the local elementary school and made just enough to take care of the basics. Besides, now that Carlos was gone, the only thing he had to look forward to for the rest of the summer was hanging out on the corner with the fellas or getting a minimum wage summer youth job.

"Man, whenever I get away from those motherfuckin' cops I feel great. I get horny and hungry, and since you a dude, even though you got a nice little bump back there..." He burst into laughter, "I'm just messin' with you. I ain't no faggot." Chulito flinched and his ears got hot. "Let's go eat. My treat. And we could talk more about my proposition."

They drove to Step In Diner in Parkchester and ate steaks. Kamikaze drank Coronas with lime, and Chulito had Cokes with lemon. Kamikaze let him sneak a couple of sips from a Corona, but Chulito didn't like it. Kamikaze was about ten years older than Chulito and it was like hanging with that experienced older cousin or cool uncle that Chulito wished he had. By the time Kaz paid the check, Chulito was well on his way to becoming his boy. That summer, he rode with him and accompanied him on special drops and pick ups. Chulito's head swelled with pride when he earned enough trust to be taken to Kamikaze's crib, where no one was ever taken. Kamikaze was a loner who never spoke about family or parents, and he never claimed any of the kids he may have sired.

It was as if Kamikaze had no history, past or connections. He only had the game.

Chulito was treated like blood and Kamikaze took him shopping to up Chulito's game from bootleg clothes to $300 Diesel jeans, Hilfiger jerseys and Kenneth Cole gear. He relished spending most of his days with Kamikaze and felt like a member of the Terror Squad when, even though he was underage, he strolled into the night clubs alongside Kamikaze. He felt protected in the no nonsense way that Kamikaze looked out for him. Just as importantly, he felt like he mattered when he was introduced as "my protégé" to rappers and fashion kings and queens. He got a thrill and felt grown when he learned to shoot a gun, in case shit went down.

But Chulito liked it best when it was just the two of them, like that first day in his room, or when they'd sit and watch *Scarface* in his crib and order his favorite rib tips and beef fried rice from the Chinese spot. He felt most connected to Kamikaze when they spent hours talking about "the game" and what the future could hold for him. Their closeness reminded him of the way he used to hang with Carlos, before he changed.

The sound of laughter from the party posse brought Chuilito back to his room. He got up from his bed to lower his window and saw the white Range Rover pull up in front of the building again. Carlos got out of the car with his mother, and they talked to the blond driver. On the opposite side of the street the "party posse" was in full swing.

Chulito froze as his phone rang.

"I can see you, bro," Kamikaze said. "What you doing standing in your room? Git ya ass out here, ahora." He hung up without waiting for Chulito to respond. Then, the party posse started chanting, "Chu-li-to. Chu-li-to. Chu-li-to."

Chulito darted out of the apartment building and avoided making eye contact with Carlos as he passed. A roar of cheers rose from the guys. As he was engulfed by the throng shouting happy birthdays, Chulito saw Carlos watching. He felt trapped. He wanted to apologize to Carlos and promise to make it up to him, but for the fellas he had to act as if Carlos didn't matter.

Papo, Chin-Chin and Davey were coming from the liquor store, bottles in hand, with Looney Tunes who was not invited. Not to be left out, Looney Tunes offered a gift. "I got you a little bottle of Hen, Chulito."

"Thanks, bro, we'll see you mañana," Chulito said. "Be cool."

"C'mon, Davey, let me get in your car," Looney Tunes said. "You got room."

"Drop it already," Papo slipped on his shades. "Look at you. You always look wrecked and you always trying to ride another nigga's wallet. The way you roll, you ain't never gonna be invited to a party posse."

Chulito and the guys headed toward Davey's car that was parked on the corner where they always stood.

Chulito heard the blond guy turn on the ignition on the Rover. He turned and saw Carlos walk to the driver's side, reach in and shake the guy's hand. As he shook his hand, Carlos flipped his hair out of his eyes and Chulito realized Carlos' hair was a little longer, almost touching his shoulder. Carlos stepped away from the Rover, waved good-bye to the blond boy and went into the building with his mom without looking back at the guys.

Papo pulled Chulito close. "See him shaking that dude's hand? Guess we taught that faggot a little lesson about kissing his boyfriends on our block."

Chulito didn't like Papo referring to the guy as Carlos' boyfriend. He doubted that was true because even though Chulito wasn't up front about his feelings, he figured that Carlos knew something was up and wouldn't show up with another dude.

"Bye, papi." Looney Tunes shook his ass, ran after the Rover and waved good-bye frantically.

Puti, the drag queen who lived with her mother in the first floor apartment across from Chulito, was perched on her window sill. "¡Sángano!" she yelled out to Looney Tunes.

"Fuck you!" he yelled and the fellas laughed.

"Oh, really? With what?" she challenged.

Looney Tunes grabbed his crotch with both hands. "Wit dis, you sorry faggot."

"With two hands full of bootleg jeans? I don't think so." She extended one long slim arm toward Looney Tunes and gave him a loud snap of her fingers. "Pleeeease." Then she disappeared into her apartment.

Looney Tunes kept his head up as the guys laughed and got into Davey's car. "Yo, fuck Puti. She's always got some stupid shit to say."

Davey imitated Puti by extending his arm out his car window and snapping at Looney Tunes. "Puh-leeeze."

Chin-Chin nudged Davey. "Yo, Puti's window is low and she gonna hear you and start shit with you, too, Davey."

"I got no beef with Puti. Maybe we should invite her to the club to celebrate your birthday, Chulito," Davey joked.

"Men only!" Papo said.

"So that's why we left Tunes out," Davey said. They all laughed.

"Technically, Puti is still a man, right?" Davey asked.

They considered the thought as Chulito noticed Brick from the travel agency coming down the block. Brick looked up at the azure sky and squinted to see the first few twinkling stars before continuing down Hunts Point Avenue.

Chulito knew Brick wasn't coming down to join the party posse because he wasn't down with Kamikaze and especially because he was carrying Crystal, his three-year-old daughter, on his shoulders like she was a princess riding a float at the Puerto Rican Day Parade. Chulito couldn't see where he held onto her slim white stockinged legs because they were covered by the mucho ruffles of her soft pink dress. She waved with small, strong arms and blew a kiss with both her hands to Gil who sat on a white plastic chair in front of his liquor store.

"Hola, mamita." Gil waved to Crystal. Her Shirley Temple curls bounced wildly as Brick walked over to Gil. "¿Qué pasa, bro?"

"Nothing, just going to meet Jennifer's mother at the train station," Brick responded.

"Oooi, la Sueeeegraaaaa." Gil shivered.

"No doubt. That's why I got some protection right up here on my shoulders. She don't start no shit with me as long as I got this sweetie with me. Right, mamita?"

Crystal kissed the top of her daddy's head.

"Need a light?" Gil asked, nodding to the unlit cigarette that dangled from Brick's lips.

"Nahhh, nigga, you crazy." Brick looked up to Crystal.

"Oh shit, sorry, bro. So, you going out with the fellas to celebrate Chulito's birthday?"

Brick looked down at Chulito and the fellas on the corner. "Nah, I stay away from Kamikaze. I had my days of dealing drugs and dodging bullets. I got more important things to do." Brick kissed Crystal's ankle.

"I hear you. I'll probably pass through after I lock up. They expect to go all night."

"Well, I's gots to be moving 'cause la suegra don't like walking alone." He said good-bye with an upward flick of his chin. "Say bye to Gil, mamita."

"Bye, Gil."

"Bye, mamita," Gil said.

"Yo, Majora!" Brick shouted to a Black woman with a vibrant tangle of dreads. Majora grew up in the 'hood and formed the local environmental group that rented a storefront next to the liquor store. Brick was placed in her program where he got paid to clean up the Bronx River and take tour groups canoeing.

"Hey Brick, you're working next Saturday, right?"

"Word!"

"See you then. Hi, sweetie," she said to Crystal.

"Hi, Majora," Crystal responded as Majora stepped behind her agency's glass doors.

"Look, Daddy!" Crystal pointed to Julio who owned the travel agency where Brick worked part-time cleaning up and delivering plane tickets to the old folks.

Julio came to the door. "Oh my God, who is that big, beautiful young lady on Daddy's shoulders?"

"Hi, Julio, you got lollipop?" Crystal asked.

"Yes, mamita, right here." He handed her a red lollipop.

"Eat it later, ma," Brick warned Crystal. "I don't want you to get dirty before Grandma sees you."

"Oh, so grandma is coming to visit?"

Brick rolled his eyes. "Yeah, so do you need any help?"

"I'm closing soon, but you can work a couple of hours later tonight organizing that mess in the back. I'll leave you the keys to lock up."

"Definitely! Anything to get out of my house. I'll build the shelves for the supplies."

Chulito was intrigued by Brick and Julio's friendship because Brick was über macho and Julio was über gay. Julio would dress in drag every Halloween, usually as a stewardess or a cruise director. His family had owned Cruz Travel Agency for years and when his father died, Julio took it over. The fellas didn't bother Julio, because they grew up with him and he kept to his place. They also knew he had a registered gun on the premises. Having Brick around also helped.

Brick was strong, stern, and puro hombre with an old soul that could be seen in his dark eyes. If beauty was a mark of leadership, Brick was destined to rule the Bronx. He only stood at 5' 9" and weighed in at a slim buck fifty. But size mattered in other places. First, were his hands, which he now used to do odd construction jobs and other forms of physical labor. He also had a big heart and thought of others in addition to thinking of himself. And word on the street was that he was a condom stuffer, a gift he shared with any woman he chose.

Chulito remembered when Julio used Brick in a promotional campaign to drum up the travel agency's business. The ad was a simple poster of Brick shirtless with a seductive stare in his eyes and the tag line, "Come away with me." Every store owner in the neighborhood put one up, and Brick became a local celebrity. In addition to being displayed all over Hunts Point, the fellas found out that the poster was also hanging in every gay bar in the city and in ads in gay magazines. Brick's stock rose one thousand percent with the women, but the guys gave him lots of shit, asking him if he was turning because the ad looked gay. Brick loved the attention and ignored the guys.

He got about three other, high-paying modeling gigs off of that. Julio managed his budding career, and the fellas teased Brick non-stop, calling him a homo-thug. Eventually, Brick stopped accepting offers for gay campaigns, but his short-lived venture with Julio cemented their friendship. When some rough necks from the other side of the Bruckner Expressway gave Julio some trouble, Brick intervened.

Brick was his nickname, because his birth name, Alejandro, was too old and formal for the twenty-four-year-old former street gangsta. Alejandro was a name he would have to grow into, if ever. Brick worked well with the shorties and it commanded respect from the brothers.

Lost in thoughts, Chulito realized that Brick had almost reached the corner when Looney Tunes waved his hands in front Chulito's face. "Yo! Wake up, bro. Your posse is gonna leave you behind." Chulito looked away and saw Kamikaze beckoning him over. "Later, Tunes." Then he looked back as Tunes dashed toward Brick.

"Yo, Brick!" Looney Tunes called out, stopping him in front of the pawn shop three doors down from the travel agency.

"'Sup Tunes?"

"Those suckas won't let me go with them, so I'm gonna hang out with my girl." Looney Tunes was feeling the new girl who worked in the pawn shop. Whenever he visited her, she'd send him back and forth getting her coffee or something from the doughnut shop.

"Your girl? Right." Brick smiled and kept walking down the

block toward Chulito and the fellas.

"Yo, what you mean 'Right?'"

"Forget it, man, you da boss."

"That's right and don't you—" Looney Tunes was interrupted by Crystal's voice. "Bye, Tunes!"

"Hey, mama, don't you look beautiful today. Is it your birthday?"

"No, Grandma's coming."

"Happy birthday, mamita!" he yelled and disappeared into the pawn shop.

"Yo, Brick! You coming?" Papo yelled. Brick waved and pointed up to Crystal.

But everyone knew Brick stayed away from Kamikaze and from doing things with "the pack." He was a bit of a lone wolf, played on the low with his share of women and he had a Jesus tattoo on his back. There were several stories about that tattoo, but no one seemed to know the real reason he had it done. With Crystal on his shoulders and Jesus on his back, Brick checked out the cars as they filled with the guys and took off into the night to the Gentlemen's Lounge in Yonkers.

From the passenger's seat in Kamikaze's ride, Chulito watched Brick cross the street with Crystal bobbing on his shoulders. He wondered how Brick managed to stay friends with Julio and stay ahead of all the homo rumors.

chapter three

A strong stream of piss splashing loudly in a toilet bowl across the room brought Chulito back to the conscious world. His auditory nerves twitched and his eyelids lifted slowly to reveal a fuzzy view of a ceiling fan spinning lazily and sending down a soft warm breeze on his face. Ah, he could feel his face. With every blink, the room came more into focus. He was in Kamikaze's crib called cielo which means heaven, but was just on the other side of the Bruckner Expressway near Longwood Avenue in a building that got fixed up and went condo. Kamikaze had BG, one of the guys from Tats Cru Graffiti Mural Kings Inc., paint the apartment's ceilings and walls to resemble a sunny blue sky with puffy clouds that glowed in the dark so they could be seen at night. Plush white carpets covered all the floors in the apartment except for the kitchen which had smooth, white, marble tiles. The white overstuffed couches were like giant, cumulous clouds parked around the expansive sunken living room. Kamikaze believed that with all the shit he'd done on earth, he'd never make it to heaven, so he created it in the Bronx.

Chulito's neck muscles joined the awakening and he turned to see Kamikaze standing over the bowl with his back to him and from between his legs the golden pee shimmered in the late morning sunlight. He wore briefs (he only wore briefs because he said his low hanging balls needed support) and the elastic waistband dug into the top of his ass as he pulled down the front. His legs were hairy, which contrasted his smooth back and on his wide shoulders he had KAMIKAZE tattooed in cobalt blue letters with red, orange and yellow flames rising from them. His waist was small and although his butt was covered Chulito could see the two indentations that sat right above each cheek.

The pissing trickled and stopped. The last few drops were squeezed out and Kamikaze tucked himself away. Chulito shut his eyes so he wouldn't get caught watching, then as the toilet flushed he pretended to wake up. Kamikaze turned. "Glad to see you survived last night."

Chulito sat up on his elbows and felt like the room shifted forty five degrees, so he plopped back down.

"Suffer, papa. ¿Pa' eso bebe? Hope you learned your lesson not to mix liquor." Kamikaze teased.

Chulito pressed his knuckles into his temples. "What the fuck happened, Kaz?"

"You couldn't get hard." Kamikaze ran and leaped onto the sofa bed.

"Ow, don't make the bed shake, bro."

Kamikaze sat cross-legged on the bed. Chulito could see the folds of skin from a hairy testicle through the loose leg band. The stale smell of Kaz's cologne sent an electric thrill through Chulito that made his heart race. He turned on his stomach to press down on the awakening in his groin.

"You got fucked up within an hour after we got to the club. We had the hottest mamitas over to lap dance and you kept saying, 'My shit won't go up. Somebody put something in my drink so my shit won't go up.'" Kamikaze laughed and smacked Chulito's butt.

"Ow. Chill wit dat, yo."

"Man, you held on to those dancers like your life depended on it. Remember the one named Veronica who was into you? She buried your face in her tetas and the guys chanted, 'Dale leche, dale leche.' Man, she would have been here, too, if you hadn't passed out." Kamikaze stretched out beside him and hugged a pillow. He raised his two thick, beautiful, black eyebrows. He looked like he was half Chinese and half Puerto Rican. His skin was the color of soft chocolate ice cream, with a short nose and high cheeks. Kamikaze trimmed his moustache close to his lip to the point that it was barely detectable but emphasized their fullness.

Kamikaze's unusual beauty and irresistible charm made it easy to like him. He was open and happy, not like typical dealers or thugs who were all dark and moody.

Chulito stole a glance at his torso, which was smooth except for a small mass of hair in the center of his chest that trailed down the center of his stomach. He pulled the thin white sheet over his head, but in his mind's eye he could still see Kamikaze's long body hugging the pillow, facing him. "Yo, Kaz, keep it down."

He apologized and continued to tell Chulito about the night. How at one point Chulito got up on the low table in their booth to dance with one of the strippers.

"I danced? I don't dance, bro," Chulito protested, defending himself.

Santo, one of the Tats Cru guys, said that he used to strip in a gay club in Puerto Rico and got up on the table to demonstrate. The fellas joked and gave him shit, calling him a fag.

"Shut the fuck up," Santo had said. "I don't let the patos touch nothing, pero I used to make good tips."

Chulito had shoved him off table and tried to imitate him. The German twins from Tats Cru said that they went to a club in Spain where the patrons licked the dollars and stuck them to the stripper's skin. Chulito then pulled the front of his shirt over his head so that it rested on his shoulders and exposed his stomach and chest, and the guys licked dollars and stuck them to him. Even Veronica the stripper licked one of her tips and stuck it on Chulito. After management made him get off the table, he gave his tips to Veronica.

Chulito recalled the evening in small flashes. He remembered feeling jealous when he saw Kamikaze flirting with a blonde dancer with long legs. He remembered that Chin-Chin cried because he hadn't seen his daughter since his ex moved to Florida a year ago. He remembered how the women in the club were all over the German twins because they are blanquitos with blue eyes.

Damian, one of the auto glass guys, was a great dancer and tore up the small dance floor with one of the strippers. He remembered Damian kissing her hand like a gentleman when they finished then rejoining the group, saying that he would eat that dancer alive starting with her pussy.

The three guys who founded Tats Cru—BIO, Nicer and BG—basically hung together and did their fair share of tipping. One of the dancers, a Latina with huge hair, told BIO that he was the man of her dreams. He jokingly told her to keep dreaming 'cause he was already taken, but that she could live a little of her dream right then. She responded with a lap dance. Orlando, the young guy who worked at the corner bodega, showed up to wish Chulito well and had a couple of drinks and a lap dance before leaving. Several other guys from the neighborhood did the same.

Chulito remembered that with each shot of Patron, with each Corona, with each Jack and Coke, with each Cuba Libre he thought of calling Carlos and cursing him out for not calling back. He remembered going to the bathroom to text him: sorry sorry sorry please call me or hit me back. Chulito checked his phone. No texts from Carlos.

Chulito knew that at that very moment any of the guys who were not hung over like him were at the corner or at Tats Cru's offices buzzing with stories from their night out.

"Hey, Chulito, I'm going to take a shower. I made some coffee if you want, but I gotta get something to eat. You wanna come or you can just chill here?"

"I'll go." Food was the last thing on his mind.

"Cool, buzz your mom. Someone's been calling your cell all morning, probably her and she won't relax until she hears your voice." Kamikaze tossed Chulito's phone over to the bed. "Yo, Chulito, I got Veronica's number for you. I told her you were twenty one and she believed me. So if you want it I could do you the favor…"

"Don't do me any more favors, and what do you mean if I want it? You into her?"

"She was hot, bro. All I'm saying is that if you don't want her, toss her this way. And pa, she ain't no Yolanda." Kamikaze went into the bathroom, pushed the door but it stayed ajar and turned on the shower.

Yolanda was another one of Kamikaze's favors. A year ago, when Chulito first met Kamikaze, during one of their three o'clock in the morning, deep soul conversations, Chulito confessed that he'd never had sex.

"What the fuck are you sayin' to me, Chulito? All those shorties buzzin' around you and you ain't poked not even one of them. They ready to hand they shit over to you, m'brother."

Chulito said that he was a virgin out of respect for his mom and church.

Kamikaze laughed.

Chulito covered his face and shook his head realizing how lame that excuse sounded once it came out his mouth.

Kamikaze looped his arm around Chulito's neck and kissed his temple. "We gotta change that shit right now. You fifteen years old, pana, and way past due."

Chulito pulled away. "Yo, Kaz, don't do some crazy shit."

Kamikaze laughed again. "I'm gonna call Yolanda and she will fuck your brains out, papa, tonight! Nah, fuck that shit, she's gonna do it now!" Kamikaze flipped open his cell phone and pushed one button.

Chulito's hands sweated. "Nah, man, I...I...I'm not ready."

"Shut the fuck up and get ready to have your first taste. Hey, mamita, it's Kamikaze. What you doing right now?"

Chulito's mind raced. No fucking way! No fucking way! And he ran out of Kamikaze's apartment.

Kamikaze chased him down the block, and caught him, "Yo, nigga, what the fuck is wrong with you? You gay or something?"

It was like the air had been sucked out of the world and Chulito could hear just hear his heartbeat. He knew at that moment that he would have to fuck Yolanda.

"Nah, man, I'm just scared. There are all those diseases and she could get pregnant."

Kamikaze took a deep breath, looked him in the eye and smiled. "Chulito, there ain't nothing to be scared of, ah-ight? Listen, Yolanda is a professional. It's her job. So forget about all that pregnant shit and diseases. Besides, your shit will be wrapped." Kamikaze looked up into the dark sky, thought a moment, and then looked back at Chulito. "So, this is what we gonna do. She's gonna come to my place and we gonna do her together. Fuck, I might as well get a little some'n, some'n out of this, too."

"Together? I don't think so." Chulito loved the idea of Kamikaze being in the room with him and Yolanda.

"Ah-ight, so do her by yourself."

"Do her?"

"Chulito, what is up?"

"It's just that…" Chulito thought of the times he saw Kamikaze in his underwear when they chilled in his crib. He recalled the dreams he'd had where it was just the two of them wrapped in each other's arms.

"Look, you want me to be there? I'm wit it. I'll get her all warmed up and then pass her to you. I'll be your coach."

"My coach?"

"Yeah. I didn't need no coach, but you so scared I want to make sure you don't fuck it up, and I want to make sure you go through wit it."

Chulito suppressed a smile. "O.K., but don't tell anybody."

"Who the fuck am I gonna tell?"

So they went back to Kamikaze's apartment and waited for Yolanda's arrival. They took showers, separately, as Yolanda requires of her clients before she arrives. She also only goes out, never has men to her apartment. She has two daughters and a son and doesn't want them seeing any activity going down.

Yolanda showed up all mighty and voluptuous. She had lots of curves and wild curly hair that she had tied up in a tangle on the top of her head. She took out a napkin from her purse and stuck the gum she was chewing in it, then wiped dark red lipstick from her mouth. She looked at Chulito and smiled with wide bright teeth. "Hey, baby, I'm gonna pop your cherry."

"Don't look so fucking scared, man." Kamikaze counted out four hundred dollars and handed it to Yolanda. "She ain't really gonna pop something. You ain't no chick."

"I know," Chulito lied. He knew that when women had their cherry popped something inside them broke and there was blood involved. He imagined that the head of his dick would pop like a pimple full of blood and burn with searing pain.

"Listen up. Me and Yolanda are gonna go get busy and I'll call you when she's ready for you." Yolanda rolled her eyes and followed Kamikaze.

"Ah-ight," Chulito said as they disappeared behind the bedroom door.

Chulito looked around Kaz's living room. Most of the furniture was custom made and even the television and remote where white. Money was no object for Kamikaze. One day he hoped to have a place like this.

The couch's imported white Italian leather was soft as suede and Chulito sank deeper into it. They'd sat on those couches for hours watching TV, getting high and had fallen asleep a bunch of times without pulling out the bed. He started to drift off when he heard Yolanda moaning and Kamikaze growling, "Yeah, mama." His heart was slowly climbing up his throat. Everything felt moist, his brow, his palms, the crack of his ass. He got up and walked slowly toward the door to leave the apartment. As he reached for the doorknob Kamikaze yelled, "Yo, Chulito!"

His stomach gurgled and he went into the bedroom. The air was thick and he could smell sweat. Kamikaze and Yolanda were in his round white bed under a thin sheet. Yolanda sat up. "Come here, you cute motherfucker. You are so beautiful, Chulito."

He moved to the bed as if he were sleepwalking.

She grabbed his belt, undid it, and his loose pants dropped to his ankles. Chulito felt his dick shrinking into his body.

Kamikaze said, "Yo, relax Chulito. You look like you gonna shit your pants."

The sound of his voice reminded Chulito that Kamikaze was there on the bed, behind Yolanda. Excitement got added to his nervousness.

Yolanda pulled down his boxer shorts and he felt generations of Catholic shame wash over him.

Kamikaze appeared at her shoulder, kissed it softly and slowly and didn't make eye contact with Chulito. As Yolanda stroked Chulito, he watched Kamikaze's thick rough hand caressing her large smooth hip. Then Kamikaze looked at Chulito, raised his two thick eyebrows and smiled —all teeth framed by thick lips. The warm air of a nearby fan tickled Chulito's pubic hairs and his dick awakened.

"Ah, good, he's finally starting to grow, look," she said.

"I don't want to look at his shit!" Kamikaze buried his face in Yolanda's hair.

"C'mon on, papito," she said coaxinxg Chulito to join them on the bed. "Move back, Kamikaze."

Chulito took off his shirt, kicked off his sneakers, stepped out of his pants and boxers and got into the bed beside her.

She told him to lie on his side and she faced him. With a determined look in her eye, she reached down, grabbed his dick, slipped on a sticky condom and slipped him inside her. He instinctively began moving his hips in and out. It was warm and wet and their genitals made a slick, slippery sound.

"Very nice, Chulito. Keep moving, papito." She pulled him closer to her. As Chulito put his arm around Yolanda, his hand brushed Kamikaze's chest and he quivered.

Chulito and Yolanda developed a rhythm. His sweat dripped down his face, neck and chest, but it felt as if someone were pouring seltzer water all over his body and the tiny bubbles were bursting and tickling his skin. He held onto Yolanda's hips. To his surprise he liked almost pulling all the way out of her and then shoving his hips forward into her while pulling her toward him. Each long deliberate stroke brought him higher. He felt as if he would float to the ceiling still attached to her. His head bobbed back and forth and he grunted with each thrust. Kamikaze watched. "Look at chu, Chulito. You don't need me here. I'm bouncin'."

Yolanda stopped him. "You and your dick ain't going nowhere."

"Ah-ight, but I'm not just gonna watch," Kamikaze challenged. "I'm all horny and shit."

So they made a Yolanda sandwich. Chulito continued to pump deeply from the front while Kaz kissed the back of her neck and squirmed against her ass. Kamikaze then lifted Yolanda's leg and Chulito felt Kamikaze's cock poking at her pussy too, then it slipped and nudged his balls. Chulito shuddered, but kept pumping. Kamikaze persisted until Chulito felt it. Kaz's cock pushed inside Yolanda, rubbing the underside of his own dick as it slid inside. They all sighed simultaneously. Chulito breathed in small gasps and felt like he was going to pass out from the sensation of Kamikaze's hardness gliding against his dick. He pressed his face into Yolanda's breasts to keep from popping.

"You're a fucking freak, Kaz. Open me up, motherfuckers." Yolanda bit the top of Chulito's head.

Her voice was distant, as if she were in the next room. Chulito thought his body was going to explode all over the place. He thrust himself faster, imagining what their dicks looked like wrapped together insider her. He released one hand from Yolanda and reached to hold onto Kamikaze, who pushed his hand off and pulled out. The quick retraction brought Chulito to the edge. Kamikaze whispered, "Can we try the position I like before I bust my nut?"

Yolanda turned to look him in the eye. "Only because you gonna pay extra…and I like that position, too."

Like a group of acrobats they maneuvered and ended up with Yolanda on her back with Kamikaze's balls in her mouth and Chulito inside her.

Chulito and Kamikaze were facing each other. It was wild for him to see Kamikaze naked, sweaty and holding his big, hard, shiny dick. Kaz was thick and long. Chulito had never seen a dick like that in gym class. He wondered how he measured up for Yolanda after having a dick that size inside her.

Kamikaze jerked his cock while Yolanda lapped his swollen nuts and slurped each ball in her mouth. Chulito felt his orgasm rising and shut his eyes, because the image of Kamikaze jerking off was bringing him there. That vision burned on his brain along with the memory of Kamikaze's stiff prick pressing against his.

Kamikaze's deep low moans grew louder. When Chulito looked he saw Kamikaze's eyes rolling back into his head as he murmured, "I'm coming, mama."

The first shot hit Chulito right below the chin and the second shot hit him between his nipples. The rest landed on Yolanda's round breasts and soft belly.

Chulito was buzzing. He wiped his chin and continued to hump, but held out for Yolanda. He felt like she was close by the way she shoved her hips into him. She looked at Kamikaze's dick and flicked her tongue in its direction. His dick had become softer, but didn't shrink like Chulito knew his would after he came. Yolanda's arms scooped underneath Kamikaze's legs and her nails gripped his thighs. "Don't just sit there," she said to Kamikaze. "Play with my tetas! Kiss them! Kiss me!" Kamikaze obeyed by smearing his cum around her dark brown nipples and squeezing their tips. He then wiped one clear and sucked it. She trembled and let out a series of short breaths combined with high yelps. Kamikaze sat up to watch Yolanda come while he cupped her breasts with his hand and rubbed the nipples with his thumb. She shouted a litany of curses in Spanish, "Carajo, coño, puñetaaaa," and let out a gasp that made her deflate to almost half her size. Then she looked up at Chulito, smiled and nodded. "You worked me, you cute fuck." She continued to move her hips in slow small circles. Then she reached up and wrapped her manicured hand around Kamikaze's soft cock. When she squeezed it, Chulito saw a white pearl of cum ooze out of his slit. He knew he shouldn't be looking at Kamikaze's dick so he quickly diverted his stare from it to Yolanda's eyes.

Chulito was about to pass out from holding back his orgasm, so he pumped harder and boom! His entire body convulsed like the Pentecostals he spied on in the churches on Manida Street. He wondered if getting the spirit felt the same way. His knees gave and he toppled onto Yolanda slick with sweat and Kamikaze's cum. When Chulito opened his eyes, Kamikaze dick was inches from his face and Kaz was smiling. Chulito smiled back, pulled himself out of Yolanda and slipped beside her on the bed. The condom drooped with the weight of his cum and Chulito's dick began to shrink. Yolanda pressed her lips to Chulito's mouth and he smelled the musk from Kamikaze's balls all over her lips. When he pushed his tongue in her mouth, it was coated with the taste of Kamikaze. He kissed her hungrily, licking the roof her mouth and the insides of her cheeks. One of Kamikaze's wiry pubic hairs got transferred into his mouth. He pushed it under his tongue and held it there.

Kamikaze laughed. "You ain't no virgin no more, little nigga." He wiped some of his own cum off his hand then raised it up. Chulito licked Yolanda's lips one last time, then leaned on one elbow and slapped Kamikaze high-five with his cleaner hand and their fingers laced together. "You did it, Chulito. I was a witness. Hey, Yolanda, we just birthed a sex son."

She sat up and pushed her curly locks away from her face, "Ay, what the fuck are you talking about? Mira, get out of my way so I can clean up. That was good Chulito, but this don't make you a man or nothin'. It takes a lot more to be a man than just fucking a woman." Then she got up and went to the bathroom.

Kamikaze laughed and fell back on his bed. Chulito loved how Kamikaze was comfortable being naked. He started getting hard again, so he reached for a small towel by the side of the bed and wiped himself.

"You missed a spot." Kaz pointed to the glob of cum that had landed on Chulito's chest. "Sorry about that, bro, but having my bolas sucked drives me wild. You should have it done some time and see what I mean." Chulito rolled the hair around the inside of his mouth and imagined rolling his tongue around Kamikaze's balls.

Kamikaze wiped his hands with another towel, flipped Chulito with it, then tossed it on the floor. "Wanna smoke?"

"Sure."

He lit a joint and danced around the room, "Chulito ain't no virgin no more."

Chulito smiled at the memory of his first time and heard Kamikaze in the shower. He watched steam escape out the door and dissipate as it hit the dry air in the room. The ceiling fan caused some of it to swirl around the apartment filling it with the sweet, fresh scent of the minty liquid soap Kamikaze loved. He imagined the light lather all over Kamikaze's body, small bubbles sliding down his legs with the hair all matted down and sleek. With his eyes closed he could see Kamikaze soaping up his crotch and the foam mounting as he rubbed it in.

Chulito shook his head to clear it, then called his mom and assured her that everything was O.K. He apologized for not coming home and in order to calm her down, he made a list of promises to her like he would get his GED, would call her in the future no matter what, and he wouldn't get any girls pregnant.

There was a mounting pressure growing in Chulito's bladder. He tried to hold out until Kamikaze finished taking a shower because it was difficult peeing with a hard-on. He'd decided to go to the kitchen, stand a foot or two away from the sink and pee like an erect fountain boy when Kaz's cell started ringing with Fabolous's "Keepin' it Gangsta." The phone was clipped to the pants hanging on the bathroom door handle.

"Yo, Chuly-chu, get me my phone!"

Chulito scurried to the bathroom, unclipped the phone, entered the steamy room and handed the phone to Kamikaze. "Yo, I gotta take a leak."

"Ain't nobody stopping you." Kamikaze kept his head out of the shower to keep the phone from getting wet.

Chulito pulled down his boxer briefs, sat on the bowl and pushed his erection down to pee into it. Chulito felt every muscle in his body relax as the urine flowed out of him, while Kamikaze talked with one of the suppliers who had a stash ready for disbursement.

"See you at three." Kamikaze ended his conversation and handed the phone to Chulito. "Should I leave the water on?"

"O.K.," Chulito responded. Kamikaze slid the curtain open, stepped out, grabbed a towel and dried himself.

Seeing Chulito sitting on the bowl he reacted. "Fo! You taking a shit? I thought you said you had to pee, nigga."

"I am peeing, it's just…"

"Oh, I see. I guess things are back in working order down there. Maybe you should give Veronica a call now." Kamikaze pumped his hips. "We could do her like we did Yolanda back in the day."

"Bet." Chulito finished peeing, but sat pressing down on his erection waiting for Kamikaze to leave the bathroom.

"I gotta go see Hank at three for a pick up, you comin'?"

"Yeah." Chulito stayed seated on the toilet. "But I gotta go home first, O.K.? Show my face."

Kamikaze dried his hair with a towel then wrapped it around his waist. He went over to the mirror, wiped off steam and put shaving cream on his face. Chulito realized that Kamikaze was not leaving the bathroom any time soon so he got into the shower quickly.

Seeing Chulito's erection bounce, Kamikaze said, "Don't be taking a long shower and shit. It's already after eleven o'clock and if you want to come with me we gotta eat and stop by your house before heading up to Hank's in Connecticut."

Chulito tried to ignore his erection as he washed himself, but the memory of the Yolanda incident and seeing Kamikaze naked again had him horned out. He squeezed his cock and felt a rush through his body accompanied by guilt. Kamikaze continued to talk and shave.

Chulito washed his underarms, bolas, ass crack, and feet. Then he gave his dick a few strokes and jerked off as quietly as possible. It could be fast, he thought. The sink water went off. Good, Chulito thought, Kamikaze would leave the bathroom and he could just finish the job. Then the hair blower come on. Chulito continued to stroke himself and circle his nipple with his thumb sending waves of pleasure up and down his body. The intensity built quickly in his balls. He held his breath as the first stream of cum shot out of him. Kamikaze turned off the blower. For the second and a third squirt he was was silent, but by the fourth shot a short gasp escaped from him and he continued to tremble.

"Did you just come, nigga?" Kamikaze asked matter-of-factly. "You better make sure none of that shit sticks to the tub when you're done, and hurry up 'cause we gotta go, or I'm gonna leave ya ass."

Chulito stood in the warm shower, his knees weak. He never thought that he would do something like that, and Kamikaze treated it like no big deal. Nothing was too weird for him. It was one of the things that made Kamikaze different from any of the guys in the neighborhood. Chulito loved that about him.

chapter four

Chulito watched as a warm, powerful blast of wind shoved Carlos around the corner of Garrison and Hunts Point Avenues. Chulito's heart shifted into high gear, as it always did, when he saw Carlos suddenly appear half a block away. Outwardly, Chulito stayed nonchalant, as if he had been leaning on the car in front of their building by chance, but he had been there hoping to run into Carlos.

A week had passed since the party posse, and Carlos was like a phantom walking by without making eye contact, as if Chulito, or anyone else on the block, didn't exist.

Now, as Carlos came closer, Chulito's pulse quickened. Carlos' shopping bags swung out of control, his hair flew wildly obscuring his face, shorts flapped around his legs and his loose shirt ballooned all around him occasionally revealing a small line of smooth skin on his stomach. It was like Mother Nature wanted to see Carlos naked and was threatening to blow off his clothes.

Since the fellas weren't on the corner and it was too early for many people to be around, Chulito decided to not let Carlos just walk past. He distracted him from his struggle with a loud, "Yo!"

Carlos looked at Chulito leaning on the car.

"Hey, Carlos, how you been?" Chulito braced himself for Carlos' tirade.

Instead, Carlos ignored him and continued to walk into their building.

"Hol' up, Carlos, please?" Chulito checked to see who was around then stood up. "I called and texted you a couple of times to apologize."

"Hey, Chulito, they still call you that, right? They haven't changed your name to Thug or Nigga?"

"Nah, it's still Chulito."

"What's with the braids? Your curly hair is too soft? Looking for new ways to look gangsta?"

Chulito patted his head. "I had them done this morning. All the cool reggaetoneros are sportin' them. You know I like to keep up. What do you think?" Chulito winked.

Carlos shrugged. "What do you want?"

Chulito looked away. He'd wanted to talk to Carlos, but now that he had his attention he didn't know what to say. "Can we go talk privately?"

"No. If you have anything to say, say it now. Here." Carlos stood still, but the wind continued to animate his clothes and hair. "Well?'

Chulito looked away from Carlos. "I'm sorry about not keeping our plans that—"

Carlos interrupted him. "You already apologized. I got your texts and your phone calls. Consider them sufficient."

Chulito's palm sweated. He wanted to say that he wished they could rewind and go back to the phone calls they were having. He wanted to say how excited he was anticipating Carlos' return. He wanted to go up to Carlos, whose arms were weighed down by the two shopping bags and hug him tightly. Then help him carry the bags. "Gimme a second, Carlos, please?"

Carlos put down one shopping bag and pushed his hair out of his face. Chulito realized that this was the first time in over a year that he was seeing Carlos' face up close and it was all eyes like Japanese animation characters. A lock of hair was caught on one of his eyelashes and it reminded him of the morning Carlos was leaving for college.

Carlos was outside, on the very spot where they both now stood, with his maletas, boxes and shopping bags. Clara, the marimacho who always wore plaid shirts and who worked at Borinquen cab service, was going to drive him out to Long Island. His mom stood there looking so proud of him. People kept stopping by to say "good luck." Chulito's mother brought Carlos a container with arroz con gandules and chuletas she'd cooked the night before. Chulito saw all this through a slit at the bottom of his shade. He felt as he did now, full of thoughts and feelings about Carlos but unable to express them. Earlier that summer the bottle incident had happened and they never spoke about it.

Just about everybody loved Carlos. He was so smart that he got skipped twice—once from the third to the fifth grade and again from the seventh to the ninth. Chulito admired that about him, especially since he hated school, but he liked hanging with Carlos, so Chulito did his best to keep up.

That morning was windy, too, and Chulito watched Carlos packing the back of Clara's taxi. His loose stringy black hair kept falling in his face and he kept brushing it back. A few strands got caught on some of his long eyelashes and he blinked to try to get them out of his large copper colored eyes which looked brighter against his pale, creamy skin. And his smooth lips looked especially kissable. Chulito knew that he was not supposed to be noticing Carlos that way, but as he sat all pissed off in his room watching him pack the cab that day he thought Carlos was cute. Ever since he saw Carlos with that guy the day of the bottle incident, he was feeling an urgency to be real with what he was feeling. Sooner or later Carlos was going to fall in love with someone, then Chulito would have to keep his feelings on permanent lock down. He didn't know how he could risk being as real as he needed to be with Carlos.

As Chulito watched Carlos hug everyone good-bye, he wished that he'd had a pause button so that the whole world would stop. Then he would go down and hug him without anyone seeing him and say, "Do your thing, Carlos." But he couldn't do that. People might think some shit. So instead, Chulito just peered through the slit in the shade. He watched Carlos give a final hug to his mother, climb into the cab and disappear down Garrison Avenue.

As he sat in his small room, Chulito couldn't make up his mind whether he was more angry at Carlos for leaving or at the whole 'hood for thinking that it wouldn't be cool for him to be friends and hug a nigga that everyone called a pato. Who made up those rules? Chulito wondered.

Talking to Carlos that first chance since he was back from school was bending those rules—breaking them.

Chulito looked into Carlos' eyes. "You have every right to be pissed."

Carlos shook his head and put down the other shopping bag.

"I'm pissed at myself for expecting something different from you."

Chulito took one step toward him then stopped. "I didn't know about the plans the fellas made."

"But you went along. You picked hanging with them over hanging with me."

Chulito moved closer and whispered, "What was I supposed to do? I was hoping we could have gone out the next day."

Tears began to pool in Carlos' eyes, but he looked angry not hurt. "Talking to you every day for the last month made me feel connected, like we were friends again. But when we're alone it's different than when we're here." Carlos looked around the neighborhood as if in disgust.

Just then a car that pulled up in front of their building and Looney Tunes popped out. Carlos wiped his tears. Looney Tunes pushed back his tangle of hair he never combed, wiped his hands on his dusty denim shorts and pulled down his faded T-shirt with a Budweiser logo on the front and a rip in one of the sleeves. He tripped on the curb and one of the flip flops fell off his white socked foot. He winked at Chulito with his green eyes, which were his calling card, he thought, for all the chicks in the neighborhood. Chulito thought he looked like he had a hangover and got dressed in the dark.

"Hey Chu-li-to, my man, wassup?" He clapped/shook hands with Chulito and they gave each other a shoulder bump.

"Chillin'," Chulito responded. Looney Tunes nodded to Carlos.

"Hey, Looney Tunes," Carlos said indifferently.

As he stepped into the building, he looked back and wiggled a limp wrist behind Carlos. Then his burst of laughter echoed through the empty lobby.

"He's a crazy nigga," Chulito said.

Carlos bent down to pick up the shopping bags. "No, he's a fucking asshole."

Chulito moved in to pick up a bag. "I was really looking forward to hanging with you. I still want to."

Carlos yanked the bag from him. "Why? It seems to cause problems. Chulito, on those calls we talked about how we've changed. Those changes just get in our way."

"More college talk?"

"Fuck you, Chulito. Don't act like you don't understand me."

"Sorry. Damn. So you saying we can't hang?"

"Why would you want to anyway?" Carlos asked, his expressive brows arched like two parentheses framing his eyes.

"You're different."

Carlos was always different. Chulito liked that Carlos stayed out of trouble and never hung out on the corner. He was a bookworm and talked about the novels of James Baldwin, Gabriel García Marquéz and Virginia Woolf and would get heated and say "The schools are leaving out our Latina writers from our curriculum like Sandra Cisneros, Julia Alvarez, Isabelle Allende and Esmeralda Santiago." He loved reading out loud from contemporary cats like Abraham Rodríguez and Junot Díaz. Chulito connected to the stories about the Bronx or the hood and loved talking about them with Carlos. Also, Carlos always knew what new movie was out, especially the ones that didn't make it up to the Bronx multiplexes, and he listened to music different from what everybody else jammed to. Chulito could hear Carlos' music coming down through the ceiling. Carlos was down with hip hop and salsa, but he also listened to rock and jazz. Carlos had a special love for Nina Simone and once proudly told Chulito that she lived in France because of racism. Carlos had no issues doing his own thing because being different, in some way, meant that he was better than everyone else.

"You're different, too, Chulito. That's why you and I connect and I don't connect with all those other fucks." Chulito looked away and down the block as if he were searching for someone.

Carlos picked up his bags and said under his breath, "Why do I fucking bother."

"Wait, Carlos, why you so heated?"

Carlos shook his head and looked at Chulito. "On the ride back here from school I couldn't wait to see you again. I called you about four times, and when you didn't answer I felt something was up. Then I saw you on the corner, I got scared because I thought I'd come back to the same old shit. I don't want to get hurt."

"You don't ever have to be scared of the fellas on the corner again. I got your back." Chulito slapped his chest with the flat of his hand.

"My hero? I can't trust you to protect me. Besides, I've taken pretty good care of myself." Carlos chuckled.

Chulito's anger rose. "Don't laugh at me, bro."

"I just think it's funny that you say you have my back and you threw a bottle at me." Carlos' face went red and the tears returned. "How do I know you won't do that again—or worse—next time?"

Chulito felt like his heart was going to shatter as he saw a tear slide down Carlos' cheek. "Sorry, pa, I swear I'll never do that again. I told you I got your back. I'm dead serious."

Carlos put down a bag and wiped the tear. "You might mean what you say, but I never thought you would do it in the first place. Look, I wasn't coming back home after the semester. I planned to get a job out in Long Island and do my internship with the *New York Daily News* so that I could stay the fuck away from here. But after talking to you again I came home to continue our connection. Then when I heard those guys chanting your name, it was like nothing had changed. So I don't think it's a good idea for us to be friends again."

Chulito felt stuck. It was tough enough for them to just be seen together, so how could they have a friendship, let alone open up what he felt for Carlos? "Whatever." Chulito turned away from Carlos and looked up at the windows and across the street to see if anybody was watching. "So it's like that?"

"How can it be any other way?" Carlos sounded forlorn.

"Then don't let me hold you up." Chulito leaned back on the parked car and lit a cigarette like he didn't give a shit, but tried desperately to figure out what he could do.

Carlos took two steps toward him. "Chulito, I know why this isn't easy for me, but why is this so hard for you?" He searched Chulito's eyes more intensely than he ever had before.

Chulito turned away and shrugged, but wanted to burst out and say, "'Cause I'm feeling you, ah-ight? But we gotta keep it on the low."

Before another word was said, Damian approached, shirtless and doing trunk twists. Chulito was annoyed by the interruption. "Nigga, why you always gotta be showing off?"

"'Cause I got a lot to show off." Damian rubbed his abdomen.

"Jail. That's what you got to show off. Y'all niggas always come out looking all buff and then you let shit go. Watch, next summer, if you still here, you'll probably have a little belly and shit."

Damian looked at Carlos. "What you looking at? This ain't for you." He turned to Chulito. "Is that little faggot giving you lip, Chulito?"

"Nah, it's cool."

"Fuck you." Carlos' tears were back. His face flared with rage.

"What?" Damian walked toward him. "You betta watch your fucking mouth."

Chulito got in between. "Chill, Damian."

Damian backed off. "You betta watch your fucking self, Carlos." He returned to searching for cars.

Carlos picked up his bags. "I hate this fucking neighborhood."

Chulito turned to Carlos. "Yo, Carlos, wait a second. You said that you know why this is tough for you. Why is it?"

Carlos turned to Chulito, took a deep breath and exhaled. "It's because I dig you, Chulito. It's the one thing you and I don't ever talk about, but I get so worked up and angry when we don't connect because I dig you, and not like when we were kids."

Chulito looked away from Carlos to hide his grin. He had imagined a more dramatic declaration, but Carlos was smooth and hearing him say those words made Chulito want to leap in the air and shout, "Yes!" But he suppressed his feelings and just shook his head. "Wow, don't hold back."

Carlos shrugged. "Now you know." He turned to go into the building but stopped to find his keys. "So what do you think?"

Chulito wanted to say, "Me too, Carlos, I fuckin' dig you, too." But he just nodded his head. "I don't know what to say."

"Yo! Chulito!" Kamikaze called out as he bopped toward them.

"Well, I better go," Carlos nodded toward Kamikaze, "before the next asshole gets here."

"He ain't like that. Kamikaze is real cool." Chulito got up from the car and straightened out his Yankees jersey.

Carlos smiled. "His name is Kamikaze? Classic. I'm sure he's cool." Carlos looked down the block at Kamikaze. "And he's cute, too. Is he my competition?"

"Yo, don't be going all crazy and shit. Kaz ain't like that."

"Chill, Chulito, it was only a fucking joke. You don't have to be so sensitive, blood. Take care." Carlos vanished into the dark lobby of their building before Kamikaze reached them.

Kamikaze held out his thick palm high in the air ready to collide in a powerful high-five with Chulito. Then he slipped his arm around Chulito's neck, pulled him close and kissed his temple.

"Yo, cut that shit out." Chulito protested and looked back at the building entrance to make sure Carlos hadn't caught it.

"What the fuck? I can't kiss you? Since when?" Kamikaze teased.

Since thirty seconds ago, Chulito thought. "I dig you, and not like when we were kids." Carlos' phrase was like a wrecking ball slamming into the bricks of Chulito's mind. Chulito struggled to not cross the pato line. Now Kamikaze's brotherly kiss felt weird even though at times they'd sit in their underwear and smoke weed or sit side by side near the Bronx River sipping Hennessey and watching the sun rise. They were just two niggas hangin'. They didn't cross the pato line and Chulito could keep his feelings in check.

Kamikaze had a serious look. "Hey, Chulito. I love you like you was my little brother."

Chulito looked into Kamikaze's eyes and said earnestly, "I know."

"So because you turn sixteen, you too old for me to be kissing you? Who gives a shit?" Kamikaze shouted like a town crier. "This is our neighborhood and we do whatever the fuck we want, right?"

"Yeah," Chulito said hesitantly. "It's just that..."

Since he was a couple of inches taller than Chulito, Kamikaze bent his knees to look at Chulito eye to eye. "¿Qué pasa, panita? Did I do something? 'Cause I know you get all silent and moody when something is up."

"Nothing is up. Just don't kiss on me out on the block in front of everybody. O.K.?"

"Whatever you say, little bro. If you too grown for me to be expressing my love for you, I got it." He winked at Chulito and laid out the day's plan.

Damian's cries of "Auto glass! Auto glass! Auto glass!" sliced through the sounds of salsa and hip-hop music streaming out of apartments, kids playing on the sidewalk, trucks booming down the street, and an old man calling out, 'Coco! Cherry!" as he pushed his cart filled with fruit flavored ices.

Chulito watched Damian flash a bright white smile at a female customer then throw his head back and laugh as he ran his hand across his smooth chest letting his thumb linger over one swollen brown nipple. He looked over to Chulito and nodded at him. The sun made Damian's skin glow and his pale brown eyes look like they were lit from within. He scratched his cleanly—cropped fade haircut along with his freshly clipped moustache and eyebrows. Damian's body was tight with long, brown arms that ended with big, strong hands. A thin line of hair ran down the middle of his rippled stomach and disappeared behind the elastic waistband of his underwear, which Damian wore low. His pants were even lower. Chulito could see the tops of his lean hips, and a hint of his pubic hair.

Kamikaze followed Chulito's gaze and made eye contact with Damian.

"Yo, Hercules," Kamikaze called out as a big eighteen wheeler rambled down Garrison Avenue, spewing thick gray smoke into the Hunts Point air.

"Kaz! You got my message?" Damian swaggered across the street with his hips leading the way.

"Yeah, I called you back, nigga, and your girl answered."

"Yo, yo, yo! Ex-girl. Man, that's over. I had enough of her shit. I get out of Rikers and you would think she would be happy to have me back, especially wit all this." He held his arms out and turned around to display his buffed body. "But hellll no! After two days it was back to the same old shit. The rent! She wants kids! She needs money for this or that! Fuck, I don't get paid from this shit job for another two weeks, I'm living off of the tips and commissions." He shoved his hand in his pocket and pulled out a fistful of dollar bills.

"So, get yourself another one." Kamikaze held up his hand and Damian high-fived him. "Damian, I don't get why chicks always want to sink in their hooks. Like that chick Brenda is always trying to pin her baby Joselito on me. That chick's had every dude from Bryant Avenue to Manida Street, how does she know that kid's mine? No way. Just trying to pin me down."

Damian nodded. "That's what I'm talking about. Chulito, little bro, look and learn from your elders. So check it out, I bounced and moved in with Lefty until I could get my own place. So just use my celly when you want to connect."

"So why you call?" Kamikaze asked.

"I want my usual. You got something with you?" As Damian talked he looked up and down the block and kept rubbing and caressing his chest and shoulders. Chulito stole glances at Damian's hands.

"Let me call one of my boys to swing by and take care of you, but I got a little personal gift in my car." Kamikaze winked.

"Vamos, vamos, before my boss gets back."

The three of them continued down Garrison until they reached Hunts Point Avenue and waited for the light to change. Chulito turned his head to look back at the spot where he and Carlos had been talking. The warm breeze that had pushed Carlos around the corner was now traveling through Chulito's braids tickling his hairs. A chill ran through his body.

"C'mon, Chuly-chu," Kamikaze called from the middle of crossing the street. Chulito straightened up. He narrowed his eyes and walked across the street tough and strong. As he reached the other side, the spicy, fried smells from the Spring Garden Chinese take-out floated up his nostrils and gave him a craving for some chicken wings. Chulito jogged to catch up to Kamikaze and Damian.

Their conversation was in full swing. Damian leaned in close to Kamikaze. "So I'm gonna call up some of my dogs and we gonna chill at Lefty's place, smoke up some weed, get some bitches and fuck up a storm, straight up and down! You two wanna come through?"

"Maybe for a minute. I gotta take care of business, Big D. I'm a working dawg." Kamikaze went to private parties, but it was usually for sales or to make an appearance that could lead to future sales. He was never a part of a crew, just his own man, so in a way a part of every crew. No one was close to Kamikaze except Chulito.

"How 'bout chu, Chulito? You wanna come? Since you sixteen and all you can hang with the big boyzzz." Damian's big smile glowed against his brown skin.

"Thanks, bro. Maybe I'll come through, but I gotta take care of this nigga," he said, pointing a thumb at Kamikaze who was getting into his car.

"Git ya bump in the car," Kamikaze ordered, slamming the door shut.

"Thanks, Kaz," Damian called out. "Later, Chulito. Try to come through." Damian turned and walked back down Garrison Avenue. Chulito watched the muscles in Damian's back flex and sway with each step.

Chulito got into the car. Big Pun protested through the speakers about the plights of poverty and making wrong decisions, all set to danceable beats. Kamikaze looked at Chulito and bopped his head. "That is the shit." He made a U-turn on Garrison and stopped at the light. As Damian crossed Hunts Point Avenue, Chulito watched him run up to Martha and put his arms around her. She shrugged him off and he tried again. As the traffic light changed, Kamikaze lowered the radio, rolled down the dark window. "Hit it, Damian. Don't take no for an answer."

Damian gave up on Martha and stepped off the curb. "Fuck it, there are plenty more women who know a good thing when they see it."

"Good thing?" Martha defended herself. "Just because you worked out in jail and look all diesel, don't change a damn thing about you. I don't have time for a bunch of weed-smoking, Hennessey-drinking, hanging-out-on-the-corner niggas. Get your shit together, then maaayyybe we could talk."

Puti, who watched from her window cheered Martha, "Tell them, sister!"

Martha nodded at Puti who reached down and offered her flat palm. Martha slapped it five and marched down the block.

Damian waved off Martha and Puti and joined his co-workers in the "Auto glass! Auto glass! Auto glass!" chorus.

"I feel like some chicken wings. How 'bout you?" Kamikaze

asked.

Chulito nodded and looked out the back window. Damian's body grew smaller and smaller until it became an indistinguishable dot in the portrait of his neighborhood.

chapter five

"Auto glass! Auto glass! Auto glass!" Damian yelled outside Chulito's window, waking him from a deep slumber.

Chulito had trouble falling asleep for two reasons. One reason was because his thoughts were wrapped around Carlos' words "I dig you, and not like when we were kids." The other reason was because when he and Kamikaze stopped by Lefty's party, Chulito saw, on his way to the bathroom, Damian's bare ass rising and falling slowly as he ground himself into a skinny chick with long red nails. The image of Damian fucking in that bedroom was burned into Chulito's brain.

"Auto glass, mamita," Damian continued to yell from across the street. Chulito rolled over on his stomach and lifted the shade to peek out. Damian leaned on a car with a cracked windshield speaking to the driver. The sun gave him a heavenly light and his baggy shorts and boxers were slipping exceptionally low. As he spoke to a bleached blonde Latina, he shifted his weight from one foot to another and rubbed his biceps as if they were sore. He nodded his head a couple of times, smiled and pointed her toward Master #1 Auto Glass Shop. Nailed. As she drove away, he stretched his arms and did a couple of trunk twists knowing full well that someone, somewhere was watching. In this case it was Chulito laying on his morning hard-on.

Chulito rolled onto his back and looked down at his own slim body. He could see Papito through the slit in the boxers. He rubbed his chest and slid his hand down to give it a little squeeze. The warmth in the room was soothing and comforting. He didn't have to keep himself in check. He closed his eyes and imagined that he was standing on the ledge of his first floor window. Legs apart. Knees slightly bent. Boxers around his ankles. One hand holding on to the top of the window and the other stroking himself slowly for all to see. He wanted to shoot and cover Garrison Avenue with a thick white coat of Chulito juice. He sleepwalked to the window and began pumping his hips on the dusty glass. His stiff cock was making strange shapes as it pressed against the glass. The auto glass guys noticed. "¡Mira! ¡Mira!" they yelled. To their surprise, they sprouted their own erections—Benny El Loco, Miguelito and Freddy El Dominicano. Then Damian rose out of his beach chair and walked directly to the yellow garage right across the street from Chulito. Damian had the biggest bulge of all. It pressed against his baggy gray sweat pants and looked like he'd stuffed it with a sandwich from Hero City on Spofford Avenue. Everybody knew their heroes had the most meat.

Damian undid the drawstring tie and the size forty-four sweats slipped past his thirty-inch waist and dropped to the pavement. He grabbed the sides of the elastic waistband of his boxers and bent all the way over as he slid them off. Damian began to stroke himself with both hands, peeling back his dark foreskin and revealing his slick pink head. The only barrier keeping them apart was Garrison Avenue.

Chulito's hips shoved the large glass pane out onto the street. He stroked himself and synchronized his rhythms with Damian. All the other auto glass guys grimaced as they rose to their climaxes. Chulito and Damian moved their hips making circles and swinging back and forth. The other guys started shooting. Benny El Loco, then Miguelito, then Freddy El Dominicano— one by one all the auto glass guys up and down Garrison Avenue came like geysers.

Chulito felt the dizzying familiar tingle build up in his balls and travel up his dick. He gripped the top of his window, locked eyes with Damian, and simultaneously they shot one long forceful stream that connected in an arc in the middle of Garrison Avenue, right above the street's mustard yellow double painted lines.

When the streams met they bathed the block in a white, luminescent light then exploded into a tidal wave of jizz—splashing down the walls of his building, dripping off the newly painted fire escapes, covering the bright auto glass shop signs, all the cars, the hydrant near the corner, and milk crates in front of Rivera's Bodega. The street was filled with cum and all the guys collapsed with pleasure. Damian sunk into his beach chair, rubbing his palm from his stomach to his chest with his eyes closed as the rivers of cum slipped down the sewers.

Chulito awoke. He looked over at his window. The shade was still pulled down and the glass was intact. Nevertheless, a small puddle filled his navel and spilled down his side. The clean, sweet smell of himself mixed with the smell of freshly brewed Cafe Bustelo coming out of his mother's kitchen. He felt comforted by the two scents and nervous that he'd had the dream.

He wondered if the dream meant that he was actually gay. He'd had sexy dreams before, but he usually stopped the action before anything happened. But this was only a dream and he was safely in his room—the one place he could take off his South Bronx armor. The worse that could happen right now is that his mother would walk in and catch him spent with Papito resting and dripping down the side of his hip.

He figured that as long as he didn't do anything physical he was not gay. A dream wasn't going to turn him.

He started to drift off to sleep again, when he heard Carlos' footsteps above him. "I dig you, and not like when we were kids." Chulito shifted his thoughts to the day ahead. Kamikaze would pick him up at ten A.M. Then they would go to El Papa's place to pick up. Hopefully, he would be done by one P.M. and he could go get his braids redone, then go to the Boulevard and buy something for his mom's birthday. He had to figure in the ten minutes it took him to get away from Catalina, who stopped him every time he passed the nail salon where she worked. He could hear her yelling now, "Hey, Chulito, when you gonna take me out?"

"Auto glass! Auto glass! Auto glass, mamita!" Damian yelled and before Papito woke up again, he knew that it was time to go.

chapter six

Chulito spent the next couple of days debating whether he should call or text Carlos, who hadn't made any attempts to contact him. Chulito knew it was on him to make the next move and decided that he didn't want to let another day go by without telling Carlos what he was feeling. In doing so, he knew that he would be crossing a bridge, making a move that felt scary but essential.

From Carlos' room above him, Chulito could hear Nina Simone asking for some sugar in her bowl. The music stopped before the song ended. Carlos is leaving. Chulito quickly put on his new, dark brown Timberland boots. When he heard the upstairs door slam, he abandoned lacing the second boot and ran toward the door in an attempt to run into Carlos in the hall. Too late, he saw him exiting the building. Chulito was about to call out Carlos' name from the doorway when he saw Martha and her sidekicks Debbie and Brenda, who held her baby, Joselito, sitting in front of the building.

"Hey, Chulito, where you going all in a rush? Think you too good for us, just gonna run by and not say nothing?" Martha spoke so quickly that Chulito understood what she said about two seconds after she had said it. "So where you going looking all cute and everything?"

"He's always cute," Debbie and Brenda chimed in.

Chulito smiled and nonchalantly looked across the street to see Carlos disappear around the corner.

"You are lucky that I'm twenty-four and don't want to rob your cradle," Brenda warned.

"Well, I'm closer to your age, Chulito." Debbie swung her wavy brown hair away from her face and placed elaborately manicured hands on her slim hips. "Legal and tender."

"Wow, mamita, I hear you. And yo, Brenda, you make me wish I was twenty-four." Chulito played along, hoping that they would not connect his rushing out the building with one of his laces untied with the fact that Carlos had just come out moments earlier.

"Yeah, right, tell me another one." Brenda shifted little José from her right hip to her left.

The threesome had stopped in front of the building to decide whether they should go to the Boulevard or visit Catalina at the nail salon.

"You seeing Catalina?" Debbie asked suspiciously. "'Cause she be talking, but I ain't never seen you two together."

"Something like that." Chulito checked Debbie out as if she had a chance with him.

"Damn, you are fine, fine, fine!" Debbie high-fived her cohorts.

"Down girl," Martha squeaked. "He has got playa written all over him. I can smell it from he-ah." She smoothed back loose wiry strands of hair that had come undone from her small stiff pony tail.

"The only thing I can smell is some CK One and it smells mighty good," Debbie said, circling Chulito and sniffing him out.

"Don't embarrass your ass out in the street and everything. Damn!" Brenda handed José to Martha so that she could look in her bag for his bobo.

"Hey, I'm single now." Debbie looked Chulito up and down.

"Single my ass," Brenda said. "Chulito, Benny's in jail. He was stealing money from the Bravo Supermarket where he worked."

"What?" Chulito said, pretending to sound interested as he looked over to where Carlos had just disappeared.

In one breath, complete with neck rolls and nods, Martha said, "He's a stupid motherfucker, excuse the French, because they had made him assistant manager and he was definitely gonna be a manager and now he fucked it all up, excuse the French again, and now he's in jail and Debbie is out here acting like a ho."

"Uh-hmmm," Brenda agreed and took her son from Martha.

Chulito tried to think of an excuse to leave the women and catch up with Carlos. He wanted to be having different conversation. He loved how Carlos matter-of-factly said he dug him. That was up front and gangsta. Carlos was all smarts and could have his pick of any college dude, but he came back to the hood for Chulito. Chulito wanted to tell him that he dug him, too, since forever, even though the thought that anyone in the hood might ever find out still terrified him. He wondered how he could tell Carlos and still keep himself in check.

"Martha, you better watch your mouth," Debbie said defending herself. "Just because you're going to college, don't be thinking that you could tell everybody else how to live."

Martha responded in kind. "You could come to college with me and meet some smart educated guy, not the riff raff walking up and down these streets, no offense, Chulito. You fine and all that but you know what I'm talking about."

"You gotta get all serious and shit." Debbie moved in so close to Chulito that he could feel the heat rising from her skin. "I'm just playing with him. I'm not talking about marriage or anything. I'm just looking to have a little fun."

"Uh-hm, then Benny finds out and he have someone kick Chulito's ass and fuck up his face and shit," Martha said.

Chulito put an arm around Debbie. "Hey, Martha, I can take care of myself."

"It's your life, but what I see is that we keep spinning the same old circles. Getting pregnant, going to jail, selling drugs." Martha paused and Chulito imagined her totaling the cost of his fitted authentic Yankee cap and jersey, gold chains, Fossil watch, Tommy Jeans, and custom Timberland Roll Top boots. "But we got to educate ourselves and do something else."

Debbie crossed her arms and glared at Martha. "You're worse than those fucking Pentacostals preaching in front the train station on Saturdays. All preach, preach, talk."

"Debbie, take a look at me, 'cause I ain't all talk. I'm doing something. Just like that guy Carlos."

Debbie sucked her teeth. "The faggot? Please."

The word stung Chulito and his blood rushed to his ears.

"Faggot or no faggot, he's going to college and doing something with his life. Brenda here fell into the trap. Started fucking Mr. Fine Ass Kamikaze, a drug dealer, no doubt. Got all hooked on him. Got pregnant and look, she's walking around carrying José 'cause her carriage broke, and the drug dealing daddy keep saying he's gonna get a new one. Where is it?" Martha said. "All that damn money and zero responsibility."

Brenda looked at Chulito. "You seen Kamikaze?"

"He's coming to pick me up in a bit." Chulito slipped down and tied his boot.

"Are those new?" Martha asked suspiciously.

"You know it," Chulito said.

"So, Kamikaze has money," Martha said. "It's dirty money, but he's has it. Lots of it I'm sure."

"He didn't buy these for me. I earn my money."

"But Kamikaze pays you," Martha moved in close, looked down at Chulito and whispered, "from drug money."

Chulito straightened up. "He always takes care of business."

"What about Joselito?" Martha asked and stroked the baby's cheek. "He's Kamikaze's business and he never takes care of him."

Brenda got comfortable on the parked car and sat Joselito between her legs. "I called him a hundred times and he doesn't call me back, so if he's coming here then I'm waiting for him."

Chulito knew that Kamikaze doubted that Joselito was his son, but what if Kamikaze was wrong? "Kaz hasn't called you back?" Chulito asked.

"Not once," Brenda said. Debbie hissed out a "tsk, tsk, tsk" and sat next to Brenda. She pulled out a compact and applied a rose colored lipstick.

"Your macho, super hero buddy will dump cash on all his friends but he doesn't bother to provide for his son—typical," Martha said.

"Maybe you could talk to him, Chulito?" Brenda asked.

Chulito shook his head. "I don't get involved in his personal business."

Martha joined Debbie on the car. "Forget him. They just keep protecting each other. Brenda, you corner him and make him pay for a new carriage. Buuuut if you had your own job you could say fuck him and buy Joselito whatever he needs instead of depending on Kaz's lame ass."

"Go on Miss Independent Women's Lib," Debbie said, "all those Women's Studies courses you takin' are gonna make you a lesbian." Then she offered her lipstick to Martha. "This might help."

Martha refused it. "I'd rather be a lesbian who has her shit together than some stupid bitch whose making an ass out of herself trying to flirt with a fourteen-year-old while her boyfriend's in jail!"

"Oh, no you didn't." Brenda laughed and kissed Joselito who seemed to be engrossed in the conversation.

"Yo, I'm sixteen," Chulito said proudly, as he walked toward his building. He didn't want to be there when Kamikaze arrived.

Debbie shifted her gaze slowly from Chulito to Martha. "I don't have to take this shit from you. I'm out. Chulito, you going inside? You want some company?" She looped her arm around his.

"My mom's is upstairs, girl."

"Wait, Debbie," Brenda called out.

"Nah, wait nothing. I mean we're supposed to be going out to have fun and friends are supposed to be fun. You, Martha, are a fucking bitch. I don't need to be put down by you all the time. You do all this talk of women's lib and sisterhood, but it's all shit 'cause you just cut us down. We are supposed to be your girls. I'm outta here."

"Debbie," Martha said softly touching Debbie's shoulder, but she shrugged Martha off. "I just care about you, girl. I don't like seeing you be—"

"Be what? What?"

Martha draped her arm around Debbie, who stiffened up, and pulled her close. "You just stronger than how you act. And I know we can't always be perfect."

"We? So you mean you, too?" Debbie said, surprised to hear Martha admit to not being perfect.

"Yeah, I get tired, too." Martha fixed Debbie's hair, pushing it behind her shoulder. "I feel like I gotta fight for myself or else I'll end up like my mom and sister who just watch TV all day or I'll get pregnant, making life harder."

Martha led Debbie to the car and put her other arm around Brenda. "I love you both and I want us to be strong together."

Debbie looked at Martha as if she were speaking a foreign language. Chulito watched the three friends sitting on the car with little Joselito staring up at the women and for a moment he was transfixed. He never saw the fellas act this way toward each other. The women whispered to each other and then Debbie smiled and nodded her head. For a moment, Chulito felt like he didn't exist. He turned to enter the building.

Debbie looked over to Chulito. "Where you goin', Chulito?"

"I was just gonna give you all some room to do ya thing."

Martha warned. "Don't call Kaz to warn him that we're here. We are gonna see his face and make him pay up."

Debbie jumped in, "And make him pay for more than a fucking baby carriage. He wants to be a big ass drug dealer and roll around in his loot. The least he could do is take care of his responsibilities. It's not like he ain't got it. You dress good, Chulito, so somebody's gettin' it."

"Yo, I told you I work for my shit." Chulito looked around agitated. "Kamikaze will be here and he'll pay up. He's got the money. I know that."

"Why doesn't he return my calls then?" Brenda asked resting her chin on Joselito's curly head.

"I don't know. He's busy."

Martha made a sound like air being released from a tire, "Pssssshhh, don't make excuses for him. He's an asshole. C'mon, he can give Brenda a hundred and fifty bucks for a fucking baby carriage."

Debbie snapped her fingers in the air. "I've seen him shove that kind of shit down some saggy tit stripper at El Coche."

They all stared at her.

"Back in the day. When Benny took me there with the guys."

Martha rolled her eyes. "Classy."

Small, tinny tones of Big Pun's "Still Not a Playa" came out of Chulito's cell. He saw Kaz's number on the display and flipped it open. "Yo, wassup." Kaz had spotted the women, so to avoid Brenda and the ambush, he asked Chulito to meet him near the McDonald's down the block. "Cool, I will see you there, pa."

"Girls, maybe we should go," Brenda said. "I think we're wasting our time."

"Call him back," Martha said stepping up to Chulito.

"Forget it, Martha. He ain't gonna answer." Brenda handed Joselito to Debbie so that she could slide off the car.

"He will answer Chulito's call. Phone him from your cell, Chulito."

"That wasn't him," Chulito said.

"Give me the phone," Martha demanded.

Chulito hated Martha for pressuring him, but knew she was

right and was pissed at Kamikaze for ignoring Brenda and Joselito. It didn't make sense to Chulito because he'd seen Kaz peel off bills with ease in social situations. He paid for everything when they went out and he always bought the rounds at bars. He kept his crew well paid because as he often told Chulito, "Sharing the wealth is good karma. It builds trust, loyalty, and keeps the natives at bay."

Chulito looked down Garrison Avenue in the direction of the McDonald's and adjusted the tilt of his baseball cap. "O.K., I'll call him."

When Kaz picked up the call, Chulito said hold on and handed it over to Martha.

"Hey, Kaz, it's Martha. Look, Brenda and Joselito need some help from you. Joselito's carriage broke and Brenda has been carrying him around, and it would make things easier for her if you could help them out with at least buying a new carriage for him." Silence.

"Let me talk to him," Brenda whispered.

Martha put up her hand. "O.K., that's cool, Brenda wants to talk—O.K., O.K., I will tell him. Thanks." She flipped the phone shut.

"What the fuck?" Brenda complained.

"He didn't want to talk to you."

"So?"

"I'm sorry girl, but I wanted to deal with one issue at a time," Martha said. "He's gonna pull up on the corner in front of Rivera's and he'll give Chulito some money to bring to us. We should just stay here and not go to the car. He's on his way." For a moment, Chulito saw a shimmer of defeat in Martha's face, but just a shimmer, because she'd won a small battle.

"That's fucked up, Martha. I wanted to talk to him."

"Brenda, he didn't want to talk to you. It's hard to hear that shit but try to understand."

"He's an asshole." Debbie bounced the smiling Joselito in her arms and sang, "Your daddy's an asshole."

"He's paying for a carriage," Martha said. "I thought that's what we wanted."

Kamikaze pulled up in front of Rivera's, windows shut up tight, air-conditioning on high inside, and the beats of Fat Joe buzzing through the speakers. Chulito walked down the block to the car. Kamikaze handed him a roll without looking at him. Chulito stood for a moment, staring at Kamikaze who then turned to him. "What the fuck are you looking at? Give her the shit and get back here." Then the window rolled back up.

Chulito handed Brenda a fist full of Benjamins.

"Holy shit," Debbie said. "Look, Joselito, your mami and your two titis are going to buy you a super deluxe baby carriage." She clapped his hands.

Chulito walked into the building to get his wallet.

"Hey, Chulito," Martha called out. "Thanks." Debbie and Brenda chimed in their thanks as well. Chulito was glad that he could help and felt that it was worth any shit Kamikaze might give him.

Chulito nodded, then ran inside, grabbed his wallet and ran out to Kamikaze's car and slipped in. The doors locked. "Wassup." Chulito greeted Kamikaze who made a U-turn on Hunts Point Avenue without talking. As they passed the building Chulito saw the women waiting to cross the street. Brenda had her eyes locked on the car, as if she could see through the dark windows. Martha passed Joselito off to Brenda to distract her and they scurried across Garrison Avenue.

Chulito got startled when Kamikaze slammed the gas and the car jerked forward. One of its custom features was to go from zero to sixty miles per hour in 4.8 seconds. Chulito scrambled to put on his seatbelt as they zoomed down Garrison. The light on Longwood Avenue turned red, but Kamikaze sped right through it. A few blocks later at a corner he slammed the breaks. "Don't you ever do anything like that again!" he yelled pounding on the dashboard. "I handle my own shit! Don't forget that. There's no proof that Joselito is mine, ya hear? And what's with you helping those bitches out? Don't be getting soft on me."

Chulito was out of breath and for a split second he feared for his life. It was the first time Kamikaze had directed his rage at him. He'd heard how much of a roughneck Kamikaze was when he was running corners back in the day and he had witnessed it only once when Mikey, one of Kamikaze's new boys, tried to get over. Raheem, the lieutenant overseeing the bars in the Upper East Side, reported that cash receipts were low from the lounge where Mikey was stationed. Mikey ignored several warnings until one day Kamikaze cornered him in the men's room at a bar. He pressed his boot against Mikey's stomach and shoved him against the wall. Kamikaze pulled out his gun and pointed it at Mikey's crotch. "You've got fifteen minutes to call Raheem to hand over the cash or the stash!" Mikey nodded as a puddle of piss formed around his feet.

"What the fuck are you looking at?"

For the most part, it had all been smiles, good times and feeling Kamikaze's protection. As they continued down Garrison Avenue with the New York City skyline in the hazy horizon, he realized there were lines he couldn't cross and didn't want to discover what would be done to him if he did so again. "Sorry, Kaz."

Kamikaze looked at him, then reached over and squeezed the back of his neck. "You still my boy."

Chulito flinched. Kamikaze's hand felt cold.

chapter seven

Chulito walked up Hunts Point Avenue toward Cruz Travel Agency. His mother had asked him to go pick up their tickets to Puerto Rico before she left for work that morning. Carmen worked as a lunchroom attendant at P.S. 48 and left her house every school day morning at 5:45 A.M. She was looking forward to taking Chulito to spend the summer with her mother and older sister. It was only June 1 and they were set to leave on July 9 after the neighborhood's big Fourth of July party. At first Chulito didn't want to go, but lately he was feeling like he needed to get away from Kamikaze, the fellas, even Hunts Point.

In P.R. he could take time to get his head straight again. He was having second thoughts about telling Carlos that he dug him, too. Then what? What would they do? Be boyfriends? That shit was whack, right? Besides, he hadn't heard from Carlos since their conversation in front of the building over a week ago. Maybe since Chulito didn't reciprocate, Carlos' feelings changed.

When Chulito reached Cruz Travel Agency, Julio, or La Julio as he was sometimes called, was at his desk talking on the phone and Brick was sitting in a chair in front of him. He leaned the chair back and balanced it on one leg and rocked. Chulito nodded a greeting to him and Brick responded by raising his eyebrows.

Chulito was about to take a seat on the couch when Julio waved him to the empty chair beside Brick.

Julio covered the receiver on the phone with his slim hand. "Have a seat, papito. I got your tickets." Julio placed a thick envelope on the desk. "Just sign for them, and I'll print out a receipt."

"You taking a little trip?" Brick asked as Chulito sat next to him.

"Puerto Rico with my moms." Chulito leaned forward to sign for the tickets, not making eye contact with Brick.

"For about six weeks," Julio added as he hung up the phone.

"Wow, that's a long vacation. Did Kamikaze give you time off?"

"Not yet, but it's not a problem."

"Kamikaze must have changed." Brick got up and served himself from the water cooler. "You want some, Chulito?"

Chulito looked over and nodded. Above the water cooler there was one of Brick's posters. The seductive stare in his dark eyes was familiar. He had a tight fade haircut and his skin glistened. His chest was small, but his arms and shoulders were big.

Chulito's gaze traveled from the poster back to Brick who had his back to them. Brick's crucified Jesus tattoo could be made out through the worn white ribbed tank top.

"Bring me some, too." Julio snapped his fingers, then answered the phone.

Brick handed them their waters and took a seat next to Chulito. "That poster's dope," Chulito said.

Brick craned his long neck to look back at it. "Thanks."

"Was it fun to do?"

Brick nodded. "It's always fun working with Julio."

Julio smiled and covered the receiver. "Gay boys from all over were booking their cruises with me. Great for business." Then he returned to his call.

Brick leaned toward Chulito over the chair's armrest. "And I make good clean money here. I don't have to be risking my life."

"So it's worth all the shit the fellas be giving you?"

Brick snickered. "In the big scheme of things those fellas don't matter. Half of them don't work, and they definitely don't sign my paycheck. Besides Julio is good people, and good people are good people. Period."

Chulito felt defensive. "Well, Kaz's good people and he got my back."

"No doubt. You a cool cat, but you playin' a dangerous game. You may be tough enough to be in it, but you can't think about just you, you gotta think about the people in your life, especially the ones closest to you." Chulito remembered how Brick usually walked around with his daughter on his shoulders. He had a family with Jennifer and her son from a previous man, and he helped with the neighborhood barbecues and block parties. Whereas Kamikaze didn't reveal whether he had family and as far as Chulito knew, he was the only close person in Kamikaze's life. He imagined it was because of that danger Brick had alluded to.

Chulito nodded. "Right now, it's just me and my mom."

Brick leaned back in his chair and put his feet up on Julio's desk. He wore flip flops and the nails on his long toes were clean and clipped. Strong veins ran up his feet, across his ankles and up hairy shins.

Julio slid an envelope to Brick and shoved his feet off his desk with one hand and handed papers to Chulito with the other. He then raised one finger signaling him to wait a moment.

Brick counted money from the envelope, then folded and pocketed the bills. He flashed Julio a bright smile. "A pleasure doing business with you." He extended one of his large hands and offered it to Julio to shake. When Julio shook it, Brick bent over and playfully kissed Julio's hand. Julio pulled his hand back and hung up the phone. Chulito wondered how clean that money was and if he were being paid for more than just maintenance and handiwork.

"You're a fucking tease, a fucking bugarrón. I only put up with you because you make me wet." Julio smiled as he tore off the receipt and handed it to Chulito.

"You wish I was a bugarrón."

Chulito didn't know what bugarrón meant, but he wondered if Brick might be gay on the low. He seemed comfortable and playful with Julio, and Chulito didn't know any other man who behaved like that with a gay guy.

"Check the tickets, Chulito, to make sure everything is O.K.," Julio said.

Chulito nodded. Brick sat on the desk and put his bare foot on the chair he had just been sitting on. The flip flop remained on the floor. Chulito checked the tickets and stole glances at Brick's bare foot.

"Get your ass off my desk," Julio said playfully.

"Chill, Julio. I'm bouncin'," Brick said with a smile. Chulito had never seen Brick so relaxed. He usually walked around with a scowl.

Jennifer, Brick's woman, popped into the shop mid-smile. "Brick, how long you gonna make me wait, it's hot out here."

"Be right there." He flashed her a stern look—a look that Chulito was much more familiar seeing on him.

"What the fuck are you doing? Did you get it?" Jennifer asked.

"Yes, I'll be right out." Brick turned to Julio. "Sorry." Then he gave Julio a kiss on the cheek and left. Through the travel agency's large window covered with posters, Chulito watched Brick and Jennifer continue to argue. Their voices were muffled and the loud, rattling air conditioner made it difficult to make out their words.

"What took you so fucking long, Brick?"

"Enough, Jennifer. Ya, let's go."

"If you don't want to go shopping, just give me the money and you stay here. I don't care. Crystal needs shoes."

Julio talked to Chulito but watched the argument. "Have a good trip and tell your mother to call me if she needs anything."

The fellas from the corner walked up and pretended to pass by but watched the spectacle.

"Jennifer, don't raise your voice to me."

"I'm not raising my voice," Jennifer shouted. "I just want to go and you're sitting in there hanging out and taking your time. Just give me the money and let me go."

"Jennifer, chill."

Chulito felt like he was trapped in the agency by the argument. "Brick's woman is pretty tough."

Julio nodded. "To be with Brick, a woman has to be strong."

A small crowd had formed.

"Fuck you, just give me the fucking money so I can go," Jennifer said.

Without warning, Brick's large hand swiped Jennifer's face.

For a moment she stood there stunned. The crowd recoiled. Julio ran out front. Jennifer's eyes narrowed and she lunged at Brick. Brick lifted his hand.

"Brick, no!" Julio cried out, but Brick's hand came down on Jennifer and she fell to the ground. Crystal wailed and ran to her mother. Jennifer's mouth was bleeding and her teeth were red.

"Let him go, you motherfuckin' faggot," Jennifer yelled. "Don't hurt my baby."

"Brick!" Julio shouted.

Brick gave Julio a look that warned him to stay out of it.

Chulito took two steps toward the door and Julio stopped him.

Someone yelled, "Call the cops!" Jennifer got up and pulled Crystal to her.

Jennifer looked at Brick with defiance as she walked past him with her child sobbing. He glared at her with his hands balled into fists.

Jennifer spit at Brick. The red bloodied glob landed on his cheek right below his eye. He flinched as if to lunge at Jennifer, but held back. The spit slipped down his face and stained his white T-shirt. Brick's eyes were closed and flickering as if he were having a seizure. Jennifer walked toward their building.

Julio led Brick back into the travel agency. He sat on the couch, covered his face with his big hands and cried, his whole body shaking. The crowd peered into the shop through the posters. Chulito wanted to chase them away but he couldn't take his eyes off Brick. He'd never seen him so broken and vulnerable, and at the same time Chulito despised him for hitting Jennifer. He wondered if his own father ever expressed such remorse after hitting his mother. If so, Chulito never saw it. He mainly remembered his father's anger, depression and drunkenness. And the times his father hit Carmen, he would always leave the house in a rage.

Brick put his head on his knees and held himself with his strong arms, sobbing and shaking, no one dared to touch him, not even Julio.

"I can't believe I hit her, Julio. I can't believe that shit. I broke my promise." He looked up at Julio, his eyes were red and tears dripped off his chin and made small spots on his T-shirt next to the blood stain. Brick saw Chulito watching him and covered his face.

Chulito wanted to do something. He went to the water cooler and got some water for Brick. Julio smiled at Chulito, took the water and gestured for him to leave.

A police car pulled up to the travel agency and the crowd dispersed as quickly as it had assembled.

The fellas swarmed Chulito as he came down the block.

"Yo, what happened?" Davey asked, licking his lips.

Chulito shrugged and continued to walk toward the corner with the fellas. He was too stunned by what he'd witnessed and the look of horror on Brick's face to speak to anyone.

"She shouldn't have mouthed off like that to him," Papo said.

"What you talking about?" Chin-Chin asked. "A man never hits a woman. Didn't your mother teach you that, Papo?"

"Not unless she deserves it. A chick like Jennifer needs to be smacked down, especially if she's disrespectin' you out on the street and shit," Papo answerd.

"Yo, the cops are in Julio's place," Looney Tunes said as he ran over to them. "Do you think they gonna arrest Brick?"

"They could, if Jennifer presses charges," Chin-Chin said.

"She won't," Papo said. "She loooves him. And besides they

have kids."

Chulito noticed Carlos walking down Hunts Point Avenue and enter the pizza shop. I dig you, and not like when we were kids. That phrase was on constant replay in his mind.

"Did you see the way he hit her?" Davey asked.

"That shit was foul," Chin-Chin said shaking his head. "I got heated when I saw that."

Papo noticed Chulito's silence. "Yo, Chulito, you O.K.?"

He'd been staring at the doorway to the Bella Vista Pizza Shop way down the block. "I'll be right back fellas. I'm gonna get a slice."

"Yo, bring one back for me," Looney Tunes yelled as Chulito jogged across the street.

As he reached the pizza shop, Chulito's heart raced, his mouth got dry and his footsteps became slower. On cue, Catalina came out of the nail salon, next door to the pizza shop and intercepted him.

"Hey, Chulito, you finally coming around to see me?" She smiled and looked dark and beautiful in the orange glow of the sun. "I haven't seen you since you went out with the fellas and I know I was pretty pissed then, but I'm ready to talk to you now."

"Wow, Catalina, you look great." Chulito walked toward her and as he passed the pizza shop, he looked out of the corner of his eye and saw Carlos sitting at the counter eating a slice.

Chulito adjusted the baseball cap to block the setting sun out of his eyes, but he knew pulling down the hat made him look sexier. "I've been busy and giving you your space. I called you, right?" They stepped away from the entrance to the nail shop and Chulito positioned himself so that he could face Catalina and watch the doorway to the pizza shop.

"I got your messages." She looked beneath his hat brim to see his eyes.

"I meant what I said about wanting to go out with you for my birthday. I just didn't know the fellas had made that big surprise, and then like I said, I've been busy with Kamikaze. But maybe we could go out in a few days or I could take you shopping?" Chulito flashed a smile. He was on automatic pilot. Like many of the fellas, he knew when to smile and how to look seductively into a girl's eyes. But he was distracted every time someone walked out of the pizza shop.

"Well, I'm going to the Dominican Republic for the summer and since we haven't talked I was wondering where we stood."

They had only gone out a couple of times in the previous three months. They had dinner at the G-Bar near the Grand Concourse, he took her to see her favorite band, Aventura, at the United Palace in Washington Heights, but the intimacy of the last date freaked him out a little. He'd taken her to the movie theatre in Parkchester, the same theater he always frequented with Carlos. He felt wrong about that, as if he'd betrayed Carlos by bringing her to their theater.

Afterwards, she and Chulito walked over to the big fountain. They talked and stared into each other's eyes a lot. Then, he made out with her on one of the benches. He got turned on so he touched her neck and shoulders and felt her stiff nipples through her black silk blouse. Even though they didn't seal any deals, she acted like they were together ever since. Out of a sense of obligation, he'd bought her jewelry since that date, stopped by the nail salon a few times, and walked around the neighborhood with her one or twice on one of her breaks. Chulito loved the props he got from the fellas, but the more into him she got, the more he stepped away. He had wanted to do enough to keep her interested, but not so much that she would get hooked. But Carlos changed all that. He didn't see himself going out with her again.

"I don't know, mama, our schedules don't click. You work all day and my work is mainly evenings and weekends."

"Oh, so we don't go out with each other because it's a schedulin' problem." She laughed, touched his cheek then ran her hand down his neck, shoulder, arm and laced her fingers through his. Chulito began to sweat because he didn't want Carlos to catch him holding Catalina's hand. She looked over her shoulder at the fellas who watched from the corner and were blowing kisses and sarcastically saying, "Oh, how cute."

Chulito shook his head and smiled. "Those sánganos."

Catalina laughed.

He squeezed her hand. "But since you going away, and I'm gonna be going to P.R. with my mom, maybe we could take it easy."

Just then Carlos emerged from the doorway. Chulito dropped Catalina's hand and the playful smile was suddenly gone from her face. As Carlos approached the couple, Chulito made direct eye contact with him for the first time since they'd talked. Carlos had on a bright red T-shirt, which gave his skin a smooth glow. He slowly looked away from Chulito and shook his head with revulsion.

Catalina took no notice. Instead she lit into him. "So, where is this coming from? What? Next are you gonna say that you want to see other people? You probably got your eye on somebody else? My girls keep telling me that you a big ass playa."

"What are you talking about, Catalina? You act like we seeing each other or that we got some big thing going on," Chulito said loud enough for Carlos to hear as he passed them.

"Act like?" Catalina slowly placed fists on her hips and planted her feet. She was like a statue, completely still except for the two pearl droplet earrings that swung on each earlobe. "You mean we not? Uhh, didn't we go out a couple of times? Don't you stop by here on the regular, except for the last two weeks? Didn't you buy me a gold chain, these earrings and this charm bracelet?" She held the bracelet up to his face.

Chulito turned and saw Carlos waiting for the light to change to cross underneath the Bruckner Expressway.

"Baby, right this minute is not a good time to…" he said as he backed away.

"Don't be fucking calling me 'baby'. Hold it. Where are you going?"

Chulito's anger rose and he wanted to run up to her and place his hand over her mouth to shut her up. He thought of Brick and Jennifer. "Look, stop pressing me. I told you now is not a good time to talk. I have something to do." Chulito looked over his shoulder and saw Carlos walking down the steps into the number 6 train station.

"Pressing you? Chulito, you better not go 'cause I'm tired of chasing you."

"So stop chasing me then."

"Are you breaking up with me?" she shouted. "I need to know because I am not going to be all faithful to you while I am in the D.R. and you're gonna be chasing other bitches back here in the Bronx and in Puerto Rico."

"Now you know I'm not like that, Catalina, but—" Chulito closed the gap between them and whispered, "maybe it's best if we're just friends. I mean, you going away and shit. And I'm going to P.R. with my moms so…"

Catalina stood firm with her arms crossed in front of her ample breasts. She stared at him defiantly, waiting for him to finish his response.

"So? What are you sayin', Chulito?"

"So…" Chulito checked out the corner where several of his buddies bopped to a beat he couldn't hear.

Chulito turned back to her. Her eyes were filled with tears that just sat in her eyes as if she could control when they would spill down her cheeks. He didn't like hurting her. He knew it hadn't been fair to lead her on.

"So I think that…uhh…since you going away and all…that maybe we should, you know…"

"I'll finish for you. So this relationship is OVER!" she blurted as her tears fell.

"I'm sorry, ma—"

She put her hand up to stop him from speaking. "You go your way and I go my way. I'm done chasing you, Chulito. You can walk past this store and not worry that I am going to come out after you. I liked you 'cause you're not like the other niggas around here. You a gentlemen. You took me out. You didn't try no shit, and you kissed me when I said it was O.K. But I am serious about you, and maybe it's because you just a kid, but you're not serious, and can be just as much of a playa as the rest of those assholes over there," she said, pointing to the fellas on the corner. "But all that jewelry you gave me I am keeping 'cause they were gifts, right?"

Chulito nodded. Although he felt guilty for playing Catalina, he felt relieved.

"Mira, I'm leaving next week to the D.R. and I'll be back here before school starts. You take some time to think about what you want. And if you need to find me you will figure something out 'cause you a smart boy. But I'm over feeling stupid." She pushed past Chulito and went back into the salon.

Chulito turned and ran full speed toward the train station. He dodged cars under the Bruckner Expressway, ran down the stairs to the train station, looked around for cops and jumped the turnstile. He bounded down the stairs to the downtown train, but saw the fading lights of one that had just left the station. Carlos was gone.

He wondered whether he would ever catch up with Carlos or if he'd spend the rest of the summer chasing him and his world beyond Hunts Point. Chulito knew there was more to life and Carlos was it, but whatever it all was remained out of his reach. If he just got on the next train and went downtown, to the Village, he might see Carlos. How big could the Village be? Weren't Villages small, like in the old vampire movies? Weren't they this little area where everybody knew everybody? He could go find Carlos and maybe there they could talk, smile and not worry about the fellas and the neighborhood, but he didn't know where it was. Maybe he could ask someone, but would they think he was gay? He checked out the subway map. There was an area called Greenwich Village and an area called East Village. He didn't know there was more than one.

A young couple about his age came down toward him. The dude held the young girl's hand and nodded a greeting to Chulito. The young girl stole a glance. They took each other's hand and Chulito wondered whether he'd ever hold Carlos' hand. The thought seemed ridiculous and pointless. He would never hold Carlos' hand up there, in Hunts Point. It was a waste even to think about it. From the hot, dark subway, he looked up at the crisp blue sky, heard the rumble and whoosh of the Bruckner Expressway and wiped sweat from his brow. He took another step, then another, then another and soon reached the top. He looked around at women walking from the beauty salons with large pink rollers in their hair, blue-mouthed kids sucking on piraguas, Mexican women selling carved up mangoes with chili and lime, as the cars honked, the busses zoomed, and people laughed. Chulito realized he hadn't moved until a small Chihuahua barked at him. The old woman walking her dog yanked the chain. "Macho, stop it." She looked at Chulito and apologized. "He's little but tough."

Chulito crouched down and extended his hand toward Macho and the dog bared its crooked fangs. Chulito stood up.

"Sorry, he doesn't like to be petted. He's very protective." The woman walked away and Macho looked back at Chulito and barked a few more warnings then trotted beside his owner.

Chulito wiped his brow again and shook the sweat off his hand. His heart slowed down. He looked down the subway stairs one last time and considered going after Carlos, then walked back toward his 'hood. As he waited for the light to cross underneath the Bruckner, he wondered where else he could go.

The light changed and he crossed. He walked on the other side of the street to avoid the salon. The heat was rising in waves from the concrete on the sidewalk and tar from the street. It distorted his vision as he saw the fellas on the corner and Damian sitting in his beach chair. It was as if they were swaying from side to side and would melt into the ground. All of Hunts Point was caught in the heat and looked like it would all dissolve. Then the whole neighborhood wouldn't exist and he'd be free to go wherever he wanted. Through the heat's blur he could make out Davey waving to him from the corner. He lifted his arm to wave back. It felt heavy, but he managed to wave. He felt as if he were walking through sand as he took one step, then another and another toward the fellas. Chulito felt like he was caught in a force field drawing him to the corner. He could hear congas playing from the barber shop, where every Friday the owner, a few barberos, the conga teacher from the local community center, Mr. Rodriguez, and some local men jammed. He wanted to resist the corner, but the pull was too strong. The drums continued, *tuka tun, tun, tun—tuka, tun, tun, tun—tuka, tun, tun, tun* and he glided toward the fellas. For the first time he listened to their beats and his heart kept rhythm with each *tun, tun, tun*. He remembered how when he took classes as a little kid, Mr. Rodriguez would tell them, "Listen with your heart." Chulito didn't understand until this moment. Those thumps from the congas were always a part of his world, whether he heard them from the barber shop or a street corner or from a picnic in Pelham Bay Park, but today they sounded different. He heard their echo from the mountains of Puerto Rico and the shores of Africa.

"Yo, yo, yo, Chulito." Davey's voice sounded distant and muffled as if he were talking from behind a closed door. "We saw Catalina wildin' out over there. She was pissed."

Chulito spoke slowly and carefully. "Yeah, she's going to the D.R. for the summer and wanted to seal some kind of deal between us."

As the fellas spoke, their voices sounded muffled and distant. "I know that shit," Chin-Chin said. "My girl went to Puerto Rico last summer, and she was like, 'We gotta get engaged...'cause I ain't gonna be over there and you over here doin' your shit.'"

Chulito knew the fellas were trying to connect to him, but the sound of the drums amplified. "What?"

"Hey, Chu, you sure you're O.K.?" Papo touched his shoulder.

He looked into Papo's eyes and they turned from light brown to black as a dark cloud blocked the sun.

Chulito nodded, but he wanted to keep walking. He wanted to go home. He needed to move away from the corner. But it was as if his heavy boots were anchored there.

Davey piped in. "You all talk, Chin-Chin, because you got engaged."

"But I still fucked around with whoever I wanted." Chin-Chin slapped high-fives with Davey, Looney Tunes and Papo. He held his hand up to Chulito who stared at it a moment before high-fiving him.

Papo shook his head. "No way a chick is gonna pin me down with some shit like that. I just tol' my girl, 'You could trust me, baby. I only got eyes for you, baby girl.'"

The fellas laughed and nodded. Chulito wondered if they wanted women only for sex, holidays and family gatherings because otherwise it seemed like they didn't spend time with them. He rarely saw them holding hands with their partners like the young guy he saw at the train.

"Yo, Chulito, what happened to my slice?" Looney Tunes asked. To shut him up, Chulito handed him a $5 bill, as a large raindrop slapped his hand. Then another, then another and then, as if someone had given a good twist of the wrench to a fire hydrant, the rain poured down on Hunts Point.

"Holy shit!" one of the fellas yelled and they all ran for cover in the bodega. The auto glass guys ran into their shops and within moments the sidewalks that had had people walking and babies in strollers, old men and women with canes, and kids on bikes and skateboards, were empty. Chulito stood in front of the bodega, the rain soaked into his braids and ran down his neck. The drops pelted his shoulders and slipped underneath the fabric of his jersey. It ran down his arms, past his watch and dripped off his fingers.

"Yo, Chulito!" Papo held open the door to the bodega. He flicked his head, inviting Chulito inside. "The rain's gonna mess up ya gear." Chulito looked down at his Yankee jersey that he'd just taken out of the dry cleaners, his Tommy jeans and his boots that were going from tan to dark brown as the rain drops splashed them. Watching the droplets dance around his feet, they dripped from his nose and chin. He took one soggy step away from the corner, then another and another and another. The rain washed down the sides of his building, slid along the parked cars and created a small river in the gutter carrying an empty, crushed bag of Cheez Doodles toward the drain.

When he reached the entrance he looked over his shoulder. The light posts and traffic lights were still there. The wire garbage cans filled with trash, and the milk crates that served as sidewalk stools were still there. The Chinese restaurant and bodegas were still there, the cars were parked, but the people had vanished in doors. And as he took in the streets that were now clear of people, standing under the downpour, he could still hear the pounding of the drums.

chapter eight

Chulito slipped off his boots, peeled off his wet clothes, shook out the plane tickets that were in his back pocket and placed them on his dresser. Naked, he tip-toed, so his mom wouldn't catch him, into the bathroom to hang his clothes to dry, then returned back to his room. He lay on his bed, gave Fat Joe and Big Pun a break and listened to the distant drumming. The congueros were now singing. Although he didn't understand their incantations, he recognized Elegua, Yemaya and Chango, names of the Orisha Gods. He hugged his pillow which felt soft against his cool skin and watched the rain blur the pane. He sank into his hurricane of thoughts.

At the center of the storm was Carlos and his desire for him. Then swirling around in the debris was Kamikaze, the fellas, his mother, Catalina, the auto glass workers, Martha, Brenda and Debbie, the Tats Cru guys, Brick, even classmates he hadn't thought of before that moment but he feared what they would think about his desire.

Chulito gripped himself tightly. He felt his protective wall crumbling because strange things were happening to him, like the dream with Damian and how it had become more and more difficult to keep his emotions for Carlos in check.

The drums continued. "Elegua, Elegua."

Chulito's mother knocked on his door. He took the thin, gauzy sheet that had belonged to his grandmother and covered up. He used to play the game where he'd cover his face and his grandmother would pretend that he disappeared. "Where's my little Chulito? Where can he be?" The sheet was soft and he could see her through it searching for him. On her last visit, a few years ago, she had anointed it with Agua Florida, saying that it would bring him protection, peace and comfort.

"You want some food?" Carmen asked through the door. She cooked every night, even if Chulito was not going to be home for dinner.

"I'm not hungry." It was an automatic answer, but he, in fact, was ravenous.

"O.K., I'll put the food away."

"Wait." He got up, wrapped the sheet tightly around his waist and opened the door. "I got caught in the rain."

"I figured. I saw your clothes hanging in the bathroom." She tilted her head as if by doing so she would be able to see him better. "Are you O.K.? You're not getting sick, are you?"

Chulito smiled. "I don't think so, but whatever you made smells good."

Carmen raised her eyebrows. "Chuletas."

"Damn! I'm gonna have me some of those."

"Qué milagro, you actually want something to eat. You don't

have some place important to run off to?"

He smiled. "I'm supposed to hang out with Kamikaze later, but I wanted to ask you what you wanted for your birthday."

Carmen was going to turn thirty-seven the next day.

"For my birthday? Vamos a ver, you know what I would like? I would like for you to go back to school and get your diploma."

Chulito sighed. "Ma, you know I ain't down with school. Plus I ain't got Carlos to help me." He grabbed the tickets and handed them to her.

Carmen headed toward the kitchen. "Don't blame him for dropping out. You could at least get your GED, even though it's not the same as going to school. Think about it, Chulito. You only missed one semester. You could go back in September. That would make me very happy."

"O.K., I'll think about it. But would you like a perfume or how about something for the house?" Chulito took the serving spoon from his mother. "Sit, I'll serve myself."

She smiled and sat. "Pass my coffee. You sure you're O.K.?"

Chulito sat at the table, stabbed at the rice and beans on his plate then bit into a crisp fried chuleta. The flavor of the fresh pork and rich garlic overtook his mouth. "These are the best."

"Don't talk with your mouth full. You gonna choke." Carmen sipped her coffee. "You don't have to get me anything for my birthday. Just stay out of trouble and get your GED. You can't be a messenger your whole life." Carmen chose to believe the lie Chulito told her that he was a messenger for the health clinic on the other end of Southern Boulevard rather than a runner for Kamikaze. If she confronted him, he would just defy her and keep on working with Kamikaze and if she threatened to throw him out, he would just leave and he knew that she didn't want to be left alone.

"O.K., so what if I promise to sign up for a GED course when we get back from P.R., I could still buy you some perfume or a bracelet?"

Carmen got up and stood next to Chulito. "I will love whatever you get me and if you do sign up for that course, Carlos could help you since he's back. I know he will."

Chulito both loved and was annoyed by how his mother persisted. He would eventually either do the course or go back to school, but it would be only to make her happy. "I don't know about Carlos helping me out."

Carmen sat beside him. "I try to stay out of your business, but what happened? You were so happy he was coming home and Maria and I were happy that you two were talking."

Chulito stared down at the food that remained on his plate. He couldn't tell his mother that he was feeling Carlos and that he didn't know how to handle that. So he shrugged his shoulders and continued eating.

"You know what?" Carmen got up and turned on the radio. A salsa song played. "Your titi Nelly in Brooklyn wants to cook dinner for me on Sunday. I know you don't like doing the family stuff, but I would love it if you could come with me. It's gonna be a party." She danced around the kitchen.

Chulito swallowed the lump of meat he'd chewed and stuffed two forkfuls of rice and beans into his mouth.

Carmen waited for his answer.

He nodded. "O.K., 'cause it's your birthday."

"Really?" She touched his forehead. "Are you sure you're not sick? You really want to do this?"

"Most def. I've been thinking a lot about what I could do for your birthday. I know you got big plans to go out dancing with Maria tomorrow night, but we could go eat breakfast or lunch tomorrow at the diner in Parkchester and then we could go to Macy's." Chulito finished all the food on his plate. He wanted to wash it down with a beer but settled for Coke.

"I would love that." She leaned on the table and looked down at him. "Thanks, papa, but is there something else on your mind? You seem preocupado."

"Nah. Nothing."

"Is it about Puerto Rico? Do you still want to go?" She picked up the tickets from the table and examined them.

"Puerto Rico is cool." He took one of the tickets and looked for his name. "I'm thinking it would be good to get out from the 'hood for a while. I still have to ask off from work, but even if they don't give me the time…" he paused. "I'm thinking of quitting." Chulito realized what he'd just said and felt a flutter in his stomach. Could he just quit? He never made an official pact with Kamikaze, but there was this unspoken understanding that once he was in the game, he was in it for life. Also, quitting wouldn't be like leaving a job; Kamikaze was the person closest to Chulito. They spent most days and nights together. And Chulito liked moving in and out of clubs with ease. Besides, the only time he ever had any goods on him was when he made deliveries to some of the celebrities they handled. He remembered being backstage with Kamikaze at Madison Square Garden at the Titans of Hip Hop concert. They kept the scene well supplied and Chulito got to hang out underneath the stage as one rapper after another climbed up on the platform that elevated them to the spotlight. The crescendo of cheers had sent a thrill through his body.

"Is that what you have on your mind?" Carmen poured hot

milk from the stove into her mug and added more coffee.

"I just thought about it right now." Chulito took a bite of food. He remembered that Brick had been in the game and somehow managed to get out. He should find out how he did it. Brick would probably help since he had such disdain for Kamikaze and the whole scene.

"Well, you could go back to school full time, just so that you have more options. You could even go to college like—" Carmen stopped herself, almost as if she knew not to keep mentioning Carlos' name.

"Like Carlos?" Chulito finished her sentence. "He's got his shit together, right? He always did, but you know school is not really my thing."

Carmen sat down across from Chulito. "Well, when you applied yourself, you did good."

"You mean when Carlos was helping me, I was doing good."

She hesitated a moment. "I don't care what people say about him. I've known Carlos since he was a little boy and he's a good person. You and Carlos were friends before, why can't you be friends now?"

A small chuckle escaped from Chulito. It sounded like his mother was trying to hook him up with Carlos.

"What's so funny?"

"We never talked about Carlos being, you know, gay. We all just act like we know it and that nothing's different."

"What is there to talk about? He is living his life, going to school and he doesn't bring home any trouble. Maria and I have talked about it. It hurts her a lot, but she feels like she has no choice. He's her son, and she loves him. What else could she do?"

Chulito gave a shrug that betrayed all his macho posturing

and he let his mother see that he was a sixteen-year-old boy with a lot on his mind.

"He was your friend before any of those guys on the corner, before ese Kamikaze, so you can be friends with whoever you want."

Chulito wanted to phone Carlos that very minute to say he had his mother's blessing. "Maybe I'll call him, but it's not that simple, Ma. We've changed a lot and you know how the fellas are about that stuff." He wanted to just spill it out and tell his mother that he was feeling for Carlos. He wanted to tell anyone. She always said that he could tell her anything and that what made him happy would make her happy. But he didn't think his feelings for Carlos would make her happy. Keeping everything locked inside was making his temples throb. "I don't know if that would be a good idea."

Carmen watched him. Chulito felt like she was trying to read his thoughts, then he rose and put his plate in the sink.

Without speaking, Carmen began to put away the food.

"Did you eat, ma?" She shook her head and continued to place pots in the refrigerator and poured beans into plastic containers. "Do you still cook every night to keep Pop's memory alive?"

She smiled sadly. "Is that what's going on? Are you thinking about your father?"

"Nah." Chulito was relieved to not have to add his father to his worries.

"No matter what you remember about your father, he loved us in the way he knew how."

As for his father's love, Chulito remembered the opposite. He barely spoke and when he did he complained about everything from the meal, to Carmen talking on the phone, to a hat Chulito may have left on a chair—"Take that fucking thing to your room. You don't own this house." A few times his father hit his mother and Chulito suffered a few blows in his attempts to defend her. But his dad mostly went to work at the dry cleaners on Hunts Point Avenue, came home, watched the news on Univision and drank a lot of Budweiser. His father often said that it was a mistake to get married so young. Chulito believed that if his father hadn't been killed driving drunk, he would have eventually left.

Still, he saw how his father's death was liberating for his mother. In the six years since he'd passed, Carmen grew younger in Chulito's eyes; she went out more, she dressed better, and spent time with Maria and her friends.

"I'm gonna go listen to some music in my room. Kaz's coming by in a few. We gonna hang in El Barrio." Chulito left the kitchen.

Carmen followed him. "Chulito, are you in some kind of trouble? You can tell me anything."

"Lay off!" Chulito caught himself. "Sorry, Ma. I just feel tired and there was a lot of ghetto drama today."

"Do you mean that fight this afternoon? I heard."

"That and more so I'm gonna chill until Kaz gets here, O.K.?" He smiled at her. "Thanks, Ma."

"You're welcome, papito. I just love you."

Chulito looked at his mother standing in his doorway and saw how beautiful she was, not only in how she kept herself up, but how easily she was able to say I love you to him. "I know, Ma." He wanted to say "I love you" back, but the words were caught in his storm. He wanted to curl up on the sofa with her in the living room, rest his head in her lap and feel her caress his forehead like when he was a little kid on those days when he stayed home from school because he had a tummy ache. She stayed home from work and they'd both sit on the couch underneath a blanket and watch TV.

He wanted to tell her that he couldn't stop thinking of Carlos. That he wanted to be near him, go downtown with him, discover new things and talk to different people other than the fellas who usually talked about the same thing over and over. He knew there was more to life than his neighborhood and Carlos knew the road to those places. He also wanted to say that he loved Carlos' smile, how his skin looked soft, the way he blinked when his hair got caught on his lashes and how he made his eyebrows squirm like two black worms. He wanted to say, "Ma, I think I'm in love." Instead he looked away from her loving stare. "I'm cool." Chulito could feel the lump pulsing in his throat; the dam was going to break. He had to be alone in his room.

His mother retreated, then he locked his door. He realized that he was alone and that solitude was what he was yearning for. He didn't want to see anybody, not even Kamikaze. He needed to be in his room and figure out a way to deal with his pain and hunger for Carlos. He needed to make sense about how everything—his neighborhood, its people, the cracks in the sidewalks, even the stray dogs—was recognizable but they all seemed strange and unusual, too.

He sunk into his bed, slipped on his headset, put Tupac's *Thug Life* on continuous play and let the tears roll.

chapter nine

Chulito woke up with the sound of the front door slamming shut as Carmen entered the apartment. The blue light from the clock on his stereo system showed that it was eight A.M. He'd been sleeping for over twelve hours. He looked at his cell, which was on vibrate, and the red message light was blinking. Tupac was still rapping about not having time for bitches, threatening anyone who got in his way with a beat down, advising real niggas to stick to the game and laying out the law of thug life—do what you gotta do. Chulito pulled off his headset, reached for the cell and listened to his messages. There were three from Kamikaze who'd been looking for him. Chulito turned off his phone and rolled over on his side. He thought he should call Kamikaze back, but he was enjoying being invisible for the moment and being away from the game.

He awoke again at around ten-thirty A.M. by his startled mother's "Ay dios" upon entering his room and seeing him on the bed. "Chulito, I thought you were out. I did laundry today and was leaving some clean clothes for you. You scared me, papa."

Chulito sat up in his bed and nodded. "I guess I was more tired than I thought."

"You've been sleeping all this time? Are you sure you are feeling O.K.?"

"Yeah, I feel better now." He responded with a groggy smile. "Happy birthday, Ma. You hungry so we could go out for your birthday breakfast?"

"I was thinking maybe we could eat here and go out tomorrow?" Carmen set a small bundle of clean socks and underwear on a chair.

"I don't want you making breakfast on your birthday." Chulito sat up and covered his crotch with his thin, gauzy sheet.

Carmen explained that she had a lot to do in preparation for going out to the Copacabana for her celebration with Maria that evening. So Chulito scrambled eggs and made toast for her at home and they agreed to go out for breakfast the next day, before they went to Brooklyn. After breakfast, Chulito gave her $500 that he said he'd been saving up. She reluctantly accepted it and spent the day shopping on Southern Boulevard and at the salon.

Chulito called Kamikaze after he washed the dishes.

"Yo, Kaz, I am so sorry about last night. I fell out. Was everything cool?"

Kamikaze was pissed, but said that he mainly missed Chulito's company as he made the rounds at some local clubs and discos. "Don't fuckin' disappear like that. For a minute I thought some shit had happened to you. But I got you tonight, Chuly-chu, right? It's Saturday night."

"Most def," Chulito said hesitantly.

"I'll pick you up at eight. Are you O.K.? You sound different."

"I'm cool. I'm just feeling wrecked. I'm gonna lay down again."

"Maybe you caught a bug, little bro?"

"Nah, I'll see you tonight. Peace."

Chulito took a shower, a long one, and let the steam ease his mind. Then he laid back down on his bed and fell asleep.

Chulito's nostrils filled with the rich smell of garlic and cilantro. His head was heavy and he felt even sleepier than when he awoke in the morning. He opened the door and heard his mother singing along to an old Hector Lavoe song. The way in which he had Big Pun, Tupac and Fat Joe in constant rotation on his CD player, his mother had Hector, La Lupe and Luis Miguel on the CD player in the kitchen.

"You went back to sleep? Ay, papi, I think you're coming down with something?" Carmen was wearing a house coat, but her hair was blown and styled and her nails manicured.

Chulito sat up in bed. "I'm just tired, but look at you."

"You like my hair?" Carmen swung it from side to side. "Catalina did my nails and she told me that you two broke up."

"We was never really together. We went out a couple of times and I bought her some jewelry, but that was it. And she's going to the D.R. for the summer and I'm gonna be in P.R., so what's the point?"

Carmen shook her head. "Well, papa, you say it doesn't matter, but you haven't left the house since yesterday afternoon and all you do is sleep." Carmen lifted the lid on a pot of simmering red beans and stirred it. "It's O.K. if you feel a little broken-hearted."

"I'm not broken-hearted."

"Catalina's a sweet girl and she's pretty. I understand if breaking up has you down." Carmen scooped up a small amount of the beans, blew them and tasted them.

"Ma, I don't give a shit about Catalina. I'm tired. That's it."

She slammed the spoon on the counter and faced Chulito. "Don't get disrespectful, Chulito."

"I'm sorry, Ma, but can't I just be tired?"

"Then you should have a blood test done at the clinic where you work. You could be anemic."

"I'm fine, Ma. I just needed some rest. I feel better already." He flexed his small bicep and winked.

Carmen smiled. "Well, the food should be ready in about a half hour. Remember that I'm leaving at six o'clock to go out with Maria and the girls."

Chulito got dressed and peeked out his window. He saw Papo and Davey on the corner. He thought of going out, but instead sat in his room and looked for some music to play. He flipped through his CDs: Trick Daddy, Ja Rule, Noreaga, Wu Tang Clan, P. Diddy, Notorious B.I.G., Jadakiss, DMX, Ludacris, Nelly, Snopp Dogg, Junior M.A.F.I.A. and a continual procession of every hot rapper that money can buy. He turned on the radio and switched from station to station and heard Alicia Keys wail, "I keep on falling in love...with you."

Chulito sat still and listened to the pop song, his soul swallowing each word. The melodies blew over him like a warm breeze. As he shut his eyes, he remembered how sometimes he'd walk into the kitchen and his mother would be standing with her eyes shut, singing along with Hector Lavoe. "Tus ojos más lindos, más lindos que el mar."

As Chulito surrendered to the simple lyrics and the sweeping keys of the piano, he felt excited and scared at the same time. When the song ended, he wanted to hear it again. The light station continued to play love song after love song and Chulito rested on his bed, looking up at the ceiling.

Over an hour had passed when Chulito heard Carlos' footsteps above him. Chulito turned down the station really low to hear Carlos' movements. Carlos danced to some old school Madonna. Chulito couldn't tell if it was "Borderline" or "Holiday," but whatever it was it reminded Chulito of his mom. When he was about four or five years old, she'd play that old school Madonna and wild out with her friends when his father wasn't around. She'd pick up Chulito and dance with him. Carmen had the songs on cassettes and once during an argument, Chulito's father stomped them into pieces. Carmen went out and bought all the music again and listened to the songs on her walkman, but the dancing stopped.

When six o'clock came, Carmen transformed into a sexy mamita with a spaghetti-strap burgundy dress that stopped with a flair at her knee. She wore black high heel suede shoes and a black, sheer shawl around her shoulders. She came into Chulito's room to show off her dress. Upstairs Carlos was playing "Like a Virgin" and she did a little shimmy and kicked up her leg.

"Wow, Ma, maybe I should go to protect you."

"I look good, right?" She proudly patted her upswept hair. Two glittering diamond earrings hung from each ear with a simple matching teardrop diamond hanging from a gold necklace.

"We're gonna take a cab down to a restaurant near Times Square and then over to the Copacabana." Madonna continued to squeal and his mother invited him to get up and dance with her.

"Ma, I don't know if you noticed, but I don't dance."

"Oh, you used to love dancing around with me. C'mon, get up. It's my birthday."

Chulito got up and flailed his arms around without moving his feet and made a crazy look with his face.

"O.K., sit down, you could hurt yourself," She said with a laugh. He loved hearing her laugh.

"So you gonna go get me a daddy with that dress."

The smile left her face. "Don't be silly, it's just me and the girls."

"And a club full of sharks."

"I can take care of myself," she said playfully, regaining her spark.

"But I'm your back up." He said that in earnest even though it had come out sounding playful.

She came over, kissed him then wiped her lipstick off his cheek.

The music stopped upstairs, and they both looked up.

There was a knock at the front door. Maria called out, "The cab is coming, they said two minutes."

She gave Chulito a hug. "Tomorrow it's you and me, right?"

He nodded and smiled. "Have fun, Ma."

He looked out his window and saw his mother and Maria get into the cab. Carlos was with them, standing outside the cab and giving his mother a kiss. Chulito could tell from the black tank top with tight black jeans and black boots that Carlos was ready for a night out. As the cab sped away down Garrison Avenue, Carlos looked back at Chulito's window. Chulito ducked out of view. When he looked back out Carlos had crossed the street on his way to the subway station.

For the rest of the night Chulito stayed home. He ate the pork chops, rice and beans his mother had cooked. He washed the dishes, turned off his phone and lit a healthy blunt and smoked it, freely blowing smoke throughout all the rooms of his apartment like he'd seen his grandmother do with a cigar to bless her house. He went to his mother's room and sat on her bed. He saw the shoes she'd tried on for the night out and rejected. Her make-up containers were all over the dresser. Pictures of him and his father were wedged to the sides of her mirror. He remembered when he sat on that very edge of the bed and his feet couldn't touch the floor. He'd watch his mother put on make-up and she'd make funny faces at him. He felt like they were the only two people in the world. He felt safe.

The sun was still out so he didn't need to turn on a light, but as night fell he sat in darkness. Since it was easy to see into his apartment from the street and he didn't want anybody to know he was home, including Kamikaze. He knew he was taking a big risk but he turned off his phone. He watched television in the living room because the windows faced the inner courtyard and nobody walking on Garrison could see its bluish light, or see him sleeping in front of VH-1's "I Love the 80s" as old school Madonna danced into his dreams.

The next morning, his mother was brewing that richly fragrant Bustelo coffee. It said espresso on the can, but to Chulito, his mom, and most Puerto Ricans it was simply café. When he sat up on the couch he saw his Tims were neatly set on the floor and the television was off. He felt fully awake and alert. Then he panicked because he had missed two days with Kamikaze and knew that he'd be pissed.

He had to respond to the missed calls and messages from Kamikaze. He flipped it open without checking them and called Kamikaze. He was relieved when the machine picked up: "Yo, yo, yo. This is the Big K. You know the drill…spill it. Peace!"

"Hey, Kamikaze. Sorry about last night. You were right, I caught a bug or a stomach thing and I was laid out." He paused, feeling obligated to call Kamikaze, but he wasn't ready to see him. Besides Kamikaze reserved Sundays for recuperating from Saturday night. "I'm cool now and since it's my mom's birthday we headed out to Brooklyn to visit family and we staying over. I will catch up with you tomorrow, promise, promise, promise. I'm really sorry about last night, bro. I hope everything was cool. I'll hit you up when I get back to the Bronx."

His phone beeped as he was ending his message.

"What the fuck happened?" Kamikaze demanded without saying hello.

"Kaz, I was just going to, uh, ring you up last night, man. I was in bed all day. You were right, I think, I think I caught a bug or something." Chulito waited for Kamikaze's response.

"Be straight with me little, bro. If you sick, you sick, but if some other shit is up, spill it the fuck out right now." Kamikaze sounded impatient and angry.

"Nah, ain't nothing but a bug, stomach thing. On the real." Chulito wanted to get off the phone. He wanted to retreat back from his neighborhood and his life.

"Fuck. The only reason I'm gonna buy what you sayin' is because you been on the level with me, but you better stay healthy or I'll fucking make you sick." Kamikaze laughed. "I'm joking."

Chulito was relieved to hear Kamikaze laugh. "Thanks, Kaz."

After sharing a cup of café with his mom, he stripped out of his clothes, did some push-ups and sit-ups and took a shower. He put on a white short sleeved button down shirt by Polo that had thin aqua blue horizontal stripes, a pair of khaki colored cargo pants that were nice and loose with a brown belt and chocolate brown Timberland boots. He wrapped his head with a white du-rag and slipped on light blue Kenneth Cole shades. Even though Parkchester was just five stops and less than ten minutes from Hunts Point, he didn't want to talk to anyone so he called a cab.

He saw the fellas hanging out on the corner, but he went right into the taxi with his mom without acknowledging them.

The rest of the day went smoothly. Brunch at Step-In's. The long train ride to Brooklyn.

Then on the cab ride back from Brooklyn, as his mother slept, Chulito thought about the last few days. He realized that he needed that time away from everybody, time away from the noise and opinions on the corner, time away from Kamikaze and the business, time away to figure out what he wanted to do next. There wasn't a lot of figuring, it was more trying to find the courage to go for what he wanted. And he wanted Carlos. He wished that he was going to Puerto Rico with just Carlos. Then they could hang out and go to the beach and not have to worry about the fellas, Kamikaze or anybody.

When the cab arrived in Hunts Point, it was two o'clock in the morning. The streets were deserted and all the lights were out in Chulito's building, except for Puti who slept with the light on.

Chulito could barely sleep, anticipating what he was going to tell Carlos. He fell asleep going over the script in his mind. At five in the morning, he was wide awake. He heard his mother in the bathroom preparing for work. School would be out in a couple of weeks and she wouldn't have to get up so early.

As he lay on his back with his hands behind his head, he looked up at the ceiling as if he could see right through it and watch Carlos sleeping in his bed. Chulito wanted to wake him. "Hey, Carlos, I'm ready."

And he was ready. That morning Chulito was sitting on the steps inside his building's vestibule, so that Carlos couldn't leave without seeing him. He rubbed his sweaty palms together, blew on them and waved them to dry and shake off the nervous feelings that where urging him to go back into his apartment. He cracked the muscles on his neck, rolled his shoulders and in his mind practiced what he would say. He'd keep it simple. Be up-front.

He leaped up when he heard the door to Carlos' apartment open. The jingling of keys sent Chulito tip-toeing toward his own apartment. Then he stopped and returned to the foot of the stairs. He wasn't going to retreat. No more running away. For the first time ever, he felt as if his knees were going to give way. They trembled and buckled. He balanced himself by holding on to the wooden handrail coated with decades of black paint, then held looked up the worn marble stairs as Carlos' footsteps echoed in the hall. Carlos was startled at first but recognized Chulito and stood still, placing his hand on the handrail at the top of the stairs. The window on the landing bathed Carlos in a soft light. He looked puzzled. His brows were gathered tightly then they relaxed. Carlos' smile triggered a calmness in Chulito. He still felt nervous but he no longer felt like he would be sick. Then Carlos began descending and Chulito began ascending the stairs. When they met up Chulito faced him. He had to say what he'd practiced, regardless if a door opened or if someone walked into the building. He was not going to back out of this moment. He looked around the hallway and whispered, "I dig you, too, Carlos. And not like when we were kids."

"What?" Carlos searched Chulito's eyes to see if his heart was aligned with his words.

"You heard me right." The urge to touch Carlos overcame

Chulito reached out and gently ran his fingertips along the sleeve of Carlos' crisp white shirt. Then, he dropped his hand and shoved it in his pocket. But all the while he held Carlos' stare.

Carlos looked at where Chulito had just touched him. "What are you saying? What are you doing?" There was a tinge of anger in Carlos' voice, as if he thought Chulito might be playing with him.

Chulito hoped he hadn't made a mistake. He felt his heartbeat pulse in his ears. "Carlos, I been feeling you for a while. I just didn't know what to do. What we'd do?" He continued to speak softly. "I don't know what to do next, but I figure I say what I got to say. Let you know how I feel and then we can see wassup."

Carlos sat down on the steps. "I never thought you would own up to how you felt."

Chulito wanted to sit, too. But the reality that someone could catch them sitting made him choose to keep standing. "You knew?"

"I had a pretty good idea." Carlos smiled and checked his watch. "Your timing sucks. I'm going to be late for my internship." Carlos got up and dusted the seat of his pants.

"I been thinking of telling you for days. What do we do now?"

Carlos shrugged.

Chulito smiled. He felt light in his chest. "Can I pick you up when you get out?"

"Call me and we'll work it out. I promise to take your calls now."

Chulito held out his hand.

Carlos chuckled. "What are you doing?"

"I don't know." Chulito wanted to do something, but a hug would be too much and a kiss was not right. Being caught talking on the steps was one thing but anything else was too much. So a handshake felt right. Not the kind you do when you greet your buddies, but the old fashioned, seal-a-deal kind.

Carlos shook his hand. "Sometimes you can be such a trip. Call me later?"

Chulito walked Carlos to the doorway. They both walked slowly side by side, prolonging the moment. Carlos stepped out of the building and paused. He shook his head. Chulito beamed and watched him cross Garrison Avenue. Carlos looked back, still shaking his head. Chulito's heart was racing and his heavy breathing dried up his throat, making it hard for him to swallow. He wiped his moist palms on his shorts, then he grinned and whispered, "Holy shit."

chapter ten

Kamikaze's phone message was direct. "Be ready at ten A.M., nigga, 'cause you been incognito and there's a lot of work to catch up on." It was ten A.M. am on the dot according to Chulito's Fossil watch. Damian, who had already taken his post, waved to Chulito, who waved back, then looked away and snickered, remembering their dream encounter.

Chulito flipped open his cell, called Carlos and left a message. "Yo, Carlos. It's Chulito. I know you probably still on your way to work, but I wanna just let you know that I'm thinking about you, bro." He smiled because he'd always wanted to leave him a message exactly like that one. "Turns out I gotta be with Kaz today, but I should be back around the 'hood around six. Hit me back." He sat on the stoop, pushed earphones on and bopped to Biggie. He couldn't wait for Carlos to call him. How would he answer? "Wassup, beautiful." Too corny. "Hey, babes." Too soon. "Holla." Too ghetto.

Chulito looked at the corner and recalled Carlos struggling with the wind and the grocery bags that day and the smile that wouldn't leave his face broadened. Then he imagined the fellas on the same corner and knew that he would have to deal with them at some point.

Twenty minutes passed and Chulito got up and paced.

"Pssst, hey Chulito."

Chulito pulled out his headphones, looked up and saw Puti in her window.

Puti snapped her fingers. "You got anything for me?"

"Nah," Chulito said annoyed. "I don't got anything,"

"Ah, c'mon. Not even a little something? I ain't got no money but te lo chupo like nobody could, trust me. It's top dollar." Then she did the international gesture for a blow job, jerking her hand in front of her mouth and with each pump bulged out her cheek from the inside with her tongue.

"I told you I ain't got nothing. I don't carry shit on me. One of the neighborhood boys should be around soon." Chulito got up and walked away from Puti.

"Is Kamikaze coming? Maybe you could get something for me? He won't give me nothing. I owe him money from way back, but maybe you could help out." Puti whispered, "Come up. I could perform CPR on your pee-pee now and you'll see how good, then you could get me something from Kamikaze."

Chulito looked at Puti. She'd seen him grow up. She and her mom even babysat for Chulito when he was little, and now Puti was offering to suck his dick for a fix. He hated seeing this part of the game. It was different going from club to club feeling like a top cat and seeing people partying and getting high. Seeing people in his neighborhood addicted to their drug of choice or of availability was another thing.

"Nah, Puti, it's not gonna happen. Kaz and I never walk around with shit, you know that."

"Fuck you!" she said in full voice.

Chulito walked toward the corner.

"Wait, Chulito, come back, I'm sorry," Puti said, back to whispering.

Suddenly, Chulito could hear Fabolous's "Keepin' It Gangsta" vibrating from Kamikaze's Lexus. He pulled up to the front of the building and rolled down his window. "Y'all know whoooo, keepin' it gangsta. We come thruuuuu, keepin' it gangsta. How we dooooo, keepin' it gangsta. I'll hol' truuuuu, keepin' it gangsta." Now, Chulito knew that Kaz liked to make an entrance, so he probably just hit #2 on the CD as he rolled up the block. Chulito tapped his Fossil to signify that Kamikaze was late.

"I may come late, but I's always cum on time, squirt." Kamikaze tilted his Yves St. Laurent shades with the light blue lenses and shouted, "Yo, Chu! My little brother. Panito, what is up? Why you hiding from me?"

Chulito hesitated before getting into the car. "Nah, Kaz, I was really sick." Chulito paused then confessed, "I also just got a lot of shit on my mind these days, but things are cool."

Kamikaze slapped the passenger's seat. "So why you ain't call me? I thought if there was something on your mind you would call me. You know you the first person I would call if I had shit on my mind. Especially if it was you who I had beef with."

Chulito climbed in and strapped on the seat belt. "Sorry, Kaz. But it was nothing like that. Where we off to?" The tinted window rolled up to create a cocoon of rap music and air-conditioning. He looked over to Puti who was staring at the parked car as if she could see through the dark windows. Her mother, who looked like a sixty-five-year-old version of Puti with the same wispy hair and gaunt face, appeared and shoved her aside to make room at the window.

Kamikaze reached over, put Chulito in a headlock and kissed his temple. He then leaned back. "Let that be the last time you do a disappearing act on me, understand?"

Chulito nodded. Kamikaze was smiling but the severity of the warning came through clearly.

Kamikaze nudged him with his elbow. "I thought you were pissed because of that shit with Brenda. It takes a lot for me to lose my cool, but we good, right? I missed you, nigga."

Chulito wasn't sure how to read Kamikaze, but chose to go with the jovial Kamikaze he knew and loved. "I missed you, too."

"Really, nigga? Get outta here." Kamikaze flashed his bright smile. "So why you didn't call me? You had me all wondering like some bitch that something was up." Then he laughed out loud.

Being the closest person to Kamikaze, Chulito knew just about everything there was to know about him, even his real name.

Kamikaze was born Roberto Jimenez, but after chasing him three times in one week when he was running corners the cops christened him Kamikaze. The first time he was chased he jumped from the roof of one building to the next and ran down into the apartment of one of his women to hide from the cops. One cop jumped and didn't make it. The others didn't even try. He got away.

The second time he was chased to the Bronx River, where he dove in and swam to the other bank. They fired warning shots at him, but he escaped again.

The third time he was being chased, he leaped like a gazelle onto the back of a truck that was heading up the ramp to the Sheridan Expressway. The cops followed but they couldn't out run a truck and he got away. So whenever the cops wanted to bring Roberto Jimenez in for questioning they said they were going on a "kamikaze mission."

"We headed to El Barrio, Chuly-chu, to pick up some good super hydro shit. Fuck, from the way they talkin', I am going to have to charge more and shit." He said that all proud, then he put an arm around Chulito and leaned in real close to his face. "And we's gots to have a little sample to check it out, so we get to do a little partyin', too." He playfully kissed the tip of Chulito's nose.

Chulito wiped it. "Yo, what's up with that?"

"You know you love it. Besides nobody can see."

"Chill, man, let's just go do this."

"Yo, what's with you? You all serious and shit. You gettin' enough pussy? I could hook you up with Yolanda again." He put his hand up to give Chulito a high-five. Chulito reluctantly responded. He knew Kamikaze loved him in his own way, but this morning, after being open with Carlos and spending those days away from his surroundings, being with Kamikaze felt like putting on a pair of his favorite sneakers that he had outgrown. Kamikaze laid out the day's activities, his arms moving opening up wide to leave the steering wheel unattended for a few seconds, his head nodding and his talk non-stop.

Chulito felt different and stared at him trying to see if something had changed with Kamikaze, too. But it was all familiar. He knew how it would go down.

Noticing Chulito watching him, Kamikaze asked, "What's up, Chulito?"

"Nothin', I'm cool."

"Ya mom alright? She had a good birthday?"

"We had a great weekend celebrating. Nothing's up with her."

"Well, my little bro, you know I got your back unconditionally, and whatever is up you'll tell me when the time's right, right?"

"I'm cool, Kaz. But chu right. I know we tight and I can share any shit with you," he said but thought not really.

"Now that's what I like to hear," Kaz said. He rocked back and forth singing along with both hands on the steering wheel.

For someone so straight up gangsta, Kamikaze pushed the limits when it came to clothes. He was dressed in a turquoise Adidas running suit and pale blue Timberlands. Chulito remembered last Easter when he dressed in all baby blue except for a pair of pink Timberlands with a pink suede fedora. Nobody said shit about his flamboyance when it came to dressing because he had the women and the babies to steer them away from taggin' him a 'mo.

Kamikaze cranked up the sound system. "You know whooooo, keepin' it gangstaaaa," Chulito, Kamikaze and Fabolous sang as they crossed the Third Avenue Bridge into Manhattan.

Chulito waited in Kamikaze's car on the corner of 106th Street and Second Avenue. Kamikaze slipped his gun into the waistband of his briefs and went up to see El Papa, one of the local suppliers. They were supposed to pick up Friday night, but since Chulito was incognito, and Kamikaze never does a pick up alone, he put El Papa off.

As Chulito sat in the car, Carlos returned his call. "Hey, Chulito," he whispered. "I'm not supposed to be on my cell phone when I'm at work, but I wanted to hear your voice."

He liked hearing the hushed excitement in Carlos' voice. Chulito whispered, too, as if somebody could hear him. "You being a tough boy, breaking rules to talk to me? I told you. You gangsta."

"Stop playing. So can you meet me or not?" Carlos asked very matter-of-factly.

Suddenly, Chulito looked up and saw Kamikaze, a turquoise streak, running toward the car with his gun in hand.

"Oh shit!" Chulito dropped the phone, scooted over to the driver's seat and turned the ignition. Chasing Kamikaze were two guys, a tall skinny Latino man with a pony tail wearing a black Adidas running suit and a buff, Black guy with a mohawk, dark shades and black tank top and dark gray jeans. Chulito shoved the car in gear as Kamikaze pulled the door open. The Latino guy pointed a gun at Kamikaze. "Gimme ya gun, motherfucker!"

Kamikaze froze and handed him the gun. The Black guy went over to the driver's side and pointed his gun at Chulito. He never had a gun pointed at him and felt as if he was going to shit his pants.

"Get in Kamikaze and unlock the back door, now."

Kamikaze sat in the passenger's seat and the Latino guy got in the backseat and told the Black guy to get in beside him. He pressed the gun to the back of Kamikaze's head and the Black guy had his gun on Chulito.

"You didn't see shit, ya hear?" the Latino guy said.

"Nothin' man, I didn't see nothin', Rey."

Chulito realized that this wasn't some random thug, but Rey himself. Whatever was going down was big for Rey to be chasing Kamikaze. Chulito wanted to get a better look at him, but thought it best to stay still.

"I'm serious Kamikaze. The only reason I ain't poppin' you and your boy is because it wouldn't be good for business. 'Cause

I got zero love for you. That's the difference between me and El Papa; I just focus on business and the numbers. That fat fuck got weak lettin' small time niggas owe him money just 'cause they had history. I knows you don't have that problem, but effective immediately we under new management, ya hear." He shoved the gun into the back of Kamikaze's head. Chulito thought of the scene in a movie where the gun went off in the car by accident and splattered its victim's brains all over the back window. He had trouble breathing and his eyes were moist.

"I got chu, Rey." Kamikaze didn't move. Chulito followed his lead.

Rey moved in close and Chulito could see him in his peripheral vision. Rey wasn't covered in tattoos and greasy looking the way Chulito had imagined him. His skin was light and he had black, trimmed moustache. He wore a white Kangol hat pulled down low and a light green plaid shirt. Although he was sweaty from running he smelled like the fresh Florida water Chulito's grandmother used in her rituals. Rey growled into Kamikaze's ear. "So you saw nothing, right?"

"Nothin'," Kamikaze responded quietly.

"You got the loot?"

"It's in my pants. Can I get it?"

"No, Kaz, you keep you hands on the dash board. Felix, get it," Rey said to the Black guy.

"It's under my balls," Kamikaze said.

"Get it, Felix." Felix lifted the waistband to Kamikaze's blue sweats and reached in, pulled out a bundle of money and handed it over to Rey.

"I'll send Felix down with your shit. Wait here, but I ain't playin', Kamikaze. You say something or you don't play straight,

I'll order a Diallo on you and your boy here." Then Rey dropped Kamikaze's gun into his lap and he got out of the car with Felix.

Kamikaze looked pale. "This ain't good, Chuly-chu."

"What happened, Kaz?"

Kamikaze told Chulito that when he went up to El Papa's, Felix answered the door. He thought something was up when he saw Rey instead of El Papa. When he asked for El Papa, Rey said he was out, then Rey and Felix laughed like they had a secret. Then Rey said, "You wanna see El Papa? He's in his room. Go ahead. Go see him." He opend the bedroom door and El Papa lay on the carpet with his throat slit. They wanted to show off and show him who was the new boss. Kamikaze bolted out the apartment.

"Rey was El Papa's right hand man, Chulito. This ain't good."

The excitement and bling had been taken out of the game for Chulito and the danger kicked in full force. In the year that he'd been working with Kamikaze it had been mostly smilin' and glidin'. Now he wanted to get out of the car and run away. Take Carlos and get far away from the city. Carlos! Chulito picked up his cell phone, which was still flipped open. He held it to his ear, and then closed it. He wondered if Carlos had heard a play by play of what just happened. "Should we go? Get the fuck out of here?"

"You crazy? Rey is no joke. He just slit his boss' throat. Now if he got orders to do it, then it's just a change in management. But if he's being maverick, things are gonna get crazy and we are gonna have to lay low to see what's up."

Felix came down with a big Duane Reade bag. It was stapled shut at the top. Kamikaze got out of the car.

"Who the fuck told you to get out of the car?"

"Sorry, man." Kamikaze started to get back in.

"Hold up, nigga. Here, take your shit." Kamikaze took the bag, opened the trunk and looked inside the bag.

"It's all there."

"I'll call in a couple of days." Kamikaze locked the trunk and replaced Chulito in the driver's seat.

They distributed their booty as quickly as possible and collected loot the whole day. Kamikaze hardly paid any attention to Chulito but made several calls, his forehead creased with worry the whole time. He even spoke aloud in the car, trying to make sense of the situation and figure out what was next. "Gotta check the account...I gotta call up Rodrigo in the Bahamas just in case we need to bounce...Make sure all my boys are locked and loaded."

Kamikaze took his personal stash and when they were done with business, they headed back to his crib. "We gonna have to lay low here until I find out what the deal is. Call your mom, and let her know you wit me. I'm thinking a day or two tops."

chapter eleven

The night after the incident with Rey, Chulito sat eating rib tips and beef fried rice with Kamikaze in front of the TV, wondering what was going on in Carlos' mind. He felt like he blew it again. Chulito was freaked out by what went down and he couldn't imagine Carlos wanting to see him again. Instead of doing something to bring them closer, he'd given Carlos a solid reason to stay the hell away from him.

Kamikaze was on the cell a lot, getting the lowdown on El Papa and Rey and keeping in touch with his team. He had them get extra muscle because business had to continue. He connected with his special clients and told them that he would be out of town but that they could call him if they had an emergency. It was early in the week, so they had time to recoup before the weekend demand.

Kamikaze picked up a white take-out container and poked around in it with chopsticks. He popped a piece of sesame chicken into his mouth and sat beside Chulito. "Sorry about all this, little bro, but I'm glad you were with me. I hate this part of the game, but unfortunately it's just a part of it and we can't pick and choose the parts we like from the parts we hate." He raised his thick eyebrows and searched Chulito for a response.

Chulito shook his head. "To be straight up, I ain't never been so scared in my life. When they had those guns pressed up on us…"

Kamikaze slid over, wrapped his arm around Chulito's neck, pulled him closer and kissed his temple. "I try to keep you protected from all that, but either way I got your back. You know that, right?"

For a split second, feeling close and protected, Chulito thought of sharing what he was feeling about Carlos, but he backed off. What if I got all open with Kaz, risked my friendship with him, and Carlos is not even feeling me anymore? Besides, Kamikaze had bigger concerns at the moment.

Later, as Kamikaze slept, Chulito found a quiet moment to finally call Carlos. "Hey, Carlos."

"Chulito, are you O.K.? What happened?"

Chulito realized that maybe Carlos had heard something. "What did you hear?"

"You said, 'Oh shit,' then I heard fumbling then the phone when out. I called you back but it kept going to voice mail so I thought something must have happened to your phone and I was busy at work, so I put my phone on vibrate and waited for you to call or text."

Chulito sighed. He'd been all worried that Carlos had heard the whole deal and he would have to give a big explanation.

"Hey, Chulito. What happened?"

"Nothing. My phone just…" Chulito stopped.

After a few seconds Carlos said, "Hello? Are you there?" Then he said to himself, "His phone must be fucked."

"I'm here." Chulito took a deep breath to calm himself. He looked over to make sure Kamikaze was still asleep. "Carlos, some crazy shit went down."

"What? Are you O.K.?"

Chulito liked hearing the concern in Carlos' voice. "Yeah, I'm cool but…" He paused. He felt that if he came clean about what happened he would lose Carlos, and the same time he felt he had to be real and Carlos needed to know who he was if they were going to even try this. "Some crazy shit happened." Chulito gave Carlos a play by play of what went down. All the while Carlos was silent, but Chulito pushed on and when he was done his armpits were soaked.

"So, I been at Kaz's all day. We layin' low as a precaution, but I think everything is O.K. Sorry I didn't call you right away. Been feelin' like shit."

He heard Carlos breathing heavily. Then Carlos said coldly, "I don't want to be involved in anything like that."

Fuck! Chulito thought. "Hold up, Carlos, please." Chulito shut Kamikaze's bedroom door and sat on the couch to calm himself, because he knew Carlos' next words would be about staying away from him. "Carlos, I'm thinking of getting out of this game, but I can't just now. You hear me?"

"I hear you, but how are you going to do that?"

"I'll work that part out. It might take some time." Chulito rubbed his chest. "Damn, I really want to see you. I want us to be together."

"Chulito, maybe we shouldn't see each other, well, not until you get out of the game. If you do get out of the game."

Chulito felt as if he'd poured gasoline all over himself by coming clean and Carlos' words were like a match igniting the flame. He continued to whisper, "Carlos, how you gonna say some shit like that? If I could get out and it be clean, I would do it this minute, but you know it ain't that easy."

Carlos was silent.

"Please don't do this to me." Chulito pleaded. "Not when we are getting so close, pa."

"I didn't do anything to you. I don't want any of that drug shit in my life. What you said about the guns and the threats scares the shit out of me. Not only am I going to have to worry about my own life, but I'll be worried about you, too."

"You will?"

"Chulito, don't try it."

"O.K., sorry 'bout all that, about everything. I promise you, Carlos, I will get out of the game. Please stick with me. I will keep it all away from you, but don't leave me before we even got started."

Carlos was silent, then said, "Let's talk face to face."

Chulito jumped up and pumped his arm up in the air as if the Yankees had hit a home run. He tried to not sound excited. "O.K., but I gotta lay up here in Kamikaze's place one more day, just to be sure things are cool. What time do you get off work Friday?"

"I'm off on Fridays."

Chulito had to do runs with Kamikaze, but he thought it would be best not to mention that. "I should be around the block at, like, four o'clock. You gonna be around?"

"Yeah, but I was gonna get together down in the Vil with some friends who are home from school. You willing to come downtown?"

Chulito hesitated. He wanted to hang with Carlos but not with a bunch of friends, especially college friends who might put him down. "What time do you gotta meet them?"

"Like seven or eight, it's kind of flexible."

"O.K., maybe I could ride down with you and we can talk on the train. Then I'll head back uptown and let you do your thang with your friends."

"You can come to the Vil, too."

Chulito was excited and concerned about going to the Village. Concerned because he felt that was moving faster than he wanted. At the same time he had wondered for so long about Carlos' world and knew that if he wanted to get closer to Carlos he would have to go to where Carlos wanted to go, so he agreed. He shrugged his shoulders and laughed quietly. "What the fuck?"

Chulito didn't make it back to Hunts Point until six. He dashed into his room and heard music playing above, so he knew Carlos was still home. He tried not to sound out of breath from running as he held his cell phone with his shoulder. "Yo, Carlos, wassup?"

"Hey, Chulito, I thought you chickened out."

"Yo, I did not chicken out. I just got delayed."

"You're still coming downtown?"

"Well, I don't know," Chulito said playfully. "I was gonna hang out with some friends who are home from college for the summer, too."

"You're making fun of me, Chulito?"

"Listen to you getting all huffy. Don't get all protective and shit."

"Then stop playing."

"I just gotta change right quick, give me five. Why don't you head out to the train and I'll meet you there?"

"I can wait."

"Nah, go to the train. I'll met you there."

"Don't take long or I'll bounce."

"Bounce? If you the Carlos I know, your ass will be right there waiting."

"Leave my ass out of it. All of me will be there but not forever, Chulito."

"You always gotta be messin' around. Give me five, O.K., ten tops. I'll meet you at the bench inside the station before the stairs you go down to the trains."

"I'm serious, Chulito. Don't take long. You've had me waiting long enough."

Chulito checked himself out in his mirror. He studied his profile, smoothed out any loose hairs and pressed down his eyebrows. He knew that Carlos liked what he saw, so he had to be perfect. But he suddenly felt nervous. What did Carlos want with him besides what he could see in the mirror? What could he offer Carlos? He didn't have a real job or even a high school diploma. What if Carlos got bored with him? And who were these friends in the Vil? Were there any past loves?

Chulito shook off his doubt and looked out the window. He saw Carlos crossing the street and checking out the corner where the fellas had already begun to pass around a bottle of Hennessey. He continued across the street and headed to the train station.

Chulito pulled off the yellow FuBu Shirt he was wearing and pulled the plastic off of a red Rocawear jersey he had taken out of the cleaners. He couldn't just put it on after running around all day with Kamikaze, so he undressed and took a quick shower. Back in his room he sprayed CK One all over himself, including his ass and his balls, and flinched because he never got used to the alcohol's sting. He put on clean socks, boxers, and the size thirty-eight Levi shorts that came down to his shins. He put on the red Rocawear jersey without a t-shirt underneath it. It was short sleeved and had snaps on the front that he closed except for the last two on top and the last two on the bottom. He checked out his braids and pulled on a red du-rag. He tied it nice and tight and topped it all off with a Yankee cap fitted to size. Then he slipped into a pair of dark blue Timberland boots. He checked himself one last time in the mirror, grabbed his wallet, watch, keys, and phone, turned off the light and yelled, "¡Bendición!" out to his mom as he slipped out the door.

"Chu-li-to!" Papo yelled from the corner as Chulito crossed the street to go to the train station. The ten minute mark to meet Carlos was just about to strike. Shit, Chulito thought.

"Gotta run, fellas, gotta meet up with—" He was going to say Kamikaze but then he saw Kamikaze's car parked near the fellas, so he jogged over to the corner.

"Man, you looked pressed." Davey swiped his lips with his tongue. "Where you goin'?"

"Downtown. I'll catch you tomorrow." Chulito turned away.

"Hold up. You been missing for days." Papo placed his arm around Chulito's shoulder and pulled him close. "You don't want a little shot with your boys before you go?"

"Yeah, it's just that I'm running a little late."

"Don't be letting no pussy whip you, little bro." Papo released Chulito. "Whoever she is, she gonna wait. And if she don't," Papo pretended to kick a can, "kick her to the curb."

Chin-Chin and Davey both laughed.

Kamikaze stepped out of Gil's Liquor Store and came down

the block.

"What are you knuckleheads up to?"

"I think our boy here has got some chocha plans," Papo said.

"'Bout time," Kamikaze said, "'cause I was getting worried about you acting all moody. Glad to see that you putting Catalina behind you."

"So, who is it?" Davey passed Chulito the bottle.

Chulito took a swig of Hennessey. "It's not like that. I'm going to hang with my cousin."

"In El Barrio?" Kamikaze asked. "I'm headed that way."

"No, in Brooklyn." Chulito handed the bottle to Chin-Chin.

"Brooklyn? You hung with them last weekend." Kamikaze said.

"Well, since you and I are off this weekend, I figured it would be cool to go back out there."

"You guys are off?" Chin-Chin asked.

"You ain't heard about the crazy shit going down?" Kamikaze said.

"Look, fellas, I gotta run." Chulito crossed Garrison Avenue. Midway across the street Papo yelled, "You ain't going to hang with no cousins."

Chulito turned and gave them a sly smile.

"I knew it," Papo yelled.

"Dále webo," Davey yelled as he did a hump dance, putting his hands behind his head and pumping his hips.

Chulito ran toward the train station. When he arrived, he didn't see Carlos on the bench. He swiped his Metro card, ran down the stairs and found Carlos on the platform.

"You were gonna bounce?" Chulito asked as bopped over to him.

"I waited fifteen minutes. You're lucky I gave you the extra five."

Chulito stood side by side with Carlos and scoped out the subway platform to see if there was anyone he knew. He looked at Carlos out of the corner of his eye. "How many trains did you let go by?" he asked and smiled.

Carlos smiled back. "Only one."

"I knew you were gonna wait for me."

"So you took your time?"

"Nah, I was right on time, and then I ran into the fellas."

"I figured."

The train pulled in and Chulito sat across from Carlos rather than next to him. There were only three other people in the car—a young couple kissed deeply, pink tongues slipping in and out of brown lips and a teenager moved to music on his headset as his blond dreadlocks bounced to the beat.

They rode silently, stealing glances and reading the subway ads. Carlos looked fresh and clean and good enough to lick. Chulito leaned forward to ask Carlos where exactly they were going, but it didn't matter what he asked he just wanted to talk to him and hear his voice. But as the train filled with goth kids, young women headed to a nightclubs, rambunctious teen-aged boys and nurses and security guards in uniforms heading to work, Chulito lost his nerve to speak to Carlos. He didn't want anyone else to hear.

At 125th Street most of the passengers switched to the express train, but Carlos moved to a corner seat and called Chulito over. They sat side by side. Sometimes their shoulders touched, sending a chill through Chulito. Carlos leaned in. "You're so quiet. I thought you wanted to talk."

"I want to talk to you, not the whole train."

"Nobody can hear us unless you shout. I'm glad we finally got to hang."

"Me, too," Chulito said. "I was scared that you wouldn't want to see me again, after what went down in El Barrio."

"Everything is not cool, Chulito. I'm still not sure what to do. I bust my ass to go to school and stay clean. I really don't feel like I want to get involved in some crazy shit. As much as I feel you."

Chulito nodded and looked away. "I hear you. Damn, you was bold when you came out with whole 'I'm feeling you' thing."

"Don't change the subject." Carlos smiled. "Let's just hang and see what happens."

Chulito smoothed out his pants and adjusted his baseball cap. "I'm glad you giving me a chance to hang with you. I'm glad we here."

"I was tripping myself up with my feelings. I can't explain it. And when you didn't keep our plans for your birthday, I was wrecked."

"I'm sorry about—"

"That's in the past, but I was really hurt. I still went ahead with the plans, but instead I just took my mom and Andrew instead."

"That blond dude in the white Range Rover?"

"He's a really good friend from school." Carlos sat up and looked at Chulito in the eye. "And since you blew me off, I invited him and my moms out to City Island."

"I love the seafood out in City Island."

"I know."

Chulito nudged his knee against Carlos'. "I'm sorry."

Carlos looked at Chulito and then away. "I was so upset because those phone conversations we had before I came made me feel close to you again. I love hearing your voice and you are so beautiful Chulito…you a pretty thug."

"Damn, Carlos. Don't hold back now." Chulito smiled, but looked nervously around the train car.

"But I just figured, let me just say what's up and at least let it out, because as long as it was inside me, I was just making myself crazy thinking about you."

"I think about you too, a lot."

Carlos smiled. "C'mon, it's clear that you dig me, too."

Chulito smiled to mask his nervousness. "It wasn't that clear to me, but I knew I was feeling something."

"What do you feel, Chulito?" Carlos' eyes stared expectantly as if their next blink depended on Chulito's answer.

Chulito couldn't put words to what he felt. The question raised sensations in his body—a flutter in his chest, a chill up his spine, a tingle in his balls. "I don't know. I think about you, too. I love to see you smile. But a dude ain't supposed to be saying shit like this to another dude, so I bug out." Chulito paused while their train stopped in a station, then once it resumed he continued his conversation under its rumble. "Like when you started being all gay and shit and everybody was talking, I stayed away because I didn't want to be seen with you. And, even though I could never admit it to anyone, not even myself, I missed you. And I could see you were hurt when you tried to talk to me and I'd just say 'wassup' and keep walking. I wanted to do something else, but if we stayed friends, everybody would think I was gay and I'm not."

Carlos sat up. "So what are you doing here? Why did you say what you said to me on the steps?"

Chulito was caught off guard. He thought he had a handle on the situation, but labeling what he felt for Carlos as gay didn't seem correct. He looked at their reflection in the window across from them, sitting side by side, Carlos awaiting his answer. He then looked at the passengers as if they could help him formulate an answer—among them was a beautiful young woman with big tangled hair, a tight dress that showcased her dark, round breasts and stiff nipples. She was checking him out, too. Could she stop him from where he had every intention of going with Carlos? Was she an angel who'd come to save him from himself? He nodded to her and she smiled.

Noticing this exchange, Carlos started to stand up, but Chulito touched his arm. He leaned over, cupped his hands around Carlos' ear because he didn't want one syllable to escape into the clatter of the subway car, and whispered, "I'm here because I like you Carlos, and I think about you constantly."

Carlos played along and whispered into Chulito's ear. "What do you think about when you think about me?" His lips brushed Chulito's lobe and Chulito quivered.

"I wonder what your job is like. I wonder where you go when you go out? I think about the conversations we used to have." Chulito wanted to add, I think about your smile and how it gives me chills. I think about how beautiful your face is, especially your big eyes and how you can make your eyebrows dance. I think about the day when I saw you coming around the corner, and the wind blew your shirt up how I could see your skin on your stomach and how that moment is on constant replay in my mind. I think about what it would be like to hold you. But he didn't. He wasn't ready to dive in.

"What about our conversations?"

"I feel like we here," he said forming a "V" with fingers and drawing a line from his eyes to Carlos' eyes and back. Carlos sat back on the seat and rested his head against the wall. Chulito did the same. Simultaneously, they looked at each other. Chulito chuckled and Carlos shook his head and smiled as they reached Astor Place.

Navigating the mob headed toward the turnstiles, Carlos leaned into Chulito. "I'm glad you're here."

"No doubt, but don't get all open leaning up on me." Chulito smiled then leaned into Carlos.

"I'll make sure to keep my distance." Carlos playfully pushed him. "Wouldn't want any of these strangers to get the wrong impression about you."

Chulito looked around and realized that he didn't know anybody. This was strange because he was so used to spending most of his time on his block where he knew everyone and everyone's business, which affected how he behaved. But here he didn't know anybody and nobody knew him, so he could behave however he wanted.

As they climbed the stairs, Chulito checked out Carlos' ass and wanted to give it a playful smack.

When they emerged from the train station, Carlos asked him what he was smiling about.

"Nothin'." Chulito looked around and felt a little claustrophobic by all the people scurrying around. The only time the streets in Hunts Point were this populated was when there were street festivals or block parties.

A corner Starbucks was full of people sitting at a ledge in the window typing on laptops, talking on cell phones and with one another. Across the street, in the middle of a concrete island, there was a black cube the size of a small house but it was standing on one of its points. He thought it looked strange and wondered what was the point of it being there. Chulito checked out the skinny boys on skateboards with plaid shirts tied around their waists whizzing by the sculpture, some kids with pink and purple hair sat on the curb near it, and a woman with a guitar and a guy with a flute played beneath the cube to a small crowd. The air smelled of coffee and sweet roasted peanuts. Chulito looked around. There were a couple of old looking buildings, a K-Mart and a Walgreens, but no big gothic sign that read "Welcome to the Village."

"So we here?"

"This is the East Village. We're going to the West Village, but I came down the east side so that we could have more time to talk as we walk across town. And it's a perfect evening. Sun is still out and it's after seven P.M., and it's not humid."

As the two began their walk they heard Carlos' name being sung out in a falsetto faux operatic voice.

"That's my friend Kenny," Carlos said as Kenny waved to them from across the street. "You want to come say hi or do you want to wait here?"

Chulito went with Carlos. There was no doubt in Chulito's mind that Kenny was gay. Chulito checked out Kenny's tangle of bleach blond curls held away from his face by a red bandanna. He wore red Adidas running shoes with black hip-hugging jeans and pink tank top that was cut to just meet the waist band of his pants. Kenny was slim but muscular and a gold loop pierced his eyebrow. The one thing that didn't match Kenny's look was a small tattoo of the Dominican flag on his shoulder. Chulito shook his head and wondered if all of Carlos' friends looked like this.

Carlos hugged Kenny who looked over Carlos' shoulder at Chulito and panned him from head to toe.

"I heard you were back," Kenny said to Carlos but didn't take his eyes off Chulito.

"Been back a couple of weeks, but I haven't seen you around."

"That's because I was giving the West Village a rest, and spending time in the East." Kenny raised his eyebrows and pointed at Chulito.

"This is my friend from my 'hood," Carlos said.

"He's from your hood? I thought he was from Planet Yum. Yum, yum, yum. I'm liking your look. Very thug, very Jay-Z. Are you a homiesexual?"

Chulito's eyes narrowed and a flash of anger shot through him. "What?" he growled. "Get the fuck outta here!"

"Oops, sorry," Kenny said. "Didn't mean to rush the issue. Take all the time you need."

"No," Carlos jumped in. "He's just a friend from my 'hood. His name is Chulito."

"Chulito? Oh, that's perfect. Purrrfect." Kenny danced around repeating "perfect." "Damn, Chulito, you are over, ovah. So are you two together?"

Chulito looked at Carlos. "What the fuck is his problem?"

"Chill, Kenny, we've known each other since we were little kids and we haven't had a chance to hang out since I've been back, so tonight worked out. I invited him to come with me to the pier. But we just hanging."

Kenny waved his hand in the air. "Whatever."

"It's his first time coming to the Village." Carlos nudged Chulito. "Right?"

Chulito nodded.

"Really?" Kenny's voice raised several octaves.

Chulito shrugged his shoulders. "Never had no reason to. I

got all I need right up in my hood in the B.X. My friends, my family. Me and my friends go out sometimes, but I basically stay in my nabe."

"So you're going to the pier? With him? Then I'm going." Kenny hooked his arm around Carlos' arm. "I can't wait to see the looks on their faces when they see…Chulito." Chulito started to think that he should have stuck to his plan to just ride down with Carlos and then head back up to Hunts Point. He didn't like Kenny being so touchy feely with Carlos. Did they have some history?

Chulito felt uncomfortable walking with Kenny, so he lagged a couple of paces behind them as Kenny and Carlos were catching up on news. Chulito knew what everybody in the 'hood knew about the Village. Faggots and freaks hung out there. He pictured the Village being like one in an old Dracula movie with a big gate in the front, cobblestone streets and gray stone houses. As they walked he saw what he imagined were college students because they dressed like Carlos, then he saw a group of gay guys who looked like Kenny and they were loudly calling each other girl and Miss Thing. Chulito decided he couldn't do it.

"Hey, Carlos, can I talk to you?" Chulito looked away and adjusted his shirt while Carlos approached. "Yo, I want to head back home."

Carlos looked at Chulito's eyes. "It's O.K. Why don't I tell Kenny that we changed our plans and we could go do something else?"

Chulito nodded.

Carlos turned to Kenny, "Change of plans. We're not going to the pier."

"No!" Kenny stomped over to them as if he were having a

tantrum. "Let's go. Please? Come to the pier, Chulito. I promise to behave."

Chulito folded his arms across his chest. "I just don't wanna be tagging along."

"I'm sorry, you guys were off on your evening and I jumped into your business."

"We ain't got no business. What the fuck is he saying, Carlos?"

"It doesn't matter." Carlos said, "Kenny, we're gonna do something else."

"Oh, go to the Village, Chulito. You came all this way. And the pier is fun. There's all kinds of people there and some bring boom boxes, people dance and hang. And sometimes we go eat something. At least check it out and if you don't like it, then you guys leave."

Chulito admitted to himself that he was curious about going to the Vil and the pier. He wanted to see Carlos' world, and Kenny was right, he could leave if he didn't like it. "Bet," Chulito said, nodding in agreement.

"You sure?" Carlos asked.

"We check it. If it's not cool, we bounce."

They talked about their ages, about Kenny being born in the Dominican Republic, but he lived in Puerto Rico until he was ten when his family moved to New York.

"I bet you like rap music," Kenny said to Chulito.

"It's my shit."

"Who's your favorite?"

"Pun, no doubt."

"Classic. Love him. And he was from the Bronx, so you got the Bronx connection thing going with him."

"I like the old school rappers like Fat Joe, Tupac, Ja Rule but I been rockin' Fabolous, too."

"Holla back, young'n, whoo, whoo." Kenny sang and Chulito laughed.

"I didn't know you were into rap music," Carlos said to Kenny.

"Honey, I'm into rap music lovers. I got me a bad case of thug passion."

"I know what that is," Chulito said. "Hennessey and Alizé."

"Yes, that and it's also me getting all stupid over guys like that brother over there."

The trio had reached the corner of Seventh Avenue and Christopher Street. Chulito discovered there was no big gate or gray stone houses in the West Village either. Nothing special. It looked just like all the small streets they had passed. Christopher Street was narrow and lots of guys were checking him out. He was used to women staring him down, but not guys, not like this. Usually, when guys checked him out they were nervous and looked away, but here they held the stare, and a few even shared comments—"Damn," "Want some company, papi," "Are you my baby daddy." Chulito liked the attention.

"Kevin!" Kenny called out in the same falsetto he'd used to call Carlos. "Let's go say hi."

Kenny led the trio over to Kevin who was dressed like a hard up thug—du rag tight around his braids, open Enyce jersey, loose shorts and Timberland boots. "Wassup, m'brother?"

"Chillin'," Kevin responded. "'Sup, Carlos. Ain't seen you in a minute." Chulito watched Kevin hug Carlos and didn't like him pressing Carlos against his bare chest.

Carlos pulled away from Kevin. "This is my friend Chulito."

Kevin held up a fist, and Chulito bumped fists with him.

"'Sup Chulito. I ain't seen you around here before." He crossed his arms and sized up Chulito.

"Chulito and I grew up together," Carlos said. "It's his first time in the Vil."

Kevin pulled down his shades to reveal light brown contact lenses. He chewed on a toothpick that sat in the right corner of his mouth. "Welcome downtown, little brother, you in good hands with these two. Kenny will get you in trouble and Carlos will get you out of it." Everyone but Chulito laughed.

Kenny lifted one of the open flaps of Kevin's unbuttoned Enyce jersey. "Well you looking good, Kevin. Been hitting the gym, I see." Kevin tapped his hand away.

"Sorry. We headed over to the pier." Kenny said. "Wanna come?"

"I just came from there."

"Who's there?"

"The usual suspects. I might hit The Monster, since I turned twenty-one a few weeks ago."

"Happy belated birthday." Kenny kissed him on the cheek.

"Chill, Kenny, don't be slobberin' all over me. Stop acting so hungry."

"The Monster is one of the oldest gay bars in the Village," Carlos explained to Chulito, pointing to it, "but we have to be over twenty-one to get in."

Chulito looked over to The Monster. He had been to so many bars and lounges with Kamikaze that he figured the gay bars looked the same, except for guys and women it would be guys and guys. He could make out men sitting in the big windows with drinks in hand.

"Well, enjoy the Monster," Kenny said. "It's just the pier for us young queens."

They continued down Christopher Street, stopping to look at windows of shops that sold Speedo swim trunks, tight form fitting clothes displayed on shirtless mannequins with big bulges, sex toys, exotic soaps, candles, and porn magazines and DVDs. Chulito thought that it was wild for everything to be out in the open.

"Let's go in." Kenny stepped into a shop that had a mannequin wearing leather chaps, a harness and mask.

"Nah." Chulito said looking down the block. "Y'all go on. I'ma be right here."

Carlos shook his head and smiled. "You don't have to be afraid."

"I ain't afraid." Chulito folded his arms across his chest. "It just ain't my scene."

Carlos laughed. "Yeah, right." He was unphased, relaxed and even laughed a lot more than he did walking down Garrison Avenue.

By the time they reached the pier, Kenny and Carlos had greeted about fifty people and had as many mini conversations about as many topics. Chulito felt out of place. He longed to go back to the 'hood.

The sun was setting over the Hudson River with its rays dancing on the rippling waves and the warm light casting long shadows. The pier was buzzing with young people, rollerbladers, joggers and vendors selling ice cream, hot dogs and shish kebobs. Chulito thought it looked more like a park than a pier. There was a small plaza at the entrance and a long expanse of neatly trimmed grass full of people relaxing. "This is dope. I wish we had one of these back up in Hunts Point."

Carlos smiled. "Glad you like it, Chulito. This is where I spend most of my time. It's free, there are always lots people, there's food and there's even a bathroom."

Chulito continued to check out the scene and wondered if the group of break dancers, spinning on their backs and uprocking, were gay. There were guys who looked like Papo, Davey and Chin-Chin from his neighborhood, except these guys were holding hands or making out. "I'm a little bugged out," he said with a laugh.

"What's so funny?" Carlos asked.

Kenny leaned into him. "Culture shock, honey."

The trio walked over to a couple sitting on the grass. Pito was a slim Black, Cuban guy wearing baggy sweats, high top New Balance sneakers and a ribbed, white tank top. He had his arms wrapped around Sebastian, a creamy colored Latino with sky blue eyes who was short, very muscular, shirtless and also wore sweat pants.

Kenny plopped down next to them. "Hey, lover boys, this is Chulito, Carlos' friend."

They both said "wassup" to Chulito. Pito kept nuzzling Sebastian's neck and kissing his ear. Sebastian winked at Chulito who looked away.

A short drag queen in high heels called out to Kenny, "Bitch, where have you been?"

Kenny jumped up and ran over to her. The two hugged and had a conversation that was all arms.

Carlos sat on the railing near the couple and invited Chulito to join him. Chulito just leaned beside him.

"Kenny's talking to Lady Elektra," Carlos said. "You O.K.?"

"This is not what I expected, but niggas are definitely doing their thang." Chulito looked at Pito and Sebastian who were locked in a kiss.

"Well, you wondered where I go. This is one place. We're too young to get into clubs or bars. The Gay Center sometimes has parties and there is Kurfew, an under twenty-one party, which is fun. We go to the pizza shop we passed on Christopher Street, too."

Two tall white boys who reminded Chulito of slightly younger versions of the German twins from Tats Cru walked over to them. ·They were slim with tattoos on their arms. Both had on eyeliner, which made their blue eyes brighter.

"These two lucky suckas are models," Carlos whispered to Chulito.

"We got a call back for an A and F campaign, but another set of twins got it. They asked Sean over here to come back, though," Siobhoan said of his brother.

"I'm not going. We're a team," Sean said.

"You are going, 'cause money is money, right?" Siobhoan asked. Carlos nodded.

Sean leaned on his brother. "So then you go. Those assholes are not going to be able to tell the fucking difference."

"Guys, this is my friend Chulito."

Sean and Siobhoan raised their eyebrows simultaneously. "Very nice," they said in unison.

Kenny danced with the drag queen and some other young folks. The break dancers joined them and started voguing and striking poses to the beat from a boom box playing house music. Carlos swayed.

Chulito was amazed by so much activity. He thought the Village would be overrun by goth kids and drag queens, but he was excited to see so many guys who looked like him.

Carlos hopped off the railing. "You wanna dance, Chulito?"

"You crazy? I don't dance," Chulito responded. "But go do ya thing."

"I don't want to leave you by yourself."

"I'm cool."

Carlos ran over to Kenny and danced. The twins joined the crowd, and soon about thirty or forty people were dancing wildly and freely to the music under a streetlight. Meanwhile, Pito and Sebastian kept kissing and Chulito noticed Pito slip his hand inside of Sebastian's sweats, grabbing hold of the bulge that had grown.

Embarrassed, Chulito walked away from the couple and wondered if everybody on the pier was gay. His question was answered when he recognized Damian dancing with one of the strippers from the club they'd gone to for his birthday. A salsa song had come on and some people left the dance area while others broke into pairs and started salsa dancing—boys with boys, girls with girls, and boys with girls. The little bit of ease and fascination that Chulito had with the pier quickly shifted to panic. What the fuck was Damian doing there?

Carlos and Kenny came over to Chulito, laughing.

"We gotta bounce," Chulito said abruptly.

Carlos followed Chulito's line of sight and saw Damian spinning the young woman around. "Is that Damian? I've never seen him here before."

Kenny looked over. "You know that guy dancing with the stripper? I've never seen him either, but she's always here. That's Lady Elektra's sister. Anyway, some of us are gonna head over to Kurfew. You two wanna come?"

"Let's get out of here." Chulito pulled his cap down low and stormed off. Carlos and Kenny followed.

Kurfew was like the pier, except multiplied by a hundred. Young people danced under elaborate, flashing lights and the entire room vibrated from the massive sound system. The bar area was lit from below so the bartenders, male and female, looked like alien beings. All around the periphery of the dance floor there were tall tables and clusters of writhing, dancing young people around each one.

Pito and Sebastian danced crotch to crotch on the dance floor and kissed continuously. The twins danced together and Lady Elektra gave an impromptu show. Kenny, Carlos and Chulito were drinking sodas and Kenny was giving Chulito the gossip on just about everyone in their sight. Hunts Point and the fellas on the corner seemed far away.

Carlos sat across from Chulito at one of the tall tables and because the music was so loud Kenny sat beside Carlos and talked right into his ear. Even though Carlos listened to Kenny he stared at Chulito. They held one another's gaze and smiled. Chulito's dick stirred. He looked at Carlos' fingers wrapped around the glass of Diet Pepsi. With his index finger he touched one of Carlos' neatly clipped fingers. All around him young couples were embracing, kissing, laughing, dancing. He wanted to go around the table and take him into his arms and finally feel him pressed close.

Chulito checked the crowd every so often to see if he spotted anyone he knew, but the coast was clear. Remembering Damian at the pier, he realized that the world of Hunts Point and the pier were not completely exclusive of each other. And even though the young people at Kurfew where all types, like flamboyant Kenny, conservative Carlos, fellow thugged out dudes and everything in between, they seemed to get along and be happy. This was their place, Carlos' place and a place he could be with Carlos.

Big Pun's "Still Not a Player" mixed in to the beats and Chulito bopped.

"This is your boy, Chulito, you wanna dance?" Kenny shouted.

"Nah," Chulito said.

"C'mon, Carlos let's go dance." Kenny said, then darted to the dance floor and wedged himself in between the twins.

Chulito waved Carlos toward the dance floor. "Go dance, I'm cool."

Carlos imitated Chulito and bopped his head. "This is Pun, right?"

"Yeah, but I can't dance." Chulito did a little awkward shimmy.

"Liar, come dance." Carlos grabbed Chulito's hand tried to pull him to dance.

Chulito yanked his hand out of Carlos' grip. "Yo, chill, don't get open, you buggin'?"

"Oh, just come stand and bop your head. You could do that." Carlos dragged Chulito to the dance floor. Chulito squeezed Carlos' hand, followed and stood in place bopping his head from side to side scanning the crowd. Kenny came over and danced around Chulito before going back to the twins. It seemed like the whole club knew the words to the song as they all sang along with Pun. What would Pun think about a club filled with gay young people groovin' to his music? The song by J.Lo and Ja Rule thumped into the mix. The crowd once again sang along. The beat was slower, so Chulito moved his shoulders a little. He watched Carlos who was singing along with Jennifer Lopez, looking so happy. Then Ja Rule's part of the song came along and Carlos sang along with the gravelly voice. He grabbed his crotch and pretended to be a thug and bopped over to Chulito who laughed.

Kenny became thug number two and they bumped chests and pretended to fight. When Jennifer came back, they both imitated her and blew kisses at each other and the two Jennifers danced around Chulito.

When the music changed to a house music song that had a lot of piano playing in the beginning, Chulito backed off the dance floor and Carlos followed.

Carlos picked up the soda he'd been drinking earlier and said teasingly, "I thought you didn't dance?"

"I was not dancing. You and those people were." Chulito pointed to the crowd. "You got some moves, Carlos. And your J. Lo wasn't too bad."

"What about my Ja Rule?"

Chulito smiled. "No comment, but I could help you if you want."

"Oh, you're gonna give me thug lessons?"

"If you want." Chulito struck a tough pose.

"Let's go."

They waved good-bye to their friends on the dance floor. Kenny blew kisses to them with both hands and danced back into the crowd.

Chulito and Carlos ate pizza on Christopher Street and then strolled through the neighborhood, passing brownstones, theatres, cabaret lounges, bars and restaurants with white table cloths and little candles on them. They talked about Carlos' college and internship at the *New York Daily News*, Chulito's adventures with Kamikaze, and about their mothers. Carlos bought some books from a street vendor and at two in the morning they were eating strawberry shortcake and drinking milk at a diner on the Westside Highway. There were moments of long silences where the two just walked side by side or simply looked at each other. When the sky started to lighten they found themselves back on the pier. This time it was deserted, except for an occasional jogger running by as the sky went from black to cobalt blue. They sat leaning into one another facing the Hudson River. Silently. Staring out into the dark water, stealing glances, sharing smiles.

Carlos tapped the brim of Chulito's Yankee cap. "Eventually we're going to have to head back to Hunts Point."

"No doubt," Chulito said sadly.

"But this is always here," he said, looking around, "and knowing that helps me deal with the neighborhood."

"You were going to stay out in Long Island but came back because of me, right?"

Carlos nodded. "And my mom is in Hunts Point, so I'll always come back, but it's tough living there. And at the same time, I can't live here. It's expensive for one. And for me to find roommates and live in a place like Spanish Harlem wouldn't make sense. I might as well stay in Hunts Point. At least I know the thugs on the corner."

"True. I didn't know what to expect, but tonight was pretty dope. I met so many new cool people, including Kenny, that nut. And the disco was a riot. The Village wasn't what I expected, but I can see why you come here so much." Chulito moved closer to Carlos and their legs touched. "Everybody is so open. I can't wait to hang with you again."

Carlos smiled. Chulito stood up, extended his hand, and pulled Carlos up.

He didn't want to release Carlos' hand. Chulito wanted to walk hand in hand, fingers laced, but he released Carlos' hand, dusted the seat of his pants and said, "Let's bounce."

They walked across town to the six train in the pre-dawn light. Chulito watched Carlos sleep on the ride back to the Bronx. Carlos' head leaned against the subway map and his stringy hair fell on either side of his face. As the train screeched and jerked, Carlos awakened, smiled and fell back to sleep. Chulito didn't look away. Since there weren't many people in the subway and most of them were asleep, he took Carlos in watching his slim chest rise and fall, then following a vein running down his right forearm and imagined what it would feel like to trace it with his finger. Carlos' hands loosened their grip on the plastic bag with the books he'd bought. Chulito wanted to press those hands to his face and kiss each finger tip. He burned to walk across the train, kneel before him and press his face to Carlos' stomach and hold him close, feeling his warmth, breathing him in. He felt himself lengthening in his pants and leaned forward, resting his forearms on his knees as he pressed his erection with his elbow enjoying the rush.

As the subway clambered up to the Bronx, Chulito finally looked away. The night he'd just spent with Carlos confirmed that he knew exactly what he wanted. The question he now asked himself was whether he had the balls to go through with it. It was one thing to feel and acknowledge the desire he felt for Carlos. Acting on those desires would take things to another level. What would it mean if instead of just staring at Carlos' mouth, he actually kissed it. If he actually held hands with Carlos, or hugged him close. Would he be gay? Or bi? Just by spending this night with Carlos, something had shifted and he wanted more. Of what? He wasn't sure yet. They'd be home in Hunts Point soon. He thought about *The Wizard of Oz* and how throughout the whole movie Dorothy was trying to get home. That night, the Village was like Oz bursting with color and strange new sights. He always thought being in Oz was way better than black and white Kansas.

Chulito took the sleeping Carlos in one more time, then walked across the empty train car and pushed a strand of hair away from his face. The feel of it made his crotch stir. Carlos continued to sleep. Chulito adjusted himself and was grateful for his baggy pants. He took one last longing look before shaking him. "Yo, we home."

chapter twelve

As Chulito and Carlos climbed the steps out of the train station, Chulito noticed Brick sitting on the ledge at the top of the stairs. Chulito backed off into the safety of the subway station.

"What's the matter?"

"That Brick nigga is up there. I don't want him to see us together."

"Chulito, we were just hanging."

"I know, but you know how people are."

Carlos rolled his eyes. "Well, we're back in Hunts Point." Then he exited the train station and passed Brick. They made eye contact and nodded.

Chulito waited ten minutes for the next train to arrive before coming out of the station. He hoped Brick would be gone, but he was still there. As Chulito climbed the stairs, Brick stared him down. " Kaz had you workin' all night, little bro?"

"Nah, I's just chillin'."

"C'mere a second." Brick hopped off the ledge.

"Wassup, yo, I'm tired."

"I just wanna ask you why you wasting your time with that Kamikaze dude. He's bad news." Brick lit a cigarette and blew out smoke.

"That's my business." Chulito took a few steps away.

"You're right, but I heard about what when down with El Papa, and stuff like that is why I had to get out of that game."

Chulito wanted to ask him how he did it, but said instead, "Look, Brick, I know what you trying to say, but I make my own decisions."

"If you say so."

"I know about you and what you went through, and that you have beef with Kamikaze."

Brick interrupted him with a shake of his head. "I don't have beef with Kamikaze. The way he runs his shit, I did the same in El Barrio. Me, Rey and another cat, Crazy Joe, were like brothers. Rey took care of shit below 106th, Joe was above 116th up until 125th and I took care of the middle from 106th to 116th Street. The bosses wanted to consolidate shit and get rid of one of us." Brick took a long drag before continuing. "El Papa told me I had forty-eight hours to off Rey or Crazy Joe or else they would off me. But he said the same shit to Rey and to Joe. Ain't that some shit? We all like brothers and then we all trying to kill the other one off. For a whole day I just laid low, trying to figure things out. Jennifer was pregnant with our baby, complaining that she can't take it no more and that she wants me to get the fuck out of her life. Then I got word that Crazy Joe was dead." Brick blew out smoke and shook his head. "Rey just went to his house and slit his throat. I wondered if Rey had picked Joe or if he just found him first. Man, Joe was probably laying low in his crib trying to sort things out, too."

"So Rey picked Joe."

"I don't know for sure. Now they got Rey to off El Papa. That's how things are done."

"But you got out. How?"

"It cost me and I'm still paying." Brick flicked his cigarette into the air. "It cost me my grandmother and my—" Brick stopped. "My grandma was real special to me."

"They killed her?"

"Well, first she got robbed and beaten to scare me, which it did. They thought that after my grandma I'd give in and come back to work. I didn't. Then a week later she gets out the hospital and she gets hit by a car. An accident. She was the only family I had. My dad died in jail and my mom died of AIDS when I was ten. Then they said Jennifer was next and she was pregnant with my son and, well, she lost the baby as a result of all that stress."

With all the gossip and dipping into people's business that went on in Hunts Point, Chulito was surprised that he hadn't heard Brick's story before. "I didn't know about that," he said. "I'm sorry man."

"Oh, there's more, but you just need to know what you up against. I see you dressed fine, and the guys taking you out and all, and you and Kamikaze livin' it up, but there's more to all that. And you got a nice mom, and they don't play."

Chulito thought of Carmen. How she got up at dawn to go to work and how she was so happy to get that job when he was little so that she could be home for Chulito when he got home from school. He thought of all she endured with his father. He wanted to make her life easier and he would protect her no matter what.

Besides, Kamikaze wasn't like those crazy cats from El Barrio. He wouldn't kill anyone.

Brick looked up at the large Mega Millions lottery sign that loomed over the gas station and laughed. "But who am I to be giving advice, right? I really fucked things up, and now I'm just hanging around catching glimpses of my daughter as she goes out with her mother. They should be by soon, I hope. Jennifer works the early shift today and since I ain't home she's taking them to her moms. I can't go near them, though. Jennifer has a fucking order of protection out against me. I don't blame her. I owe her a lot. Jennifer took me in when nobody wanted a wired up nineteen-year-old street thug. Not even my grandma at that point. Now, I'm twenty-four and trying to figure shit out. But if I had to do it all over, I'd make different decisions."

Chulito appreciated Brick being so open with him. He felt for him and understood some of the heaviness with which he walked the neighborhood. He wanted to say something, but all that came out was, "Thanks, Brick."

"You remind me of myself when I was your age, so I'm just trying to look out."

Across from them on the wide street, Jennifer walked by holding Crystal's hand. Jennifer didn't look over to Brick, but Crystal waved to him. Brick waved back. "There goes my heart."

chapter thirteen

When Chulito arrived at Poe Park in the Northwest Bronx, the setting sun was putting up a fight with its final bright rays of hot light. Everything was orange—the majestic oak trees, the young guys break dancing near the benches, the empty gazebo, the Art Deco buildings on the Grand Concourse, the poet Edgar Allan Poe's cottage at the north end for which the park was named, and Carlos, who blazed a bright creamy orange as he sat on a bench, chin resting on his left knee. He was reading a book, eating an apple and his hair had fallen into his face. Chulito watched for a moment, and then, as if by instinct, Carlos looked up.

Chulito waved. "Yo, wassup!"

"Hey, Chulito." Carlos smiled, closed his book and took one last bite out of the apple before tossing it into the garbage can.

Chulito ran over and sat next to him, but not too close.

"Sorry I'm late, man, my moms wanted something from the store as I was leavin'."

"It's alright. I got a mother, too. Besides I was reading."

"Is that a book you bought last night?"

"Yeah, it's really good. I'm almost finished with it."

"Get the fuck out of here." Chulito looked around the park to see if anybody was watching them.

"I've been reading it all day."

"Fuck, a book that thick would take me forever. I don't think I ever read a book that wasn't for school or something."

"I'll lend it to you when I'm done."

"Take your time, yo, I'm in no hurry."

Carlos smiled and looked up at the sky. "Check out that sunset."

Chulito loved the way Carlos always noticed everything—even things that didn't seem important.

"It's beautiful, don't you think, Chulito?"

"Now that you mention it, it is pretty dope. Your face is all orange."

"Yours, too." Carlos gazed into Chulito's eyes.

Chulito jerked away. "We two orange niggas."

Carlos laughed.

Being with Carlos in Poe Park with the fading sun reminded Chulito of the last time they were there together.

It began with a race to the man selling Italian ices. Chulito and Carlos ran as fast as their young legs could carry them and yelled out their favorite flavors. "Cherry!" "Blueberry!" They watched with excitement as the strong, old man scooped out frosty mounds of iridescent ice. They slipped behind the park's information center to eat their treats where no one could see them. Chulito looked at Carlos' face with its curly lashes, tar pit eyes and skin that reminded him of the sweet creamy chocolate milk his mother made each morning.

That whole summer they had been inseparable. Since their rooms were right over each other's, they would sneak out on the fire escape, spy on Doña Andrea on the third floor who walked around her apartment naked. They would secretly go up to their roof and Carlos would read Greek myths aloud, and sometimes they'd sword fight with broken TV antennas. They'd look out on the vast South Bronx landscape. Yankee Stadium in the distance became Mount Olympus, especially during night games when the stadium lit up the brooding urban sky with a supernal glow.

But that afternoon in the park, while eating their ices, they sniggered and stole glances, speaking their own language of gestures and expressions. Chulito checked to make sure no one was around and then he pressed his bright red cherry ice stained mouth to Carlos' lips. The cherry and blueberry flavors swirled around for a quick moment when their tongues met. Chulito never forgot how when they separated he saw Carlos' hot, turquoise tongue disappear inside of his blue smile.

"So, what's up?"

"So, I asked you to meet me here 'cause I wanted to thank you for taking me down to the Vil last night." Chulito rubbed the red and white religious beads he wore around his neck.

"You're welcome, but it—"

"Wait." Chulito stood up, took two steps, hiked up the pants that he purposefully wore three sizes too big, turned to Carlos and spoke in one breath. "I just wanted to show you how much I appreciate you hanging with me, again, after all these years. I mean we used to be tight as kids, and we took real separate roads, and I didn't think that we…"

Carlos stood up. "Relax, Chulito, it's just me."

Chulito wanted it to be just Carlos, his best friend since he was five, but after the night they spent in the Village, Chulito's feelings about Carlos excited and scared him. He knew that by going out the night before with Carlos and now by asking him to meet him away from their neighborhood to thank him for the good time they had in the Village he was moving closer to him. He was aware that he was making the move he'd been avoiding.

Chulito had stayed away because Carlos didn't hide being a faggot. And the code of their neighborhood was that if you hang out with faggots then you must be one—as true now that Latinos and Blacks lived there as it was when Jews, Italians and Irish folks first came. It was as if that code was mixed into the concrete and asphalt that was used to build the neighborhood. It was also why, in order to be open, they had to leave Hunts Point.

"Just follow me." Chulito led him to the front of Edgar Allan Poe's Cottage at the north end of the park. His thoughts were louder than a block party in full swing. Carlos is my friend and so what if he's gay, he does his thing and says fuck you to anybody who messes with him and that is what being a man is about so Carlos is a man and when we're away from the 'hood, it feels real cool so it's alright for me to be hanging with him and nobody needs to know jack.

Chulito looked back at Carlos. "You ever been inside?"

"No, it's always closed."

"Not tonight."

Carlos stopped in his tracks. "You breakin' in?"

"Nah, I know you're a goody, goody, and I don't want to get you into any trouble. Keep walking, bro. Since you were talking about old furniture last night I remembered my friend Angel worked here so I cashed in a favor."

"We're going inside?"

Chulito saw the excitement on Carlos' face and smiled.

As they approached the gate, Angel, a round man with thick glasses, came out to meet them.

"Yo, wassup, Chulito?"

"Wassup, pana?" They shook hands and half hugged, and Chulito slipped Angel a nickel bag of weed. "This is my friend Carlos. The one I called you this morning about who's doing the report on this Poe nigga."

"Wassup, Carlos?" Angel looked suspiciously at Carlos because he wasn't dressed according to ghetto Bronx code.

Carlos deepend his voice, "Hi." Then he looked past Angel at the modest wood frame farmhouse.

"So, you guys got a half hour and then I gotta lock it up. Don't fuck with anything."

"Angel, man, I helped you clean that house a hundred times and I know all the shit in there, so go get your forty and let me show Carlos around. I want to show my college friend that I got some brains, too."

Chulito led Carlos past the thick black gate. He ran up the painted wooden stairs and held the door open for Carlos. When Chulito shut the door behind them, they were no longer in the center of the Bronx but in a place far away. The sounds of the park—the radios, the kids, the barking dogs, the whizzing cars—were sealed out. The musky scent of damp oak filled the air and the floor boards groaned and creaked as if they would snap with the weight of each footstep. Chulito watched Carlos look from the small gift case at the entrance containing magnets, Poe Cottage wooden blocks, and brass Raven bookmarks, to the main room with an old wicker rocking chair and a dark wooden desk that had on its top an open book and a white quill pen below an electric candlestick. Even though Chulito had seen the Poe Cottage before, bringing Carlos made him see the house differently. The main room was like the rest of the house in that it was set up as if Poe and his wife Virginia were out for a stroll. A tea pot was set on a small table with two ivory cups sitting on matching gold rimmed saucers and the cast iron pots in the kitchen were resting on the squat wood burning stove.

Carlos checked out a desk, touching the edges and looking underneath it. Chulito wondered if he were trying to figure out how it was made. Carlos pointed toward a room and Chulito nodded. Carlos climbed over the thick rope and stepped into the room and did a slow three hundred and sixty degree turn with a chuckle. Chulito realized that that was the first sound either of them had uttered. They had been moving through the house communicating as if they had discovered the language of Poe Cottage and all they had to do was look and point. Chulito's heart was beating so hard he thought Carlos could hear it.

Carlos walked over to an ornate floor lamp and pulled the cord. The dim light it gave was no match to the setting sun that was fighting to the end. Carlos went to the window. The pattern of the lace curtains made it look as if his face were tattooed. Chulito smiled at the thought of Carlos, the goody, goody college boy with any kind of tattoo.

"What are you smiling at?"

"Nothing. Well, you. The curtains look like…whatever," he said trailing off, enjoying his private joke.

"What?"

"Nothing."

"Check out the sun. It's almost all gone."

Chulito walked over, stood by him and felt the temperature in the already warm room rise about twenty degrees. Carlos turned his head to look at Chulito. They were about two inches away from each other. Chulito imagined himself jumping back saying, "Yo, you invading my space, bro." But he stood there, staring into Carlos' eyes, feeling the heat of the sun, the heat of the room and the heat from Carlos' body.

"Thank you, Chulito."

"I thought you'd like it."

"I love it."

Chulito thought that he should be turning away at that moment, but he didn't. He should put on the brakes, because he knew where this was heading, but he didn't. He should have been doing a lot of things, but instead he leaned forward and closed the small gap of space between them and their lips met. They kissed gently at first. Almost as if their lips were accidentally bumping into each other. And then the small kisses grew longer. Carlos slipped his smooth, velvety tongue into Chulito's mouth. Their tongues swirled slowly, one over the other, and Chulito could taste the apple Carlos had been eating earlier. It was the sweetest taste. Chulito reached for Carlos and caressed his bare arms, sliding his hands up to his shoulders and drawing him close. Carlos slipped his hands around Chulito's waist and they gripped each other for dear life. When their chests met, Chulito felt Carlos' heart beating just as hard as his, like two drums conjuring up dangerous spirits. The heat continued to rise and they continued to kiss without coming up for air. It was as if they had dived into an ocean and discovered they could breathe underwater. As they embraced tighter, Chulito could feel Carlos' erection against his own.

How many people have kissed in this room? Chulito thought. He didn't know the answer, but if the spirits were watching, he didn't think they ever expected two Puerto Rican boys from the South Bronx to be locked in a kiss whose passion challenged that of the setting sun. And kiss they did, defying their neighborhood, defying their macho Latino culture and embracing each other.

Chulito touched Carlos—his back, his neck, his hair, his face—consuming him with his hands and breathing him in with his kisses—which went from strong and consuming to gentle and peaceful. Chulito opened his eyes to see Carlos watching him and he traced his lips with his tongue. When Carlos smiled, Chulito licked his smile, too. When their eyes opened, the sun had set and the only light in the room was from the dim lamp. They looked at each other, smiled and rocked gently. "Your friend should be back soon."

"Damn. I should just send him out again, but—"

"Let's go then." Carlos leaned down and picked up his knapsack that had fallen during their kiss. Chulito turned out the light, the two adjusted themselves and felt their way out of the house. In the darkness, Chulito took Carlos' hand and led him to the front door. As they waited for Angel, they sat on the steps and looked up at the deep indigo sky with a few stars trying to push through ridges of white clouds.

"Wow!" Carlos said. "Look at the sky."

"Yeah, look at the sky," Chulito repeated, but all the while he looked only at Carlos.

chapter fourteen

After leaving Poe Cottage and saying good night to Angel, Chulito and Carlos headed toward the Grand Concourse. They walked silently, sharing the secret they held along with all the ghosts in Poe Cottage, the only witnesses to their kiss.

As they neared the bench where they first met up that evening, Carlos broke the silence. "Now what?" A question that had a thousand echoes. Chulito was jolted from the kiss' trance and realized that he had stepped through the mirror to another world. It was as if three drag queen spirits—incarnations of Julio the travel agent, Carlos' friend Kenny and Lady Elektra from the pier—had sprung from Carlos' words and were standing side by side behind him. Each guardian angel was decked with extravagant gowns and overloaded with accessories: hats, gloves, umbrellas, and lots of glittery jewelry. And all three swarmed Chulito snapping their fingers in the air asking, "Now what? Now what? Now what?" They stared and waited for his response.

Chulito looked around as if the Grand Concourse would yield an answer. He didn't know what was next. His thoughts were back in the cottage. He wanted to be there.

Carlos interrupted his thoughts. "Wanna go back to the Vil?"

The "Now whats?" approved, shouted mock hallelujahs and glamorously disappeared into the night.

Carlos shook him. "Well?"

Chulito sat on the bench where they'd first met up. "I can't. I gotta meet up with Kaz." He flipped open his cell to check the time and realized that it was later than he thought. "C'mon." Chulito stepped off the curb to hail a cab.

"Where are we going?"

"Fuck, I gotta get back." Chulito wished that instead of cabbing it to Hunts Point that he could escape with Carlos. He spoke to the cab driver through the bullet proof partition, "We going to Hunts Point, Garrison Avenue. Swing around and go down to the end of the Concourse and then loop back up along Bruckner Boulevard."

"That's the long way, brother. I'm gonna have to charge you more."

"Whatever." Chulito wanted to stretch out this time as much as possible. "I ain't in no hurry. You in a hurry, Carlos?" Carlos shook his head and smiled.

It was a struggle for Chulito to keep his cool. He could still taste Carlos.

The cab sped down the Grand Concourse. On the radio the DJs talked Spanish at a rate that was faster than the local speed limit. Chulito didn't want to go back to the 'hood because he knew that whatever had just happened between him and Carlos was not going to continue in Hunts Point. But he didn't know where else to go.

Carlos had one leg up on the seat between them and his head rested on one arm. He looked peaceful in the pinkish streeetlight shining through the back window. The bold multicolored lit signs from the beauty salons, health clinics, and block after block of bodegas that lined the Grand Concourse streaked through the window as the cab whizzed by.

"Wassup?" Chulito managed to squeeze out of his throat.

"Do you have to go meet up with Kamikaze? I want to stay with you." Carlos offered his hand. Chulito looked at it like something he had never seen before. He checked out the cab driver first, and then slowly reached out and their fingers interlocked, low, out of view from anyone, should the car stop at a red light. And their hands remained that way as the cab passed East Tremont, passed Bronx Lebanon Hospital, passed the Bronx Museum, passed the Bronx County Courthouse, passed the General Post Office and Hostos Community College down to the end of the Grand Concourse and up the ramp toward Bruckner Boulevard.

Chulito wanted to stay with Carlos, too, but as the cab approached Hunts Point, he put on his armor, piece by piece. First he unlocked his fingers from Carlos. Then he moved to the further side of the cab. He sat up in his seat, adjusted the baseball cap he was wearing, sharpened his glare and soon had the "don't fuck with me or I will fuck you up" look he used to ward off anyone who might think of starting shit with him.

When the cab reached Garrison and Longwood Avenues, Chulito told the cab driver to pull over.

"Wassup, Chulito?"

"Look, nothing personal, but it ain't gonna look cool if you and I pull up to the building and get out of a cab together."

"This sucks."

Chulito was surprised to see how Carlos' face had changed. His eyes had narrowed to defiant slits and he turned away. Chulito tapped on the bullet proof partition to get the cab driver's attention. "Stop here, bro." He wanted to assure Carlos that he too wanted drive far away to a place where he could hold him and tell him that their kiss had ignited feelings which were exploding like fireworks on the Fourth of July.

He didn't touch Carlos. "Sorry, pa, I'll check you later, ah-ight?"

Carlos sat frozen.

Chulito slipped him a $20 bill and got out the cab. He stood in the middle of the street and watched the back of Carlos' head through the rear windshield. Carlos turned to look back at him as the cab continued down Garrison.

Looney Tunes was walking along Longwood coming from the Bruckner. "Yo, Chulito, what chu doin' standin' in the street? You high or somethin'?"

"Nah, nigga. I'm headed to The Wedge to meet up with Kaz."

"So why you gettin' out the cab here?"

He wondered what else he'd seen.

"I guess I am feeling pretty nice and I just wanted to walk to straighten up a bit, before meeting Kaz. You know, we's got business."

"Hey that's cool, so lemme walk wit chu to The Wedge. I ain't got nothin' else to do. Buy me a drink?"

"Damn, Loon, don't you ever have any money?"

"Nope."

"C'mon."

They walked up Longwood Avenue, past the warehouses, as

Looney Tunes talked incessantly about all his imaginary women.

With every step Chulito took he remembered that taste of apple.

chapter fifteen

Chulito was sitting at The Wedge with Looney Tunes, who was feeling up a stripper, when Kamikaze arrived. "You brought this clown?"

"I couldn't shake him." Chulito shoved Looney Tunes.

"Stop playin', yo." Looney Tunes cupped the strippers bottom. "Gimme a dollar, Kamikaze."

Kamikaze gave him the middle finger and sat next to Chulito. "Oh, there was some excitement in front of your building. Damian was kicking the shit out of that stupid little pussy faggot." Kamikaze laughed.

Chulito thought of Carlos and panicked. "What? Who?"

"Forget it, it's over. How are things here? Any customers?"

"Yep, but Mikey's not here. What happened on the block?"

Kamikaze waved him off. "Forget it, I said. It's not important. Just stupid ghetto shit."

Chulito flipped open his phone and pressed Carlos' speed dial number. "I told customers that you'd be here, so they waiting on you."

"Mikey's a lazy fuck. Where you going?"

"Be right back." Chulito darted into the bathroom. Once inside he got him on the line. "You O.K., Carlos?"

"Yeah."

"I heard some shit went down on the block."

"Damian and Brick had a fight, but I'm O.K."

"Fuck. Kamikaze said that—" Chulito's heart beat slowed. "Well, he didn't mention Brick's name just called him a pussy faggot and I panicked. Sorry, but you know how niggas speak and I thought…Well, I'm glad you alright. What happened?"

"I got Brick here."

"Where?"

"My room."

"What the fuck is he doing in your room? I don't trust the nigga." Chulito recalled Brick's playfulness with Julio and didn't want him making moves on Carlos.

Looney Tunes knocked on the bathroom door. "Chulito, you stinkin' up the bathroom? I gotta whizz."

Chulito leaned against the door. "I'll be out in a second." Chulito heard Carlos speaking to Brick. He was saying you're welcome, no problem, anytime.

"What do you mean by anytime?"

"Brick just left. He's fine and all that, but you don't have anything to worry about. You better chill out Chulito." Carlos took on a playful tone. "Just because you kissed me doesn't mean you own me. And kiss aside, which was amazing, you still on probation."

Chulito's anger melted away. "Is he gone? Does he know it

was me on the phone? You can't be talking like that in front of people."

"Why not?"

Chuilto cleared his throat. "'Cause I says so. I'm just playin'."

"You better be. I wish you were here."

"Me, too, but I gotta work. I'll call you the minute I'm done. Someone didn't show up, so Kamikaze had to bring stuff, but I wanna hear what happened. I'm glad you O.K., though."

"I saw everything as I got here and Brick just told me the rest. And excuse my language, but this neighborhood is fucked."

"Listen to you. You kiss a thug and getting' all gangsta."

Carlos laughed.

"Seriously, Carlos, I don't trust Brick. He tries to be on the level, but I feel there ain't something right about him." Chulito didn't worry about the white college boys who buzzed around Carlos, but Brick was a thug like him and Chulito didn't want competition.

"Well, I didn't really know him until tonight, but he's pretty cool."

"You think he's pretty?"

"Pretty cool. Now finish up with Kamikaze, so I can tell you all about it."

"You got it."

It was almost two-thirty A.M. when Kamikaze dropped Chulito off. Chulito could see that Carlos' light was still on so he called him on his cell. They talked for almost an hour while Carlos told him all about what had happened.

"Apparently, Brick was passing Puti's window and she had sung, 'Oh, he's a Brick. House. He's mighty, mighty, just letting it all hang out. Ow!'"

Chulito laughed. "That Puti is somethin' else."

Carlos continued, "Then he told her to check herself. Meanwhile, Damian and a couple of the auto glass guys were leaning on a parked car that was in between Puti and the corner where the fellas were assembled. Brick passed Damian and pointed to Puti and said something like 'She's a loco loca.' And Damian said 'I guess she knows a sure thing when she sees it.' Then he started ribbing Brick because he works for Julio, the super fag."

Chulito sucked his teeth. "Damian's a fuckin' asshole."

"Well, Damian didn't let up saying that the rumor in the 'hood was that he bitch slapped Jennifer because she suspected that something was going on between Brick and Julio."

Chulito didn't want to hear the rest of the story. It was confirming all his worries about the what the fellas would think if they started seeing him hanging with Carlos again. It didn't matter if a dude went that way or not, if you hung out with a gay person then you got implicated.

Carlos didn't stop. Chulito felt as if he was telling him the story to shake him and make sure that he knew what he was getting himself into. "It didn't help that the fellas start in with laughing and saying, 'Oh shit you gonna let him say some shit like that to you?' Brick said that he tried to wave him off, but then Damian started saying that Jennifer told him herself about her doubts and, hear this, then Damian said right to his face that he thinks he's a faggot, and then said that he, and this is how Brick relayed it, that Damian fucked Jennifer last night. Boom! Brick slammed his right fist into Damian's head, which knocked him against the parked car and set off the alarm. I love that detail, I have to admit."

Chulito sighed. "That is some nasty shit. But Damian is like that." Chulito began to figure that this was a warning. He was going to have to keep things in check with Carlos while in the 'hood.

"So they started brawling and Damian kept calling him a faggot and the guys on the corner got into it. And then that's when I must've arrived because I saw them rolling on the ground and punching each other. It was scary but you know how the ghetto gets when there's a fight. There were people looking out the windows and a crowd had formed to watch and cheer. Then they got separated and Brick was kneeling on the sidewalk. Damian was being held back by some auto glass guys but he kept yelling, 'Get up, faggot! Get the fuck up!'"

Chulito felt nervous and started to regret kissing Carlos. "Listen up, Carlos, you gotta be extra careful!"

Carlos reacted to the change in Chulito's voice. "Are you worried?"

"Yeah, well I was worried for you. But you safe and shit, right?"

"Yes, but it was so wild because I felt that in a way Brick was fighting for us. Damian was acting like it was correct to call Brick out as gay and Brick was defending himself. I know it's just me projecting, but Brick never said he wasn't. He just fought back."

Chulito felt confused. "Hold up. You sayin' Brick is gay?"

"No, just that it felt good to not hear him denying it like it was wrong. Well, then the police sirens made the crowd break up and something strange happened. As everyone was scurrying away, Brick got up and straightened himself out. He had scrapes on both his elbows, a cut near his ear and his left eye was beginning to swell, but he got himself together. I expected him to run, too, but he looked at me and then turned and went calmly into our building. I saw Damian get into a car with two auto glass guys and he was pretty messed up too—bloody nose, swollen lips and scrapes all on the side of his face.

I walked behind Brick. I wondered where he was going since he didn't live in our building. Puti held her door open and urged him to come inside but he just shook his head and started walking up the stairs. I kept some distance but I had to go up the stairs, too. When I reached my apartment, I saw that he stopped midway between the second and third floor. He sat on the steps, covered his face with his hands and began to sob."

Chulito shook his head. "I'm tellin' you, I don't trust that nigga. He used you to hide out. He knew the cops wouldn't find him there. Fucker."

"Chulito, you better chill with the macho ownership shit. I can take care of myself. Well, when I heard the cop cars screeching in front of the building I invited him in. My moms was asleep, so I took him to the bathroom, gave him some paper towels and showed him the medicine cabinet. I didn't really know him, but I told him that a friend of La Julio is a friend of mine. Then he said that he appreciated me letting him in because his baby moms has an order of protection out on him and he would have gone to jail if he'd been caught in Hunts Point."

Chulito felt like he had heard enough. "Well, I don't know why you gotta be all open with him, but like you said, you your own person."

"Don't be jealous."

Chulito scoffed. "I ain't got nothin' to be jealous of."

Carlos chuckled. "You are so jealous. Well, I'm not into him like that and besides I asked him directly if he was gay. I figure he could tell me, right?"

"What?!"

"I'd heard the homo thug rumors and I wanted to find out if there was any truth, but he said that he wasn't but that he had, in his words, mad love for Julio and he wasn't gonna let anybody misconstrue, that's my word, their friendship."

Chulito didn't like Carlos bringing Brick into his house. He decided that he had to step up his game with Carlos because maybe Carlos was exploring his options. Chulito lay in his bed looking up at the ceiling where he knew Carlos was also laying on his bed. They said good-night about six times yet after each time they stayed on the phone.

"I wish I could kiss you goodnight," Carlos said.

Chulito relaxed. "That would be dope."

"Wanna come up?"

"You crazy? What if your mom sees me? What are we gonna say?"

"That you came up for a goodnight kiss and that you will be gone right quick?"

"You funny."

"Can I at least see you? Look out your window."

"You crazy, Carlos. But O.K., 'cause I wanna see you, too."

Chulito looked out and checked the block. It was pretty deserted except for a homeless guy walking over by the auto glass shops. Then, he looked up and saw Carlos looking down.

Still talking on his cell phone, Carlos said, "There you are. You are so beautiful."

"Shhhh, I'm a pretty nigga, right?" Chulito whispered into his phone. "I love looking at you, too."

"I gotta kiss you, or I am not going to sleep tonight."

Chulito checked around the block again and blew him a kiss.

"Mmmm, but you're a fucking tease."

"Hey, I'd kiss you if I could, but you know that can't happen."

"Meet me in the hall."

"No way, anybody can walk out."

"How about the roof? We could be real quiet, and nobody would be up there."

Chulito was excited at the thought of holding Carlos again. "True."

"C'mon, Chulito, a quick kiss. I feel like I'm going crazy."

"Nigga, you can only see my face. But you got the rest of me pretty worked up."

"Meet you on the roof?"

"Bet."

Chulito closed his cell phone and headed up the stairs quietly. Carlos waited at the roof entrance and led him out into the cool night air. Chulito pulled Carlos to him and they kissed stumbling back against the raised wall to the roof entrance. Their kissing expanded to grinding their hips into one another, which sent tremors through Chulito's body. He licked Carlos' neck slowly, tasting every inch of his smooth flesh. Carlos reached down and squeezed Chulito's dick through his pants, which made Chulito let out a soft, "Oh, baby." Carlos unsnapped the front of Chulito's baseball shirt. The two stared into each other's eyes and their vision adjusted to the darkness. They leaned in for an easy kiss, a lick of the other's lips and a kiss to the tip of a nose. With the snaps all undone, Carlos ran his hand over Chulito's chest, and torso. He kissed Chulito's Adam's apple and licked small circles around it with the tip of his tongue. He then traced a line of kisses down Chulito's chest and ended right below his navel. Carlos pressed his face to Chulito's erection.

Then, Chulito saw the glow of a cigarette on the far side of the roof.

He pushed Carlos off, buttoned up frantically and ran into the building.

Carlos was startled and looked around and saw the faint glow of the cigarette, too. When the person took a puff, the tip glowed to reveal that it was Brick. He had been sitting in a dark corner. Carlos felt like shit. Every step with Chulito was so difficult because he feared being discovered and with the way he freaked out Carlos knew things would be set back. He wished he hadn't pushed for them to meet on the roof, but the kiss they shared at Poe Cottage earlier left him wanting more. Carlos went into the building without saying a word.

Carlos called Chulito on his cell, but he had turned off his phone.

Hours later, Chulito and Carlos sat in their respective rooms, looking out into the street until the sunrise service churchgoers paraded down the block with their king-size Bibles.

Chulito awoke with a start. He had on the same clothes. He remembered the glowing cigarette. How did he not keep himself in check? It had only been a week since they talked on the steps and less that two days since that trip to the Village and here Chulito was acting like a gay guy, doing romantic things like arranging dates and blowing kisses. Had he forgotten who he was or where he lived? What if his mother found out? The fellas? Kamikaze? This was all moving way too fast. He knew that he loved Carlos, but maybe not enough to risk his whole life and his rep over it.

He sent Carlos a text: I need to think about everything I need some time.

chapter sixteen

Carlos spent Sunday with Kenny in Brooklyn and went to see Julio first thing Monday morning before going to his internship at the *New York Daily News*. With all the grandstanding and complaining he did about the homophobia in the neighborhood, he realized that the only time he reached out to Julio was when there was a major crisis. He told himself that even though Julio was gay, he was from another generation and wouldn't really understand him. But he wondered if he, too, was reacting to Julio being flamboyant. He always greeted Puti, the drag queen, but he never really stopped to talk to her or get to know her either.

Although it was early, he saw Chulito on the corner with two of the fellas. Carlos almost decided to skip going to Julio's because he would have to pass the corner but pushed on. He made eye contact with Chulito but said nothing.

Before Carlos could tell Julio the reason for his visit, Brick, who was usually clean and groomed, walked in right after Carlos, looking grungy, unshaven and bruised.

"Oh my god, what happened?" Julio said.

"You didn't hear? I had a fight on Saturday night with Damian." Brick filled Julio in on the details. "And this little nigga here saved my ass. Thanks, Carlos." Brick went into the back.

"Hey, hands off, Eve Harrington. Brick is all mine." Julio poured coffee. "After their fight, Jennifer left a garbage bag out front filled with Brick's clothes and a box with all of his stuff, like colognes, razors and CDs. So he keeps his things in the back in a small storage cabinet." Julio offered coffee to Carlos who refused. Julio called out back. "Brick, I don't know how you can think straight. Jennifer. Crystal. And now Damian and those crazy assholes out there. You need to shift your position, papito. It's like if I sit in this chair, all I can see is what's out that window. But if I get up," Julio rose and went to the window, "and change my position, now I can see what's up or down the block, and I can decide if I want to go up, down or stay inside."

"I hear you." Brick walked into the office area with his face covered with shaving cream and shaved in the small sink next to the coffee maker. With each stroke, Julio and Carlos watched his face reappear. And even though his eye was discolored and the split in his lip was evident, Brick was still beautiful. Carlos felt a little guilty because he was there to talk to Julio about Chulito, but he shared Julio's attraction to Brick. He loved how Brick was Hunts Point in the same way that Chulito was Hunts Point. They were tough and kind, rugged and smooth, and to him they were undeniably sexy and unquestionably beautiful.

Julio continued. "Glad to hear it, papa. I pay a woman on Eighty-eighth and Broadway good money once a week to help me see shit like that. And I give it to you for free. So, you need to get away. Go to a place that is not connected to all the crap here."

"I got an uncle in P.R."

Julio clapped. "Perfect." He searched for flights on his computer. "When do you want to go, tonight?"

Brick wiped his face. "I need to call my uncle."

"Let's call him now."

Brick called his great uncle who agreed to have him come for as long as he wanted. Julio went online and printed an open ticket departing in a week, because Brick wanted his face to heal before leaving.

A cleaned up Brick stood at the front door. "I'm gonna get some breakfast. You two want anything?"

Carlos shook his head and Julio held up the coffee. "My figure doesn't permit me to have breakfast."

Brick stopped next to Carlos. "Look, whatever is going down between you and Chulito ain't none of my business."

Carlos had been thinking about Chulito all night again. He hoped that the kiss on the roof had not ended something before it had a chance to take off. He wanted to give Chulito space, but at the same time he felt like he needed to do something to reconnect with him. "Thanks, Brick. I think Chulito is freaked out. I saw him on the corner with the fellas. He doesn't know it was you on the roof. Maybe you could tell him that you won't tell."

Brick shrugged. "I owe you, but that kind of thing is between you two." He turned and shut the door.

"Be careful," Julio called out, then sat next to Carlos on the couch. "My god, he's the man of my wet dreams."

Carlos laughed.

"O.K., enough about Brick. What's going on, lindo? First, it's a miracle you're here," Julio said. "So, this must be big. You?

Chulito? The roof?"

Carlos covered his face with his hands. He was surprised to feel tears welling up in his eyes. He worked so hard to keep himself together and felt like he was going to loose it. "I don't think I can even tell you."

"Let me guess, you're pregnant."

Carlos laughed through his tears. "No, in love with a thug."

"Get in line. It forms to the left." Julio laughed and wiped Carlos' tears.

Carlos told him about Chulito and Poe Cottage, the rooftop and Brick, and Chulito's text message. Julio locked the door and posted the closed sign. He put down his coffee and took out some rum with ice and lime. "You want some?"

"No, I gotta go to work soon and I'm only seventeen."

"You're only seventeen? How could you be in college? You are much too serious for your age."

"I got skipped twice, and I'm going to be eighteen in September."

"Don't tell your mother I offered you rum."

"I've had rum before, please." Carlos looked out the window. "I just saw Chulito on the corner with the fellas. When things get heavy, he runs to them."

"Are you in love, kiddo?"

Carlos nodded. "I think so."

"So give him his space, but let him know how you feel first then give him space."

"He doesn't answer his phone."

"Leave a message or do that texting thing you kids do or write him a letter."

"A letter?"

"You kids with internet and e-mail are missing out on one of the most classic forms of romance. Give him a handwritten letter and let him know how you feel." Julio took hold of Carlos' shoulders. "Tell him you won't wait forever, though. How about a song? Do you two have a favorite song?"

"We haven't had time. Besides he just listens to hip-hop."

"I don't know hip-hop. Do you know a song?"

"Madonna or Nina Simone have some good songs."

"Does he listen to Spanish music?"

"*I* don't listen to Spanish music."

Julio rummaged through a stack of CDs and pulled out a Barry Manilow CD. "Do you know him?"

"Yeah, 'I write the songs that make the whole world sing.'"

"Good. I was thinking maybe Barbra Streisand, but that might freak him out. When my first boyfriend broke up with me in college, Barry and Barbra got me through it."

They popped the CD into the small player and listened to songs. He settled on "Can't Smile Without You."

That evening Carlos wrote a letter to Chulito, burned a copy of the CD and told him to play #11. He ended the letter saying, "I'm hurting. I miss you, but if you are not ready to keep going, tell me. I have to shift my position to see something else. Let me know before the weekend. Love, Carlos."

He left the small package with Chulito's mother, saying it was a late birthday present. She placed it on Chulito's bed.

Carlos went home and listened to his own copy of the CD. He put it on repeat and fell asleep with the headphones on.

Chulito arrived at about one A.M. The instant he turned on the light he saw the bright blue package sitting on his bed. He sat next to it and kicked off his Tims. He knew it was from Carlos and was restraining his urge to tear it open and see what he'd left him. He took off all his clothes and sat cross-legged and naked on his bed. He read the letter and listened to the song, he laughed and thought the song was perfect. He called Carlos.

Carlos sprang to pick up his cell phone when he heard it ring.

"I got your package," Chulito said. "That song was sappy, but right on. Thanks. Nobody has ever done anything like that for me."

"I meant every word I wrote and I agree the song is sappy, but it's how I'm feeling."

"Me, too. And you signed it 'Love, Carlos.'"

"I mean that, too. So how much longer will you need space?"

Chulito didn't want any more space. He wanted to see and be with Carlos that very instant. When he was on the corner with the fellas and saw Carlos walk by, he wanted to say that he missed him right there and then. "I want to see you right now, but we gotta be careful, Carlos. Brick spoke to me, which bugged me out a bit, but how do I know that he's not gonna tell anybody? And I saw you go into Julio's. So I guess you told him, too."

"Julio and Brick are not gonna tell, but I hear you. I won't let anybody else know."

Chulito relaxed and lay down on his bed and ran his hand down his body. "I just don't understand what's going on with me. All I know is that I felt really good with what you wrote. And I don't want you hurting, not when I am feeling the same shit. I just need to take it slow."

"So when do I get to see you?"

"Now," he said jokingly. "Wanna take a cab down to the Vil?"

Carlos chuckled. "If that's the only option, but I got to be up for my internship in the morning."

"O.K., I don't want to be corrupting you by taking you out at all hours of the night."

"You know I'll go."

"Nah, get your rest, but what if I meet you when you get out of work?"

"What about the rooftop, now?"

Chulito laughed. "You are buggin'."

"I could check it out first, with a flashlight."

"Let's leave the rooftop alone."

"O.K., then tomorrow. I get out at four."

"Good night, Carlos. I'm gonna listen to the sappy song again. Who is this cat singing?"

"Barry Manilow."

Chulito snorted. "It's more like Sappy Manilow."

chapter seventeen

Chulito waited outside the *New York Daily News*, listening to Sappy Manilow through his earphones, but when Carlos appeared he closed his eyes and bopped his head as if he were listening to Pun or Tupac. When Carlos reached him he shoved his shoulder.

Chulito lowered his shades and continued to bop. "This is the shit."

"Big Pun?"

Chulito slipped an earphone in Carlos' ear.

Carlos smiled. "Sappy Manilow? You're listening to Sappy Manilow outside your room? The thug police are gonna come and arrest you."

Chulito bit his lower lip. "Man, I wanna kiss you right here."

"I dare you." Carlos puckered.

Chulito adjusted Carlos' collar saying, "I don't want to wrinkle your pretty, white shirt."

Carlos tapped the brim of Chulito's fitted Yankee cap.

"Chicken. Wanna go upstairs and check out the offices?"

"Really? But I ain't dressed right." Chulito gestured to his ribbed, white tank top, long, baggy faded blue jeans, and white New Balance sneakers. "Look at you all khaki Dockers and I look like—"

Carlos interrupted him. "You look fine, trust me. You look damn fine. C'mon, I asked my boss before I came down if it was O.K." Carlos turned and Chulito followed him through the large glass doors. "They're just a bunch of offices, I can't go to where they print the newspaper and stuff, but I can show you where all the reporters sit and the meeting rooms."

They walked by the security guard. Carlos said hi and showed his badge and Chulito signed in. Upstairs, Carlos gave him a tour of the offices. He introduced him to his boss, Maite Junco, a Latina who wore glasses, had a mass of thick shoulder length hair and who didn't talk much because she was on deadline.

When Carlos showed Chulito his desk Chulito sat down and pretended to type on the computer. "This is pretty dope. You got your own desk. So what do you do?"

Carlos explained that he scheduled appointments or interviews for his boss and he printed out press releases announcing events and logged them in. He answered the phone, filed reports, proofread articles and took lunch orders.

Chulito jumped up from the seat. "That sounds like a lot. You ain't afraid of fuckin' some shit up?"

Carlos shrugged his shoulders. "I think I do a good job."

"I bet you do. Nobody better mess with you."

Carlos showed him a large conference room where the writers from the entertainment section were having a meeting and Chulito recognized some of the movie critics from their picture in the newspaper. All around there were people typing on computers and others were rushing around.

"Wow, Carlos this is the real deal."

Carlos smiled and nodded. "Yup, I really like it, too." Carlos leaned on the edge of his desk and Chulito settled in Carlos' rolling chair. "I feel alive here. This is what I want to do because journalists have to be in touch with the world and report back on what they experienced and learned. Then people read newspapers to get information that we provide and that helps them form opinions, learn about the world, even make decisions about what movie to see or what book to read."

Chulito loved the energy in Carlos' eyes and at the same time felt small and unimportant because he had no legit plans for his life. "Well, you always had the brains and you're on your way, right? Doin' ya thang here?"

Carlos smiled. "Yep. I wish I could start working here right now, but I'll finish school first, maybe even go to Columbia School of Journalism after." Carlos tapped the brim of Chulito's baseball cap again. "Let's go."

Chulito and Carlos walked from West 33rd Street to the pier.

"That was so dope. So you gonna get a job there when you finish all your schoolin'? Am I gonna be seeing your name in the paper?"

"I'll work there or at some newspaper, but what about you? What might you want to do?" Carlos stopped at a cart and Chulito paid for a Coke and a Diet Pepsi.

Chulito shrugged. "I used to think that I wanted to be a rapper, but I think I just wanted to be famous."

"I only ask because you said you wanted to get out of the game, right?"

Chulito nodded and looked over at the Hudson River which glistened in the late afternoon sun. He'd said it, but faced with coming up with an answer, he felt at a loss. He was familiar with the benefits and risks of the game, even dealing with crazy scenes like surviving the one with Rey.

Carlos leaned into Chulito. "You are so beautiful you could be a famous model, Chulito. That sunlight just loves your skin." Carlos pretended to snap his picture.

Chulito puffed up his chest. "No doubt." He nudged Carlos. "You beautiful, too, Carlos. I can't believe I'm saying shit like this, but it's what's going on in me."

"Thanks, Chulito." The smile on Carlos' face made Chulito realize how much he liked that Chulito expressed his feelings.

Chulito liked where they were heading together. "What else you like about me?"

"Everything."

"Like what? Because I be thinking about you and me a lot. And not, like, us just right now, I think about, like, later and shit. You know. The future?"

Carlos nodded and sipped his Diet Pepsi.

"And you got your shit together and I, well, you got me thinking about what I'm doing, like I ain't finish high school, and my job is, let's just say, not legit. And I know you got fellas up at school, educated and shit, sweatin' you, so—" Chulito didn't know where this was coming from. When he got ready to meet Carlos, he was just excited to be seeing him, especially since he freaked out after being caught on the roof.

"Chulito, you want to sit a moment." Carlos sat on bench along the West Side Highway. Chulito stood next to the bench, put one foot on it and leaned against his knee.

"I'm sorry, Carlos, I don't know what I'm talking about."

"Chulito, I love being with you because we're from the same place. I get you and you get me. I'll admit, I hate Hunts Point sometimes. Well, a lot, but that neighborhood and those people are a part of me, too. And you and my mom are reasons why I love the neighborhood." Carlos played with the laces on Chulito's sneaker. "And it feels good to know you got my back."

Chulito smiled. "No doubt." Then he checked out his surroundings before kissing Carlos' forehead.

Carlos smiled. "And some guys up at school don't get me, or they think they do. They hear I'm from the Bronx, from the South Bronx, and expect one thing. But look at us, we're both South Bronx, different in a lot of ways and the same in others."

Chulito admired how Carlos knew how to make sense of things. The fellas on the corner did a lot of talking but it very often made no sense to Chulito. They could spend hours passionately talking about Derek Jeter or the Shaq, but what did that really matter in the grand scheme of their lives? But the fellas were far away and he was here with Carlos. Chulito sat next to him, took a deep breath and when he exhaled he put his arm around Carlos. The cars whizzed by and Chulito wondered if someone he knew might drive by.

Carlos rested his head on Chulito's shoulder.

"I just get scared, Carlos. Why you wasting your time with a nigga like me?"

"I'm not the kind of guy who likes to waste time, so forget about that. I love being with you, and how excited and new everything is to you—going to the pier, walking on Christopher Street and meeting my friends." Carlos looked into Chulito's eyes. "Even this. Us sitting on this bench. I never would have thought it could really happen with you, and here we are. You keep surprising me."

Traffic started to slow down and since Chulito could see the people in the cars, he thought they could see them, too. "C'mon let's keep walking."

"I know this is tough for you, Chulito. I think about the future, too, but we're here and now and we just gotta take this day by day."

Chulito nodded. He wanted to take Carlos' hand and hold it, like that young couple he'd seen in the subway, but instead just walked side by side.

The pier sizzled with activity but Kenny spotted them.

"So, is Carlos turning you into a pier queen, Chulito? Only kidding," Kenny said before Chulito could respond, then he turned to Carlos. "Why are you dressed like you're from Planet Nerd?"

"Chulito picked me up at work and we just walked over."

Kenny pulled at the little tuft of hair he had growing under his lower lip. "He picked you up? I have several questions, but which to ask first?"

"None of them," Carlos said. "Who's here?"

"The twins are trying to pick up a couple of French-Algerian break dancers. Lee was here, but she flew away—she had to go slave for her family."

"Lee is from the Chinese restaurant on Hunts Point Ave," Carlos explained.

"From Spring Garden? He comes here?" Alarmed, Chulito looked around. "But you said he's gone right?"

"Hours ago," Kenny said. "And The Hetrick-Martin/Harvey Milk graduating class is over by the water drinking wine coolers and handing out flyers for the Gay Pride Youth Dance." He showed Carlos a lime green flyer.

"You going?" Carlos asked.

"Definitely. It's gonna be like a second prom and Lady Elektra is gonna perform. You should come."

"Maybe." Carlos looked over to Chulito who shrugged.

"Something is up with you two. And it's not my imagination."

"Kenny, we're just hanging. Right, Chulito?"

Chulito nodded and his scowl spread into a smile.

Kenny looked Carlos in the eye. "I knew it. I'm not talking to you, Carlos. I hate you." He started toward the wine coolers, then he stopped about fifteen feet away from them and turned shouting, "I hate you, Carlos!" Then Kenny laughed. "I'll save you two some wine coolers if you want. I'll be by the water, and oh, God, I hate you Carlos." Kenny ran off.

"He's a funny dude," Chulito said.

"Wanna go get those wine coolers?"

"No doubt."

They waved to the twins as they passed them. They saw Pito and Sebastian with the Harvey Milk senior class, sipping wine coolers out of brown paper bags.

"So tell me, Carlos." Kenny handed them raspberry coolers. "It was less than a week since I saw you two, right?"

Chulito and Carlos nodded.

Kenny clinked bottles with Carlos. "You work fast, bitch."

"It's not what you think, Kenny. We're just friends."

"Oh, cut the shit and spill the details."

Carlos turned serious. "Stop with the questions or we're going to leave."

Watching Pito and Sebastian make out, Chulito longed to kiss Carlos.

"O.K., so then I'll talk," Kenny said. "Guess who I finally

hooked up with? Kevin. Do you remember him, Chulito? You met him when we were on our way here the day I met you."

Chulito nodded.

"Well, let me tell you, the rumors are true. Nine by seven, he let me measure it. I gagged, literally."

"Too much information, bro," Chulito said.

"Oh, sorry, I didn't mean to excite you."

"That doesn't excite me." Chulito shook his head and looked away at a butch and femme Latina couple dancing salsa by the water.

"Well, even if nothing is going on with you two, I don't care. You look happy, Carlos, and if just walking around with Chulito makes you happy, then so be it." Kenny hugged Carlos and turned to Chulito. "This guy is my best, best friend. I love him like a sister, and if he weren't my sister I would be making a play for him myself. And there are many others who would like to sink their claws, amongst other things, into him."

"Enough, Kenny," Carlos said sternly.

"You need to know, Carlos. Since I came back here with you guys last weekend, David from Washington Heights, Calvin from New Jersey and Alex from Castle Hill, all asked me what was up with you."

"The next time those dudes asks," Chulito said, "You can tell them he's taken." He drained the wine cooler.

Kenny's mouth opened in mock shock.

"Chulito, you want to go get something to eat?" Carlos said quickly.

Chulito nodded and smiled.

"Now if I was tacky," Kenny said, "I would say, 'Oh, great, I'm famished,' but to show you I'm not, I'm gonna kiss my sister."

Kenny embraced Carlos and kissed him on the cheek, and then he kissed Chulito, who flinched.

"That's because you're family, Chulito." Kenny turned to Carlos. "Did I just get to kiss him first?"

Carlos shook his head a sly no.

"Oh, I most definitely hate you." Kenny looked at Chulito. "God, I hate you."

Chulito and Carlos waved good-bye to Sebastian and Pito and headed to the pizza shop.

"So, I'm taken?" Carlos playfully shoved Chulito.

Chulito pretended to trip. Carlos laughed.

"Damn right you taken. Right?"

Carlos nodded and grabbed Chulito's hand. "That means you're taken, too. No Catalinas. No playin'."

"You got me." Chulito still felt nervous that someone would see them and released Carlos' grip. "This don't make sense to me, but I felt like shit when we were apart, and I know I feel so good with you."

The two spent the next several weeks meeting in Manhattan. Either Chulito would pick Carlos up at his internship or they would meet at Union Square, where they would shop for music and go to the movies. Carlos took Chulito to the Strand Bookstore, but Chulito preferred hanging out next door at the comics shop Forbidden Planet. Chulito felt like he and Carlos were floating on air as they walked around Union Square Park and ate at sidewalk cafés, staring passionately into each other's eyes. It didn't matter if they walked to the East Village and drank iced mochachinos at Starbucks or ate ice cream from Häagen Dazs or just sat silently on a bench in Tompkins Square Park, Chulito felt peaceful having Carlos close to him. Every now and then they hung out at the cube and tried skateboarding with some of the guys there. As they grew closer, they made regular appearances at the pier and Chulito got to meet some of Carlos' friends from his school, including Andrew, the guy who had dropped Carlos off. By the time Gay Pride rolled around they were one of the summer's pier couples, like Sebastian and Pito.

By spending so much time with Carlos, Chulito spent less time with Kamikaze. Whereas before they'd check on a round of clubs and then hang out at one of them or go back to Kamikaze's place to watch movies and get high, now Chulito would leave when they were finished to meet up with Carlos. Or he would try to take care of whatever business he could during the day to have the late afternoon or early evening to spend with Carlos. Kamikaze knew there was someone in the picture but would just reiterate one of the ghetto's creeds: "Never pass up your bro for a shorty, because they come and go, but your bro is there for life." Chulito would nod in agreement, and things would stay cool between them.

To the fellas, his excuse for not being around as much was that Kamikaze had him busy because it was summer and business was heating up. Looney Tunes joked, "She must be ugly."

Chulito found it fairly easy to navigate the two worlds— that of his neighborhood and the one to which Carlos was introducing him. He was excited about the possibility of being a part of a world beyond Hunts Point. And Carlos felt so right. All the closeness they'd shared growing up had ballooned into a connection that made Chulito feel like he was floating whenever he merely thought of Carlos. Every love song spoke to him and how he felt about Carlos. He sent Carlos texts that simply said: thinking of you, because he was. Chulito was Kamikaze's boy, but he was Carlos' man. And Carlos was his man. The first time he said the words out loud he'd smiled along with Carlos, but terror still flickered inside him.

Gay Pride Sunday was the first day in weeks they didn't spend together. Carlos marched in the parade down Fifth Avenue with Kenny and the students from the Hetrick-Martin Institute, while Chulito worked the early rounds with Kamikaze. That evening Carlos went with Kenny and Kevin, the twins and their new French-Algerian boyfriends, and Pito and Sebastian to the Christopher Street Pier, which was jammed almost beyond capacity. The Official Pride Pier Dance that their crew, except for the twins, couldn't afford was in full swing a little further uptown on another pier. They could hear the music.

Carlos checked his cell phone for messages.

"Did he call?" Kenny asked.

Carlos shook his head.

"O.K., whoever wants wine coolers give me money. One good thing about having a man who's twenty-one is easy access to booze." Kenny took the collection and left with Kevin to the store.

Everyone turned their attention to the fireworks that lit up the sky. Alex, the guy from Castle Hill who'd been asking about Carlos, came up and sat on the railing alongside him to watch the display.

"How you been?"

"Good, Alex, and you?"

"I got a summer job at The Gap. I hear you're doing an internship at the *New York Daily News*. Sounds cool."

"Yeah, I don't get paid, but I get a stipend for lunch and an unlimited metro, so it helps."

Alex moved closer to Carlos and their elbows touched. Carlos looked out of the corner of his eye and saw the familiar tattoo of the old school Puerto Rican flag on Alex's right shoulder, and then moved a few inches away. Alex reached over and slid his thumb along Carlos' exposed arm. "So you all alone on Gay Pride?"

Carlos turned toward Alex. His face was smooth and clean except for the small crease on his forehead as he waited for Carlos' answer. Carlos looked away. "Chill, Alex. I am not all alone."

Alex hopped off the railing. "I don't see your Romeo." He ran his hand across the front of his tank top.

Carlos hopped off the railing. "He's busy."

Alex cornered Carlos by pushing him against the railing and placing his arms at either side of Carlos. A smile curled along the edges of his mouth. "You see, if it was me, I would never be too busy for my man on Gay Pride. It's the one day I would make sure we were together." He moved in for a kiss.

Carlos placed his hands over Alex's heart and slowly pushed back. "Well, that's you."

He grabbed Carlos' hands and held them. "And you, too, Carlos. I seen you around and I have a hard time picturing you two together. I mean, at school you run the fucking gay club and shit, and you're walking around with a closeted homo thug. He's fine and all, but c'mon, I ain't that bad. I got a legal job, and we go to the same school. To be honest, it's hard for me not to keep from being all over you. I've been wanting to eat you up for the longest." He kissed one of Carlos' palms.

Carlos pulled away. Alex was tough, but there was something soft and pretty about him. Maybe it was his clear green eyes and long black lashes. Carlos had been attracted to him up at school, but Alex never seemed to want to travel that road until now. He looked at Alex, his face changing from bright yellows to hot pinks from the fireworks. "Well, Alex, love is a funny thing. It strikes with some and not others."

"Ouch, pa. I'm just expressing myself."

"I'm sorry. I'm flattered by what you said."

Alex lit up with a smile. "O.K., this is more like it."

"I think you're cool and you got it going on but—"

"But you into this cat, right?"

"I got it bad," he said with a shrug.

"Damn, I was too slow. I can't believe you and I live one express stop away from each other but didn't meet until school. Think some fate shit is at play?" Alex rested against the railing and looked into Carlos' eyes.

Carlos smiled. "How come you're never like this up at school?"

Alex stood up straight. He was a little taller than Carlos and his black spiky hair made him seem even taller. "Honestly, I've been thinking about you since we got back from school. I told Andrew that I was gonna make a play for you now that we back home because up at school you're, like, untouchable, too busy being Super Freshman writing for the newspaper and involved with this club or that one. Do you make time to get laid?"

"Not really."

"Not really or no?"

"Not really."

"For real? Then we must be fucking in different circles 'cause word on campus is that you are like Mother Theresa and shit."

Carlos laughed as his cell phone rang. When he picked up, Chulito asked, "What's so funny?"

Carlos took a few steps away from Alex. "Just the guys bugging out."

"Sorry, Kaz and I just got back from Jersey. How's it going?"

"We're at the pier and there are fireworks going off and Kenny went to go buy some wine coolers with Kevin. Are you coming down?"

"I don't know. It being Gay Pride, there are probably a lot of people out there, right? Television cameras?"

"The pier is packed, but there are no TV cameras. That was at the parade. But we could meet in Union Square if you want."

"I don't think Manhattan is the ticket."

"Can you talk? Or is someone around?"

"Kaz is nearby, but I wanted to call you."

"Well, I had a great day. The only thing missing was you."

"I'm sorry, Carlos. You know I couldn't be down there. Why don't you call me when you get home? We can talk then. By the way, I'm not going to go to Puerto Rico with my mom. I told her that I couldn't get out of work, but there is no way I can be away from you for more than a day. Today has been killing me. Trust me."

"Me, too. I love you, Chulito."

"I love you, too."

Chulito surprised himself with how easily the words came out of his mouth. Just four weeks ago, before he started seeing Carlos, those words only had meaning when he thought of his mother or Kamikaze. Now he joined the lovers of the world. He had crossed a bridge that he thought he never would. Feeling love from Carlos he experienced what he thought was an impossibility, and he wanted to keep it forever. Tears filled his eyes and he fought to hold them back.

Carlos didn't hold back, and the tears ran down his face and into his smile. He didn't expect to hear those words back from

Chulito. Not that he didn't feel loved by him, but Carlos knew Chulito always kept a part of himself guarded. But he loved how far Chulito had come and hearing those words made him hopeful that they could get deeper and grow closer. "I want to come home right now, just to see you."

"I want to see you, too, but I still got some biz with Kaz, so have a good time with the guys and tell Kenny and everybody that I said hello or Happy Gay Pride or whatever. Call me when you get home. I'll ride the train downtown tomorrow with you in the morning and I'll pick ya ass up from work, then we'll hang."

"Alright, then I'll stay here for a little bit longer. I'll call you when I get home."

"No matter what time."

"O.K." Carlos slipped his phone in his pocket and returned in a daze to Alex.

"Is he on his way?" Alex asked.

Carlos smiled. "I'm gonna see him later tonight." Then he leaned back on the railing and sighed.

Alex shook his head and walked away.

Chulito flipped his phone shut and walked back to the corner. Papo asked, "So did you break her heart by breaking the date?"

"She'll live," Chulito said.

"I knew something was up with you." Davey licked his bottom lip. "We don't see you no more. You acting all secretive. And look, fellas, he broke a date and he looks like he's gonna cry."

"He got it," Chin-Chin said. "Catalina didn't do it to you, but whoever this one is, she got you, bro. It's written all over your face."

The fellas laughed as Chulito scowled. "It's cool. You know, it's a new thang. I'm feeling it out."

"That's right. Take your time," Chin-Chin continued. "'Cause the next thing she will want to be engaged and you too young."

"I'm glad you made some time to hang with your boys." Papo put an arm around Chulito. "You gonna be at the Fourth of July barbecue, right?"

"Oh, yeah," Chulito said. "Moms is making her potato salad and her guineitos, too."

"I love those shits. Man, your moms is beautiful and she cooks better than my mom," Papo said. "May he rest in peace, but your pops was dumb. He shoulda treated y'all better."

"He just got married too young," Chulito said matter-of-factly and shrugged. "He didn't want a wife and a kid. He wanted to be free."

"Then learn from your dad and have fun while you young and don't be getting too serious in relationships," Chin-Chin said.

Chulito looked across the street at the Chinese restaurant and could see Lee at work.

"Yo, I'm gonna go get me some chicken wings. Anybody want some?

"Nah, Chulito, but check this out, fellas. I was in the Village the other day with m' girl at her favorite spot, that Mexican place with the giant margarita hanging off it, and guess who I saw?" Papo said.

"Davey." Chin-Chin answered.

"Nah, shut up, stupid. It was little Lee from the Chinese place, La China, and he was all pegao with a viejo. Man, they were slurping each other down, I swear to God," Papo said holding up his hand as if he were taking an oath.

"Iiiill, that's nasty," Looney Tunes said and shuddered.

"My girl was, like, 'Leave him alone,'" Papo continued, "but I just woofed out 'Lee!' and he jumped about four feet in the air. I just kept walking and he was looking around, like, 'Who said that?' It was funny as shit." The fellas laughed, and Chulito laughed, too, but wondered what Papo was doing in the Village. He would have to watch himself.

"Lee!" Papo barked and everyone jumped, then laughed. While they cracked jokes about him, Lee was busy working in the heat, stuffing containers with rice, spooning chicken with broccoli into Styrofoam plates and pouring wonton soup into plastic take-out bowls.

Papo announced, "Yo! Give it up, papas. The Hen is getting low, I'm going to Gil's for a bottle." Hands got stuffed into baggy pants and crumpled bills appeared. Chulito handed over a ten dollar bill and repeated, "Any of you niggas want some chicken wings?"

"Nah."

"Be right back." As Chulito stepped to the curb to cross the street, Papo barked out "Lee!" and Chulito jumped. The guys' laughter reached the rooftops. "Damn, Chulito, you a crazy mother fucker." Chulito smiled and trotted across Hunts Point Avenue.

When he stepped into Spring Garden, Lee and his family were moving at a hundred miles an hour, as steam rose from woks and the frying food sizzled like rain. Lee had his back to Chulito and didn't see him walk in. Chulito checked out his slim body and small muscles flexing on his shoulder as Lee reached toward a top shelf for a white cardboard take out box. Lee wore shorts that were too short and too tight by ghetto standards.

The phone rang. Lee swung around to answer it, but dropped

it when he saw Chulito. Lee scrambled to pick the phone up. "Spring Garden, how can I help you?" He shrugged apologetically to Chulito who gave him a cold stare. "One moment, please." He put the phone on the counter. "Hey, Chulito, what's poppin'?" Hearing him try to be ghetto always made Chulito smile. "Whoa, you got a nice smile, Chulito. Always hidin' it, tryin'a look gangsta."

"What! I am gangsta, nigga. You betta watch yourself. I'm in no mood to fuck around. Now, lemme get a order of chicken wings. Extra hot sauce."

With one hand Lee picked up the phone and listened to the order, and with the other he grabbed a handful of chicken wings and tossed them into the wire fryer basket. He wrote the order down on a pad with one hand and with the other he grabbed two extra chicken wings and tossed them into the fryer and winked at Chulito. "That's for you, extra, no charge." Chulito nodded indifferently, fighting a smile. He imagined that Lee must want to be downtown celebrating with everyone else, marching in the parade, hanging out at the pier, everything Carlos was doing. But Lee was stuck working.

Chulito looked out of the scratched plastic window of the Spring Garden at the fellas across the street. Papo returned with the Hennessy. The little cork top was popped and Kamikaze spilled a little on the ground in memory of Willie then took a swig. Then Papo took a swig. Then Chin-Chin. Then Davey. Then Looney Tunes and the bottle got corked and hidden from the cops behind one of the brick pillars in front of Rivera's bodega. Even though it's a ritual Chulito had participated in over and over, he dreaded going back to the fellas. He wanted to be with Carlos, but on this day, with all the cameras and crowds, he couldn't risk being seen.

And, at the same time, he didn't feel right being with the fellas and lying to Carlos.

Chulito read the menu for the hundredth time and looked at the faded pictures of glossy General Tso's chicken, spare ribs and moo goo gai pan. Every now and then Lee checked him out and turned away. He always looked away. He knew better.

"Hey, Chulito!" Lee said with his cute accent. "Your order is ready. Extra hot sauce, right?"

"No doubt."

Lee squirted a long red stream of hot sauce into the wax paper bag filled with chicken wings. Then he meticulously folded the bag up and placed it in another paper bag and stuffed a bunch of napkins inside. "I give you extra napkins because they could be messy."

Chulito slipped him a five and got three bucks back. Lee shot Chulito the same nervous, longing stare that young girls gave him.

"Later, Lee," Chulito said.

"Later, Chulito." Lee's graduation picture caught Chulito's eye as he turned to leave. Lee looked proud in his black cap and gown with gold trim. Chulito knew his own mother would like a similar picture of him for their living room. He shrugged off the thought and in one swift move Chulito stepped out the store, pulled his baseball cap down closer to his eyebrows and bopped across the street.

"Yo, Chulito, hurry up, man," Papo yelled. "We did two rounds, you gotta catch up."

"Yo, hol' up you thirsty niggas. I'm coming."

Debbie was walking up Hunts Point Avenue and Davey chased after her. "Don't go, mama."

"What do you want? I got stuff to do. I can't be hangin' on no corner. Now, if you offerin' to take me out that's another story."

A chorus of "Oh, shits" erupted from the fellas.

"So, it's like that. Go clean yourself up and get pretty and maybe I will think about takin' you out." Davey looked back at the fellas for approval.

Another chorus of "Oh, shits!"

"Whatever." Debbie showed him her palm. As Chulito passed her, she said to him, "You shouldn't be hangin' with those ruff necks. They ain't nothin' but trouble."

"They don't mean no harm. They just see a fine mamita like you and they get all stupid."

She smiled. "At least someone around here knows how to appreciate a woman." She kissed Chulito on the cheek. "Mmmm. You always smell so good. Later, papa." She continued to walk up Hunts Point Avenue.

Chulito stood there for a moment and played his position by checking out her ass as she walked away.

"Yo, forget that ho and come drink up." Papo held the Hennessey bottle out to him.

As Chulito joined his friends, he noticed Lee standing in the doorway watching the whole scene. Then Lee took a couple of steps away from the front of the restaurant and looked down Garrison Avenue. Chulito looked to where on the horizon he saw Manhattan with its twinkling lights and the Empire State Building lit in lavender.

chapter eighteen

The day for the annual Fourth of July barbecue had come and tables were set up on the sidewalks along Garrison Avenue with several more around the corner on Hunts Point Avenue. Several barbecue pits were arranged alongside the closed gates of the auto glass shops, and by four P.M. they were yielding their first round of heavily seasoned grilled meats. Children played in the street while men and women brought trays of arroz con gandules, potato salad, marinated green bananas in olive oil and herbs, green salads, and rice and beans.

Carlos and Chulito helped their mothers carry out food, beach chairs and small coolers that held soft drinks and beer. Some people had bottles of Bacardi, Absolut, Johnny Walker Red and Jack Daniels hidden underneath the tables and the beers were served in large white Styrofoam cups.

Chulito and Carlos planned to stay at the barbecue until the local fireworks were shot, then they'd head down to the pier to continue the celebration with their friends.

As the two young men passed each other in the hall carrying out bowls of food and paper plates, they secretly shared a smile or blew a kiss. Carlos alternated between sitting at the table in front of the building with his mother and neighbors who played cards, and working one of the grills across the street. Chulito took up his post on the corner with the fellas whose families were scattered around the neighborhood.

As the hours passed, Carlos grew weary of the coy, stealing glances game and walked over to the corner. Chulito felt nervous as he saw Carlos approaching.

"Hey, guys," Carlos said to no one in particular. "Chulito, your mom needs you."

Chulito was relieved that Carlos wasn't being maverick. "What does she want?"

"I don't know."

"Mommy's calling," Davey teased.

Carlos started to walk away when he heard Chulito say, "Be right back, fellas."

"Bye, Chulito," Looney Tunes said in a voice that sounded like Tweetie Bird.

Halfway between the fellas and their moms, Carlos whispered, "I gotta kiss you. Meet me in my room."

"No fucking way, Carlos. Don't play."

"C'mon, Chulito," he pleaded.

"No."

When they reached the table Carmen asked, "You want to eat something, Chulito?"

"Nah, I'm gonna get a CD."

Carlos sat down, as Chulito winked at him and walked into

the building.

"Oh, Chulito, bring back the aguacate," Carmen said.

Carlos got up. "I'll get it. Where is it at?"

"Either on the kitchen counter or in the refrigerator." Carmen returned to her card game. "Thank you, papa."

Carlos opened the unlocked door to Chulito's apartment and went into his room. "Hey."

Chulito smiled. "One quick kiss then we back out, right?"

Carlos nodded. "I gotta bring your mom her aguacate." Carlos brought the avocado to Chulito's room and set it on the dresser and closed the door behind him.

Chulito whispered, "People can see," as he pulled Carlos away from the window and pushed him up against the wall, shoving his tongue into Carlos' mouth and kissing him deeply. Carlos reached under Chulito's shirt, but Chulito stopped him. "O.K., that's it, Carlos, let's go."

Carlos hugged him. "Let's go downtown. It's torture seeing you and not being able to at least talk to you."

Chulito kissed the top of Carlos' head. "Later. Like we planned, O.K.? This day is a big deal for my mom. She held off on her trip to Puerto Rico until tomorrow so that she could be here."

"You're hardly spending any time with her. You're just on the corner with those assholes."

"C'mon, let's go back outside," he urged, separating himself from Carlos.

Carlos grabbed his hand. "One more kiss then, if I'm going to have to wait hours before we leave." Chulito kissed him. "Make it one that is gonna last for hours, pa." Chulito smiled nervously, pressed Carlos against the wall and kissed him again. He placed his hands on Carlos' waist and pulled him toward him. Carlos unsnapped Chulito's shirt and kissed his chest and licked his right nipple.

"Oh, fuck," Chulito whispered and quickly put his hand over his mouth. Carlos chuckled silently continuing to lick Chulito's nipple as he unbuckled Chulito's belt.

"Hold up." Chulito grabbed Carlos' hand.

"C'mon. Let me at least see it."

"Now? You crazy." He smiled and released Carlos' hand. Chulito's large shorts dropped to his ankles. Carlos could see Chulito's erection shoving against his fitted boxer briefs.

"Damn, is all that gonna be mine?" Carlos asked slipping his fingers into the waistband.

"All of it." Chulito gently held Carlos' head with both hands and kissed him deeply.

Carlos began sliding the underwear down when the front door slammed.

"Chulito? Carlos?" Carmen called out.

Chulito shoved Carlos, knocking him to the floor and scrambled to get dressed.

Carmen knocked on the door and then tried to open it. When she found it locked she said, "Chulito, did you see, Carlos? He came to get the aguacate and I'm almost finished with my salad."

"I don't know where he's at. I didn't see him."

Carlos stood up and dusted his seat, and mouthed, "Liar."

"Well, the aguacate isn't here, so he got it. Maybe he went upstairs for something."

Chulito heard his mother leave the apartment. He sat on his bed and held his head. "Shit. You see?"

"You didn't have to push me," Carlos said angrily.

"We got caught!"

"She thinks I went upstairs, relax." Carlos started to sit next to Chulito who jumped up.

"We gotta be careful." He looked out the window and saw his mother sitting right below it. He pulled back and with a hushed voice said, "She'll be gone soon, then we got this place to ourselves. Now let's go. Wait, I should go first, not you."

Carlos rolled his eyes. "Chulito, chill."

"No, you chill!" he said forcefully. "This was stupid. I should have walked out the minute you came in here."

"I can't keep this up." Carlos picked up the plate of avocado from the dresser.

"What do you mean?"

"All this hiding and secrets is driving me crazy."

"You knew the deal."

"Yes, I knew the deal," Carlos shot back, "but it's not working."

"We just gotta wait 'til tomorrow and she'll be gone," Chulito pleaded.

"And then what? She'll come back in a couple of weeks and we go back to not being able to be together? Chulito, you won't even hold my hand at the pier for more than two seconds or kiss me in public because someone might see you."

"We different. You don't give a shit, but I do."

Carlos stepped toward him, staring into his eyes. "Do you give a shit about me?"

"I do. I love you, Carlos."

The anger that had flared up between them simmered. Carlos looked away as tears blurred his vision. "I'm going to the Village now, are you coming?"

Chulito didn't answer. He wanted to hold Carlos. "Don't cry, Carlos. I'm sorry I pushed you away."

Carlos left the avocado on the dresser and went upstairs.

Chulito stared at the aguacate and tried to figure out what to do with it. If he walked out with the plate, then his mother would know that he had run into Carlos and she might figure out that Carlos must have been in Chulito's room.

Chulito stepped outside with the plate of cool, green avocado. To his annoyance, Carlos stepped out right behind him; he had changed the loose shirt he had on and put on a tight black tank top.

"I'm going downtown, ma."

Maria got up and placed a hand on her son's shoulder. "You're not gonna wait for the fireworks?"

"Yo, Chu-li-to." Papo called from the corner.

Carlos looked over. "I need a change of scenery."

"Are you sure you're O.K., papa?"

Chulito set the avocado down on the table and waved to his friends to hold up.

"I'm fine, ma. I'll be better once I'm downtown."

Carlos looked at Chulito's expressionless face which masked his anger. Chulito sat next to his mother.

Carlos began to send a text while talking to his mother. "I won't be back late, I gotta be up early for work. But I'm texting Andrew who's hanging out with some friends from school at a rooftop barbecue near the FDR to let him know that I can come after all. I was gonna meet up with them later in the Vil, but the rooftop barbecue sounds like fun and it would be my first time seeing the fireworks up close. So, why not, right?"

"Be careful." Maria kissed his cheek.

"Have fun," Carmen added. "Chulito, are you hungry?"

Chulito shrugged his shoulders. "I might as well."

Carmen handed him a plate and told him to go get some meat.

"I thought you were going to serve me."

"You can't serve yourself? I'm playing cards. ¿Mira este?" Carmen said to Maria.

Carlos' phone buzzed and he checked the text message.

"Yo, Chulito," Davey called. "You're missing this."

Looney Tunes was making attempts at break dancing while Chino the DJ supplied the beat box.

"Hol' up," Chulito yelled back.

"You better hurry up, Chulito," Carlos said sarcastically. "You're gonna miss all the fun." Then Carlos crossed the street and headed toward the train station.

Chulito saw Carmen and Maria exchange a puzzled glance and realized that he'd been staring blankly at the antics on the corner while holding an empty plate.

From Garrison Avenue, they could all see the Macy's Annual Fireworks display way in the distance. Chulito knew that when it ended kids would run around with sparklers and the teenagers would set off all kinds of illegal fireworks from the streets and the rooftops.

Their kiss in his room and Carlos' tear-filled eyes played over in Chulito's mind. He started to call Carlos about a dozen times. He wanted to apologize, but he couldn't give Carlos what he was asking for. The hours since Carlos left dragged on and Chulito felt trapped. He was tired of the same jokes on the corner and he couldn't just hide out in his room.

As the fireworks in the distance ended and the ones in his neighborhood heated up, he flipped open his phone and called Carlos.

He answered in mid-laugh. "Hey, Chulito."

"Did you see the fireworks?"

"Yeah! Amazing. We're about to head over to the pier. Why are you whispering? Are you outside?"

"Yeah, on Garrison." Chulito answered.

"Then why don't you go hide in your room and call me from there." Carlos sounded tipsy.

Chulito walked away from the crowd and went toward the Bruckner Expressway. "Yo, Carlos, wassup wit' your attitude."

"My attitude?"

Chulito was still whispering even though he was a block away from Garrison and across from the elevated Bruckner Expressway. "Yes, and what did you mean by you can't keep this up and it's not working?"

"Exactly that, Chulito. I don't want this down low, keep it on the QT relationship. And stop fucking whispering. I can hardly hear you."

Chulito crossed under the expressway and spoke in full voice. "Sorry. I wanna see you."

"I thought I could handle it. But it hurt me a lot when you pushed me away today."

Chulito knew where this conversation was heading and wanted to change the course. "I'm sorry. I didn't mean to push you so hard."

"I don't mean physically."

"I'm sorry, Carlos. I freaked when I heard my mom come into the house."

"I know you did. I wish you were in a different place because right this minute I want you here with me."

"I'll meet you at the pier, right now."

"Hold it."

"What?"

"If you come, you gotta be ready to hold my hand or let me hug you or even kiss you without freaking out that someone is gonna see you. And if Damian or Lee or anybody you know does show up, you are not going to push me away."

Chulito paced the wide median under the Bruckner Expressway. "Carlos, I'm not ready for that, please."

"Then don't come. Stay in the Bronx."

Chulito stopped pacing. "What? You breaking it off?"

"I don't want to go back into a closet to be with you, Chulito." The words stung him. "Carlos, don't do this."

Carlos hung up.

A lump the size of a fist formed in Chulito's throat. He could hear the cheers from his neighborhood rising up into the night like a crowd at a Yankees game. Chulito wanted to run, but he didn't know to where. He hailed a cab to the Village.

"You gotta take care of yourself." Kenny wiped a tear from Carlos' cheek.

"I love him." Carlos sat on the cool dry grass at the pier, brought his knees to his chest and rested his chin on his right knee. "It hurt so much when he pushed me today. It was like a wake-up call. I know he needs time, but it's already been about a month and a half, I just don't think that I have the time to give him." As Kenny and the twins comforted Carlos, Kevin came over with Andrew and Alex.

"You O.K., Carlos?" Alex asked.

Kenny blurted out. "He broke up with Chulito."

"Damn, Kenny, just put my business all out there."

Kenny mouthed "sorry" to Carlos then kissed Kevin.

"I'm sorry," Alex said sympathetically. "For real. You were having a good time at the party but I noticed that you got real quiet all of a sudden."

"I'm sorry, too," Andrew put his arm around Carlos and pulled him close.

"Me too," Carlos said through tears, then sobbed on Andrew's chest.

Alex took Carlos' hand. "You're gonna be alright?"

Carlos pulled his hand away and nodded.

"Do you want to go for a ride?" Andrew asked.

"We could head out to City Island for some ice cream," Alex offered.

Carlos nodded.

"Any room for some additional pier queens in your chariot, Sir Andrew?" Kenny asked.

"Yes, but I'm not coming back into the city. So if you're cool with being left at a subway in the Bronx, you're welcome to come along."

"I'm staying at Kevin's in Brooklyn tonight, so that won't work for me."

Alex, Carlos and Andrew took off in the white Range Rover up the West Side Highway toward the Bronx.

Chulito arrived at the pier, handing the cab driver a $50 bill and asking him to wait.

He saw Pito and Sebastian leaving the pier. "Yo wassup, you seen Carlos?"

"We saw him earlier with Kenny by the water."

Chulito ran over to the water and saw Kenny, who told him

that Carlos left with Alex and Andrew to City Island.

Chulito ran back to the cab and headed up to the Bronx. When he was alone in the cab, he covered his face with his bandanna and cried. He wanted to see Carlos, hold him. Beg him for more time. Maybe they could move far away from the neighborhood and start a life together. Chulito knew he was changing. Lately, he didn't care so much about the fellas. He hardly spent time with them. And he'd decided to get out of the game with Kamikaze. He'd never felt happier than when he was with Carlos. He'd never felt love like when they were together. Then anger overtook him. How could Carlos just break things off like that? Maybe he didn't love him. Chulito slammed his fist on his knee repeatedly, then a howl grew inside and shot out of him, which startled the cab driver. He quickly assured him "I'm cool, I'm cool," but Chulito was far from cool. He felt his heart coming apart cell by cell, and the tears wouldn't stop pouring out.

When the cab pulled up to the block, all the tables and grills were gone, but the fellas were still on the corner.

"Hey, Chulito, where you disappear to?" Davey called out from down the block.

Chulito stood at the entrance to his building away from the corner. "Business guys, but I'm dead, yo. I'll see you guys mañana."

"Kamikaze was looking for you. He's up the block at Gil's," Davey said.

Chulito checked his cell phone but he hadn't missed a call from Kamikaze. "When you see him, tell him to call me."

"Yo, Chulito. You O.K.?" Davey asked walking toward Chulito.

"Just tired." Chulito leaned against the entrance to his building. He was glad he lived on the first floor because he had just enough energy to get to his door.

Papo held out a bottle of Hennessey. "Come have one little palo before you turn in."

"C'mon, we missed you. Just when all the fireworks were shooting you bounced," said Davey.

Chulito took a deep breath and walked over to the corner, where the streetlight lit his red and swollen eyes.

"Oh, shit, bro. What's up?" Davey asked.

"I'm tired. I gotta get some sleep."

"Yo," Papo said, "if it's none of our business just say so, but you don't just look tired, you look hurt, bro."

"I'll be alright. I just got some bad news is all, nothing too serious."

"Family?" Chin-Chin asked.

"Nah, it's just, whatever."

"Love?" Chin-Chin said. "Oh, shit, it's love, right?"

Chulito responded by not responding.

Davey and Chin-Chin high-fived each other.

"It's that girl you cancelled with a week or two ago, right?" Davey said. "You were all moody after you cancelled to hang out with us."

"Did you two have a fight?" Chin-Chin asked.

"Nah, sort of."

"Sort of?" Davey asked. "What happened? You look like you been crying."

The fellas laughed.

Kamikaze came out of Gil's Liquor Store and walked toward them.

"She dumped you?" Davey asked.

Chulito nodded.

A chorus of "Ay, benditos" rose up from the fellas as Kamikaze reached them.

"Wassup, knuckleheads?" Kamikaze asked then saw Chulito's face. "What happened to you?"

"That chick that Chulito has been seeing on the low just dumped him," Davey said.

"So that's what's up? It makes sense why I only get to see you when we're working."

"I guess you gonna be seeing a lot more of Chulito." Davey laughed.

"Have some respect," Kamikaze said. "Can't you see that my boy's heart is broken?" Kamikaze slipped his arm around Chulito's neck, pulled him close and kissed his temple.

"Ah, don't baby him," Papo said, taking a swig of Hennessey. "Know what I say? Fuck her. There's plenty more."

"This is love, Papo," Kamikaze said. "Look at his face. A dude only cries like that when he gets bit. You ain't never been bit, Papo?"

"Of course."

"Then have a little heart, bro. Our little brother here fell in love, gave his heart away, and it got tossed in the trash. Right, Chulito?"

Chuito nodded. "Something like that."

"What I want to know is why it was such a secret," Kamikaze said. "I thought you and me were tight."

"Yeah, Chulito," Davey said. "Was she a dog?"

Chulito shook his head. "Nah, she's beautiful. It just had to be that way." Chulito thought for a second. "She was a church girl with a strict father and nobody could know about us. Anyway, I want to go to bed." Chulito tried to pull away from Kamikaze's embrace, but he held him tightly.

"A church girl?" Davey said.

"The worse kind." Papo shook his head. "They make you jump through hoops for a little taste, and then if they give anything up, you owe them your fucking life. Sorry, bro. If you didn't keep it such a secret, we could have warned you and saved you all the heartache."

"She lives in the neighborhood?" Chin-Chin asked.

"No, in Manhattan." Chulito tried again to squirm away from Kamikaze.

"You ain't going to your room to cry." Kamikaze pulled him over in a headlock. "You coming with me. When your heart's broken, you should not be alone."

"Thanks, but I want to go to bed."

"Bye, fellas." Kamikaze held Chulito in a headlock and brought him over to the car.

Davey mock cried, "Bye, Chulito. You're gonna live. You're gonna live."

The fellas laughed.

Kamikaze pulled off and made a U-turn on Hunts Point Avenue. "You hungry?"

"No."

"I'm starving, bro. How about some Mickey D's or seafood?"

"I'm not hungry."

"Let's got to City Island."

"All the way over there? Can't you get seafood someplace else?"

"I want the best. Besides, Rey owns a restaurant out there and his top dawgs eat for free."

Chulito looked at his watch and figured that Carlos must be gone.

"Let's go," Chulito said. Before Kamikaze even reached the entrance of the Bruckner Expressway, Chulito breathed heavily and fought to hold back tears. He looked away from Kamikaze out the window. He wondered where Carlos was. He thought of texting him, of saying he was sorry, but that wasn't the issue. Carlos wanted what he wouldn't give him. Carlos wanted to be open. The pain Chulito felt was unlike any other he'd experienced. It began in his chest, right in the center, and then it spread up to his throat and strangled him. It pulsed in his temples, like his brain was being squeezed. And the tears. They kept rising and spilling. He'd lost control of holding them back and sat sobbing. Kamikaze looked over to him and swiftly pulled the car over to the side of the street. Chulito put his hands on the dashboard to steady himself.

"Wassup, Chulito?"

Chulito was on the brink of hyperventilating. Kamikaze removed their seatbelts, placed a hand on Chulito's neck and squeezed. Then he pulled Chulito over and embraced him. Chulito sobbed in Kamikaze's arms. "This hurts, bro. I feel like I can't breath, and there's a knot in the middle of my chest. My head feels like it's gonna pop, Kaz."

"I'm sorry to see you like this, bro."

Chulito pulled away from Kamikaze. "I feel so embarrassed crying like this in front of you." He wiped away at his tears. Kamikaze flipped open the glove compartment and pulled out tissues.

"It's alright. Love can make you lose your cool." Kamikaze lifted Chulito's face and examined it. "And you have definitely lost it, little bro, but you don't always gotta be cool, and definitely not with me."

"Thanks." Chulito wiped his face. "I'm O.K. now."

"Let's just go to my crib, I'll order from the Chinos instead and we got weed and Hennessey and whatever else you want. This way, if you feel like you need to cry, let shit out or whatever, you can do what you need to do. It will be just me and you." Kamikaze smiled.

Chulito spent the rest of the night in Kamikaze's apartment with its blue skies and fluffy clouds. They shared rib tips and fried rice from the Chinese joint, eating out of the same containers, drank Coronas and smoked blunts. Whenever Chulito had a crying fit, Kamikaze would hug him, place the flat of his palm on his back and move it around in soothing circles. He wished that he was hugging Carlos or that Carlos was holding him instead. They didn't talk, except for Kamikaze cradling Chulito and periodically saying, "Let it out, little bro" or "It's cool." It was strange for Chulito to feel this close to Kamikaze. He'd had fantasies of being in Kamikaze's arms, but they never played out like this. It was peaceful and easy. He liked being close. They were alone and private. Chulito knew that Kamikaze understood the deal and that they could never do this on the block. Why didn't Carlos understand, too?

Chulito fell asleep on the couch, and Kamikaze removed Chulito's Timberland boots before going to sleep.

Chulito woke up as the sky was starting to shed its darkness. He looked around the room. The air-conditioner was humming in the corner and the ceiling fan was spinning slowly above him. Kamikaze must have cleared the empty bottles of beer and Chinese food cartons. He walked over to Kamikaze's room and saw him asleep on his bed. Kamikaze was lying on his stomach, hugging a pillow while one bare foot poked out from under the plain white sheet covering him. Chulito could see Kamikaze's tattoo blazing on his back in the dim light. He taped a note to the bathroom door that read "Thanks."

It was a twenty-minute walk back to Hunts Point from Kamikaze's apartment. An hour later, Chulito found himself sitting on a rock by the Bronx River. The water moved slowly and he watched leaves, plants and an occasional can float by.

Watching the sun rise, Chulito felt angry at Carlos for asking for something he couldn't give and cried because he didn't want to think about not being with him. Chulito thought about Poe Cottage, he thought about Sebastian and Pito, he thought about the time they slow danced, how happy he felt when he and Carlos were alone. He considered telling Kamikaze the real deal, but not the fellas. Well, not all of them; maybe Chin-Chin and Davey, but not Papo. What would he say to them? "I lied about the church girl. It's really Carlos who drives me crazy and I feel happy when I'm with him." Would he tell his mother? After about his fourth cycle of being angry at Carlos, coming out to some of his friends, and deciding to just go on without Carlos, two guys showed up at the river with fishing rods. They nodded to Chulito who dusted off the seat of his pants and headed back toward his neighborhood. He looked at his Fossil watch and saw that it was almost eight o'clock. He knew Carlos would be leaving for his internship in about an hour.

Chulito walked through his neighborhood, but avoided Hunts Point and Garrison Avenues where he knew all of the auto glass guys were already lined up. He looked at his old elementary school, the NYC Parks Department gym that was being constructed and the new post office. He looked at the cracks in the sidewalk and wondered if the little blades of grass came up from some deep dark place in the earth and pushed their way through the cement, or if the seeds flew through the air and landed on the little bits of dirt. Either way that was some tough grass, he thought.

He walked by the giant warehouse with the theatre and artists studios on Barretto Street, where a woman planted flowers in small patches of dirt around new trees. He thought it was strange to see her with her long light brown hair in her face, digging into the ground. What was the point? He thought about asking her whether the grass came from underground or from the air.

The flowers were small and vibrant in shades of pink, magenta and purple. She had a bicycle with a basket in front of it that had lots of little plants and loose flowers. She wore a daisy pierced by a gold hoop as an earring. When Chulito passed her she smiled, got up and handed him a sunflower.

"No thanks." He kept walking.

"C'mon, take it," she said. "Give it to someone you love."

Chulito stopped and looked at her. She was still smiling and holding out the sunflower. He had seen her before, riding her bike. He knew that she was down with the two gay guys who ran the dance studio in the warehouse.

"Or give it to someone you don't love, but I want you to have it."

Chulito walked over to her and accepted the sunflower, "Thanks."

"Thank you for accepting it."

"Why are you planting flowers?"

"Why not?"

Chulito opened his shirt and stuck the flower inside.

"Too much of a macho to walk around with a flower?"

"Nah, I want it to be a surprise."

"Alright. But if there is some law that says a macho guy like you can't walk down the street holding a flower, I think it should be broken."

Chulito nodded and continued to walk home with the flower hidden under his shirt.

When he arrived at his building he sat inside at the bottom of the steps near his door. He knew that Carlos would be down shortly and would have to pass him. Soon he heard Carlos' door open and keys locking the door. Carlos took two steps down and saw Chulito sitting at the bottom of the stairs. He continued down and Chulito looked up at him.

"Good morning." Chulito presented Carlos with the sunflower.

Carlos stopped and accepted the flower. "Thanks. Do you have something to say to me or did you just want to give me this?"

"I hardly slept, thinking about you."

"If you gotta whisper, then you haven't heard what I had to say."

"I know what you want, and I been thinking all night, Carlos. I just need time. I'm not ready." Chulito took Carlos' hand then let it go.

"I know you're not. And I want to say, fuck it. And all night, every time I heard a car door slam or heard footsteps, I looked out the window to see if it was you, but I don't like sneaking around." Carlos realized he was whispering, too, and used his full voice. "I don't like this double life thing. I came out to my mother, to everybody and it's not easy, so I understand that. I even lost you as my friend for a while." Carlos paused and looked away from Chulito. "Now I'm losing you again." Carlos handed the flower back to Chulito and left the building.

Chulito opened the door to his apartment and saw his mother

standing in the hall.

"Hey, papa, it's good to see you, I was worried."

"I crashed at Kamikaze's." Avoiding further discussion he slipped into his room.

Carmen knocked on his door. "¿Chulito, qué te pasa? I know something is bothering you."

"I'll be alright." He wiped tears from his eyes.

"Well, I don't feel good about going to Puerto Rico and not knowing what's going on."

Chulito opened his door a crack and gave her the sunflower. "I'll be fine, ma. I just…I just have a broken heart, I guess."

Carmen reached for the flower with one hand and touched his face with the other. "Come here." She tried to hug him.

Chulito pulled away and wiped his tears. "I'm O.K. Don't worry."

"You're too much of a man to let your mother give you a hug?"

"It's not that. I want to be alone right now."

Carmen looked away and retreated from his room. "Thank you for the flower, Chulito. I love you, negro."

Chulito laid on his bed, kicked off his Tims and sobbed softly into his pillow.

When Chulito opened his eyes, the room was dark and he felt paralyzed. He was in that place between dreaming and being awake. He could hear sirens in the distance, slowly becoming more present. He knew that if he could just wiggle one small toe, it would set off a chain reaction that would shake him out of his paralysis. The sirens grew louder and were joined by the *tuc-tuc-tuc* of helicopters whose blades sliced through the South Bronx night sky. The crackle of walkie talkies joined the symphony of the raid. Chulito could hear the television from the living room. There was a newscaster who had a voice that was smooth, creamy and very official.

"We interrupt our usual programming with a message that as of midnight tonight Congress passed a bill that has outlawed macho. A special team of police has been dispatched into five major cities in the U.S. to capture and bring in all macho men with a reading of four point eight or higher on the Macho Meter. We will hear from our Mayor Margarita Lopez in just a few minutes to explain more, but, I repeat, as of midnight tonight being macho is against the law."

Each pounding heartbeat broke Chulito out of his paralysis and he sat up in his bed. The lights from the sirens were flashing in his room. He jumped up and peeked through the shade in his window and saw police trucks lined up and down Garrison Avenue. Chulito could hear heavy footsteps running down his hall, the voices calling out, "Alberto Sanchez, you have a reading of six point four. Come with us."

Men in their boxers and wife-beaters were being led into trucks and vans. Papo, Davey, Chin-Chin and Looney Tunes were lined up against the closed auto glass shops and scanned with a handheld gadget that looked like a cell phone. As the police men and women passed the scanner over them, little red lights blinked and the fellas were cuffed and stuffed into a van.

Chulito jumped away from the window and paced in his room.

Outside a woman yelled, "Llévatelo, sácalo de aquí, for twenty years you have given me hell. Take him."

"Mami, where are they taking Papi?" a young child asked.

"To make him better…Papi has a big problem."

Chulito heard Puti screaming from her window next door.

"Take that one over there, his name is Damian and he works at Master #1 Auto Glass Shop. That motherfucker threw a beer bottle at me for no fucking reason, other than the fact that I am more glamorous than any woman he could ever have. And go to apartment 7B, there is a guy named Manny and don't let his cute face fool you, he is the most macho motherfucker on the block. And Brick, he lives around the corner…Oh, shit, he's on vacation in Puerto Rico…are you people going there, too? That whole island needs to be under Macho Lock Down."

Chulito searched for clothes that wouldn't make him look thuggy, but as he tried on different clothes they got bigger and bigger—XXL becoming XXXL. He frantically looked through his closet, while outside yells, screams and cheers filled the night: "Don't take him, he really is good deep down inside." "About time some shit like this happened." "Say something now, motherfucker, huh, say something now."

On TV the newscaster was interviewing the Latina mayor who said that the men were being taken away and those who could be rehabilitated to an acceptable macho reading would be returned back to society. The rest would be put in secluded areas where they would have to live off the land or ultimately kill themselves off. Then they had a quote from the woman who invented the Macho Meter: "All men have macho in them. Even gay ones, but there are varying degrees, and while most forms of macho are lethal to the progression of the world and society, there are some acceptable levels, very low levels, that can sometimes be useful."

Chulito pulled out his graduation suit from junior high school, but it was too small. He looked up at his ceiling which had become glass and he could see Carlos in his room. Carlos was listening to music peacefully and plucking the petals off a large sunflower when his mother entered the room with a police woman, who scanned him and gave him the thumbs up. His mother hugged him.

Then Chulito heard a knock on his door; they were coming for him. Would he pass the scan? He heard his mother talking to the officials at the door. Chulito thought his heart would stop. He wouldn't pass the Macho Meter. He would be taken away. He looked up at the ceiling and Carlos was sitting on the edge of his bed, looking down through the floor at him. The sunflower petals continued to fall, filling the ceiling, obscuring Carlos.

He wanted to apologize. He wanted to say that he loved him and that they should run away together. There was a knock on his bedroom door. "Chulito?" his mother called. "You awake?"

Chulito tried to say something to Carlos, to his mother, anything but his throat was dry and no sounds were coming out.

He closed his eyes and tried to yell out, "Carlos! Carlos!"

Nothing.

The door handle turned, his mother's face appeared with the official behind her, scanner in hand. Chulito looked up to the ceiling and yelled, "CARLOS, I LOVE YOU AND I WANT TO BE WITH YOU, ON THE PIER AND EVERYWHERE. I LOVE YOU, PA!" Chulito woke up professing his love to Carlos.

Carmen had been knocking on his door. "Chulito, open up. Are you awake? What are you yelling about?"

Chulito covered his mouth, realizing that he'd been shouting out loud, and looked up at his ceiling. His face was sweaty and he breathed heavily.

Carmen rushed in and sat by him. He resisted her embrace at first and then gave in. He allowed his mother to hold him for the first time in years.

"¿Que pasa, Chulito? What were you saying about Carlos?"

"Nothing, ma. It was just a bad dream. Forget about it." Chulito held his mother tighter.

chapter nineteen

Chulito and his uncle from Brooklyn took his mother to the
airport. He agreed to call her every night and to stay in touch
with Maria, then he kissed her good-bye and went outside to
the baggage claim area where his uncle would be circling. As he
waited on the curb, Chulito felt a small nervous rush when he
saw Brick, who had just returned from Puerto Rico. They hadn't
spoken since they'd seen each other shortly after that night he
caught them on the roof. Brick had a big suitcase and knapsack
and looked tan. He saw Chulito, nodded and called him over with
a small jerk of his head.

"You goin' somewhere or coming back?"

"Droppin' my mom off."

"You ain't goin'?"

"Nah." Lately, Chulito had considered going to Puerto Rico
since Carlos broke things off.

"I was gonna catch a cab to the 'hood. You need a ride?"

"I'm waiting for my uncle, he's circling."

"Your uncle live in the Bronx?"

"Brooklyn."

"So why don't chu come with me? I'm cool with it."

As the two spoke they didn't look at each other, but stared out at the traffic in the airport arrival gate.

Chulito wished that he hadn't come over. He didn't even want to wait for his uncle. He would rather ride back to the neighborhood alone. He needed time to think. That was the main reason he decided to stay in the Bronx. He wanted the time and space to sort things out. "It's O.K., my uncle can take you back and save you the forty dollar cab fare," he said out of obligation.

"Look, I don't know if you still thinking about the roof—"

"Carlos and I aren't talking, so that doesn't matter." Chulito tried to sound matter-of-fact, but his crossed arms and clenched jaw revealed his anger, and the tears that welled up by just mentioning Carlos showed his sadness.

Brick looked at Chulito. "Sorry, bro. What happened?"

Chulito was surprised that Brick seemed concerned. "I'm not sure." Chulito kept an eye out for his uncle, wanting to escape as fast as possible.

"Well, Carlos is a cool dude and you, too. Wait, are you still working with Kamikaze?"

Chulito nodded.

"Well, except for that." Brick nudged him and smiled.

Chulito smiled back. "I don't know what's right anymore."

"I know what you mean. That's why I left for a while."

"Did it help?"

"Yeah. It's not all in check, but I'm gonna stop by Julio's first, and then go to Jennifer's and see where we at."

"Maybe I should have gone to P.R. with my moms."

"You at the airport, nigga. Ain't too late."

"Here's my uncle."

"Well, you're still welcome to ride with me and let your uncle head back to Brooklyn."

Chulito was curious. He didn't have anybody to talk openly with about his situation with Carlos, and since Brick knew the deal and his interest seemed genuine, he said good-bye to his uncle and rode back to the Bronx with Brick. He considered Brick's relationship with Julio and thought he might be able to relate. "This is all new for me, Brick. I don't feel different, except that I got feelings for Carlos. It doesn't make sense to me."

"I hear you."

"You do?

"Shit like that ain't supposed to make sense. I went through some cool shit out in P.R. I met this dude out there."

Chulito thought his suspicion of Brick being gay was about to be confirmed. He turned to face him. "You, too?"

Brick laughed. "It wasn't like that, but close. I mean we camped out in El Yunque for three days. Just him and me. I told him stuff that I ain't never told no one. Not even Julio." Brick stared out the taxi's window at the Van Wyck Expressway, but had a far away look on his face. "We got real close, real deep. I can honestly say that I love that dude. Not like I want to marry him and stuff like that, but I miss him. He made it hard for me to leave Puerto Rico and come back to all the shit here."

"Did anything happen? Did you do the deed?" Chulito was embarrassed that he'd blurted out what he was thinking.

Brick shook his head and smiled. "That whole shit took me by surprise."

Chulito faced Brick. "So what happened?"

"I'll never forget the day we met. I'd been in P.R. for about a week helping my uncle out in his farm in Bayamón. I loved doing all that physical work. I'm good with my hands." Brick held up and examined his large hands. He rubbed the calluses on the upper part of his palm. Then he winked at Chulito.

Chulito smiled and thought, "I bet you're good with those hands."

"So my uncle says that I should spend a day up in El Yunque. Do you know it?"

Chulito nodded. "I went to P.R. when I was twelve. I loved going up to that rainforest."

"Well, my uncle tells me, 'Don't miss the cascadas.' You know those waterfalls way up?"

"They're really beautiful."

"The day was hot as hell and my uncle drops me right when the sun was coming up. I get up there and the temperature drops, like, twenty degrees. There was a foggy mist everywhere. The water is pouring down the rocks and slamming into the water. Since it's so early, there ain't nobody around, and even though it's cooler than the long ass walk to get there, I'm still dripping in sweat 'cause I'm wearing Tims and overalls and shit. So I start thinking, maybe I could get in. I stand on its edge and feel the water. That shit was cold, but felt good. There were little bubbles coming up, like it was 7-Up."

Chulito relaxed into the seat. "Man, you're making me wish I'd gone to P.R."

"I can't wait to go back, for real." The far away look came back to Brick's eyes. "At the falls, I'm thinking I could take off my boots and put my feet in, but I really just want to strip down and get in right quick before anybody shows up. I started to take off my Tims when there's this loud ass splash in the water, like one of the rocks had come loose and crashed down. I'm looking into the water because even though it's clear, the bubbles don't let me see what's below it. Then, like a monster from a fucking movie, this guy comes up through the bubbles. At first I see his face, which is painted like a fucking Indian and shit."

"Sounds freaky."

"No doubt." Brick makes a fist with one hand and punches the palm of the other hand. "I get my guard up in case some shit is going to go down."

"Then what?"

"Well, the guy comes out the water and he's like..." Brick paused. "He's like some fucking, I don't know how to describe him." Brick looked at Chulito. "Yo, I'm being open with you, so just keep this here, O.K.?"

Chulito agreed.

"He was like a Taino Indian, native boy type. He had on one of those loin cloth things covering up his shit, but the only other thing he wore was paint. His face was painted with a rust colored "T" that stretched across his forehead and went down his nose. He had two yellow and red stripes on each cheek with a dark gray circle on each side. He had one reddish dot in the center of his chin. Otherwise, he ain't had no clothes on. At first I was fucking shocked, but when I saw him all naked and shit I thought 'fag.' No offense."

"Hey, bro, I ain't no—" Chulito stopped himself. It was an automatic response to deny being gay, but that was one of the questions on the table for him. He knew he was gay. Part of him always did and falling in love with Carlos—holding him, kissing him and wanting nothing more than to spend every moment of his life with him—sealed the deal. He was trying to figure out who could know and how that would affect his life. He looked at Brick who had one eyebrow raised in question. Chulito smiled and felt relieved to not have to keep up the façade with Brick.

"Yo, Chulito, you ain't gotta front with me."

Chulito sat back and rested his head against the back of the seat. "Thanks." Chulito looked over to Brick. "Do you think I'm weak 'cause I feel the way I do about Carlos?"

"Nigga, you ghetto through and through, and look who you talking to. I work with Julio and he ain't weak nohow. He gotta be tougher than any dude out there. And your man Carlos, too."

Chulito chuckled. "You know, I tell him he's gangsta being all out and shit."

"Damn right."

"So what happened with you and the naked dude?"

"Well, I start thinking that we alone and I size him up. He was about my age, same height, but he's way more buff than me. Then he climbs the rocks real fast, goes behind the waterfalls and dives through them. Splash! The nigga lands in the water again. It was out of this fuckin' world. We got to talking and he invites me to go fishing. Do you know I love to fish?"

"You fish in the nasty Bronx River?"

"So I go back to this spot where he's camped out and it's like a fantasy. Another waterfall that goes into this lake and it's surrounded by trees with bananas, mangoes, papayas, oranges, limes, coconuts everything. Now, it's all good, but I'm still thinking this guy's after my ass, and that shit ain't going to happen. Julio says I have good gaydar 'cause I'm a dude magnet. You know what I'm talking about?"

Chulito thought he had an idea but wanted to hear Brick's explanation. "Nah, what you mean?"

"I know I'm a pretty nigga. Chicks be coming on to me, but dudes be steppin' up, too. You must know what it's like to be on the train and see how dudes be checking you out but acting like they not. Or how sometimes you go to a store and one of the sales guys is being extra helpful and looks all hungry and shit."

Chulito smiled.

Brick smiled back. "You know what the fuck I'm talking about."

Chulito nodded. "Lee always gives me two extra chicken wings."

"He always gives me a double order."

Chulito sat up. "What?"

"You probably don't flirt with him. If you flirt you get more. I learned that early on. And I don't have to do shit with any dude."

Chulito wanted to say that it sounded cold to be leading niggas on like that, but he thought it might mess up the talk they were having. He looked out the window and realized that the cab was about to cross the Whitestone Bridge into the Bronx. He was glad that the thick bullet proof shield prevented the driver from hearing their conversation.

"So was it like that with this dude in P.R.?"

"Nah. His name is Taino." Chulito recognized the distant look in Brick's eye as longing. He could see that Brick missed Taino. "So we fish and eat and he's got rum and shit. I relax with him. Turns out that he has a wife and kids, but goes up alone a few times a year and goes native. He has a cell that works up in the rainforest in case she needs to reach him. So I call my uncle to say that he doesn't have to pick me up 'cause I'm gonna stay the night." Brick paused. "I stayed three nights and it was no doubt the best time of my life. No worries. Fishing, living off the land mostly, but we went to the picnic area and people gave us food. And we talked all the time." Brick stopped looked out the window at the Bronx. "I ain't never shared so much stuff with another person. I told him everything. About the block, Julio, my grandma, my fight with Jennifer. I even told him about the tattoo on my back. Jennifer and Julio are the only ones who know the whole story."

"Sounds deep." Chulito wanted to pat Brick's hand or squeeze his shoulder, but he felt physical contact would be too much.

"I ain't never been so close to someone in my whole life. Nobody. Not Jennifer, not even Julio."

Chulito suspected that Brick wasn't being completely truthful about whether he'd done the deed or not. He wanted to ask outright if anything physical happened. "What do you mean by close?"

Brick shrugged his shoulders. "I don't really know. Like he became my best friend in the whole world. We're connected. Here." He placed his hand on his heart.

Chulito nodded and watched Brick who had closed his eyes and seemed to be praying. "I feel connected with Carlos like that, too, but—" Tears interrupted his words and Chulito covered his face.

Brick smiled, pulled a bandanna out from his pocket and offered it. "Damn, he got you like that?"

Chulito felt good to be open. He wiped his tears with the bandanna. "Carlos wants to be open and doesn't want to keep things underground in the 'hood, but how else we gonna be? I don't have a choice, right?"

Brick shifted in his seat to face Chulito. "I see it as you making a choice, bro. You chosin' to keep it on the low."

Chulito sighed. "My pain won't let up. I ain't never felt anything like this."

Brick patted Chulito's thigh. "If it's a done deal and it's over between you two, I can tell you that the pain will get better bit by bit, but it might never go away completely. But it sounds like you in between two places."

Chulito shrugged.

"And am I right to say that you chose the neighborhood over being open with Carlos?"

Chulito nodded.

"You don't seem to be too happy with the choice you making."

Chulito laughed. "Why did you come back?"

"My baby girl mainly. But I came back to find out if there's a solid reason for me to be here. I feel like I gotta make a choice, too."

Chulito stopped crying. "Is going back to P.R. one of your choices?"

"Maybe."

When they arrived at Julio's travel agency, Chulito was reluctant to go in, because Papo was on the corner talking to Orlando from Rivera's Grocery Store. Chulito slipped into the travel agency while Brick paid for the cab. Julio and Brick hugged. Brick reached into his knapsack and gave Julio a picture of himself in El Yunque. Chulito sat on the couch and watched.

"Papa, with that tan, Jennifer would be crazy not to take you back." Julio snapped three times in the air.

"She's down to have a conversation, but I'm open to anything."

"Anything?" Julio teased.

"Well, not anything. I told Chulito about Taino on the way over."

"Oh, did your mother depart alright?" Julio asked.

"Yeah, I guess," Chulito responded. He felt a little awkward sitting in the agency. He liked being alone with Brick in the cab and wished he could talk more with him.

"I brought this nigga over 'cause…"

"I know," Julio said. "Carlos told me, but I wasn't gonna say anything."

"He told you we broke up?" Chulito said.

Julio nodded.

He felt a little easier. Both men listened attentively. "Everything was going fine, but I guess it started getting crazy when Brick caught Carlos and me…" Chulito looked down. "Making out on the roof."

"Lord have mercy, lock the door," Julio joked.

Chulito chuckled.

Brick poured himself a cup of coffee and sat on the desk. "So 'cause of that you two broke up?"

Chulito relaxed more into the couch with each response. "Well, not that. On the Fourth of July we started getting a little busy, if you know what I mean."

Julio fanned himself. "Spare me the details. I'm an old man, I don't think my heart can take it."

Chulito said with a sly smile, "Well, we was just kissing and stuff."

Brick turned away. "Don't hold back."

Julio playfully shoved Brick. "Let him speak."

"Let's just say that we was in my room. The door was locked, but my mom came in from outside and called for us. I freaked the fuck out and pushed him. And he basically said he didn't want to keep things underground and broke shit off." Chulito swallowed to ease the lump that had formed in his throat.

"I don't know what to do with you two. You and Carlos and you and Taino. The ghetto is coming out."

"Hold up," Brick said. "It wasn't like that with me and Taino. We didn't do the thang."

"You may as well have," Julio said.

Chulito looked at Brick and asked Julio, "Why do you say that?"

Brick handed Chulito a cup of water. "It just didn't feel right. I didn't tell Chulito about how we slept holding each other the last night in El Yunque."

"You held each other?"

"Yeah and it was cool, like he was a part of me. But that was it." Then Brick went silent for a moment. "I can say this to you because you understand. Niggas out there would be calling me gay or homo."

"What's wrong with that?" Julio asked. "They call you that anyway, just because you work with me."

"True. After I came down from El Yunque, I stayed at my uncle's a few more days, and I didn't speak with Taino until this morning when I called to say good-bye." Brick looked away. "I miss him, yo. I will never forget Taino."

"Taino sounds dope," Chulito said.

"He was." Brick stopped and sat on the desk next to Julio. "There's nothing here for me really. Except for Crystal and you, Julio, of course. So I want to talk to Jennifer to see if we could make it work for Crystal's sake."

"What if she says no?" Chulito said.

"I wouldn't blame her. I broke my promise to never hit her. But that day I felt like I was somebody else."

"But you were still you," Julio said.

"I know, so whatever rules Jennifer sets I'm gonna follow, because I want to be with my baby girl and I can't take her away from her mother." Brick went silent.

Julio smiled and patted Brick's shoulder. "Ay, muchachos, there are some sacrifices you have to make if you really want something. And if you're not willing to make those sacrifices then you might not want that something or someone so badly."

Brick nodded his head. "I really want my daughter." Brick hesitated before hugging Julio in front of the large glass windows of the travel agency. "Thank you, man. Thank you."

Chulito watched the two men hugging in Hunts Point in front of the big window with people passing constantly. It was safer to hug on this side of the window than outside of it, Chulito thought. He was glad that he rode the taxi with Brick and had had the talk with Julio. He felt like he'd entered into their private world and they into his. Now those worlds weren't so concealed. And he understood the hug between these two men. The kind of hug that shows a person cares about the other. He'd shared hugs like that with Kamikaze. Maybe Kamikaze would understand, too.

"Part of me wants to find out what it would be like to be with Carlos." Chulito swallowed to soothe his throat. "I want to say fuck it and let everybody know. But if I do, then there's no turning back."

"True. You gonna have to deal with a lot of shit. But Julio always says to me, 'Why do you keep dealing with shit? Just flush it and deal with the good stuff in your life.' "

"That's right, flush it," Julio said.

"That hard to do," Chulito said.

"Of course it's hard. I'm fifty-two and it's still hard, but I keep flushing the shit and gravitate toward the people who are on my side, like Brick and my parents when they were alive, a few friends, too."

"I know about you and Carlos and I don't give a shit," Brick said. "If the fellas give a shit, then flush them. Hang out with the people who are cool with you two."

Chulito always thought no one would accept him and his love for Carlos. He always thought that the fellas would bug out, especially Papo. But then he never imagined that Brick would be cool and that Julio could be someone he could turn to. He imagined that some people might be good with the news and others might try to mess with him. Would it be a constant fight or would he have to stop hanging out on the block or move? Where would he go? "My mother is gonna freak."

"Mothers usually come around," Julio said. "Most of them already know."

"I don't think my mother knows."

"Well, if she doesn't or does, you have to figure out if you want her to hear it from you or from somebody else, because if you want to be with Carlos or any other guy, she will eventually know."

"I don't know if I want to be with another guy. Right now, for me, it's just Carlos."

"Whatever decision you make will have its consequences," Julio said, "but there could also be benefits. If you let Carlos go, you lose him and gain what? Or if you are open to your feelings about Carlos, you get him but it might cost you in some other way."

"How do you know so much, Julio?" Chulito asked.

"I told you, I'm fifty-two and I go to a good therapist on

Eighty-eighth Street. I'll give you her card, papito. But for us, love is tough because at every turn somebody is gonna try to shut your love down. So until the world changes, we gotta fight for our love."

Brick let out a sigh, "That shit is deep, Julio."

"And you, too. You gotta fight for Jennifer, but you gotta fight even harder to be close to Taino because people want to tear that shit down." Julio imitated a tough thug, "Yo, don't you be sleeping in a cave with no nigga. That shit is 'mo.'"

Brick and Chulito laughed.

"But seriously, Chulito, it's up to you, papito." Julio put up his fists and awkwardly moved around like a boxer. Brick boxed along with Julio and then offered his chin. "Get me right here, Julio. I give you a free shot."

Julio moved in and kissed Brick's chin.

"You a crazy bitch." Brick collapsed on the couch next to Chulito. "I got your back, Chulito." He offered him his hand to shake. "Even if those niggas out there turn on you."

"Thanks." Chulito shook Brick's hand. "But that's what scares me."

"Don't worry," Brick said. "If people say any shit to me, I'll tell them to mind their fucking business—"

"No," Julio said. "You gotta do more, Brick. You gotta tell them that you think it's cool that they're together."

"Well, if being together makes you two niggas happy, which is more than I can say for most of the sorry asses around here, then that's cool."

"Thanks, Brick. Carlos' mother told me he went up to Connecticut to visit a friend this weekend."

"A gay nigga?"

"Yes. I've been sick over that, too."

"He there now?" Brick asked.

"Nah, he should be at work," Chulito said.

"You better call him up, before the next sucka moves in on your shit."

"Carlos is a catch," Julio said. "If you want to be with him, I wouldn't waste time."

Chulito panicked and flipped open his cell phone and pressed #1 on his speed dial. He wasn't sure what he would say, but he wanted to let him know that he didn't want to let him go. "Hey, Carlos."

"Chulito, I'm busy," Carlos said coldly.

"I'm talking to Julio and Brick and they said that I should call you 'cause some other nigga might be moving in on my shit."

"You're talking to Brick and Julio about us?" Carlos sounded surprised.

"Yeah, so if someone is pressing you, they better back the fuck up. Can I meet you after work?"

Carlos laughed. "Did you take a Tarzan pill or something?"

Chulito smiled and high-fived Julio and Brick.

As Chulito walked down the block he saw Papo on the corner. Papo raised one of his black eyebrows. "Making travel plans?"

"Nah, just talking to Julio."

"That stupid faggot? For what?"

Julio was neither, but for the first time, Chulito felt emboldened to speak his mind. "He ain't stupid. He's real smart." As Chulito passed him his heart pounded and he felt scared and excited. He wanted to look back at Papo but continued forward instead.

chapter twenty

Before meeting Carlos, Chulito decided to go to the barber shop. He was ready for a change. They undid his braids and gave him a closely cropped haircut. As the clippers buzzed against his scalp, Chulito watched a young kid pound on the congas in the corner. "Leave that alone," the kid's mother warned, but the barbero said it was O.K. The barbero outlined his hairline with warm shaving cream and cleaned the tiny hairs with a straight edged razor. Then he finished off his hair cut with the sweet citrus smell of Clubman's Aftershave and soft scented talcum powder that he brushed on with a small broom. Chulito ran his hand over the fuzz on his head and smiled.

Chulito went home, took a shower and dressed in all white, a FuBu shirt over Pepe jeans and Adidas sneakers, topped off with a white, fitted Yankees baseball cap.

When Carlos stepped out of the *New York Daily News* building he and saw Chulito holding a bouquet of red roses with one sunflower in the middle, he mockingly put one hand on his heart and the back of his other hand on his forehead as if he were going to faint. Chulito smiled and held out the flowers.

"Cute." Carlos accepted the flowers.

"I know I am, but what you think about the flowers?" Chulito pulled off his cap.

"Wow! You shaved your head?"

"Just about, you like it?"

Carlos nodded and checked out Chulito from head to sneakered foot. "Damn, it doesn't matter what you do, you always look good."

"But do you like this better, because I can grow my braids back?"

"I love it. It's very butch."

"Feels good. Touch it."

Carlos rubbed Chulito's head. "Damn, I didn't think it was possible for you to be hotter."

Chulito smiled. "I'm glad you like it. It feels light. I feel light."

"Is that why you dressed in all white?"

"I'm hoping for a new beginning."

They headed toward the pier.

Carlos smelled the roses as they walked. "I love all this, Chulito, but I'm still a little nervous about you. I don't trust your change of heart. All day long questions swirled in my head. I don't know how serious you are and honestly, I don't want to get closer, if you're gonna jump ship."

Chulito walked silently. True to form he imagined that Carlos was thinking with his head as well as his heart. And although Chulito was decidedly optimistic when he came downtown, he knew it was easier to do the big show there than in Hunts Point, and at that thought fear started to creep back into his heart. "I hear you, Carlos, but when you broke it off I felt like I was gonna die. I never felt pain like that. And I missed you. I missed our talks, our walks. I even missed seeing all the dudes on the pier."

Carlos leaned into Chulito. "I don't doubt it. Look at you. From throwing a bottle to showing up with a bouquet of flowers."

"Damn, you never gonna let me live that down."

"No. Because I need to remember that even if you didn't want to throw that bottle, you caved into the pressure." Carlos stopped in front of a new apartment building as rush hour traffic crawled along the Westside and looked Chulito in the eye. "I need to protect myself, but I don't want to have to protect myself from you."

It was as if Carlos had ripped open his chest. He felt exposed and ashamed. "No, baby, I promise." Chulito wanted to say more but couldn't find the words. He wanted to vow his love forever. He wanted to get on his knees and beg for forgiveness. He wished he could rewind to that moment and do something different. "I promise." Then he closed his eyes and kissed Carlos. They breathed each other in and their tongues circled. Chulito felt overwhelmed by joy and fear.

When they stopped kissing he kept his eyes closed, then opened them to see Carlos smiling at him. Chulito surprised himself, but it felt like the right thing to do to let Carlos know he was on board. Suddenly, he needed to sit so he moved to a large cement planter and leaned against it. Carlos sat too and put an arm around him.

He watched the cars whiz by, then looked back at Carlos. "I love you so fucking much, Carlos. I think I'm all strong and tough, but I'm scared as shit when it comes to this."

Carlos kissed his shoulder. "I know that block means a lot to you."

"I mean it's all I got, right? And you from that block, too."

Carlos rested his head on Chulito's shoulder and said, "I love Hunts Point and I hate it. Not everybody is fucked up. There are some great people, like Agustin at the bodega, Martha and our moms."

"We've known those people all our lives."

"And some of those people keep us apart. And even the people who are cool, are not going to be throwing us a party when they find out we're together."

Chulito chuckled. "Well, maybe Julio and Brick."

Carlos lifted his head and smiled. "I still can't get over that you talked to them. I have to let you know that when you said that, I decided to hear you out. What did you talk to them about?"

"Well, when I told them about Sappy Manilow—"

Carlos pushed Chulito's shoulder and got up. "You didn't."

Chulito nodded and dusted the seat of his pants. "Then Julio snapped his fingers high up in the air, he pointed at me and said, 'Hooked.'"

Carlos' laugh shot out loud and bubbly. Chulito laughed along with him.

Chulito stopped and placed a hand on Carlos' shoulder. "Thanks for giving me another chance, Carlos." He pulled him close as they waited on the corner to cross the street.

Carlos held on to him and spoke into his ear. "I love holding you, but I don't want to go around hiding it. I'm not ashamed of the way I feel for you."

Holding Carlos tighter, Chulito said, "That's one of the main reasons why I like you so much. You take chances and you all bold, 'Don't nobody mess with Carlos.'" He pulled back to look at Carlos' face. "And when you asked me to be open, too, part of me wanted it, but more of me wanted to keep it on the low. But I really want to be with you and if being open is what I gotta do, then that's what I gotta do." Chulito moved in and wrapped his arms around Carlos, not caring for the first time what the joggers, people walking dogs, and women and men in business suits on their way home from work thought. It felt so good to hold him. He gently released Carlos and put an arm around him as they continued to walk. "On Friday, I saw your moms and I asked about you. When she told me you had gone to Andrew's for the weekend, I almost went crazy right in front of her. I been in my room listening to Sappy Manilow all weekend." Chulito pulled Carlos' head to his. "I got some real feelings for you, Carlos."

"I went to Andrew's because I couldn't be on the block. And when I saw the fellas on the corner or the auto glass assholes I wanted to take an Uzi and mow them all down."

"Now those are some gangsta thoughts." Chulito smiled.

"Oh, I've imagined their demise lots of ways. But I could either be controlled by their stupid remarks, and be made to feel like shit, or fight back. And honestly, as much as I hate to have to always fight back, it's way better than being secretive. And that is my neighborhood, too, they need to make room 'cause I'm coming through."

"Holla!" Chulito cheered.

Carlos tapped the brim of Chulito's cap. "I'm serious."

"No doubt."

"But Andrew offered a break from all the drama and from you. And just for the record, there's nothing between me and him. But after I spoke with you I was so distraught that I knew if I were to see your light on, I would just say, 'Forget it, let's go at his pace. But as much as I love you, that wasn't what I wanted. I want a guy who could be by my side, especially when shit comes down, because we gonna get a lot of shit. Especially you with those assholes on the corner. They are not gonna let us have a minute of peace, but being with you is more important. And my mom knows how I feel about you."

Chulito stopped and asked with surprise. "What?"

"I haven't exactly told her, but I think she's hip. So our mothers will become suegras."

The thought of their mothers calling each other "in-laws" made Chulito chuckle. He wondered how he would tell his mother. "Can we take it one step at a time?"

"I'm just playing." Carlos hugged him just as they approached the pier.

A voice beckoned them from behind. "Do I detect a reconciliation?" Kenny said as the couple arrived.

"Most definitely." Chulito winked at Kenny.

"Good, 'cause, Chulito, this one over here was ugly. Tears and make-up running all over the place. I couldn't enjoy Kevin, knowing my friend here was in pain."

"Well, the pain has been lifted." Carlos put his arm around Chulito.

"Aw, how sweet. Now I can go back to hating you, Carlos," Kenny said. "Can I borrow your flowers?"

Carlos nodded.

Kenny ran off to some friends yelling, "I won. I won."

Carlos and Chulito went over to the water. Carlos sat on the railing, then pulled Chulito over and held him.

Chulito swung his baseball cap to the back. "I feel a little nervous." Then, he pressed his face into Carlos' chest.

Carlos rubbed Chulito's back. "Thank you for being here and being with me. I know this is a lot for you, but I also don't want you to do something you don't want to do."

"I want you, and though I feel nervous, I feel good, too."

Carlos leaned in and kissed Chulito's forehead, then Chulito kissed Carlos' chin.

Carlos pointed to the far end of the pier where Kenny was doing a Miss America promenade, holding the flowers and blowing kisses. As Chulito observed Kenny in the distance, he saw Lee from the Chinese restaurant walking up the path. A chill shuddered through Chulito and he buried his face in Carlos' chest.

Lee saw Carlos and came over to them. "Hey, Carlos, how you been?"

"Cool. How you been?"

"I'm glad to be away from the restaurant for a little bit. I never get to hang out. I am always in that damn kitchen, but five more weeks until I go to the University of Pennsylvania. Pre-med, baby." Then Lee pointed to Chulito. "Is that who I think it is?"

Carlos nodded.

"Hey, Chulito. I heard you two were messin' around." At the sound of Lee's cute accent, Chulito slowly turned around to face him. "'Sup, Lee," Chulito said as smoothly as he could. With Carlos still sitting on the railing, Chulito rested his back on Carlos' chest. Carlos reached around and locked his hands around Chulito to hold him. He wondered if Carlos could feel his heart slamming against his chest.

"I can't believe it. I always had a feeling about you."

"Really?"

"You're just too pretty. So, are any of your friends interested in

Korean boys? Like Brick? Or Davey? Davey is cute."

"Not that I know of, but if I find out I'll let you know."

Carlos rested his chin on Chulito's head.

"You lucky, Carlos," Lee said. "I don't mean no disrespect, but Chulito is fine, fine, fine."

"None taken, Lee, he's a beautiful man."

Chulito looked up to Carlos. "You beautiful, too.'" They kissed.

"O.K., this is too weird," Lee said. "And you're making me jealous, so I'm gonna take my single Korean butt away from you two and see if I can find my own man."

"It's a cute butt," said Siobhan, one of the twins.

Lee turned around, did a pose that showed off his ass and waved good-bye.

"There's a hip-hop dance this evening at the Center," Siobhan called out to Lee, "in case you got some Thug Passion."

"Fuck, I gotta work," Lee said.

"Thug Passion?" Kenny said as he came over. "Since my thug, Kevin, has moved on I gotta go bag me another one. Are you guys gonna go?'"

Siobhan shrugged and kissed Hamid, his latest conquest.

"Kevin broke up with you?" Carlos asked.

"I'm fine. He broke my back, not my heart." Kenny smelled the flowers. "So I'll go and see if I can find another thug."

"A whole evening of hip-hop?" Carlos asked. "I don't know. I could take a couple of songs, but a whole party?"

"What?" Chulito said. "You don't like rap and hip-hop 'cause you don't understand it."

Carlos shook his head. "What's to understand? It's either about 'keepin' it real,' 'holdin' it down,' 'livin' large,' 'bein' gangsta,' 'hangin' with my boyz' and 'bangin' the bitches.'"

"You crazy, Carlos. Rap has some deep shit, too. Like you ever listen to Tupac or Pun?" Chulito said.

"Pun used to beat his wife. That, I know," Carlos said smugly.

"O.K., besides that. They be talkin' about life in the ghetto and the situation we live in and how to get ahead."

"Maybe but I can't ignore the fucked up parts. Besides, they don't sing about getting ahead by going to school, but by selling drugs, shootin' the po-lice, or 'by any means necessary.'"

"O.K., but also about breaking free of the system."

"There is no freedom in rap. And as a gay man, that shit just oppresses me."

Chulito realized that he had to overlook a lot of what Carlos was saying in order to focus on what he felt was positive. "You like rap, Kenny, right?"

"Yeah, but don't drag me into your argument. You two just got back together and you gonna go right back to divorce court."

Carlos laughed and hugged Chulito.

"But you like rap, right, Kenny?" Chulito asked.

"I like guys who like rap, but I do like some stuff. Well, like all those boys talking about their dicks." Kenny high-fived Siobhan.

"What?" Chulito said.

"They're constantly talking about dick," Kenny said. "'I got a thing in my pants that will make you choke,' or how about 'by the look on her face I could tell she ain't never had something this long.'"

"Damn!" Carlos said. "Those are lyrics?"

Chulito nodded.

"You see, I could get into that."

"Biggie calls himself the condom stuffer." Siobhan said. "I'd love to see a bunch of those rappers naked. They should make a naked calendar of rappers showing their dicks."

"Yeah, because according to their songs, they all have big ones," Kenny said. "With the calendar we would see who's really 'keepin' it real.'"

"You all crazy," Chulito said.

"You don't wonder what Tupac's dick looked like?" Kenny asked.

"No, I never thought about Tupac's dick," Chulito said.

"I think about it," Siobhan said. "He's dead and I still think about it."

"He got shot in his balls once, didn't he?" Carlos asked.

They all looked at Chulito. He nodded.

"I think Tupac was gay," Kenny said.

"Now I know you buggin'." Chulito said.

"C'mon, Chulito," Carlos said. "Any rappers' dick you want to see?"

"Right now, I got you on my mind."

"Oh, young love," Kenny sang.

"Well, I'm happy for you two, but all this young sexual energy is making me hungry for some Hamid." Siobhan and Hamid left walking hand in hand. "I might see you at the dance."

Chulito felt Carlos' erection on his chest. "What's all that?"

"Your mother is in Puerto Rico, right?"

Chulito looked at his watch. "She should be having dinner with her mother in Bayamon about now." Chulito smiled. "Oh, so you don't want to be wastin' no time."

"I guess I'm going to the dance alone." Kenny handed Carlos the flowers. "See you around, lover boys. Have fun and be safe."

It was dusk by the time Chulito and Carlos arrived in Hunts Point. Carlos sat on Chulito's bed, but the room was much darker with the old, brown shade pulled down. Chulito knelt in front of Carlos and kissed him deeply, as Carlos took off Chulito's white baseball cap and tossed it on the dresser. One by one, they pulled off shirts, undid belt buckles, slipped off shoes until they lay naked on Chulito's bed facing each other. Carlos pressed his face against Chulito's neck and inhaled. The pinkish colored streetlight switched on, giving Chulito's smooth brown skin a soft glow. Carlos licked his neck then gently sucked an earlobe. Chulito let out a soft, "Yeah, papi." Carlos continued his journey down Chulito's body, softly biting his nipples, kissing his stomach and running his hands down Chulito's back. He held Chulito's soft round ass in his hands and pressed his face against his stiff cock. He inhaled again. He looked up at Chulito who was biting his lower lip. Carlos took Chulito's balls in his left hand and with his right hand took hold of Chulito's cock and pulled down its skin before slipping the cock into his mouth. He savored the salt and sweat that had accumulated there. Chulito let out a soft grunt. Carlos slid Chulito's cock in and out of his mouth, making it slick and smooth. Chulito started to grind his hips into Carlos' face. Carlos went all the way down, feeling Chulito deep inside his throat, and then he swallowed and the contraction of his throat sent a shiver through Chulito's body. He squeezed Chulito's nuts gently with one hand while he squeezed one of Chulito's nipples with the other. Chulito pushed and shoved himself into Carlos' mouth, then with one quick action he reached down and lifted Carlos to kiss him.

Carlos positioned himself on top of Chulito so that their cocks lay side by side sliding against each other. Chulito's hands were like vines reaching all over Carlos' back and ass. Their bodies began to sweat and soon they were like two slick seals gliding up and down each other. Carlos' cock slipped between Chulito's legs and rubbed his asshole. Chulito stiffened a little. "Relax, Chulito. We're only doing what we both want, O.K.?"

Chulito pushed Carlos on his back. He stroked his body and held on to Carlos' cock. "This is the first time I ever held a dick that wasn't my own," Chulito said. "It feels nice." He stroked it gently and then jerked it quickly. "You got a fat head, yo." And then he slipped it into his mouth and after a moment said, "Damn, that tastes weird but I like it, Carlos." He continued to suck, imitating what Carlos did to him, slowly taking it into his mouth and trying to take it down his throat. He coughed a little.

Carlos chuckled. "Don't get greedy."

Chulito looked up to Carlos and smiled. "This shit is crazy. I can't believe you here and I got you in my mouth. And the fellas are right down the block."

Carlos then swung around and they both sucked gently and hungrily on each other. They traced veins and ridges with their tongues. Chulito kept wiping sweat off his face until finally he said, "I'm gonna turn on the fan."

As Chulito walked to the dresser, Carlos said, "Damn, I think I'm gonna remember that view for the rest of my life. You have got one fine ass hiding underneath all those baggy clothes." Carlos sat up in bed. "It's hot, can we take a shower?"

"Sounds dope."

The two trotted into the bathroom and laughed at their erections bouncing in front of them.

In the shower they continued to kiss. The cool water refreshed their bodies while their hands explored each other's back, arms, shoulders and chests.

Carlos pushed Chulito against the wall and licked his back and ran his tongue right in between Chulito's butt cheeks. When his tongue made contact with Chulito's hole, Chulito jumped. "Yo, what you doing?"

"Trust me, if you don't like it, I'll stop." Carlos reached around and took hold of Chulito's cock with one hand and stroked it as he stuck his face between Chulito's two plump ass cheeks and brushed his hole with his tongue. The strokes grew broader, and Chulito moaned. Carlos tickled the hole with the tip of his tongue then slipped it in a little.

"Oh shit." Chulito pressed his hands flat against the tile wall.

"Relax, baby." Carlos covered Chulito's hole with his mouth and sucked and licked it while he jerked Chulito's cock, sliding the foreskin back and forth.

"Stop, I'm gonna bust." Chulito turned around and pulled Carlos up. "Rinse your mouth before I kiss you."

Carlos laughed. "It's pretty clean down there."

"You're a freak."

"You like it?"

Chulito nodded like a little kid saying yes to more ice cream.

Carlos lay down on the tub, spread his legs and jerked himself as he took in Chulito's body above.

"Damn, you are beautiful, Carlos."

"Jerk that big dick for me."

Chulito obeyed. "You are definitely a freak."

After a couple of strokes Chulito stopped. "I'm gonna bust, yo. I gotta chill."

Carlos got up and wrapped one arm around Chulito's shoulder. "Let's come together. I'm getting close."

They grabbed the other's cock and jerked while kissing and looking into each other's eyes.

Chulito panted. "I'm almost there, Carlos."

"Me too, keep looking into my eyes when you come."

"Bet. Oh shit, pa." Chulito looked down.

"Look at me. Oh fuck, I'm coming."

Chulito and Carlos struggled to hold the other's gaze as the climax rose up and shot out of them. Chulito felt his knees buckling as his body shuddered with every squirt. He peeked down and saw his cum sliding down Carlos' leg. When he looked back into Carlos' eyes, he felt the first few strong spurts from Carlos hit him right above his navel. When their spasms subsided, they held on to each other, their cum tangling in their pubic hairs and on their legs.

Chulito gently kissed Carlos' neck. He felt peaceful and excited at the same time. He wanted to repeat "I love you" over and over again, instead he whispered, "That was dope, nigga."

Carlos pressed his face into Chulito's neck. "What's today's date?"

"I don't know, like July 9th."

"So July 9, 2005 was our first time together." Carlos kissed Chulito's nose.

July 9, 2005 was also their second, third and fourth time together.

Around midnight Carlos called his mother and said that he was going to stay over at a friend's house.

The next morning Chulito watched Carlos sleep for a few minutes before he awoke and smiled. Carlos looked peaceful as he breathed deeply. Chulito, too, felt at peace. He didn't have to gird himself with the bravado he wore walking the neighborhood or deal with the dangers of Rey or the game. He could just watch Carlos sleep. Watch him breathe. Seeing Carlos' chest rise and fall. Chulito matched his breath—inhaling and exhaling. Chulito didn't want to wake him but couldn't resist touching him. He moved Carlos' hair away from his eyes and kissed his nose.

Carlos awakened and grinned. "Hello, lover."

"Hi, beautiful, I could get used to seeing this face when I wake up everyday." Chulito kissed Carlos' eyebrows.

"I know what you mean." Carlos laid on top of Chulito and they hugged. Their erections were ready for the next round. "I don't want to go into work today."

After two more rounds that morning, Carlos used a towel to wipe himself and slipped upstairs to shower and change.

Chulito lay on his bed, still wet from their last encounter. He could feel their cum drying on his body as he listened to Carlos' footsteps above him. Chulito got up, showered quickly and got dressed. He had to meet Kamikaze at one P.M., but he wanted to accompany Carlos on his way to work. When Carlos came down to say good-bye, he was surprised to hear Chulito was going with him.

They stepped outside and Chulito instinctively checked the corner as they crossed Garrison Avenue. It was early and the fellas were not out yet. He saw Damian looking at them. "Hey, Chulito, wassup?"

"Wassup?" Chulito passed him coolly and when he looked back he saw Damian staring at them. He turned away and grinned, feeling amazing about the sex he'd shared with Carlos. He'd fantasized about what it would be like to be with Carlos, but after having tasted parts of his body for the first time he wanted more. He wanted to run and leap and sing out Carlos' name. He looked as his hands and arms and was glad that there was no outward evidence of all the sex he'd just had. It wasn't like after having sex his skin color had changed to blue, but inside he definitely felt different.

The train was full of rush hour passengers, so the couple stood face to face. Chulito slyly rubbed his denim against Carlos' khakis. He looked at Carlos' face, his hair, his neck, his hands and recalled moments of their lovemaking. His desire rose up in him until he had to look away. The other passengers read newspapers and books, listened to music on their headphones, snoozed and stared blankly at the subway ads for English classes and trade schools. They were involved in their own thoughts and none had a clue that Chulito had just had the most amazing night of his life.

Carlos leaned in and whispered, "I don't know exactly what you are thinking, but I have a pretty good idea."

Chulito beamed then let out a small chuckle. "Damn, Carlos. I feel high and shit."

They shared a laugh and allowed the bumps and jerks of the train to press them together, resting on the other for an extra second or two before separating.

Carlos whispered. "I love you, Chulito."

Chulito nodded. "I love you, too, pa."

chapter twenty-one

Chulito sat on a parked car and waited for Kamikaze. It was after one P.M. but still early by Kamikaze's standards.

Damian crossed the street. "Wassup, Chulito?" He was shirtless as usual and his skin had turned a deep, dark reddish-brown from being in the sun.

"Chillin', waitin' for Kaz." Chulito turned down his headset.

"Did you do anything special last night?"

Although Chulito felt the heat of a nervous blush, he calmly said, "Nah, I came home early and went to bed."

"Yeah, I saw you come in, it was like eight o'clock. I was sitting in a car across the street talking to Debbie. You know I tapped that shit last night, bro."

"Debbie's hot."

"No fucking doubt." Damian trotted back to the auto glass shops.

"He's fine but the biggest asshole on this block," Puti said from her window.

"Hey, Puti." Chulito didn't look up.

"Orange is your color, Chulito, and with the white you look like a tasty Creamsicle. Can I lick you?"

"Chill, Puti."

"You ain't got something on you?"

"You know I don't carry shit."

"Not even a little personal bag that you could give to an old friend?"

"Sorry."

"Then, since I can't lick you, you want to go buy me a Creamsicle on the corner? I got a dollar."

Chulito considered her request since she hardly ever left her apartment, because she had difficulty walking after being brutally beaten in jail. Chulito glanced up at Puti then looked away. "No, Kaz will be here any minute."

Debbie came down the block.

"Debbie, mamita," Puti said. "You wanna buy me a Creamsicle? I got a dollar."

"I'm on my way to Martha's and I'm late," Debbie said with attitude.

"It will only take a second."

Debbie kept walking and glared at Chulito.

"Wassup, mamita?" Chulito said with a wink.

"Wassup?" Debbie said simply. Then Chulito heard her say under her breath, "What a waste."

Chulito looked back at Damian who was looking in his direction. Damian pointed to Debbie and pumped his hips. Some of the auto glass guys laughed.

Papo passed Debbie and checked out her ass as he walked

past her. "Damn. That body is begging for attention." Papo shook hands and bumped shoulders with Chulito. "You waiting for Kaz?"

"Yep, where you headed?"

"I'm going to enlist, bro."

"You joining the Army?"

"The Navy, bro. Enough talk. I was chilling with a recruitment officer last night at El Coche, and we made an appointment for one thirty P.M. You think about it and maybe you should enlist, too, man. There ain't shit for us here and they have a lot of jobs. I may not even go to Iraq or some fuck place, but even if I do, it's just peace-keeping shit. You have to wait until you eighteen, but you should do it, too." Papo nodded to Damian across the street.

"That's not my thing, but you go, Papo."

"I'm going. The recruiter said that after all the paper work is done I could be at boot camp by the middle or the end of August." Papo's bright smile erased any trace of the hard dude he purported to be. "See ya." He saluted and continued down the block.

"Hey, Papo," Puti said. "You looking mmmm, mmmm, good."

Papo walked over to her first floor apartment window, reached up with one long arm and slapped Puti's face.

"Ow, you fuck!"

"Cut your shit, faggot. I ain't like the other niggas around here that let you get away with that. I don't like it." Papo looked back at Chulito and pointed his thumb at Puti. "Check him out."

"You don't have to hit me, you fuck. I'm gonna call the cops and press charges."

Papo turned to her and walked backward holding his wrists up as if he were handcuffed. "Call them and try to have me arrested. You the one starting shit. I was just walking down the block."

"You gave her what she deserved," Damian yelled from across

the street and slapped a high-five with some of the other auto glass guys.

"Him. I gave him what he deserves." Papo crossed Garrison Avenue. Damian ran over to high-five him.

Puti held her face. "You lucky my girls are not around or we would fuck your asses up."

The guys laughed as Papo left for the recruitment office.

Chulito remembered that by her "girls" Puti referred to the Gay Bandits of Hunts Point, a group of drag queens who robbed liquor stores and then had parties on the rooftop. Their crime sprees lasted several summers before they were caught.

"You know about my girls, Chulito?"

He nodded and walked away from her.

"I miss so them so much. They were my whole world. Sometimes I feel like I have nothing left to live for. Betty is still in jail and Cuketa." She paused. "Those motherfuckers killed my beautiful Cuketa. They tried to kill me, too. I fought like a motherfucker, but they still messed me up. I used to be pretty, you know." She dug her bony elbows further into the dirty pillow and looked forlorn.

Chulito had distant memories of her being extravagant and wondered if she would spend the rest of her life looking out at the small world of Hunts Point from her perch, looking frail, unkempt and sad. As a kid, Puti was who he thought of when he imagined a gay person—feminine and flamboyant, but now he pitied her. Would she ever find love like he had with Carlos? Who could love someone like Puti? Then there was Julio, who was a different type of gay. He was feminine and strong. He took care of himself. There was nothing shabby or pitiful about Julio. And Carlos helped him see so much more and he met so many different kinds of gay people that, although Chulito still felt like an outsider, he knew he was part of a tribe. Chulito walked to the corner, bought Puti a Creamsicle, and handed it to her.

"You so sweet, Chulito. You gonna be a good husband." She winked at him and unwrapped the Creamsicle.

When Kamikaze rolled up to the building, Chulito slipped into the car as Damian ran up to Kamikaze.

Damian handed over a $50 bill and Kamikaze gave him a sandwich bag with some weed and vials.

"Thanks, Kamikaze. How you doin'?"

"Workin'," he said sternly. "And consider this a one-time delivery."

"I know I owe you big time." Damian tapped the 'hood of the car. "I had me some good pussy last night, how 'bout you?"

"I had me a big dick," Kamikaze responded matter-of-factly.

"What, yo?"

"My own." Kamikaze pretended to jerk himself off and they both laughed.

"You crazy, but that shit can be good, too." Damian looked at Chulito. "How 'bout you, little bro. You get any last night?" He winked and went back to chasing cars without waiting for an answer. Chulito's stomach tightened. Did Damian see something? They'd kept the shade down and the lights out. He remembered a soft breeze lifting the shade every now and then, but it was too dark, he thought.

"So, everything cool with you, Chuly-chu?"

"Good."

"No more crying fits?"

"Things are good. We talking again."

"Good. I think that nigga Damian is trying to start some shit.

This morning when he calls beggin' for his bag, he asks me if everything was cool with you. He said that he saw you and Carlos come in together last night and leave this morning. I told him that was no big deal. You and Carlos have known each other your whole lives and you guys live in the same fucking building."

Chulito felt the heat rise in his face.

"Damian is a trouble maker, so I didn't pay too much attention to him, but you know how ghettos love gossip."

"What do you think he's saying?" Chulito struggled to remain calm but his voice cracked on the word "saying."

Kamikaze moved his head from side to side, weighing Chulito's question. "He's not coming out and saying anything direct. He just said, 'Yo, I saw Chulito hanging out with Carlos, he better be careful the faggot don't rub off on him.' "

Chulito's felt his heart pounding in his ears. "He's fucking stupid."

"Screw him. If he wants to start trouble with you, he's gonna have me to deal with." Kamikaze grabbed Chulito's neck and squeezed it.

Chulito tensed up and Kamikaze noticed.

"What's going on, Chulito?"

"Nothing." The car's air conditioning was on high but the sweat trickled down Chulito's arm pits and beaded on his upper lip. "Could you pull over to that store, I need to get something to drink."

"Are you O.K.? You don't look good."

"I'm just…my throat's dry."

Kamikaze pulled over.

"You want something, Kaz?"

"I'm cool."

Chulito went into the grocery store, paced around, then flipped his cell open and called Carlos.

"Hey, this is Carlos. I can't answer the phone, but leave your info and I will call you back when I can. Adios."

Chulito felt good to hear Carlos' voice, even if it was just voicemail. "Yo, Carlos, I gotta talk to you. I think some shit is starting and I'm freaking the fuck out. I don't know if I can do this. I want to talk to you. I gotta talk to you. Call me when you get this message." Then he grabbed a bottle of water, laid a $5 bill on the counter and walked out of the store. As he approached Kamikaze's car, he could hear Fabolous playing.

He stepped into the car's coolness and looked at Kamikaze who sat there expectantly.

"Tell me what's going down. You my boy, and I know shit ain't right with you. If something is up, I gotta know now."

Chulito looked into his eyes. He could see that Kamikaze was concerned. He wanted to lay everything out—how much he loved Carlos, how happy being with him made him feel, how he was thinking of big changes and how he wanted to get out the game. He didn't know how to begin. What would be the hardest news to break? "I can't tell you. I don't understand what's going on with me."

"Is it about that chick you seeing?"

Chulito felt sick, his stomach churned. It was now or never. If Damian had figured out that he and Carlos were together or wanted to start planting that seed in the minds of the peeps in the neighborhood, then he would either have to pull out completely from Carlos and stop everything cold or go forward with loving Carlos. He was not going to back-pedal. He couldn't do that to Carlos, or to himself. As Kamikaze waited, Chulito thought that loving Carlos and holding onto that love was stronger than any other feeling he'd ever had. Stronger than being afraid that people would find out he was gay.

"Nah, there ain't no girl."

"Then what is going on, bro?"

Chulito feared losing Kamikaze as a friend, but maybe if Kamikaze rejected him, then he would find his way out of the drug game. Regardless of the outcome, Chulito had to tell Kamikaze and then he'd have to keep telling and telling and telling.

"You know last week when I was losin' it?" Tears clouded Chulito's eyes.

"Yeah."

Chulito took a deep breath and talked without pausing. "Well, it was because Carlos didn't want to sneak around anymore and he said that if we can't be open, that he didn't want to be with me. And at first I said fuck it. I ain't about to be dealing with this shit, but then I felt like I was gonna die without him—"

"Hol' up. Hol' up. You sayin' that you messin' with Carlos?"

Chulito nodded and searched Kamikaze's face for a response as he stared at him incredulously.

"Fuck." Chulito turned away and tried to get out of the car.

"Wait." Chulito felt Kamikaze's hand on his back. "You still my boy."

Chulito didn't turn to face him, but rested his forehead against the passenger door window and sobbed. When he saw Kamikaze staring at him a moment ago, he didn't think he would ever feel his touch again. Kamikaze made those soothing circles on his back like he'd done back in his crib. Chulito's heart slowed down a few beats. "I'm scared, man. I'm scared of losing you and my mom and the fellas, but I don't want to lose Carlos either." Chulito didn't turn to look at Kamikaze.

Kamikaze switched off the radio. "You sure about this?"

Chulito nodded and turned to face Kamikaze.

"Then let it go." Kamikaze tapped the dashboard and a small drawer opened. He pulled out a plastic box containing a half a dozen joints. He lit up and offered a puff to Chulito.

Chulito inhaled one long drag and relaxed into the seat. "I don't know where to start." He wiped away tears, sat up and then sunk back down. "I feel embarrassed."

Kamikaze sniggered. "With all we been through, you ain't got to be embarrassed with me."

"I know what I want to say, but the words keep getting caught in my throat." Chulito took one more puff and passed the joint back to Kamikaze. He looked down at his Tims and said sadly, "I don't know how to explain it, but I'm just feeling Carlos." He let his head drop back against the headrest. "I can't believe I'm saying this to you."

"You sure you feeling Carlos, because people in love are usually all happy and stupid acting and you a depressed motherfucker."

Chulito chuckled through his tears.

"Damn, Chulito. This is some shit." Kamikaze shook his head. "Well, it explains why you been moody and hard to reach." Kamikaze lit up. "By the way, you cannot be vanishing on me. How am I supposed to be running a business when my right hand man is nowhere to be found? In a way, I'm glad you came clean about Carlos. You don't have to be hiding and sneaking anymore."

Now that he'd broken the news, Chulito considered letting Kamikaze know that he wanted to get out the game, too, but one step at a time. He stayed quiet about that.

Kamikaze turned on the radio. "Fuck, I knew it was somebody but I had no idea it was Carlos. You definitely kept that shit on the low."

Chulito told him about the bottle, the telephone conversations and how he dissed Carlos the night of the party posse. He told him of the conversation in front of the building and the trips to the pier.

Kamikaze looked out the front windshield. "The problem is fuckheads like Damian like to start trouble. I got your back, bro, no matter what. So what are you gonna do?"

"What do you mean?"

"Is this going to be our little secret?"

Chulito shook his head. "Julio and Brick know, too."

"Brick knows? How'd he find out?"

"Carlos and I were on the roof kissin' and Brick saw us."

"Whoa, too much info," Kamikaze said, waving his hands.

Chulito chuckled. "What you mean? Me and Carlos kissin'?"

"Yeah, I'm having a little trouble taking this all in, little bro."

Chulito turned to face Kamikaze. "Well, last night we did the deed for the first time."

Then, Kamikaze sighed and laughed. "Well, you going to hell, bro."

"Don't play like that, man. You sound like those religious freaks who preach on Southern Boulevard. I already feel a little bugged out about all this."

"I'm just playing. And don't be listening to those religious fucks, man. They really get to me with their yelling and their bullhorns. I don't how that shit is even legal. Hallelujah this and hallelujah that, it's more like hallelujah, pow!"

Chulito laughed.

"Nah, that shit is serious. They claim to be trying to help people but they be beating us down with their fucking Bibles.

Preachin' hate and fear and judgement. They really need to know what love is."

"Damn, I didn't know—"

"Well, now you do. My grandma used to be religious like them, singing Jesus songs on the corners when nobody wants to be hearing their sad voices, so don't get me started. The shit they dish out gets in here." Kamikaze tapped his temple. "And fucks you up. I can't even joke with you and say you goin' to hell without you getting all serious. So ignore those fucks, especially now that you all gay and shit."

Chulito exhaled. "Wow, I hear you. I mean you mention the word hell and I get all scared and start to think of burning up and suffering and shit."

"And where the fuck do you think you got that idea?" Kamikaze shook his head in frustration. "Forget that shit. I got mad love for you and what you got going on is top priority. Since Brick knows, you think he's running his mouth to Damian and shit?"

"Nah, he's cool. He found out, like, a month ago."

"A month ago? And you just telling me now?"

"He found out by accident."

Chulito was glad that Kamikaze seemed more flipped out over the preachers on the corner that his news about Carlos. He even seemed a little hurt that Brick found out before he did. Kamikaze put his hand to his forehead. "Well, this is unexpected, but like I said, you still my boy, right?"

"Yeah, I still want to be." Even though he had said those words, he wasn't so sure anymore.

"Good, but you still going to hell." Kamikaze laughed.

"You going to hell, too, then, with all the shit you do."

"So we be in hell together, and if people want to fuck with

you, they gonna have to fuck with me." Kamikaze put out the joint and shoved the box back into the secret drawer. "With all your disappearing acts, I got nervous thinking you wanted out." Kamikaze put his hand on Chulito's neck and squeezed it, again. "Carlos knows what you do, right?"

Chulito nodded.

"He down with it or he giving you shit?"

"We don't really talk about it a lot." Chulito lied. "But he knows what's up."

Kamikaze patted the back of Chulito's head. "You need to let him know the deal. That's why I don't roll with no women and don't connect with family. They always got an opinion. But you're better than family."

Chulito smiled nervously and the phone rang.

"Hey, Carlos," Chulito sniffled.

"What's up? You sounded scary on your message."

"It's cool. I just told Kamikaze about you and me."

Kamikaze winked at Chulito.

"And?" Carlos' voice raised an octave.

"He's cool. A little freaked out, but cool. He said I was going to hell."

"Definitely." Kamikaze laughed and turned the ignition.

"I'll talk to you later, right?"

"Wow, Chulito, I'm really happy to hear that. Your message had me worried. Wish I could leave and be with you right now. Did you tell him about wanting to get out?"

Chulito looked over at Kamikaze bopping along with Biggie.

"Not yet and I don't know what time we'll be done, but I'll call you."

"Chulito, I thought this would never happen." Carlos sounded excited and hopeful. "I can't wait to see you. I don't think I've loved you more than I do right at this moment."

Chulito smiled. "Yeah, well…" He looked at Kamikaze and raised his eyebrows. "I, uh, I love you, pa." He closed his cell phone.

Kamikaze shook his head. "This is bugged out. Are you cool to come with me?"

Chulito nodded and smiled.

"Good to see you smile, nigga. Let's go to war."

chapter twenty-two

For the next couple of weeks, Chulito avoided the corner. He got picked up by Kamikaze to do runs, went to the pier, and woke up each morning with his limbs tangled with Carlos'.

Maria offered to speak to Carmen on Chulito's behalf, but decided to wait until she got back from her vacation in Puerto Rico. She knew Carmen would be worried and have questions and there was no sense interrupting her vacation.

So whenever they spoke to Carmen, they said everything was fine, and in fact it was. Maria made the young men dinner upstairs every night and Carlos and Chulito sometimes watched a movie with her. Maria was loving and supportive and Chulito hoped his mother would be as cool as when Maria first found out. She was surprised that Chulito had come around and told them to be safe, to stick together and to come to her whenever they wanted.

While Chulito created his cocoon of support and followed Julio's advice to flush the shit in his life, the rumors accumulated like debt up and down Garrison Avenue.

"So fellas," Looney Tunes rhymed to a rap beat. "The incognito, boom, boom boom, nigga Chulito, boom, boom boom, as far as we know, boom, boom boom, has become a patito." He laughed.

Davey licked his lips. "Yo, don't believe the shit that fuck Damian be saying."

Chin-Chin sat on a milk crate and fanned himself with his baseball cap, "Yo, D, Chulito has been slipping in and out with Carlos."

"He better not be perpetratin'," Papo said. "Or he should have the balls to come clean instead of being a true pussy."

"Damian said he saw them in the Village and they were hanging out with a bunch of other dudes," Chin-Chin said, scraping a stick along the sidewalk. "I ain't got nothin' against fags, just as long as they don't try no shit."

"Word," Davey said.

Papo lit a cigarette and blew the smoke toward the sky. "Well, I don't go for that, so if Chulito turned pale, then it's best he keep to his shit and stay off the corner, 'cause I don't chill with patos."

"That shit is ill, man," Looney Tunes said tapping Chin-Chin. "You think Chulito and Carlos be doin' the nasty?"

Chin-Chin got up from the milk crate and picked up the bottle of Hennessey. "Oh, c'mon, you don't have to go there with that shit."

"See," Papo slammed his fist into his palm. "I don't want that bullshit in my face and faggots never know they place or when to stay back. That's why I popped Puti the other day, because he feels like he could say whatever he feels to niggas, but I don't want a dude looking at my ass."

"I hear you," Davey said, "but, c'mon Papo, Puti's just playin'. It ain't no big thing."

"What?" Papo shoved Davey. "I don't want to hear any words come out of his dirty mouth. He needs to back the fuck up. Straight up and down."

Davey straightened his shirt out. "Chill nigga."

"He's got a point." Chin-Chin passed Davey the bottle. "I don't want niggas lookin' at my butt."

Davey took the bottle and hesitated. He took a swig and passed it to Papo. "Sorry, bro, but I don't think Puti is looking at our butts."

"Yo, what's with you, Davey?" Papo snatched the bottle. "Maybe you a little soft or something? You betta come clean nigga and don't be frontin'."

"Get the fuck out, I ain't gay. I'm just saying that if Chulito is gay, he still our boy," Davey squared off and looked at his fellas. "Right?"

"Fuck no." Papo stepped to Davey. "I don't know what he be thinkin' when he looking at me. And I don't want to have that shit around me plain and simple."

Chin-Chin stepped in between them. "He got a point, Davey."

"So, you writin' Chulito off, too, Chin-Chin?" Davey shook his head.

Chin-Chin shrugged. "I don't know, fellas. I can't see it. Chulito is hard and shit. I don't see how he could be gay. But if he is, I ain't down with him hangin' with us."

As the guys talked, Kamikaze's car pulled up in front of Chulito's building. Chulito climbed out of the car and headed into his building.

"Yo, Chu—" Papo called out, but Chulito disappeared into his building. "See? He being real slippery. Something's up."

Chin-Chin took the bottle from Looney Tunes who had been taking advantage of their conversation and drinking up the Hen.

Davey bit his lower lip and said, "I'm going to his house, I'm asking him what's up."

Papo stepped into the street. "I want to talk to Kamikaze to see if he knows what's up."

Davey headed down the block while Papo flagged Kamikaze down. Kamikaze stopped his car, rolled down the passenger window and tilted down his blue shades.

"¿Qué pasa, Papo?"

"How you been?"

"Workin'. Wassup?"

"We were just talkin' 'bout Chulito and the word on the street is the he turned 'mo. What you know about that?"

"Chulito is my boy and I don't appreciate how you coming at me."

"I don't mean no disrespect, but niggas be talking and he been incognito for weeks. I just want to know what's up."

"You should be thinking about what you doing with your own life instead of what's up with Chulito."

"I gettin' my shit together. I enlisted in the Navy, bro, but Chulito is part of my life. I just don't hang with patos and if he a pato I ain't standing for that shit."

"You need to check yourself, bro. You grew up with Chulito, you know him just like everyone else on this block, so what do you care what people be saying?"

"'Cause I don't go for gay shit."

"Why you care one way or the other unless you interested in kickin' it with him?" Kamikaze shut his window and sped off.

Papo stood for a moment with his mouth open. "What? That shit is crazy. I ain't no faggot. I don't see how that has anything do with knowing if Chulito is gay." Papo turned to Chin-Chin and Looney Tunes. "Kamikaze is buggin'."

"I don't think that if Chulito's gay Kamikaze would still call him his boy," Chin-Chin said. "So Damian is full of shit."

"You got a point," Looney Tunes agreed.

"That don't mean shit." Papo spit in the direction of Kamikaze and glared at the fellas.

Chulito expected to see Carlos when he heard the knock, so when he opened the door he was startled to see Davey standing in his door way.

"Wassup, Davey?" Chulito checked out the hall behind him to see if Davey was alone.

Davey took a step as if he was going to walk in, but Chulito didn't move. "Chillin', bro. You just haven't been around and I'm wondering how you doin'." Davey looked into the apartment behind Chulito. They could both hear door locks clicking open on the second floor. Carlos came out of his apartment, walked down the stairs and stopped when he saw Davey in Chulito's doorway.

"I'm cool." Chulito shifted his gaze from Davey to Carlos and back.

"Well, people are talkin' shit and since we ain't seen you I wanted to talk, but..." he looked up at Carlos. "If now is not a good time, we could talk whenever."

"What are they sayin'?" Chulito said coolly.

Davey looked to the ground, then he looked up at Chulito, then at Carlos. "Nothin'. Forget it." Davey walked out of the building into the late afternoon sunlight.

Chulito smiled nervously at Carlos. "Coming down?" Carlos followed Chulito into the living room where Chulito sat and bowed his head. Carlos didn't know whether he should touch him or leave him alone. Then Chulito reached out for Carlos.

Carlos took his hand and knelt before Chulito and they hugged.

"Shit is closin' in, Carlos. I was gonna tell Davey what was up, but feel." Chulito placed Carlos' hand on his heart.

Carlos patted his chest. "I'm sorry, Chulito."

"Why you sorry? You been saying we don't have to be sorry to nobody, and you took a lot of shit from them, me included, and you still did your thang."

"But I was scared, and I'm scared now of them doing some stupid shit."

"They're gonna give me shit, but they ain't gonna do anything."

"I hope not, but I never expected that you would do anything and you threw a bottle at me."

Chulito gave a look that said, "Please."

"O.K., you threw it at my date but you threw a bottle."

"No doubt, but I think they're just freakin' out, and like Julio said, if they can't take it…" Then Chulito mimed wiping his butt with toilet paper and flushing it down the toilet.

Carlos smiled. "We don't have to go to the Vil. We can just stay here and…" Carlos kissed Chulito and slid into a hug.

"You know I am always down for this. But if we want to go out, we goin' out."

"We can call a cab, and go to the number two train."

"I don't want to hide from them. Carlos, I feel real happy with you, and if you was a girl, I would be talkin' to them about you and they would be high-fivin' me and shit."

"I'm not a girl, Chulito. And I don't want you or me to get hurt."

Chulito hugged Carlos. If felt so good. Carlos was always strong and smart and Chulito didn't want him to get hurt either. At the same time Chulito wanted to be strong and smart just like Carlos and to stand up for his love. He even felt lucky to be sharing this embrace with him. Chulito leaned back to look into Carlos' eyes. "I'm hungry. Let's go get a slice on Hunts Point before we head out. We could go to the Vil or check out a movie."

Carlos took a deep breath. "You sure?"

Chulito extended his hand to Carlos. They laced their fingers and held on tightly. "Let's go."

It was just after five P.M. when Chulito and Carlos stepped outside. The fellas were on the corner. Brick was in Julio's office. Lee was working his shift at the restaurant. Martha, Debbie and Brenda were sitting on a parked car. Damian and several of the auto glass guys were still running up and down Garrison Avenue.

Davey saw them first as they stepped out of the building's dark entrance and into the open street. As they waited for a truck to pass, Puti came to the window and watched as Chulito and Carlos crossed the street. They held hands and walked. By the time they reached the middle of the street, everyone had seen them.

"What the fuck?" Papo threw his hands up in the air.

Damian jumped up and down, laughing. "I told y'all niggas, see?"

Chulito and Carlos held hands in a tight grip and took quick, sure steps. Chulito looked at Damian and some of the auto glass guys as they leaned on each other and blew kisses at him and Carlos. Chulito breathed heavily, like a bull ready to charge.

He realized that he was gripping Carlos' hand too tightly, and loosened it a bit. Carlos looked straight ahead and didn't make eye contact with anyone.

"Yo, Chulito, you fucking serious?" Papo shouted out.

Chulito looked over at him and nodded a greeting.

Looney Tunes was laughing so hard he was stomping around on the corner. Davey was silent and just watched. "Yo, that is some shit," Chin-Chin said. "I'm seeing it but I can't believe it."

As Chulito and Carlos reached the sidewalk across the street from the fellas, Papo said, "That's the kind of shit that gets to me. You see that? Walking out like it's nothing, and there's little kids around here and shit." Papo picked up a beer bottle and dumped out the dribble of beer that was in it.

"Yo, you ain't gonna throw that," Davey said nervously, licking his lips and walking toward Papo.

"Stay back, Davey, or I'm gonna hurt you."

"Chill, Papo," Chin-Chin said.

"You, too?" Papo said to Chin-Chin. As he leaned back to throw the bottle, Puti yelled. "Watch out," but the bottle hit Chulito on his shoulder and shattered in a shower of gold glass. They let go of their hands.

Carlos wasted no time. "C'mon, Chulito. Let's get out of here!"

Chulito shook the glass off and turned around to face the corner.

"Run, boys!" Puti called out.

"That's right, I threw it." Papo took a challenging stance with his arms outstretched.

"Let's go," Carlos urged.

"Listen to your boyfriend, Chulito," Damian teased.

It was now or never. He could run, but he knew better. He had to stay and fight. And he had to protect Carlos if need be. Chulito took two slow steps into the street, looked out for traffic and headed toward the fellas.

"What you gonna do?" Papo said with his fists locked and ready. "I will fuck you up, Chulito."

Carlos followed slowly behind Chulito.

As Puti saw Chulito walking toward Papo, she put on her slippers and grabbed a high heeled shoe.

"Yo, chill," Davey told Papo.

While still looking directly at Chulito, Papo said through gritted teeth, "Don't get in my way, Davey."

Chulito charged and leaped on Papo, knocking him to the ground.

"Fight!" A kid on the corner of Manida Street yelled toward a group of children playing.

Martha, Debbie and Brenda saw the kids running in the direction of the action and followed.

When Papo landed on the sidewalk, he shoved Chulito off of him, quickly got up and kicked Chulito who was still on the ground.

The auto glass guys charged over and Damian yelled, "Fuck him up."

Carlos pushed his way through the crowd toward Chulito, who had gotten up and charged Papo again and punched him in the chest, and the two shoved and punched each other. Davey got kicked by Papo when he tried to intervene. In between swings and kicks, Chulito kept shoving Carlos out of the way and told him to stay back.

When Brick and Julio saw people running past the travel

agency window toward the corner, they went out to see what was happening.

Puti limped toward the crowd with her shoe held high in the air and yelled, "Somebody help him. Call the cops." She swung her heel at Papo and caught him in the neck. With his flat palm, Papo hit Puti in her face with such a force that she stumbled back and hit her head on the pavement. Carlos ran to Puti who was bleeding from a busted lip and a cut near her eye. Puti's mother, who had followed her out the house yelled, "You see! That is what you get! You wanna be a pato? Look at you."

Puti covered her ears and yelled back, "Shut the fuck up!"

Carlos' mother ran out the building and shrieked when she saw his bloody hands. "I'm alright, ma, it's Puti's blood. She's hurt. Call an ambulance."

"I don't need no ambulance, carajo!" Puti got up, wiped the blood away from her eye, and picked up her heel.

Watching the fight unfold, Lee called the police.

Brick and Julio reached the fight as Papo hit Puti. Julio and Brick charged at Papo and Brick held him in a bear hug.

"Get the fuck off me!" Papo yelled as he struggled and kicked. Chulito was trembling and bleeding from his mouth, but he had his fists up.

When Damian saw Brick he called a couple of his auto glass buddies, and they all rushed Brick. Puti whacked one of them as they passed her. Papo broke free and he and Chulito continued to fight while Brick and Julio fought with the auto glass guys. Then Julio ran back to his agency with two of the auto glass guys chasing after him. He reached his office and locked the door. The guys banged on the glass windows and rattled his door. Julio went to his desk and looked for his gun.

When Lee saw the guys chasing Julio, he grabbed a large kitchen knife and tried to go out, but his father shut the metal gate that kept the customers out of the kitchen and locked him in. "You are staying here." Lee yelled and held up his knife to his father, but his father stood still and simply shut his eyes. Lee looked at his siblings and through tears said, "My friends are in trouble." Lee ran to the small take-out order window and looked through the clouded glass to see what was happening. His mother was crying and praying in Korean, while Lee tried squeezing himself through the take out window where only his head could barely make it through.

The travel agency window shattered and Julio fired two gun shots, which sent the auto glass guys running. When Brick heard the shots he shoved Damian away and ran to the store. As he climbed through the broken window, Julio crouched behind his desk, took aim and shouted, "Stay the fuck out!"

"Yo, it's me, Brick." Julio saw him and got up. "Yo, Julio, put that gun down, bro."

"No, our boys are in trouble and nobody is gonna help them." Brick blocked his path.

"Move, Brick. I will kill any of those motherfuckers even if I have to go to jail. They need to know that they cannot fuck with us. We are not a bunch of scared faggots who cower when they flex their macho attitudes." Julio pushed past Brick, jumped through the window and ran toward the corner. He fired several shots into the air. There were screams and everyone ran in different directions.

"Stop it, you fucking animals!" Julio shouted as he charged the corner.

In trying to stop the fight, Chin-Chin and Davey were now fighting with Papo. Looney Tunes was trying to get Davey and Chin-Chin to stay out of it. Damian and the two auto glass guys took off across the street to the shops. Chulito was bruised and bloody with his right eye nearly swollen shut. Carlos' shirt was covered in Puti's blood but he went to Chulito and held him.

Papo stood defiant. He had blood oozing out his mouth and nose, and running down his right ear and the side of his head from a gash in his scalp.

Julio aimed the gun at Papo.

"Gimme the gun!" Brick yelled.

"Listen to your boyfriend," Papo said, coughing.

"Fuck him, Julio. Just give me the gun." Brick held out his hand.

Papo smirked. "You just a faggot with a gun, Julio. You ain't gonna shoot me, and if you do, you better kill me with the first shot, 'cause if not, you going down, no joke." Julio cocked the gun and moved closer to Papo. "Enough."

When he heard the sounds of sirens in the distance, Brick put his hand on Julio's shoulder and traced it down his arm until it reached the gun. He took the gun out of Julio's hand and put it in his pants. Julio trembled with pent up rage, and walked up to Papo and yelled from the pit of his gut, "Enough!"

"You better get out my face, bitch," Papo said.

"Enough!" Julio didn't budge. "Enough, enough, enough!"

"Yo, Papo, let's bounce, man, the cops are coming," Looney Tunes said.

Julio turned and shouted at Looney Tunes "Enough!" and then he went to Davey and Chin-Chin and repeated, "Enough!" Then he looked across the street to the auto glass shops and yelled, "Enough!" and then he turned to Puti's mother and almost in whisper said, "Enough."

Martha and Brenda held on to each other. Debbie left with Damian and the other auto glass guys as Kamikaze drove up to the scene.

Orlando from Rivera's grocery store was handing out rolls of paper towels so that folks could clean up. When he offered a roll to Papo, he smacked it out of Orlando's hand. He glared at Davey and Chin-Chin. "I'm sick of all y'all." Papo wiped his hands. "I wash my hands of all of you niggas. You and the faggots are gonna burn in hell. You too, Chulito. You acting one way and being another." Papo walked casually away as the police and ambulance arrived.

"Where you think you going?" Martha said to Papo, who just turned and gave her the finger.

Carlos was not allowed to go in the ambulance with Chulito because he was under eighteen. Maria went with Chulito in the ambulance and Kamikaze drove Carlos to the hospital.

Brick and Julio talked to a female police officer in the travel agency and she filled out a report. Julio pressed charges against the two auto glass guys who smashed his window and assaulted him.

Kamikaze drove Chulito, Carlos and Maria back home from the hospital. When they pulled up in front of the building, the bodega on the corner was closed, the fellas were not hanging on the corner, and the block was fairly empty. Only Puti's blood stain remained as evidence of the battle that had taken place.

"Anybody hungry? Micky D's?" Kamikaze said.

Maria thanked Kamikaze for the ride but said frostily,

"I'm going to heat up some real food. I don't want any of that McDonald's crap." Then she got out of the car.

"I'm not hungry," Chulito said through his swollen lips.

"Not even for a milkshake?" Kamikaze asked.

Chulito smiled and winced because it hurt.

"Even all beat up, you're still beautiful, Chulito," Carlos said.

"Awwww." Kamikaze teased.

"Shup up, yo," Chulito said.

Kamikaze looked toward the backseat at Carlos. "So, three shakes?"

"Not for me," Carlos said. "I think mom's cooking is more my style. You coming, Chulito?"

"In a few. I'm gonna get a shake."

Carlos leaned forward and hugged Chulito, who sat in the passenger's seat. "I'll wait up."

He patted Carlos' arm. "Cool, 'cause I think you wants to play doctor."

Kamikaze covered his ears playfully. "Too much info, bro."

Without making eye contact, Carlos thanked Kamikaze and got out of the car.

They rode the three blocks down to McDonald's silently. Chulito knew every inch of those blocks as they passed—the order of auto glass shops, the colors in the giant Tats Cru mural, the cracks in the rose brick wall surrounding the Banknote building, the vehicle line-up of the school bus company and the ever changing oil slicks on the ground at the gas station with the Dunkin' Donuts. Everything seemed the same, but it wasn't. Whereas before the dirt and the grime were just a part of the neighborhood, he now saw them as disgusting. He had to live with the dirt all his life because he had no other choice. He had to just deal with it. But he realized that he had choices and living in Hunts Point was a choice. He tried to imagine a different life—a life where he could love Carlos and not have to fight or watch his back, where there was more good times and less dealing with shit, where he could find a new way of living, where they could wake up feeling relaxed, go to the movies, eat at restaurants without being hassled, where they could go to the beach and swim, feeling open and free. Would he have to leave Hunts Point to have this life he was imagining or did he have the balls to do it here? Was that even possible?

Kamikaze pulled up in line at the drive through. "Want anything else? Fries?"

Chulito shook his head. "Don't think I can handle anything else. My jaw hurts like hell."

Kamikaze patted his knee. "Then don't talk, little bro."

But Chulito needed to talk because every punch, shove and kick with which Papo came down on him didn't keep him down. He fought back. He stood up. And even though it felt like every bone and muscle in his body was bruised, he felt powerful.

"If I have to, I will fight every single day, but I feel like I want to go live somewhere else. Someplace where being with Carlos is not the end of the world."

Kamikaze nodded and listened.

"Look at me, Kaz, I'm wrecked and this was done by Papo. Someone I used to look up to. Someone who's known me most of my life." Chulito paused. He wanted to say the one thing he was afraid of saying to him up front. Maybe it was the adrenaline that was still pulsing through his body, but he felt it was now or never. "These streets look the same but everything is different, right?"

Kamikaze moved his head from side to side weighing Chulito's question. The car moved up and Kamikaze placed the order.

Chulito closed his eyes and breathed evenly. This was his moment. He had to let Kamikaze know that he wanted out of the game. He felt the car move forward again and heard Kamikaze pay for their order. His heart began to pick up its pace as he felt the car move and stop behind the next car. Then he looked at Kamikaze, who'd been watching him attentively. "I'm thinking, that, maybe…" Chulito paused. "I'm thinking I should get out of the game. Find a job doing something. Go legit."

Kamikaze breathed in so deeply it sounded as if he'd sucked all the air in the car, then he held it for a few seconds before letting it out slowly. "Think about what you saying. Think it through." He then looked away from Chulito. "How you gonna say something like that when I got your back no matter what, right?"

"I know, but—"

"But nothing!" Kamikaze slammed the dashboard. "Where the fuck is this coming from? Carlos? Is that preppy fuck pressing you?"

"No, I—"

"You have no fucking idea what you are asking." Kamikaze gripped the steering wheel and shook it. He banged the dashboard with his fist and without looking at Chulito said, "Get the fuck out of the car."

"Kaz," Chulito pleaded.

"Out!" Kamikaze looked straight ahead, breathing heavily. "Now."

Chulito turned slowly. Clicked the lock open. Took hold of the handle. He was expecting Kamikaze to say, "Chill. Stay in the car." He wanted him to say or do something to stop him from leaving.

Instead, Chulito stepped out and closed the door. When the door shut he heard the locks click. He couldn't see Kamikaze through the tinted glass, so he walked forward to look at him through the windshield but Kamikaze avoided his stare. Then Kamikaze began honking his horn and called out, "Hurry the fuck up in there!"

Chulito didn't expect to feel his heart break. It hurt more than the bruises on his body. Was that it? Had Kamikaze thrown him out and would he never talk to him again? He held back tears. He wanted to run home to Carlos, slip into his arms and let go. Let the tears roll. Let the hurt take over and feel the warmth and comfort of Carlos. He was too bruised to run home to Carlos. He managed to take one step after another and limped as fast as he could up Garrison Avenue, away from McDonald's and toward home. He wiped away his tears he couldn't hold back, then he had to pause a second because the pain in his chest was crippling. He reached for his phone. It was only three blocks to their building, but maybe Carlos could come get him. He breathed deeply and as he was about to dial, he heard Kamikaze's car screech to a halt next to him. The window slid down. "Here's your shake."

Chuilto hesitated. Kamikaze still looked furious.

"C'mon, I ain't got all night."

As Chulito reached for the shake he saw Kamikaze's other hand swing around and point a gun with a silencer at him. "Now, if you really want out of the game, this is how I'm supposed to let you out."

Chulito fell back against a parked car. Kamikaze held the gun steady. Chulito panicked. He could be killed right then and there. The block was empty. He shook his head slightly. He wanted to say, "Please don't, Kamikaze. Please, don't kill me. Don't let me die without seeing my mom and seeing Carlos one last time."

The words couldn't come out. He managed to just plead with his eyes. Kamikaze clicked out the gun's clip and then reached out his window and fired the gun into the sky. "Now it's empty so get in the car." Chulito was paralyzed by the fear of having the gun pointed at him and how quickly it all had happened. Kamikaze could have pumped a few into him and he'd be gone. It would be that easy.

"Chulito, please get in. One thing you have to believe is that I would kill myself before I would harm you."

Chulito's knees gave and he fell to the ground. He never would have imagined that Kamikaze would point a gun at him, and if that weren't enough, Kamikaze's deadly glare scared the shit out of him. Maybe Kamikaze had changed his mind, but Chulito knew that he had considered wiping him out. The changes in his life were happening so fast, like dominoes knocking down one after another.

Kamikaze got out of the care and came around to help him up. "Get off me." Chulito struggled at first and then acquiesced. He felt as if he'd exhausted his last reserve of energy. He was like a rag doll being held up by Kamikaze's embrace. Chulito choked on his sobs.

Kamikaze held Chulito with one arm and opened the passenger's door with the other. He helped him into the seat. Kamikaze drove around the corner and parked near the convent.

Chulito continued to sob. Letting the tears roll down his face, drip off his chin and get absorbed by his jersey.

He offered Chulito the shake. "Chulito, you think it's easy to get out the game? Once you in, you in. That's the fine print—well, more like the invisible print." He put Chulito's shake in the cup holder between them. "Maybe when you a low-level street runner it might be possible, but the deeper you go, the more about the operation you know, the more of a liability you become. And you, little brother, are in pretty deep. So you can't just quit, because for as long as you live you'll know the players, where they live, where they get their stash, and any leak of info could bring down the operation and big money will be lost. To ensure that info doesn't get out, you would get iced. Same deal if someone is a fuck up and they need to get 'fired,' they just get popped." He held up the gun. "This decides who goes."

"So you saying I can't get out?"

"Well, if I let you just walk, then I look weak and Rey might take me out and then take you out anyway." Kamikaze sipped his shake in thought. "But I'm good for business, got a good rep, lead a clean, smooth operation and it takes years to build the trust up. And money talks when it comes to Rey, so he won't take me out easily, but you're a loose thread he can cut."

"Fuck." Chulito feared for the safety of Carlos and his mother. "And what about Brick? He got out?"

"Brick was tough and smart. They sent a couple of dudes to do him, but he was one step a head and popped the fucking assassins first."

"Brick killed them?" Chulito picked up his shake and sipped. "Damn."

"But Brick paid, too, with his grandmoms. He ain't had much family, just her and Jennifer. They knew the grandma would hurt harder, so they warned him first, just roughing her up and puttin' her in the hospital."

"I heard about that."

"Then, when he wouldn't come back, they had the old woman run over. They made it all seem like a fucking hit and run. They would have popped Jennifer next and she was pregnant, but keeping her alive was to their benefit. If they'd killed her, Brick would have had nothing to keep him from going maverick. By keeping her alive, it ensured that Brick would keep quiet. I think part of that Jesus tat on his back has something to do with his grandma."

Chulito set down his shake. "So I gotta stay in the game?"

"I'ma figure something out. Don't worry. Like I said, money talks with Rey. But you think about it. You don't got brains like Carlos, and you know the street. What are you going to do?"

Chulito shrugged. "I haven't thought about what I would do. It would be legit, though."

"Well, one thing you know is that you ain't going to be pulling in the loot like now. And even though your moms looks the other way, she benefits from having a light financial load."

Chulito nodded.

"Seriously, is Carlos pressing you?"

"I'd been thinking about getting out."

Kamikaze nodded. "Sorry for blowin' up at you and the gun and shit, but I got heated." He looked at Chulito. "It ain't like I'm just losing an employee. I'm gonna miss you, Chulito. You're my blood. What am I going to do without my boy, huh?" Kamikaze slurped the last of his shake.

Chulito sat up. "Wait, we can't still chill?"

Kamikaze shook his head. "You'll become a liability to me. They'll know that and they could get to me through you and I can't have that. That's why you wanting to get out hurt so much." Kamikaze picked up Chulito's shake and took a deep sip.

"Yo, that's my shake."

Kamikaze smiled slyly. "I bought it, nigga."

Everything was changing faster than he thought. Even though he hadn't been hanging out with the fellas lately, he wouldn't be back out on the corner, and now losing Kamikaze, too, seemed like too much.

Kamikaze handed the shake back to Chulito. He sipped it. "I don't know what I'm gonna do without you Kaz."

"You could change your mind." Kamikaze raised his eyebrows and waited for an answer. "Well, you know that you can always call on me and if you ever in a spot, I'll help out."

Chulito passed the shake to Kamikaze. "Don't you ever think about getting out of the game?"

"Nah. This is what I know and I'm good at it."

"Don't it ever bother you?"

"What? That our peeps be hooked on it? Yeah, it bugs me a bit, but shifting from street level to the clubs makes it a little easier, and I focus on the business aspect. And I ain't responsible for the decisions that addicts make. It's on them." Kamikaze turned on the ignition. "You've had a big night, and 'sides you got someone waiting."

He pulled out and drove to the front of Chulito's building. "So, little brother, I'm gonna consider this like they do in the corporate world and take this as you giving me notice, O.K.? Give me a couple of weeks so I can figure shit out and get some help."

Chulito nodded. "However much time you need. Hey, what about Miguel who runs the east side clubs for you?"

"I'll handle figuring that part out. Yo, you ain't gonna get jealous when you see me rollin' with another cat in that seat?"

"Of course I will be."

Kamikaze smiled. "You better."

With great effort Chulito pulled his aching body out of the

car. He watched the red and blue taillights become dots and disappear in the distance before he went inside.

When Chulito arrived at Carlos' apartment, Maria was putting plates in the sink and Carlos was seated at the table eating. Although Carmen wasn't due back from Puerto Rico for another two weeks, Chulito knew that bad news and drama travelled fast, so he called her to clue her in.

"Chulito, what happened? Of all the years we lived there, nothing like this has ever happened."

"Papo just started some shit and I couldn't take it. But I'll let you know all the juicy details when you get back," he joked.

Carmen sighed. "If anything were to happen to you, I think I would die. Ay, I'm coming home on the next flight."

"Chill, ma. Everything is fine now, for real. See? I wasn't gonna call you because I didn't want you to worry or cut your trip short."

"I want to be there for you and I can't help but worry."

Chulito looked at Maria and Carlos. "Maria has been looking out and Carlos and I are tight again." He smiled at them both. "I do miss you, but I'll see you in a couple of weeks." Chulito blew a kiss through the phone. "There are a lot of changes. Good ones."

"Just tell me now," Carmen urged.

He took a breath. "O.K., I'll be changing jobs is one. Can you trust me on sharing the rest when you come back?"

"Changing jobs? Really?" Carmen sounded pleased and surprised.

Carlos looked at him questioningly.

"Really. I want to be honest with you. I spoke to Kamikaze and it's gonna work out. Send abuela and everyone my love and next summer I will definitely go with you. Maybe we could take Carlos and Maria, too."

"Alright, papito, but if I can't relax, I'm coming home."

"Do what you gotta do, Ma. But I want the best for you, for all of us."

"You sound so grown, Chulito."

"It's gotta happen sooner or later." Chulito chuckled.

Chulito and Carlos said goodnight to Maria. She didn't stop washing dishes, just glanced up a moment. They saw a hint of sadness in her eyes, but they went downstairs to Chulito's apartment.

Chulito's arms, shoulders and back were bruised and sore, so Carlos helped him undress. "I feel so lucky and proud to be with you, Chulito."

The aches in his body made Chulito moan. "Ain't no turning back now, right?" He touched Carlos' cheek. Despite the heaviness of the night, Chulito felt light. The weight of all the secrets he'd kept inside was slowly lifting. He wouldn't have to lie or hide.

"Today has been one of the toughest days of my life." After Chulito shared what went down with Kamikaze, Carlos kissed Chulito's bruised knuckles. "You're my hero."

"And you're mine." Chulito touched Carlos' face. "It feels weird knowing that people know about us, but it feels good, too. How are you feeling?"

Carlos hugged Chulito. "Happy. Because I have you and because of what happened. I remember Julio, seeing him tremble with anger and strong with power. And how about Puti? I haven't seen her out in the street in years. I was beginning to think she did't have legs."

Chulito chuckled.

"And you probably couldn't see what was going on, but people took sides. And not everybody was on Papo's side. Davey was trying to stop him. Some of the auto glass guys stayed out of it, Martha was with us and even Orlando from the bodega was sympathetic. Today I had hope for Hunts Point, just a small glimmer of hope. And I can see why you're so close to Kamikaze. He has a big heart."

Chulito smiled. "I don't think they gonna be throwin' no block party for us any time soon."

They lay down on the bed beside one another. "No, but you stood up. You represented. I don't feel so alone here any more."

That night Chulito and Carlos slept in each other's arms. It was the first time they slept together without having sex. They found a profound peace in simply being close. The next morning they continued to hold on to each other.

chapter twenty-three

Damian and Papo were both arrested and released. Papo, who was going to go into the Navy, ended up going into the Army instead, because the Army would take him with the criminal charge. By the middle of August, he was off to Army boot camp. Chin-Chin, Davey and Looney Tunes went back to hanging on the corner and Damian was riding out the last shirtless days of summer.

When Carmen returned from Puerto Rico, their sleepovers ended.

The first morning Chulito was up front with her about his love for Carlos.

"Chulito, I appreciate your honesty, but I'm going to need time to take this in." Carmen said through tears. "This is tough for me."

Chulito nodded. "I know, Ma. It's been tough for me, too." He watched the coffee she had poured grow cold. He hated seeing his mother cry. This was the hardest talk he'd ever had.

"And even if it were Catalina or another girl, I wouldn't allow you to…to be together in this house."

Chulito nodded. "I know we young in one way, but we know what's up. And, Ma, I may not look like it right this minute, because it kills me to see you looking so hurt, but nobody has ever made me feel happier."

Carmen wiped her tears and sat up. "In a way, I'm glad that it's Carlos and not ese títere Kamikaze."

Chulito laughed. "Are you serious?"

She nodded and smiled. "If Carlos had anything to do with you changing jobs, then he's good for you."

"He's great, ma." Chulito extended his hand across the table. "You know I'm gonna start working part time at Jimmy Jazz? The pay sucks but I get discounts on clothes."

Carmen took Chulito's hand. "I love you, papito, but it's gonna take time and I'm gonna need help. You are all I have and I want the best for you."

Chulito squeezed her hand. It felt warm and moist. "Carlos is the best."

When he'd played this scene over and over in his mind, there had been tears, but also rage and it usually got to a point where Carmen would throw him out. But here it was happening and the smell of the coffee and the touch of her hand gave him hope that his mother would come around. "Maybe we could help each other because I ain't got this all figured out either."

Carmen smiled then she stood up and outstretched her arms.

Chulito slipped inside of her embrace. "I love you, Ma."

Chulito and Carlos took to spending time in each other's arms on the roof and listening to music on a boom box. Sometimes Kenny would come over from Brooklyn and they'd drink wine coolers, or Lee would come up to the roof and bring chicken wings from Spring Garden. But mostly it was just Chulito and Carlos looking out over the horizon with the Manhattan skyline shimmering in the distance and Hunts Point bustling below.

Carlos' internship ended, and the night before he was to leave to Long Island to start his second year at Adelphi, they had a private celebration on the rooftop. They bought a bucket of fried chicken with lots of fixings, set up two beach chairs, a blanket and had Asti Spumante because it was step up from wine coolers but still sweet.

A cool breeze swirled around them, causing Carlos to embrace Chulito tighter. "Seeing Yankee Stadium glowing over there reminds me of when we were like eight or nine years old and we would sneak up here to play."

"Yep. You used to read those Greek stories and then we would have sword fights," Chulito said. "Yankee Stadium was the mountain where all the Greek gods lived."

Carlos watched the stadium glowing in the distance. "Mount Olympus."

"I can't believe you going back." Chulito felt Carlos' heart gently beating on his back.

Carlos lifted his head that had been resting on Chulito's shoulder and kissed his ear. "I wish you were coming with me."

"You could transfer to a school in Manhattan or here in the Bronx, so you wouldn't be so far away." Chulito had been thinking that despite having Julio and Brick, he would be alone with Carlos gone and Kamikaze staying away.

"You make it sound like I am going to the other side of the country. Long Island is close. You could take the train out, or by car it's less than an hour."

Chulito turned around. "That shit is deep. You ain't even gone and I miss you."

"If you get your GED, I could help you get into my college and then we could be roommates." Carlos made his eyebrows dance and Chulito kissed them.

"We wouldn't get any work done 'cause I'd be all over you every chance I got." Chulito tickled Carlos. "Well, my moms keeps pressin' me about getting' my GED. Now I got a real reason to get one."

"There you go, but you'll visit me for my birthday, right? I'm making arrangements with my roommate to have the place to myself that night."

"September 17th. There is no way I am going to miss your eighteenth birthday. I been thinking about getting my own crib, so you and I don't have to do all this schedulin' just to be together." Chulito smiled but it quickly faded, "But who is gonna rent an apartment to a sixteen-year-old and how am I gonna pay for it?"

"Well, I'll be eighteen, so maybe it could be in my name?"

"But there's still the question of paying for it. Maybe Kamikaze could help me out until I get on my feet. And where would I live?"

"You wouldn't get it here in Hunts Point?"

Chulito shrugged. "This is the only place I know, but I'm thinking if I live somewhere nobody knows me, I can start clean. Look at you, Carlos, when you left you was not plannin' to come back."

"Sometimes you have to leave your home to grow up, Chulito. To change."

Chulito nodded.

"Or you can be maverick here and make people change."

Chulito weighed that option. "I think of that, too, right? Fuck it, everybody here already knows."

They both laughed.

"If we did get our own place, would you want it to be somewhere else, Carlos?"

Carlos nodded. "Most likely, but I don't think the perfect place exists yet. Here at least we understand the people and everybody looks like us, more or less. Some gay neighborhoods are mostly white, and we may not fit in there either."

"This is our 'hood, Carlos." Chulito looked down at the people walking the streets going in and out of the bodegas and shops, the fellas on the corner, the auto glass guys zipping up and down the block and buses and cars making their way up Hunts Point Avenue. "This is our history. This is where we're from."

Carlos sat on the blanket. "It will always be a part of who we are, but this neighborhood doesn't get to define us, we define ourselves. That's what we did. We decided we wanted to be together which goes against the rules, right? But we say how we live our lives," Carlos pointed down to the street, "not them."

Chulito sat, faced Carlos and took his hands. "I don't want you to go, but I know you gotta do your thing."

"And I don't want to be apart from you, but I can come home some weekends and we could bug out at the pier."

"I'm afraid of losing you out there."

"Don't worry about that. You got my heart."

Chulito smiled. "I like hearing that, and like you said, I could take the train. Just to let those college cats know you got a dude."

Carlos laughed. "You gonna show up growling like a pit bull."

"If that what it takes to make them back the fuck up."

"Well, I will be coming home more 'cause I know I won't be able to go long without seeing you and holding you." Carlos kissed Chulito's nose.

"Me, either." Chulito kissed Carlos' neck and nestled into its warmth. He felt the rise and fall of their breathing.

chapter twenty-four

Chulito could hear Carlos' footsteps and the suitcase rolling along the floor above his bedroom. Andrew's Rover was parked outside and packed with boxes, bags and suitcases. Chulito watched Carlos and Maria bringing out more things. He wanted to help, but felt a heaviness knowing that Carlos was leaving and that the next time they planned to see each other was for Carlos' birthday in three weeks. He had a picture of Carlos and him hugging at the pier that Kenny had taken stuck to the edge of his mirror. They were smiling and glowing, and seeing it Chulito felt pleased, with no regrets for being true to himself and to Carlos. He kissed his fingertip and pressed it to Carlos' smile in the photo.

Chulito looked out the window and saw Carlos alone stuffing a bag into the Rover. He couldn't wait to hold him one last time, so he ran downstairs and grabbed Carlos from behind.

"I was just gonna go knock on your door," Carlos said. "You been hiding?"

"You know where to find me. Hey, wassup, Andrew? You gonna let all those niggas out there know that Carlos' man is gangsta, and if they know what is good for them, they gonna see the 'off limits' sign he got tattooed on him."

Andrew smiled and shook his head.

Maria and Carmen were in front of the building talking about going out on the weekend to see a salsa concert, while the fellas, Davey, Chin-Chin, Looney Tunes and a new kid named Felix the Cat, were hanging on the corner.

Carlos handed Chulito a gift bag. "I got you some house music."

"You giving me a present? Thanks, pa. Now I could listen to it and imagine you and Kenny and all the guys doing your thang." Chulito did a little dance, imitating Carlos and their friends.

"Look at him," Carmen said. "Since when did you start dancing again?"

"I'm just imitating these dudes that be buggin' out downtown to this music." He pulled out the CDs from the gift bag.

"That wasn't bad," Carlos said and Andrew agreed.

"I got you something, too, but I want to give it to you in private. Come upstairs."

They headed inside to Chulito's room. Sitting on the bed, Carlos unwrapped the bright blue tissue paper to find a carved, wooden paperweight from Poe Cottage.

"I saw it in the gift case and I went back and got it for you. Well, I got two, so that I could have one here."

Carlos held the gift to his heart. "I love it."

"It's the scene of the crime," Chulito said. "Where it all began."

Carlos got up from the bed and came to Chulito. "It began long before that for me."

Chulito nodded. He couldn't remember a day when he didn't think Carlos was the most beautiful boy in the 'hood. "Me, too, but that day, after we kissed, I knew that I wanted to be with you."

They hugged, neither of them stopping.

"I love you, Carlos. And I don't want to let go of you."

"You got me."

Chulito could see Andrew and their mothers right outside his window. But he didn't care if they saw them embracing. He was full of love and felt courageous being with Carlos. Still, they shared a nervousness because with all the vows and assurances they'd made, they both knew that anything could happen and that being apart meant that things could change.

Maria finally called out that Andrew was waiting and that it was time to go.

Carlos got into the passenger's seat of the Range Rover, and Maria shared parting kisses and hugs with him. Chulito walked over to Carlos and looked at Andrew. "Remember what I told you." Andrew smiled again.

"Go do your thang, Carlos." He touched the side of Carlos' face. With everything that had happened, loving Carlos felt right, and he would do it all and more to have this moment, staring into Carlos face and feeling love bubbling in his heart.

Carlos mouthed, "I love you."

Chulito mouthed, "I love you, too." Then he kissed him. Carmen looked away as Maria put her arm around her.

As the Range Rover took off down Garrison Avenue, Carlos looked out the window and waved. Chulito and Carlos kept looking at each other until the Rover turned a corner and vanished.

Chulito looked to his mother who smiled at him, then with Maria went arm in arm inside the building.

Inside his room. Chulito knew he wouldn't hear Carlos' footsteps above him for a while. He turned on his sound system and Tupac started singing about being buried a G. Chulito listened for a few seconds and turned it off. He looked back at the picture on his mirror. He touched Carlos' cheek, just like he'd done a few moments ago. Then he grabbed the boom box and the CDs Carlos had given him and headed to the roof.

He tucked the piece of wood they used to keep the door jammed shut and sealed himself on the rooftop. To the south he could see Manhattan in a distant haze. To the north he could see the Whitestone and the Throggs Neck bridges, where Carlos would be crossing any minute on his way to Long Island. On the street below the fellas were on the corner and Brenda pushing Joselito in his baby carriage while Martha talked on her cell phone walking alongside them. On the north side, down on the street, Chulito could see the red awning of Julio's agency, and Gil, the liquor store owner, talking to Brick, who had Crystal on his shoulders, and across the street from them was Spring Garden. Back over on Garrison Avenue, the auto glass guys ran around chasing cars and Kamikaze was coming up the block in his royal blue Lexus with the silver trim. It was as if they had all assembled on cue.

Chulito hit "play" on the boom box and the first chords of a piano accompanied by percussion filled the air. The chorus began singing "It's alright. I feel it." They repeated it several times as percussion tumbled into the song. Chulito moved his hips a little and then let his shoulders join in. Next, his head wiggled from side to side and he closed his eyes and let the music travel into his limbs.

"Dance for me," he could hear Carlos saying. "Dance for me, Chulito."

Then he started to softly strut around while continuing to move as much of his body as he could. Chulito bent his knees and bounced to the music. "Can you feel it?" The woman in the song asked. "Stand up. It's alright."

Chulito remembered how Carlos and Kenny and all the guys on the pier went crazy when this song came on. "Dance with me, Chulito," Carlos would scream out to him.

Chulito continued to dance on his rooftop. He spun around and felt the gravel roll under his Timberland boots. The muscles in his back loosened. He had the freedom, so he let go. He leaped and turned and kicked up the dust under the gravel. He shook his shoulders, kicked his feet and even jumped around. His arms reached out as if he could embrace Carlos. And Chulito danced. He danced for Carlos. He danced for Puti. He danced for Lee. He danced for Julio and Brick. He danced for Kamikaze. He danced for Kenny and all his friends on the pier. He danced for Davey and the fellas. He danced for his mother and Maria.

Chulito danced because it was alright and he felt it.

Thanks...

To my literary madrina, Marcela Landres.

To Don Weise for being a caring editor and for making it possible for it to be in the hands of readers.

To Junot Diaz, Sandra Cisneros, and Jaime Manrique for their generosity and blurbs.

For the opportunity to develop portions of the book in various workshops: David Mura at VONA Voices of Our Nation Writers' Conference, Percival Everette at Bread Loaf Writers' Conference, and David Leavitt and Brian Leung at the Indiana University Writers' Conference.

To Erasmo Guerra for giving me honest and caring feedback for a stronger edit.

Thanks to Fernando Ramirez for his legal guidance and concern.

To The Saints and Sinners Writers Conference (where I first met Don Weise) and where I was embraced as a writer before I'd completed a book, and the Lambda Literary Foundation, where I have found a queer community of support.

To Katherine Berger and the Byrdcliffe Guild Artists Colony in Woodstock for providing the environment to write the first draft of this book.

To Paul Adams of the Emerging Artists Theater for giving me my own writers retreat in his beautiful home up in the Catskills.

To the Macondo Foundation's Casa Azul, where I got to work on a section and vibe off the energy of writers.

Sarah Schulman for being a literary guide and force in my life, and Rigoberto Gonzàlez for his caring support.

To the dynamic movers and shakers who were a part of my social therapy group who live between the lines of text and in my heart, including but not limited to Kelly McGowan, Tia Lessin, Carl Deal, Hamid Razik, Majora Carter, Beth Tilson, Maria Petulla, Frankie Fuentes, Alice O'Malley, Isaac Butler, Anne Love, Jamal Brown, Fran Vogel, Emily Choi, Mary Pratt, and Jack Kupferman.

To my sisters Denise and Lisa, my nieces Miranda and Jocelyn, and my stepdad, Salomon, for their encouragement and support.

To editors Steven Berman, Moises Agosto, and to Goddard College's Pitkin Review for publishing sections of the book in their anthologies. A special thanks to Charlie Vazquez, who published in the anthology *Best of Panic!: En Vivo from the East Village* a section that I loved but had to edit out called "Hallelujah Pow." I'm glad that the section lives in print.

To Matt Brim for including an excerpt in his curriculum and inviting me out to the College of Staten Island for an unforgettable afternoon with his students and for reading a portion of the book and giving me feedback.

To my soulmate writers Ru Freeman and Donnelle McGee, who endlessly inspire me and support me "no matter what."

To my BAAD! family for being with me through every word: the amazing Elizabeth "Macha" Marrero, Damon White, Richard Rivera, Carlo Quispe, Ruben Thomas, Shizu Homma, Monica Figueroa, Mike Diana, Cándida Carrasquillo, Bryan Glover, Mili Bonilla, and Edgar Rivera Colón.

To photographer Ricardo Muñiz for a gorgeous cover and to model/dancer Noel Rodriguez, who danced at BAAD! with Violeta Galagarza's KR3T dance group.

To many people who encouraged me along the way including Jane Gabriels from Pepatian; Bill Aguado, former Executive Director of the Bronx Council on the Arts; Charlie Vázquez (fellow scribe) from the PANIC reading series and his beautiful partner, John Williams, manager of the Nowhere Bar and the Phoenix; Ron Kavanaugh from Mosaic; Sofia Quintero and Elisha Miranda (also fellow scribes) from Sister Outsider Entertainment; Jorge Merced and Arnaldo López from Pregones Theatre; Jenn DeLeon (another fellow scribe); dancers Rokafella and Kwikstep; Bronx poet and artists Caridad De La Luz (La Bruja); Mildred Ruiz and Steven Sapp from Universes; my life partners in the "unholy trinity," Bianca López and Diana Sándigo-Cabrera; Nicholas Boggs from Queer Readings at Dixon Place; and the dynamic duo of inspiration, Bill T. Jones and Bjorn Amelan.

And last, but certainly not least, to the amazing community of people in Hunts Point who inspire me endlessly, including Cybeale Ross, Cynthia and Rupert Phillips, Sidney Boone, Alfonso "Hammer" Ramirez, Ruben Morales, Puni, TATS CRU—Nicer, BIO, BG-183, How, Nozm and Sandro, the Auto Glass guys, and the late Martin from Rivera's bodega.

It's often thought that writers create alone. All mentioned here and more contributed to the creation of this book.